THREE
WISHES

KRISTEN ASHLEY
NEW YORK TIMES BESTSELLING AUTHOR

Three Wishes
Kristen Ashley
Published by Kristen Ashley

This book is a work of fiction. Names, characters, places, and incidents are the product of the author's imagination or are used fictitiously. Any resemblance to actual events, locales, or persons, living or dead, is coincidental.

Interior Design & Formatting by:
Christine Borgford, Type A Formatting
www.typeAformatting.com

Cover Art by:
Pixel Mischief Design

Copyright © 2016 by Kristen Ashley
ISBN-13: 978-1542559195
ISBN-10: 1542559197

First ebook edition: April 9, 2011
Latest ebook edition: February, 2017
First print edition: January, 2017

Discover other titles by
KRISTEN ASHLEY

DISCOVER ALL OF KRISTEN's titles on her website at

www.kristenashley.net

To Mark
Whose hand, while we sat in the Registry Office,
came out to grab hold of mine in a strong, reassuring grip.

Part One

ONE

Sarah, Fazire & Rebecca

April 1943

SARAH READ THE TELEGRAM in her hand again and sighed.

She would only allow herself a sigh. No use worrying about what she didn't know. Not yet anyway. That's what Jim would tell her. She had enough to worry about today. She would allow herself to worry about it tomorrow. Or maybe the next day. Or maybe (she hoped) there was nothing to worry about at all.

She walked through the house Jim had built her with his own two hands, well most of it anyway. A sweet, somewhat rambling Indiana lime-stone house surrounded by ten beautifully lush acres. Smack in the front yard there was a large pond. In each windowsill, even though the house was nowhere near grand enough to carry them off, were slabs of marble. Jim had wanted her to have something spectacular and elaborate. The only bit he could afford to make elaborate on his teacher's salary were those Italian marble slabs, and by damn he got them for her.

She entered the back bedroom, walked to the crib and stared down at Rebecca who was taking her afternoon nap. Her baby lips were puckered into a sweet frown as if she too knew the contents of the telegram.

Sarah felt the tears crawl insidiously up her throat and she swallowed them down with determination.

Jim would not like it if she cried.

She would worry about it tomorrow.

Maybe.

May 1943

THE PACKAGE CAME AND IT was battered so badly Sarah was certain whatever it carried would be broken and useless.

This upset her tremendously because it was from Jim.

Sarah thought the arrival of this package was a good sign even though the letter he'd written was from months and months ago, weeks before his plane had been shot down over Germany and he'd gone missing. They still didn't know where he was, if he survived and was captured or if he was struggling to find a way home or if . . . something else.

To her surprise, the item in the package was safe and sound, a pretty, fragile-looking bottle made of swirly grape and turquoise-colored glass. It was elegant, elaborate and spectacular. It had a full base, a thin stem that led to a wide bubble, which went into another thin stem and up to another smaller bubble then a slender neck on top of which was an extraordinary twirly stopper.

It was beautiful.

Jim wrote a letter to go with the bottle and told her he found it in a market somewhere in London and thought she simply had to have it.

Jim, as always, was right.

Sarah loved it.

However it could have been the most hideous piece of bric-a-brac on earth and Sarah would still have loved it.

She set it, pride of place, on the chest in the dining room.

Every time she cleaned, she'd carefully dust the beautiful, exotic, fragile bottle.

And she'd think of Jim.

And she'd hope he was all right and that soon, he'd come home.

December 1945

THE WAR WAS OVER AND a lot of the boys were home.

Not Jim.

Sarah waited but no word.

She phoned, still no word.

She wrote and no word.

She visited the War Office.

No word.

Jim, she feared, was gone.

She cried as she dusted the bottle, his last present to her, the last thing that he touched that she would also touch. Sarah had lost weight, her eyes were sunken in her head and deep, dark circles had moved in to stay underneath them.

Three-year-old Rebecca played on the floor in the dining room as blindly, and not as carefully as normal, Sarah dusted the bottle. She rubbed it frantically, maybe a little madly, almost like she wanted to rub the color right off of it.

The dust rag fell out of her hand and she didn't notice it. She just kept rubbing the bottle with her hands, her fingers, rub, rub, rubbing it. She thought a little hysterically that she might just rub it forever.

The stopper fell out and she didn't even notice.

Rebecca, seeing the pretty stopper, toddled over, grabbed it and immediately put it in her mouth.

But Sarah didn't notice her daughter, she just kept rubbing.

And then she stopped rubbing because in a grand poof of grape and turquoise-colored smoke that shot out of the neck of the bottle, a shape had formed.

The shape was a fat, jolly-looking man wearing a grape-colored fez with a little turquoise tassel on the top. He had a bizarre outfit of turquoise and grape with an embroidered grape bolero vest and billowy turquoise trousers. The trousers ended in purple shoes that had little curls at the pointed toes. He had long gold bands affixed to his wrists that went up his forearms heavily and were embedded with blue and purple jewels and thick, gold hoops dangled from his ears. He had a shock of jet-black hair and a jet-black goatee pointed arrogantly from his chin. He had sparkly brown eyes that tilted up at the corners and looked like they were lined in black kohl.

He floated in the air, his arms and legs crossed, and he stared down at her from his place about two feet below the ceiling.

Sarah thought she'd finally gone mad. Perhaps she should have worried about Jim the minute that awful telegram came. Perhaps she should have quit wishing and hoping and thinking everything would be okay for Jim, for Rebecca and lastly, for Sarah. Maybe she should have come to terms with losing her dearest Jim, being alone, sleeping alone, eating alone and raising a child by herself on her own single teacher's salary. Maybe, since she didn't, it all crept over her through the years and made her insane.

Because only crazy women saw men floating in their dining room wearing fezzes, curly shoes and sporting goatees.

"You, my mistress, have three wishes," the man said.

Sarah's mouth dropped open and if she had been looking, she would have noticed that Rebecca's did too, and the stopper dropped out of Becky's toddler mouth and rolled, unseen, under the cabinet.

"Who are you?" Sarah breathed.

"I am Fazire. I am a genie. And I am here to grant you three wishes," he stated grandly and rather pompously.

Sarah stared. Then she closed her eyes and shook her head as she mumbled to herself, "I've lost my mind."

"You have not lost your mind. I am a genie. I am here—"

"I heard what you said!" Sarah snapped at the astonished genie then leaned down and snatched her child from the ground and held Becky protectively to her trembling body. She backed away slowly, whispering, "Go away."

"I am Faz . . . er, what?" he started to say in his overblown genie voice but stuttered to a halt at her words. No one had ever told him to go away before.

Ever.

They were usually very happy to see him and quite quick with their wishes. Great wealth, which he could do. It was a snap, literally. Long life, a bit harder, and eternal life was not allowed in the Genie Code. Vengeance, he didn't like to do that but a wish was a wish. And so on.

But no one had ever told him to go away before.

Ever.

And no one had ever snapped at him.

Unless, of course, they wished for something silly and it backfired on them but that wasn't Fazire's fault.

He tried again. "You have three wishes. Your wish is my command."

She was still backing away. And blinking. A lot. Every time she closed her eyes and opened them again, it seemed she was shocked to see him.

Then she ran from the room.

He floated after her, repeating over and over the many statements of introduction that he'd been taught in Genie Training School. She was ignoring him. So much so, hours later she packed her bags, took the pretty child with her and got in her car and drove away.

Two days later

SARAH CAUTIOUSLY APPROACHED HER PRETTY limestone house. It seemed quiet and normal.

She and Rebecca had stayed with her mother. Sarah had ranted and raved and even, somewhat to her horror but she couldn't stop herself, blasphemed.

Then she'd cried, a whole day and a whole night.

And after that she'd slept while her mother cared for her daughter.

And now she was home.

And her heart was broken.

Because she knew Jim would never be home.

And she decided that if Hitler wasn't already dead, she'd hunt him down herself and wring his silly little neck.

Invading Poland, what kind of a fool idea was *that*? Didn't he know the trouble he'd cause? So many lives, destroyed. Entire families, gone.

And Jim, vital, strong, tall, clever, wonderful Jim. He'd never again play tennis like he was doing the first time she saw him. He'd never again turn the rich, dark soil in the garden. He'd never again present her with one of his luscious Indiana tomatoes. He'd never hold her in his arms. He'd never lay eyes on his beautiful daughter.

She had to blame someone so she blamed Hitler. He was, of course, to blame for a lot of things, and Sarah was happy for her religion (even though she'd cursed God only the day before). She was happy for it because her religion meant she could visualize, quite happily, Hitler stretched over a charcoal pit, twisting on a rotisserie, roasting in agony for eternity.

Regardless of her vengeful thoughts, Sarah was still weary, immensely sad and forever and ever broken, such was her love for Jim.

But, she thought, she was no longer crazy enough to see genies floating around in her house.

She no sooner opened the door and got herself and her daughter inside when the genie floated forward and shouted somewhat peevishly, "Where have you been?"

She started and then whirled to go right back out the door.

"No, don't go! Just give me your three wishes. I'll grant them and go back in the bottle." She hesitated and the genie forged on, "That's how it works. I go back in the bottle. You put the stopper on and then you give me away, or sell me, or . . . whatever. It just can't be to a member of your blood family or a friend and you can't tell anyone what the bottle does. I have to go to someone you don't know and they can't know what I do. And you can never tell anyone I was here or a thousand curses will fall on your bloodline forever. Those are the rules."

Sarah had never thought genies would have rules. She'd never thought genies existed at all.

No, she shook her head, she *still* didn't think genies existed at all.

Fazire watched her and realized she was still not going to believe in him.

Tiredly, because usually his task took him about five minutes, not *days* (people knew exactly what to wish for and didn't dally about getting it), he said, "Just wish for something, I'll show you what I can do."

Sarah didn't hesitate. "I want Jim back."

Fazire's levitated body came down a couple of feet as he saw the raw pain on her face.

Magically, of course, he knew exactly what she was wishing and he shook his head.

That, unfortunately, as well as world peace and the eradication of all disease, poverty, ignorance, bigotry (which was also just ignorance), pestilence, plague, yadda, yadda, yadda, he could not do.

Those were the rules. The Big Rules in the Genie Code that no one broke.

The Jim he *could* bring back, if he broke the rules, would be no kind of Jim she actually wanted back.

"I want Jim back!" she shouted when Fazire didn't respond. "I wish for my Jim to come back! That's what I wish. That's all I wish . . . for Jim to come back."

After she shouted at him, her voice half an ache, half a passionate scream, she collapsed to the floor and cradled her toddler in her arms, rocking the child back and forth as the pretty little girl's lips began to quiver with fear at her mother's breakdown.

Fazire found himself floating lower to the floor. He didn't like to float low and it had been *years* since his feet actually touched the earth (the very thought made him shiver with revulsion). Still, something about her forced Fazire to come close to her.

"Woman, I cannot do what you ask, your Jim is gone," he told her gently. "I cannot bring him back. You must wish for something else."

She shook her head mutely.

"Fame, maybe?"

More shaking of the head.

"Riches beyond your wildest dreams?"

Still she shook her head.

"Good health?" Fazire tried.

She simply shook her head, still holding her child carefully and rocking the toddler back and forth.

"I just want Jim." Her voice was broken and Fazire was at a loss. He'd not come across this form of human before. Usually he just saw the greedy ones or ones who turned greedy and grasping and hateful the minute they realized they could have anything they desired.

This was an entirely new experience for Fazire.

He didn't know what to do. He thought about going back to his bottle and channeling the Great Grand Genie Number One to ask, but instead Fazire followed his instincts.

And, as the years slid by, there would be many a time when he thought he regretted this, but in reality it was the best thing he ever did in his very long genie life.

He reached out and stroked her pretty white-gold hair.

He'd never touched a human in his hundreds and hundreds of years.

To his utter shock, she turned her face into his hand and rubbed her cheek against his palm.

"I miss him," she whispered.

"I know," he whispered back even though he *didn't* know as he'd never missed anyone but he could tell by the awful tone of her voice.

"I'll give my wishes to Rebecca," she said softly.

Fazire reared back an inch and stared at the small child.

"But she can barely talk!" Fazire objected.

Sarah stood up, let the child down to toddle off in some child direction with some unknown child intent in mind as, in horror, Fazire watched her go.

Then Sarah straightened, squared her shoulders and looked at Fazire.

"Well, I guess you're going to be around for a while," she said quietly.

July, many years later

FAZIRE WAS SUNNING HIMSELF IN the front yard holding under his chin the tri-paneled, cardboard-backed mirror Sarah got for him in order to get double sun access on his face. The golden rays were glinting happily off the pond and it was hotter than the hinges of hell and Fazire knew this to be true. He'd had a friend who visited one of his masters in hell and he'd described the excessive heat to Fazire during a channeling, and humid Indiana heat in July sounded *exactly* like what his friend described.

He'd been there years and neither Sarah nor Becky had used a single wish nor had they shown any signs of doing this.

At first most of his genie friends thought this was hilarious, Fazire being stuck with a family in a small farm town in Indiana, of all places, and they poked great fun at him.

Fazire, walking on the ground like mere mortals.

Fazire, wearing real clothes like humans did.

Fazire, eating blueberry muffins and strawberry shortcake just like people.

Fazire, getting a stocking filled with goodies at Christmas time.

Fazire, taking his young Rebecca on the bus to baseball games (Fazire liked . . . no, *loved* baseball and Becky absolutely lived for it).

Then Fazire would explain to them what homemade blueberry muffins, fresh from the oven and slathered in real butter, tasted like. He also went into great detail about what he received in his stocking. And he could wax poetic about a grand slam home run for more than fifteen minutes.

When he told them these stories, his genie friends got a little quieter when they were making fun. Then they got jealous. In the end they settled in and couldn't wait for Fazire to channel to tell them what he was up to next.

And Fazire was always up to something, usually with Becky.

Fazire leaned to his left and picked up the dripping wet, sweating glass of sweet, grape-flavored Kool-Aid, his most favorite human drink. That was to say, in the summer. He loved Becky's hot chocolate with marshmallow fluff melting on top in the winter.

He slurped a big swallow out of the cool glass and spied Becky walking down to him.

She was round and jolly, just like him, and very tall. She was also very lovely with pretty green eyes and her mother's white-gold hair. Fazire, although he would not admit this out loud to *anyone*, genie or human, thought of her a little bit like *his* child. He had helped to raise her in a way, if getting her into trouble and coaxing her to do naughty things was raising her, which Fazire preferred to think it was.

Now she was a part-time photographer. She'd won a few awards and she'd even taught Fazire how to take photos. And she was married to Will Jacobs who thought the sun rose and set in her.

Fazire liked Will. Will had moved in with them rather than taking Becky away and Fazire approved of this. He found he very much liked having lots of people around the house and lots of conversation and more food on the table. Will was a bit intense but only in the best ways. He loved deeper, thought harder and cared more for people than, well, almost than Sarah and Becky did.

He also could hold a pretty mean grudge so Fazire tried to stay on his good side.

And he knew what Fazire was and he didn't mind a bit.

And, lastly, he liked baseball.

Yes, Will was okay in Fazire's Book and Fazire did, indeed, have a book.

Becky waved at Fazire before she collapsed into the grass beside him. She was barefoot and wore a pretty dress. She smiled such a quirky, sweet smile it almost took your breath away. She also liked the sun, just like Fazire, and they used to spend hours outside in the summers baking away.

"Good day, Mistress Becky," Fazire greeted cheekily.

"Quit calling me that," she replied but it wasn't in a nasty way. In fact, she had a smile in her voice. He only called her that because it annoyed her and she was very easy to annoy. And sometimes when she was done being annoyed, it made her smile or giggle and even Fazire's best wish granted was nothing to one of Becky's smiles or giggles.

She *was* his mistress though and he tried to explain this to her so often, he lost count.

"You're getting brown," she observed, looking down at Fazire's nicely tanned, suntan-oil-slicked, very-rounded body exposed by the swimming trunks.

"Do you want to go swimming?" he asked hopefully. He and Becky had gone swimming in the pond more times than he could remember. And today, such a hot day, he felt it was the perfect idea.

She turned on her side and shook her head. He noticed for the first time something was on her mind.

He threw aside his sun-reflecting mirror and turned on his side too.

When Becky had something on her mind, Fazire was always there to listen.

He didn't say a word. He just waited.

"Fazire . . ." she began and then looked away. "I'm scared even to ask," she whispered.

"You can ask me anything, Becky." And it was true. He didn't know much and she'd figured that out years ago, considering she was very clever and she realized he spent most of his existence living in a double-decker bottle, but he would do his best.

She nodded and looked back at him, her green eyes warm but, indeed, frightened.

"Will and I have been trying to have a baby for years."

"I know," Fazire nodded sagely. She'd talked to him about this before. She talked to Sarah about it too. She'd tried and tried to have a baby but each time she tried, she lost it. Sometimes this was painful, sometimes she would bleed. A lot. Sometimes, no, actually every time, this was very scary for Will and Sarah *and* Fazire.

Losing a baby always made her sad and it was worse and worse every time.

"I want to have a baby," she said in a rush, almost as if she was afraid of the words, afraid to hope, *to wish*. "I won't be greedy, just one. I don't care if it's a boy or a girl. It doesn't even have to be perfect, just someone to love. Someone that Will and I made. Someone—"

Fazire went quite still.

All these years.

"Are you asking for a wish, Becky?"

She looked at him carefully, silently, before she nodded.

He couldn't believe it, after all these many, many years. She was older than most women who had babies these days but this, *this* was a wish he could grant.

He smiled at her and he reached out and touched her belly.

He looked her straight in the eyes and said, "Your wish is my command."

BUT FAZIRE DIDN'T DO EXACTLY what she said.

He *did* make her perfect.

He made her bright and funny and very, very talented.

He made her sweet and thoughtful and very, very caring.

He made her generous and kind and very, very loving.

He decided *not* to make her beautiful, at least not at first, because she should know humility and not grow up with conceit.

Though, she would become a beauty, a splendid beauty beyond compare.

Just . . . later.

TWO

Fazire & Lily

October, many more years later

FAZIRE WATCHED LILY AS she pushed her bike up the lane, which was awash in the vibrant autumn colors he liked so much in Indiana.

He was frowning and he was doing this because he saw that Lily was sad.

He didn't like Lily sad, but Lily was sad a great deal of the time these days.

She never used to be sad.

She was so very loved, so loved that the minute she was born—well, a couple of hours later because luckily Fazire had not been present at the birth, he'd heard stories about it and felt his absence was a wish granted to *him*—Becky had given her two last wishes to her new daughter.

Lily was so smart. She walked before other babies did. She talked before they did. Later, she read before other children did. Now she was two grades ahead of the other kids at school, she was so smart.

And she was supremely vivacious, happy, smiley and loving. One hug from Lily and your whole world turned golden. She gave the absolute best hugs.

And the minute she could string three words together, she started to tell stories. And they were always the best stories . . . *ever*.

If she was talking about something that really happened, she could make the most mundane happening entertaining. But it was even better when she made up stories from scratch. Those were the absolute, most bestest, *best*.

And she was funny. She could make even Old Lady Kravitz laugh and Old Lady Kravitz never laughed.

Everyone loved Lily, even Old Lady Kravitz.

There was a lot to love. Lily was, quite simply, perfect.

Except . . .

Fazire had to admit that he had made a wee, little mistake when he healed Becky's womb and made it fruitful and set the wish that would be Lily.

He should have made her become beautiful a little quicker.

Or, at the very least, pretty.

He used the excuse to himself that he didn't know.

He'd been created by the Divine One as a full-grown genie. Then he'd gone to Genie Training School where you had to pay attention because if you didn't and you messed up a wish or didn't follow Genie Code, well, the consequences didn't bear thinking about.

Fazire had never been to human school. He didn't know how cruel children could be.

And Lily, although not ugly, was plain. And being so smart made other children think she was strange. Therefore they made fun of her.

Sarah, Becky and Will worried about Lily. Well, Sarah and Becky did, it made Will madder than the dickens (this, a phrase Sarah had taught him and Fazire still didn't know what "the dickens" was but he figured it was pretty bad by the way Sarah said it).

As the school years went by, more and more Lily would come home like she did today.

Sad.

He hid himself as she came into the house (as he did most days) and watched her surreptitiously steal the three Baby Ruth candy bars (named after one of Fazire's heroes, Babe Ruth, a great baseball player who was nearly as round as Fazire).

She grabbed her ever-present book (another in a hundred romance novels that he knew she read) and ducked back out of the house. Fazire watched as she walked down the sloping lawn to hide herself in the trees at the bottom by the curve of the graveled lane.

He knew exactly what she'd do. She'd eat the candy bars. She might even steal a few more. Then she'd have a big dinner and dessert. She would also, maybe, steal something else to eat before she went to bed.

Fazire liked his food but Lily didn't. She didn't eat because she liked it. She ate because . . . well Fazire didn't know why.

And Lily was getting heavy. Not *getting* heavy anymore, she was beyond chubby.

Furthermore she read those books like . . . well, he knew why because Becky told him. They were her escape.

Somehow, Fazire knew, this was all because of the kids at school.

Now was the first time he ever wished one of his mistresses would ask for vengeance. If he even heard one of children saying cruel things to her like what Will told Fazire they were probably saying, he might do a wish for himself which was outside of Genie Code, and blast the consequences.

Stupid, ignorant, jealous children.

He waited until she'd eaten the candy bars and hidden the wrappers like he knew she did then he walked down to join her.

She was sitting in a bed of dried fallen leaves the colors of red, brown, yellow and orange, some of the leaves even had all four colors in one single leaf. Her back was pressed to the trunk of a tree. Her white-blonde head was bent over her romance novel.

But she wasn't reading. She was crying.

"What's happened, Lily?" Fazire asked quietly.

She jumped and stared up at him, the tears glistening wet on her face.

"Fazire!" She tried to hide behind her smile but it was shaky. He'd seen her don her mask of false happiness a hundred times but he caught her before she could slip it firmly in place.

"Don't you try hiding from me, Lily-child. This is Fazire you're talking to. I know all," he stated grandly in his best genie-in-a-bottle voice.

To his shock she didn't make a joke or a further attempt to hide. She burst into uncontrollable, body-wracking, fourteen-year-old girl tears.

"Oh, Fah-Fah-Fazire. It was *awful*."

Without hesitating he sat down next to her in the leaves (oh, his genie friends would just be horrified at him putting his greater-than-the-earth genie bottom on a bed of dead leaves), pulled her in his arms and let her cry it out.

"Tell me about it, Lily. Get it out. Your grammy said to me that she didn't talk about her Jim missing in the war and she should have right when she knew it happened. Don't bottle it in, my lovely. *I* know what being bottled in is all about!"

She giggled just a little and shook her head, getting herself under control.

"It's silly, Fazire." She tried to be brave but wasn't succeeding. "Just . . . a boy at school said something about me . . . about, well, about me being fat." She gave a little shudder and continued to look at the ground.

"You aren't fat!" Fazire snapped in outrage although it wasn't exactly true. She was past chubby but he'd *never* describe her as fat.

Her eyes flew to his and her mouth did some funny movements as if she didn't know whether to laugh or cry.

"I am fat, Fazire," she said quietly and then pulled the Baby Ruth candy wrappers out of her jeans pocket and showed them to him.

"Oh Lily-child," he moaned and did a little bit of genie magic, magic that was allowed for no one liked litter, not even genies, and in a snap of his fingers the wrappers were gone.

She stared at her hand. She knew he was a genie but it was always a bit shocking to be confronted with magic even though she'd seen it dozens of times before.

"Do you want to use one of your wishes so I can do something to this boy? Give him horns and a tail? Make him big as a blimp?" Fazire asked hopefully.

She shook her head, her mouth moving definitely in the way of one of the quirky smiles she'd inherited from her mother.

Her eyes, which had always been pretty no matter what anyone said (they were pale blue on the inside of the iris and dark, smoky, midnight blue on the outer edges), became thoughtful. Fazire thought her eyes were startling and lovely. Will swore they were from his side of the family though Fazire liked to take most of the credit for all that was Lily, he just didn't tell Will that.

Now he looked into her extraordinary eyes and waited.

"I do want to make a wish though," she whispered.

Fazire was shocked.

Two wishes!

If she made a wish that would be two that were used, leaving her with only one.

This meant, if she used the last one, he'd have to go away.

"Lily, think about this, my lovely. Think about it before you go wishing one of your wishes away on some stupid boy," Fazire warned rather sagely, for Fazire.

She continued to look into his eyes. "That boy today who called me fat, I liked him. As in *liked him*, liked him. He's the cutest boy in school. The most popular. The . . ." She stopped and for some strange reason she picked up her romance novel and held it to her chest like a shield that might ward off evil.

Fazire had read a lot since becoming a human-sort-of-genie. He'd never read a romance novel though. He preferred Louis L'Amour.

"Fazire, I wish—" she began.

"Lily-child—" he interrupted but it was like she didn't hear him, she kept talking.

"One day, I wish to find a man like in my books. He has to be just like in one of my books. And he has to love me, love me more than anything in the world. Most important of all, he has to think I'm beautiful."

"Lily, I need to tell you something." Fazire was going to tell her about Becky's wish and his mistake and let her look forward to something, let her look forward to the incomparable beauty she was going to be.

Most of all, he had to stop her wish *now*. He didn't want her wasting it on some fool idea. He wanted it to be special, perfect, to make her world better like she had made Becky and Will's and, indeed, his.

But again she didn't hear him. Her eyes were bright and they were steady on his.

"He has to be tall, very tall and dark and broad-shouldered and narrow-hipped."

Fazire stared. He didn't even know what "narrow-hipped" meant.

"And he has to be handsome, unbelievably handsome, *impossibly* handsome with a strong, square jaw and powerful cheekbones and tanned skin and beautiful eyes with lush, thick lashes. He has to be clever and very wealthy but hard-working. He has to be virile, fierce, ruthless and rugged."

Now she was getting over his head. He didn't think there was such a thing as *impossibly* handsome. How cheekbones could be powerful, Fazire didn't know. He was even thinking he might have to look up "virile" in the dictionary Sarah had given him.

"And he has to be hard and cold and maybe a little bit forbidding, a little bit bad with a broken heart I have to mend or one encased in ice I have to melt or better yet . . . both!"

Fazire thought this was getting a bit ridiculous. It was the most complicated wish he'd ever heard.

But she wasn't yet finished.

"We have to go through some trials and tribulations. Something to test our love, make it strong and worthy. And . . . and . . . he has to be daring and very masculine. Powerful. People must respect him, maybe even fear him. Graceful too and lithe, like a . . . like a cat! Or a lion. Or something like that."

She was losing steam and Fazire had to admit he was grateful for it.

"And he has to be a good lover." Lily shocked Fazire by saying. "The best, so good, he could almost make love to me just by using his eyes."

Fazire felt himself blush. Perhaps he should have a look at these books she was reading and show them to Becky. Lily was a very sharp girl, sharp as a tack (another one of Sarah's sayings, although Fazire couldn't imagine a tack ever being as clever as Lily). But she was too young to be reading about any man making love to her with his eyes. Fazire had never made love, never would, genies just didn't. But he was pretty certain fourteen-year-old girls shouldn't be thinking about it.

Though, he was wrong about that, or at least Becky would tell him that later.

Fazire realized she'd stopped talking.

"Is that it?" he asked.

She thought for a bit, clearly not wanting to leave anything out. Then she nodded.

"Are you sure you want this to be your wish?" Fazire asked.

She looked at him straight in the eye. Hers were somber and direct. Then she nodded again.

"Very well," Fazire said on a sigh.

He opened his mouth to speak but she put her hand out to stall him, resting it on his arm. "Don't forget that part about him loving me more than anything on earth."

He lifted his goateed chin in acknowledgement.

"And!" she burst out, squeezing his arm for emphasis, "The part about him thinking I'm beautiful."

"Lily, you *will* be beautiful, you already are."

Her chin quivered and he knew she was about ready to cry.

"Just don't forget those parts, they're the most important," she reminded him, her voice shaky and, Fazire thought, terribly, *unforgettably* sad.

His hand covered hers on his arm.

"I won't forget *any* of it."

Then Fazire lifted his hand, put it on her head and said softly, "Lily, my lovely, your wish is my command."

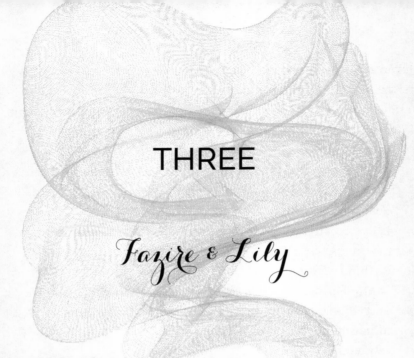

THREE

Fazire & Lily

Eight years later, Lily was now twenty-two . . .

IT WAS, QUITE SIMPLY, the worst time in his entire genie life.

And as Fazire had lived millennia that was saying quite a lot.

He thought the worst was when Sarah slipped away two years ago.

Fazire had never known anyone who'd died, and he'd known Sarah for decades. She was his roommate, his protector, his friend.

He'd had a good, long time with Sarah and he was lucky to have it. He knew that.

It didn't make him miss her any less.

She was kind to him and took care of him even on her teacher's salary. She kept him fed, clothed, happy, and showered him with baseball tickets and suntan lotion. Sarah never, even though it was her right, asked a thing from Fazire in all her years. She just gave and gave and gave.

The first and only human any genie in the entire history of the Genie race who had been entitled to but hadn't asked for one single wish.

Sarah, in Genie Land, was a legend as Fazire thought she very well should be.

She'd at least, before she died, seen the outrageous beauty Lily had become; the now well-rounded perfectness that was just simply Lily. Off gallivanting across the world, or at least England where she went to university and then decided to stay. Becoming sophisticated and cosmopolitan but never losing her down-home, Indiana-girl charm and spirit.

Lily's gold-white hair had changed. It was still golden with strands of white but also, unusually, had strands of strawberry blonde as well as copper. And just to make it that bit more interesting (not that it could get much more interesting), here and there were strands of auburn.

She'd been awarded a scholarship to go study at some place called "Oxford" in England after she won some writing competitions, creating magnificent stories that it seemed everyone wanted to read.

Once in England she became more interested in what she called "footpaths" and tramping around in cathedrals and castles and every museum in London (and a fair few shops) and writing more of her wonderful, entertaining stories, than eating. She was busy, busy, busy and the weight just melted off.

Tall, like her mother, father and grandfather before her, even though Fazire had only just seen photos of the handsome, slender Jim, Fazire knew he was tall. Lily was also curvaceous with a very small waist and a lovely hourglass figure.

She'd matured into her plain face. Her skin was always impeccable but once the baby fat left it, her intelligence and humor fixed it with extraordinary elegance and beauty.

And now, with those miraculous eyes, well . . .

She was, quite simply, stunning.

Lily was the pride of all of them: Sarah, Becky, Will and Fazire.

And she had absolutely no idea. None whatsoever.

Lily looked in the mirror and saw the old Lily, not the beauty she'd become.

So really Fazire had done his job. She definitely had humility and not the barest hint of conceit.

But now Lily looked beaten and he was very certain that this was the worst time in her entire human life as well.

She was sick every morning. He could hear her vomiting in the bathroom and he'd go in just like he did when she was a little girl and had the flu or one of her awful headaches that gave her so much pain she would get violently ill. Then he would stroke her back and hold her long, thick, glorious hair.

Fazire understood why she was ill. She was heartsick at losing her parents so close after her grandmother.

A plane crash. A horrible, hideous plane crash. They didn't even have the bodies.

One day Becky and Will were in Hawaii for a much needed vacation. They were taking a day trip to another island on a small twin-engine aircraft (this Fazire could not imagine, a plane, he thought, always needed a lot more than two engines).

The next day, they were gone.

Fazire had had to use the phone to call Lily in England. He knew how to use it, of course. He hadn't been living like a human for years and not learned how to order a pizza. But it had taken a long time to track her down. She had some job in a shop and bought a rundown house in some seaside town in Somerset called Clevedon for what she called "no money at all," which Will said laid testimony to just how rundown it was. A house that she was determined to restore to its full Victorian beauty.

Call after call, she didn't answer and Fazire finally decided she was not at her ramshackle abode.

She'd graduated from Oxford and declared she could not leave England. She loved it there. Fazire could see why from the pictures she sent home. It looked beautiful.

Nevertheless, Fazire hated it. It took away Lily and he wanted her home.

And now she *was* home, though he would never have wanted her home like this.

After contacting one of her friends who Becky had in her address book, a woman named Maxine, Fazire had eventually found Lily. Maxine said she was staying somewhere in London and gave Fazire the number.

Lily had answered the phone and had been so excited to tell him something, her voice just dripping happiness. He couldn't bear it, the sound of her happy voice while he was carrying his terrible news. He'd cut her short before she could put three words together and told her his grim tidings.

She'd, of course, taken the first flight home.

She sat next to him at the memorial service wearing a very smart black suit that looked stylish and cultured, and all the people around her didn't know what to make of her. She was very much not the Lily who had left at sixteen to go to Oxford. She was like a modern day princess—graceful, beautiful, refined and untouchable.

She held herself in a regal way that made Fazire so proud to have her on his arm it nearly edged away his bitter sadness at losing his Becky and Will.

Lily was very brave and kind to people, she nodded and smiled. After the service they went back to Sarah's limestone house, which was now Lily's, and she played hostess beautifully, making people feel comfortable and at home even though Fazire knew from her pale skin and sunken eyes she was exhausted.

There was so much food, it was everywhere and for the first time in his life he didn't eat a bite. Nor did Lily.

Everyone knew Fazire. He'd been around for decades and, of course, had not aged a single day. They thought this strange, but they figured he was from some foreign land and many of them never left the Midwest so what did *they* know about how foreigners aged? So they'd accepted him. Being a genie and thus above mere mortals, he didn't mix with them very often and now he did it only as his duty to Becky and Will and, of course, Lily. He helped Lily by playing host and kindly uncle-type figure ("uncle" was the term Sarah had come up to explain his presence in the family and Fazire liked it, always had).

Finally, hours after he thought it was seemly, the last of them left and Fazire cleaned up with a snap of his fingers because he knew Lily was too spent to do it. He put her to bed and stroked her hair until she fell asleep.

"Fazire?" she whispered right before she fell away to dreamland.

"Yes, my lovely?"

When she replied, she was still whispering but her voice held a deep sadness that scored Fazire's heart. "I'm never going to wish my last wish so you'll stay with me forever."

For the first time in his life he felt tears prick his eyes, and maybe he finally understood a little bit of what Sarah was feeling when he first met her.

"That's fine by me," Fazire whispered back but her exhaustion had already melted to sleep.

The next days she got up and was immediately sick. Furthermore, any time the phone rang, her face lit up with a strange mixture of expectation and relief and she'd rush to it. But it was always clear it was not who Lily was hoping it would be. Just a friend or family member wishing to give their condolence or asking how she was doing. Her face would fall dramatically, as if the caller had told her the world was about to come crashing to an end.

The days turned to weeks and Lily's phone rushes became more desperate. She was also making quiet calls time and again, but whatever was said made her all the more desolate.

Fazire found himself concerned.

Lily nor Fazire did a thing to work out what to do next. Neither of them had gone into Becky and Will's room, they couldn't face it. And there were a great deal of Sarah's belongings still there that should be sorted.

Lily had told him she didn't want to move back to Indiana and he, well, he'd never been in a plane. Nor did he want to after Becky and Will's awful demise. Not that *he* could die but *she* could. He could and did (very often, mostly in order to channel his genie friends) go back into his bottle and he could travel that way. But after they had this brief conversation, no plan came about.

Something else was disturbing Lily, something that had something to do with the phone and her early morning sickness that still came every day.

Finally he could take it no more. She'd been home over a month and they were both drifting through the house, Lily reading most of the time, Fazire fretting.

This just wasn't Lily.

She'd always had purpose, kept her room tidy, helped with the housework, got her homework done on time, pushed forward to submit her writing for competitions, helped with the cooking. She was a very good cook, but then again she was very good at everything, Fazire made her that way. She was a well-reared, polite, industrious Indiana girl.

Now she was tired all the time, even more cranky than Fazire (and Fazire was the King of Cranky, at least that was what Becky had called him), short-tempered and completely unmotivated.

This new behavior, Fazire thought, was not going to do.

Someone had to take care of him after all. *He* couldn't be expected to do it.

He decided it was high time to confront her. He knew she still had to be hurting about her parents, as was he, but they couldn't carry on like this forever. She wasn't even writing anymore.

"Lily, we have to talk," Fazire announced one day when he'd come upon her reading *again*.

He'd decided to float during the conversation. He did this on occasion so he wouldn't get out of practice. He also did it when he intended to put someone in their place, like he was going to put Lily now. He knew she was grieving but life had to go on. Sarah had said that after coming to terms with losing Jim, and Becky had said it after coming to terms with losing Sarah. Considering Fazire thought Sarah and Becky the most intelligent of humans, he figured it must be true. And, he realized rather shockingly, he was the only family she had left. There was no one else to snap her out of whatever state she was in.

Just him.

"Fazire, I'm in the middle of a good part," she murmured distract- edly not even looking up at him and twirling a strand of hair around her finger like she'd done while reading or watching television since she was a little girl.

He used his magic to flip her book out of her hands, levitated the bookmark sitting on the table, slapped it in her place and then the book flew across the room and set itself down well away from her.

She shot bolt upright on the couch. "Fazire!"

"You must tell me what's going on," he demanded in his best com- manding genie voice.

"I was reading," she replied, being deliberately obtuse, her elegant face settling into a charming disgruntled look that did not, at all, work on him (it would have worked on Will, her father was a pushover where

Lily was concerned).

"I don't mean now, I mean with you."

A shadow crossed her eyes. A shadow that was only part about losing both her parents in a plane crash six weeks ago.

"Lily," he went on, "I don't know if you realize this but I'm stuck in this world and it is not *my* world. Since you don't intend to use your wish then I can't go to someone else. I don't even *want* to. But in the meantime I depend on you to take care of me. I can't float around this house watching you read your books and twirl your hair forever. We have to have a plan and since I don't know anything about you mortals, *you* are going to have to make the plan."

"You know a lot more than you let on," she accused.

He got down to brass tacks (another one of Sarah's sayings that Fazire used but did not understand). "Indeed, I do, Lily-child, you would be wise to remember that. What's troubling you?"

Her beautiful face closed down rebelliously. Fazire had forgotten that she could be the slightest bit rebellious and more than a little stubborn. Fazire didn't give her *that*. *That* she got from her mother *and* her father.

He floated closer. "Lily, tell me."

"I . . . I, Fazire, I don't know what's going on. He was supposed to call. I had to leave so quickly and I wrote him a note, gave him my number here, told him what happened, told his *brother* what happened so *he* could tell him and he hasn't called." She stopped looking at Fazire and stared at the floor. "I can't believe he hasn't called, not after what I explained happened to my parents. And I've called him and the number isn't working. I know it's the right number but it's been disconnected. I called his office but he isn't returning my calls," she finished, speaking as if to herself.

"Who?" Fazire asked.

Her incredible blue eyes lifted to his and there was a world of worry and hurt in them.

Then she said, "Nate."

"Who, pray, is *Nate*?"

She fidgeted with her hands, dropping her head to stare at her nails.

"You remember my wish?" she asked.

How could he forget the most complicated wish ever?

"Yes," Fazire answered.

Her eyes lifted again and in them was something that made Fazire's genie heart beat a little faster.

"Well, it came true. His name is Nathaniel McAllister and he's the most wonderful man ever. And, I think . . . Fazire, I'm pretty sure I'm going to have his baby."

Fazire immediately stopped levitating and dropped heavily to the floor.

Then he screeched, "*What?*"

Lily shook her head and bit her lip before saying, "It was . . . I don't know. I can't think straight. It all happened so quickly. One second I was just, well, in London doing my normal London things. Going to museums, a little shopping . . ."

Fazire doubted it was a "little shopping." Lily could shop like Jackie Robinson could steal a base.

She kept talking. "The next thing I knew, I was going to fancy dinner parties and he was taking me out to romantic restaurants and midnight walks in the park and we made love again and again and again and it was so, it was . . ." She leaned forward, her eyes lighting before she whispered fervently, "*Spectacular*. Mind-boggling. You *cannot* even imagine."

Fazire tried floating again but could only get three feet off the floor. This was mainly because most of his concentration was spent on keeping his ears from burning and possibly dripping blood at his Lily-child talked about mind-boggling lovemaking.

"Then Mom and Dad . . ." She couldn't finish. They both still couldn't talk about it.

"He hasn't called," Fazire finished for her.

"No."

"Has he called, maybe, your thingie-ma-bobbie?" Fazire tried.

"My what?"

"The thing that records voices on the phone."

"My voicemail at home?"

"Yes, that."

"I picked up my messages, none were from him. He doesn't know my number anyway. I was always in London with him. He never had to phone me and I'm not listed."

Fazire thought for a while. He was, although out of practice, very good at what he did. Sometimes genies could go for years and years without having their bottle rubbed so they knew there might be magical delays and any good genie prepared well for them. Fazire, if he did think so himself, was very, very good with his wishes.

And he'd made absolutely certain sure Lily's was the best of all.

Something else must be happening with this . . . *Nate.*

Fazire peered at his mistress and made his decision.

Decision made, he declared, "Then we must go and find him."

FAZIRE WALKED UP THE SHORT staircase to the beautiful white house that Lily told him was something called "Georgian." It had black shutters and in every window there were window boxes filled so full with startling red geraniums, you couldn't tell where one flower stopped and the other started. Each box was trailing lacy, green ivy. There were fancy wrought iron fences in front of each house and all were painted a shiny, perfect black.

All the houses looked exactly the same. It was almost as if they had a pact that everyone on the whole street would have the same colored geraniums with trailing ivy so the street would look tidy and splendiferous.

Fazire very much wanted to hate this place called England, and he was pretty certain he'd really hate London for although Jim had found his bottle in a market in London, Fazire had actually come from a bazaar in Morocco and never been released in Europe at all. But even though some of London was rather shocking, busy, grimy and graffiti-filled, this street was quite lovely.

During their terrifying plane ride (neither Lily nor Fazire had a good time on that plane after what happened to Becky and Will, *and* it had far more than two engines), Lily told him some people lived in this house that knew her Nate, a man and woman named Victor and Laura. She said they were nice people, kind and caring, and they'd taken care of her after Nate had saved her life. Perhaps she'd understated the story when Fazire had been struck dumb at the idea that her life was in danger, and she explained this Nate saved her and her purse from a purse snatcher.

Lily was nervous, he could see her shaking and he stood two steps behind her. He was certain everything would be all right. This Nate had come to her through Fazire's wish, so of course it would be all right.

She knocked using the hoop that went through a brass lion's nose. Fazire thought that was peculiar. He'd never seen a lion with a hoop through its nose but he figured he'd mention that titbit later. Maybe use it as an opening gambit to some future conversation with Lily's Nate.

A dark-haired woman answered the door. Fazire was surprised that she was young, not much older than Lily. She was also crying, her face wet with tears and a mottled red with the force of her emotion. Fazire thought she might have been pretty without the tear-stained face but then decided she was not when she looked at Lily and her face contorted with repugnance and her eyes filled with hate.

"Oh, hello, Danielle, I was . . ." Lily paused then asked, "Are you all right?"

Lily stopped speaking and Fazire heard her voice was concerned as she lost all track of their quest and asked after the girl who was looking at her with such venom. Fazire wanted to grab Lily back but he stayed where he was in order to let her do what she needed to do.

"No, I'm not all right," the girl snapped. "What are you doing here, Lily?"

Fazire found himself thinking these people who lived here weren't very kind and caring at all.

Lily hesitated, somehow not surprised at this reaction from the woman, then she went on, "This is a little embarrassing but I had to leave town unexpectedly and now that I'm back, I went to Nate's and his doorman says he doesn't live there anymore. I was just—"

The woman didn't allow her to finish, her face changed to what looked somewhat sly and scheming to Fazire but he lost those thoughts at the next words she said.

"Nate's dead," Danielle informed them coldly.

Then, without further ado, she slammed the door right in Lily's face.

Lily stood staring at the door, frozen to the spot.

Fazire stood behind her, just as frozen.

And then, after what seemed like an age (and Fazire had lived many of them so he knew exactly how they felt), slowly she turned, stopped and simply stared down at him and Fazire saw that every bit of color had drained from her face.

Two years ago she'd lost her beloved grandmother. Barely two months ago she'd lost her parents. Now her new beloved boyfriend, the romantic hero that was supposed to sweep her off her feet (and at the sound of their meeting and courtship he'd certainly done that) and love her more than the earth, was dead.

She was twenty-two years old, pregnant, with only a genie to call family.

And the expression on her face showed every bit of that pain and agony.

Fazire ascended the two last steps and carefully put his arm around her fragile, tense shoulders.

"Let's get home," he murmured to his Lily-child.

She didn't move. In fact she seemed rooted to the spot.

Then she whispered, "But Fazire, where's home?"

He had no answer for that, for he didn't know.

It came to him.

"Wherever we make it, my lovely."

Part Two

FOUR

Nathaniel

THERE WERE NO GENIES in Nathaniel McAllister's life.

Nathaniel's father died before he was born. A knife fight in a pub brawl that had started because of his father's bad temper and penchant for fisticuffs and ended with him in a pool of his own blood.

Not that Nathaniel's mother, Deirdre, would have known that was his father. It could have been one of three, maybe even four, candidates. She did figure it out in a hazy way as he grew older and she'd look at her son and had some recollection of that drunken, drug-fueled night with his tall, lean, muscular, good-looking father.

Without genies or a parent who wasn't inebriated or incapacitated due to drugs all the time, Nathaniel learned early how to take care of himself. His mother was usually sleeping it off when she should have been getting him up and getting him cleaned and fed. Instinct and survival taught him to do the most basic tasks, and he could never remember a time that he didn't do all of those things for himself. Indeed, a great deal of the time he had to steal from his mother's purse or, somewhat more dangerously, one of her lovers' wallets, to go to the newsagent and get himself some milk and food. If his mother didn't have any money or there wasn't a lover around, which was often in the case of the former, but luckily, depending on how you looked at it, not the latter, sometimes he had to steal the milk and food from the newsagent. However, he learned quickly to pick ones further away from home.

Nathaniel McAllister learned everything quickly.

His mother got him into school though and he liked it there. He was smart, very smart. He knew this because the teachers told him so. Even the headmaster brought him into his office to have what the head called "a chat." They tried to tell his mother. Nathaniel, they said, should go to special schools. He was far, far brighter than most children, far more advanced, even, perhaps, a genius. Nathaniel remembered everything, absolutely everything, and he only needed to be told or shown once and he had it down pat. They said he was remarkable. They called him "gifted."

Deirdre had no money for special schools for her son and no interest in her son at all, gifted or not. So there were no special schools for Nathaniel. There was nothing special for Nathaniel.

Thus, forced to learn like normal, not-gifted children, Nathaniel became bored and restless. The teachers tried to help but there was only so much they could do. He didn't skip school, not at first. That came later. Being at school was better than being on the streets and definitely better than being at home.

Deirdre was a rather remarkable beauty and remained that way a lot longer than others would have, regardless of the booze and drugs she poured, swallowed, smoked, snorted or injected into her body. She might not have taken care of her lungs, nostrils, veins and liver but she took care of her appearance. She also had the advantage of her good, strong Scottish blood. She attracted men like a magnet and used them as best she could for whatever money, food, pills, drink or anything else she could get out of them. She allowed them to use her, debase her, abuse her, push her around and hit her, so these things would stay available in as much abundance as possible. She also allowed them to push around her son who, after a while, got pretty damned sick of it and learned to dodge the fists agilely and later, defend himself skillfully with his own.

Finally, when Nathaniel was eleven, she got herself a man who stuck around awhile. This man was named Scott. Scott hung around mainly because he liked Nathaniel, or Nate as he called him. Scott was the kind of man who recognized the promise in the boy and thought he was destined for great things. Or the kind of great things that came about in Scott's world.

Scott was not wrong, or at least not entirely wrong.

He gave Nate "jobs." Jobs that he would pay Nate to do and he'd sometimes pay even as much as twenty pounds.

Usually it was just taking packages and dropping them off at places or with people. This happened all the time—in the light of day, even during school hours, or the dead of night.

Although no adult in their right mind, although Nate knew very few adults in their right minds, would send a boy of eleven out in the early hours of the morning on the dangerous streets of London, Scott had no qualms about this. Nate was fast as lightning and learned quickly to melt into the shadows, not to mention he could take care of himself. Nate was young and knew no fear.

And Nate was very, very smart.

One night, months after Scott came into Nate's life, the drop did not go well. Nate sensed the danger with an instinct that was not only bred but born in him. He was cautious, he was quiet and he became invisible as he watched. When he knew the drop was a bust, he exited the scene swiftly and without being seen. Instead of panicking, he kept a cool head, found one of his many hiding places and stashed the package.

When he went home, Scott was livid.

"What do you mean you didn't do the drop? Mr. Roberts is going to lose his fucking mind!" Scott had shouted.

Nate had never seen Scott angry. He did not find this disturbing. There was not much that bothered Nate. He had long since learned to roll with the punches, often literally.

"You didn't lose it did you?" Scott demanded to know.

Nate shook his head. Nate didn't talk much. Nate had also long since learned to keep his mouth shut.

"Do you have it?" Scott asked.

Nate shook his head again.

"*Is it safe?*" Scott yelled.

Nate nodded his head.

Scott made some calls. He was talking on the phone in a respectful, frightened tone that Nate had never heard him use. When he was done, he turned on Nate.

"Take me to the package."

Nate again shook his head. He wasn't stupid enough to give up one of his hiding places. Even at eleven, nearly twelve, he figured he had a life yawning before him where he'd need many hiding places.

"That wasn't a request!" Scott shouted.

"I'll get the package, bring it to you," Nate offered. "Just tell me where."

Scott stared at him.

Scott, no fool (or at least not entirely a fool), knew that Nate was a tough customer. That was why he liked the kid. But Nate didn't know what this was about, how important this was. Nate had absolutely no idea how much trouble Scott was in.

Watching the boy, Scott knew he had no choice. He got on the phone and made hasty, embarrassing explanations. Then he had his orders.

Nate would, himself, bring the package to Mr. Roberts.

When Scott shared this with Nate, Nate shrugged. One drop, he thought, was the same as another.

Making certain sure he wasn't followed, Nate went to get the package and took it where Scott told him to take it. He was surprised when, on the grimy, dirty street corner, there stood an elegant, shining, long limousine. For some reason Nate didn't fear this and boldly approached the car.

The window rolled down slowly but Nate saw no one inside.

"Bloody hell, Scott. A kid?" Nate heard a rough, male voice say from inside.

"Mr. Roberts." He heard Scott's frightened voice.

"Get out," the rough voice came again.

"But, Mr. Roberts—"

"Out."

That one word should have scared Nate, the tone in which it was said would have scared anyone else. Nate just calmly got out of the way of the door.

Scott alighted from the car and looked down at the boy.

"Sorry, Nate," he said quietly then he took his chance and ran.

Nate never saw Scott again.

"Get in the car."

Nate, being a very smart boy, did as he was told.

He sat opposite a man like no man he'd ever seen before. He had thick, brown hair and assessing brown eyes and an angular, hard face. He was wearing a suit. Not the shiny, cheap kind of suit, a suit that looked like money. He had a nice, flashy watch and Nate could tell even his hair was not cut at the kind of barber that cut Scott's (Nate's mother cut his and not very well).

Nate also had very discerning tastes. He just didn't know it at the time.

"What's your name?" the man asked.

"Nate."

"Your full name."

He didn't hesitate. He also didn't fear this man.

"Nathaniel McAllister."

"That's better." The rough voice held approval. "How long have you been doing Scott's drops for him?"

Nate shrugged.

There was silence. Nate sensed something in the car he didn't understand. It didn't frighten him but another person would have been afraid, definitely a kid and also most men.

Nate, however, sat comfortably and waited.

Finally, after watching him awhile, the man said, "I paid Scott three hundred pounds for every drop you made."

This penetrated the ironclad shield Nate had around his emotions and reactions.

Instantly Nate got mad and it showed.

"How much did he give you?" the man asked.

Nate shrugged again but this shrug was different. This was a jerky, angry shrug. It was a good thing that Scott never saw Nate again.

The man sat there watching him. Nate struggled to settle his emotions. The struggle didn't last long. When he'd conquered his anger, the man smiled.

"I'm Mr. Roberts and from now on, Nathaniel, you work for me."

AND HE DID. FOR A year he worked for Mr. Roberts. He did drops, he delivered messages, he stood look out. He did a lot of things and got paid a lot more than twenty pounds.

Deirdre was thrilled. Nate began to pay the rent on the flat, paid all the bills on time and there was food in the refrigerator on a normal basis. Now *she* began to steal from *him*.

He didn't mind, there was plenty to go around, or at least a hell of a lot more than there used to be.

At twelve years old, Nathaniel McAllister was the breadwinner, the man of the house. He'd been that way since he could remember really, cleaning, tidying, holding her hair back when she'd overindulge and vomit in the toilet, dragging her in and putting her to bed when she passed out in the hall.

But now he was really the man of the house.

She, unfortunately, became stupid with their, or more to the point, *Nate's* good fortune. She bragged to anyone who would listen that her boy was working for Mr. Roberts.

She wasn't proud of his genius or of the budding good looks that were stamped on his features or the tall, lean strapping boy he had become. But she was proud that he'd become a gangster's errand boy at eleven years old.

This pride caused her death.

Drunk and bragging to her new boyfriend, an out-of-work, good-for-nothing, lazy bum (or at least that's what she called him) over and over again and very loudly. *Her* son worked for Mr. Roberts. *Her* son brought home lots of money. He bought her dresses, got her vodka.

Considering her boyfriend was drunk, high, stupid and mean he didn't take to this very well. He got fed up with it quickly and squeezed the breath out of her throat until there was no more, which, of course, made her shrill voice stop. After he did this deed, he took another, very large snort of cocaine that Nate's money had bought and he drank the rest of her bottle of vodka and he waited for Nate.

Nate didn't even have to walk into the flat to know something was wrong, but he did anyway. She was his mother. He'd been taking care of her for his lifetime. It was habit.

He opened the door and saw his mother's lifeless body. That was all he needed to see.

Her boyfriend made a grab but didn't come close.

Nate was so quick, he was vapor.

He vanished.

For a week.

And missed two scheduled drops.

Seven days later they found him, picked him up and took him to Mr. Roberts.

He sat in the back of the limousine. He'd seen Mr. Roberts twice since they first met. Both times he'd been friendly and cordial.

Now he was not.

"Would you like to tell me what's going on, Nathaniel?" Mr. Roberts's voice was very cold, and Nate knew this was no request.

"Me mum's dead."

This was met with silence.

Then, "My mum, Nathaniel."

Nate turned burning eyes to his employer. He didn't miss her, really, but she was all he had.

"My mum," he repeated sarcastically, perhaps the only living soul besides Mr. Roberts's two children who had the courage to speak to him sarcastically.

Instead of making him angry, Mr. Roberts found he admired this in Nathaniel.

"Where's your father?"

"Don't got one."

"Have one, Nathaniel."

"That either."

Mr. Roberts stifled a chuckle. It was no time to chuckle.

"Aunts, uncles?"

Nate shook his head.

"Your grandparents then."

Nate looked at him square in the eye and declared, "No one."

In his line of business Mr. Roberts learned to make quick decisions.

He liked this boy. There was something about this boy. Something special.

Mr. Roberts made a quick decision.

Decision made, he declared, "You're coming home with me."

FIVE

Nathaniel

VICTOR AND LAURA ROBERTS adopted Nathaniel McAllister.

He did not take their name, that was his decision and they allowed it.

He wanted to remember where he came from. He couldn't forget. He had to remember always what he was, who he was so he would never go back.

It would have been easy to forget with his new life.

It was almost like a genie came out of a bottle and gave him his every wish.

They were rich. Victor and Laura (he never called them Mum and Dad, even though Laura wanted him to) lived in a beautiful home on a street where all the houses were gleaming white, all the railings were glossy black and all the window boxes were filled with redder-than-red geraniums and trailing green ivy.

They had two children, Jeffrey and Danielle.

Jeffrey hated Nate with a passion.

Danielle loved him just the same.

Conversely, the first was a godsend. The second was a nightmare.

Jeffrey and Danielle had everything they ever wanted, everything they asked for, everything they desired. They had two parents who loved them and spoiled them too much, *way* too much. They had a beautiful home, beautiful clothes, food to eat that they didn't have to steal or cook, and servants to put clean, fresh sheets on their big beds and even iron their expensive clothes.

They'd never needed. They'd never been hungry. They'd never stolen. They'd never dodged a punch thrown by a grown, drunken man. And they'd never held their mother's hair back while she vomited.

Jeffrey knew from Nate's rough accent just who he was and where he came from, and he never let Nate forget it.

Never.

And this was good, Nate didn't want to forget.

Jeffrey's voice was posh from schooling at special schools. Jeffrey was the same age as Nate but would have lasted about two seconds in Nate's old neighborhood. Jeffrey knew this and Jeffrey knew his father knew this.

Jeffrey's father, he understood (though he was never told), had been like Nate when he was younger. Victor, Jeffrey had heard his father tell his mother one night, saw himself in Nate. Victor *admired* Nate. Jeffrey thought his father even doted on him and he was not wrong.

Jeffrey despised his father even before Nathaniel McAllister came into their lives. He was coarse and rough even though he tried to be polished and refined.

And he despised Nate and did everything he could to make his father's new son's life a living hell.

But nothing he did pierced Nate's armor. If anything it seemed Nate found Jeffrey amusing.

However Nate did not find Jeffrey amusing. Nate watched Jeffrey carefully. Nate trusted Jeffrey about as far as he could throw him. Jeffrey kept Nate's instincts for survival finely tuned.

Danielle, two years younger than Nate, took one look at the handsome young boy and fell instantly in love.

She wanted him. She was going to marry him. She knew this at age ten.

And everything Danielle had ever wanted, she'd been given.

So after first clapping eyes on him, she decided she owned Nate.

And she was not a girl who liked sharing.

It took Nate mere months to melt into their lives. He was a

chameleon. Even though for two years he'd barely gone to school, he caught up so swiftly he immediately became the teachers' pet. He lost his rough accent within two months, lost his tough manners at one dinner at their spectacular, shining dining table simply by watching what they did and emulating it. He wore his new expensive clothes with a casual grace that made Jeffrey seethe and Danielle's heart skip a beat. He learned tennis, how to ride a horse, how to play cricket, rugby, soccer, and in no time at all was the best. Better than Jeffrey, better than Victor, better than any boy at school or even the coaches.

Jeffrey hated it.

Danielle loved it.

Laura adored it, adored the boy, her new son.

At first her heart went out to him. Victor had sent men to find out Nate's story and this story Victor shared with Laura. Nate reminded her so of her beloved husband. She realized quickly Nathaniel's pride and history would not bear her coddling, which she *so* wanted to do. Instead she treated him with respect, almost like an adult, and *that* he responded to. He'd never really had a mother and at first he distrusted Laura, but after time she won him over. This was because she didn't treat him like a kid, she didn't treat him like he was stupid, but she did treat him like she cared because she did.

Victor grew to love the boy with a fierceness he had for neither of his other children. He felt guilty about this but as he'd been busy wiping the scum from his skin, the filth from under his fingernails, erecting a life of privilege and giving them everything they'd whined to have, they never, not once, said thank you. They never, not once, did anything but ask for more. This was partially his fault. He wanted them to have everything he didn't. And he wasn't around that often. He had not been a good father. He knew this.

Victor Roberts was also not a good man nor was he a kind man. He was a dangerous man. This was out of necessity and this was what Nate would have become.

But Victor loved his children, as hard as it was sometimes. He adored his wife. But the best thing he'd ever done, outside of marrying Laura, was bringing Nate into their lives.

And once he did he made up his mind that his fortune, his business, everything he had would go to Nate. Victor would take care of Jeffrey and Danielle, most certainly. They'd never want for anything. But he knew Nate would not let Victor's hard work, his sacrifice and the black marks he'd scored onto his own soul go to waste.

The minute Nate's adoption was legal (after a few strings were pulled, favors were called in and palms were greased), Victor Roberts went legitimate. He would not saddle Nate with a glorified life of crime. Nate had become a gangster's boy at eleven. He would be his own man, a gentleman, at twenty-one.

And thus Nate's new life led him through different challenges. Posh schools, where Jeffrey made sure all the boys knew Nate's background. This also kept Nate's instincts honed as he'd been called out for nasty fistfights, constantly, just for the other boys to test their mettle against streetwise Nate (the other boys always lost, soundly). Cambridge, where Jeffrey was thrown out for terrible marks. Country clubs, where Danielle tried to get Nate to take her virginity. This he did *not* do, instead a lifeguard did it while she convinced herself Nate was watching in jealousy, but Jeffrey was watching and laughing. Sunday rugby matches, where Nate, to Laura and Victor's delight, always led his team to victory.

All the while Victor groomed Nate for his future. Victor did this alongside Jeffrey who took no interest and eventually just took himself off and was given a nominal post that came with a very good office where he could seduce a variety of women.

Victor took his own cunning and tapped his new genius son's bright mind and together they found legitimacy and respectability, made masses of money and forged a relationship closer than blood.

Victor knew Nathaniel's future was bright. He'd taken great pains to assure it. Nathaniel would make a good marriage (if he'd simply stop sampling all the skirt that threw itself at him, Laura was getting distressed). He'd have beautiful children. He'd live in a beautiful home. He'd always take care of Jeffrey and Danielle out of duty and respect to Laura and Victor. And he'd be certain that Victor's legacy was secure.

This Victor thought was assured.

But Nate never forgot where he came from, never forgot who he was, never forgot *what* he was, never trusted what he had and always knew he didn't deserve it.

So he worked hard, harder than any man, to keep it, build it and make it strong.

So it would never go away.

So he'd never go back.

So it would never destroy him.

And he was beginning to feel his success.

And then came Lily Jacobs.

Part Three

SIX

Nate and Lily

Years later, it was the month of May and Nate was twenty-eight,
Lily was twenty-two . . .

"WE'RE LATE," VICTOR GRUMBLED.

"I know," Nate replied nonchalantly, lifting his chin in an arrogant gesture to the driver of the Rolls who was watching them walk down the crowded, tourist-clogged pavement outside Harrods.

"Your mother is going to skin us alive."

Nate wanted to laugh at this ridiculous comment but he didn't because Nate McAllister rarely laughed.

Laura Roberts didn't have a violent bone in her body. She did have a fierce temper but Nate had only seen it twice in the sixteen years he knew her. And both times, the minute it blew, she was spent. Both times, it lasted less than ten minutes. She was the kindest, gentlest, most even-tempered creature he'd ever been honored to know. That didn't mean, however, that she didn't have a steely determination when she wanted one of her children to do something they didn't want to do, she just rarely got her way.

"She'll get over it once she sees your anniversary present," Nate noted just for something to say. He knew Victor was worried about the present. If there was nothing to like about the man who had become his father, and Nate thought that there was although many people disagreed, one had to admire him for his devotion to his wife.

Though an anniversary present for Laura was a challenge.

What did you give a woman who had everything, wanted for nothing and would have lived in a hovel happily if she simply had her husband with her?

"You'd make her night if you asked Georgia to marry you this evening," Victor remarked.

He walked beside Victor to the waiting Rolls as Bennett, Victor's chauffeur, pulled open the door to allow them entry. Nate had better things to do than be on this errand with Victor, many better, more pressing, even urgent things to do.

But Victor had asked and no matter what Victor asked, Nate gave. That was the deal in Nate's mind though not Victor's. Nate owed Victor his life.

People were staring at the two men who obviously, by the look of their tailored suits, stylish silk ties, expensive shoes and gleaming watches, not to mention the chauffeur-driven Rolls-Royce, actually *shopped* at Harrods rather than visited as a tourist attraction.

Then again people often stared at Nate and most of these people were women.

He was uncommonly, one could even say *impossibly*, handsome. Very tall, lean, narrow-hipped, broad-shouldered with a wealth of thick black hair that had just the barest blue sheen to make it interesting. He had strong features, a firm jaw, powerful cheekbones and a sensual lower lip. He also had glittering, dark eyes that although he didn't know it (and wouldn't have cared if he did), were the avid topic of many women he knew. Fights even broke out. Were his eyes so gray they were nearly black or were they so blue they were nearly black? After much discussion, no answer was deemed acceptable so the battle raged on.

Nate's sensual lips thinned at Victor's words. He knew Laura wanted him to marry and settle down, give her grandchildren. But he was also relatively certain she didn't want him to do it with Georgia.

"I'm not asking Georgia to marry me," Nate stated firmly.

"Why not?" Victor asked and then went on, "She's a damned fine woman."

She was not a damned fine woman. She was a she-cat. She was nearly as bad as Danielle, if that could be credited. He'd caught Georgia snapping her birth control pills into the toilet, so he'd meticulously worn condoms. Then he'd caught her putting holes in the condoms, so he'd stopped having sex with her altogether and began the weary process of scraping her off.

He should never have dipped his foot in the family pool. Georgia was Laura and Victor's best friends' daughter. Nate even liked Georgia's parents, had known them for years.

They all had high hopes, but Georgia was history.

She'd worked hard at gaining Nate's attention. She was leggy, slender, with beautiful auburn hair and she'd always been somewhat amusing in a dry, catty way.

Therefore, Nate had rewarded her for her dogged pursuit of him. And she had rewarded him for rewarding her. As good as it was with her, and it was good, it wasn't going to last a lifetime.

Nate knew that innately. She had too much venom in her and she let it show too often. Nate had no patience for venomous women. Especially those who grew up having everything, wanting for nothing and having no reason to be the slightest bit harsh considering the privileged life they'd led.

Nate didn't know what he wanted but whatever it was, it certainly was *not* Georgia.

He was saved from answering Victor when he spied a youth wearing a gray hooded sweatshirt, the hood worn up even though it was a warm day. The boy was slouching down the pavement, head bowed, hands in the front pocket of the sweatshirt, his head swinging this way and that, looking for his mark.

Nate's guard, already on alert—always on alert—went into overdrive.

Nate's eyes narrowed as he watched the youth, and Victor started to get into the Rolls. Then, as expected, the boy darted toward his target and Nate heard a woman's outraged cry.

"Hey!" she yelled.

He watched the boy snatch the woman's purse, his body tensing for action.

And then his eyes moved to the woman and uncharacteristically, he froze.

"Hey! He stole my purse! Stop him! He stole my purse!" she shouted.

Nate vaguely registered she was an American tourist. Nate also absently noticed that no one moved to assist.

In that brief moment in time, Nate was too busy drinking in the vision that was her, he himself didn't move a muscle.

She was tall, incredibly tall.

And curvy, delectably curvy.

She had the most unusual colored hair. Hair that he knew from vast experience living in a house with Laura and Danielle for years came through a supremely talented and expensive stylist's hands.

And she had an exquisite face, flawless skin and a bearing that was extraordinary. She had been given a wide berth around her even on the crowded pavement. Not because she was screaming her head off but instead because she was majestic, radiant, elegant . . .

Untouchable.

In a stupor from simply looking at her, the boy with her purse charged right by Nate.

Not in a stupor, she realized no one was going to help her, gave up screaming and charged right after the boy.

At the noise, Victor turned away from the car and Nate shifted to watch in astonishment as she deftly and agilely dodged the crowd, her long legs a match for the short boy. Then Nate watched in stunned surprise as she jumped onto the thief's back with a graceful leap.

Everyone stared in shock but no one lifted a finger except a few started to take photographs.

"Give me back my purse, you thug!" she shouted.

Wrapping her long legs around her prey, one arm around his neck, she slapped him around the head with the other hand.

The thief staggered back then he staggered with intent and slammed her against the side of the building. Her head snapped back and cracked against the stone so loudly Nate could hear it from where he stood twenty paces away.

At the sound Nate jerked out of his stupor and forged forward.

"Nathaniel . . ." Victor called but Nate ignored him.

Regardless of the blow, she wasn't done fighting and had not eased her grip.

"Give it ba—" she started to scream but didn't finish.

The boy doubled in half and flipped her over. She lost her hold and went flying over his head, landing on her back on the pavement with a sickening thud.

The boy didn't take a single step though he started to do so. With one leg lifted to make good his escape, Nate grasped his sweatshirt in a clenched fist and pulled him back. With a violent jerk, Nate yanked him off his feet, around towards the side of the building, and let him go, brutally slamming him against the stone wall beside a huge display window.

Swiftly Nate's hand settled on the thief's throat, squeezing savagely and lifting until the boy was on his toes.

"Drop the bag," he ordered in a voice cold as ice with an edge akin to that of a razor.

The thief immediately dropped the bag.

"I-I'll call the police." Her low, rich American voice, a voice that had a strange twang to it, stuttered from beside him as she cautiously leaned forward to grab her bag. Nate noted she wasn't moving cautiously because of fear but because she was hurt.

Nate turned to watch her, her head was bent as she searched through her bag and then she pulled out a mobile and lifted her eyes to him.

The moment they hit his, Nate froze again.

Her eyes were simply indescribable. A pale blue that was bottomless, inescapable, the irises rimmed by a smoky midnight that was so alluring, he thought for a moment he'd leaned toward her, he was so drawn to her eyes.

They widened upon looking at him almost as if she recognized him.

A gasping noise came from the thug.

Nate didn't move. He stared in frozen fascination as she stole closer.

Without taking her unbelievable eyes from his, her hand settled gently on the forearm that was holding the thief against the wall. When it did, fire shot up his arm from where she touched him.

"You're choking him," she whispered.

His hold loosened and her hand dropped. With effort he tore his eyes from hers and dropped his hand only to grasp a handful of the thug's sweatshirt at his throat, jerk him forward a few inches and slam him viciously back against the wall.

The boy grunted in pain.

"Hurts, doesn't it?" Nate snarled and fury unlike anything he'd known ripped through him as he looked at the boy.

"Bennett has called the police. Bloody hell, girl. Are you all right?" Victor was at their sides, had his hand on the girl's shoulder and was bent into her, peering at her to ascertain the answer to his question.

"I think so. Just had the breath knocked out of me, that's all," she answered.

"What were you thinking, leaping on him like that? You could've been hurt," Victor admonished because she was not all right. She was holding her body like it was made of crystal. She was not as deft and loose-limbed as she had been while flying toward her assailant.

Victor slid his arm around her waist in an effort of support because of the way she held her body.

"He took my purse," she answered Victor's question.

"It was still bloody dangerous," Victor carried on with his gentle remonstration.

"I *like* this purse," she returned with a slight teasing lilt to her tone and a quirky, shaky smile.

Witnessing that quirky smile Nate found he was having trouble breathing.

Victor's head came up at her smile and then snapped to look at Nate. Or more to the point, he took one look at the way Nate was looking at the girl. Victor looked again to her. Then back at Nate.

Then he made a quick decision.

"Nathaniel, wait for the police. I'm taking her home to Laura and calling our physician."

"No, please, I'm fine. I'll stay to talk to the police," she resisted.

"Nathaniel will bring them to the house. You can talk to them at home. Come with me." Victor was using his no-nonsense, no-argument voice, a voice that sent shivers up grown men's spines.

She completely ignored it. "Really, no. I should stay."

"Go with him," Nate's voice rumbled this command and her head jerked round to look at him. She regarded him for a moment and he wondered what she'd do.

It took a moment but she nodded.

Nate watched over his shoulder as Victor put her in the Rolls and it swept cleanly away.

Not long after, the police arrived.

LILY CAREFULLY UNFOLDED HERSELF OUT of the decadent bath-tub, snatched a velvety-plush, peach-colored towel from the heated rail and wrapped it around her sore body.

Laura had forced her into a hot, scented bath even though Lily resisted because she wanted to be available for the police when they arrived.

The physician, who was at the doorstep of the house within moments of their own arrival, as Victor phoned from the car and told him to "get his ass to the house," had told her to take some ibuprofen, a long, hot bath and told Laura and Victor to keep an eye on her for a couple of days. Lily had no broken bones, no cracked skull. She was fine but just in case she was not, the physician said she should be looked after.

After a brief but earnest talk Lily had seen them have in the hallway, Laura, with Victor's adamant concurrence, insisted she stay the night with them rather than taking the train back to Clevedon. Then they insisted she take a bath.

Without the strength to resist them, or, indeed the ability (they were *very* insistent, very nice but not the kind of people who took no for an answer), there she was in their Georgian mansion, in their opulent bathroom that was off an equally sumptuous guest bedroom decorated in what she had counted were at least seven different but coordinating shades of pale peach.

And she'd finally met the man Fazire had sent to her.

Lily was certain of it. As certain as she was that she was Lily Sarah Jacobs, daughter of Rebecca and Will Jacobs and a Hoosier born and bred. And there was no denying any of that.

When she'd lifted her gaze to look into the eyes of her tall defender she'd nearly fainted. Swooned. Fallen to the ground in an unconscious heap.

If he hadn't been imminently facing a life sentence for strangling a man to death, regardless if he was a nasty purse snatcher, she would have done it.

And now . . .

Now . . .

Now what?

She didn't know what to do. She couldn't exactly throw herself at him. Tell him she'd wished for him to come to her through her own personal genie that just happened to live at home with her parents in a small town in Indiana. She couldn't seduce him, because since she was a virgin, she wouldn't even know how. In fact he probably, considering how handsome he was (*impossibly* handsome), didn't know she existed as a female with all the right parts in all the right places and with all the yearning she felt for him even though she only knew his name.

Nathaniel.

That was a very, *very* good name.

"Lily, my dear, the police are here," sweet, kindly Laura called from the other room.

Lily had taken to Laura immediately. The older woman was petite and slightly but pleasantly rounded with middle age. She had a soft dark-brown bob that framed her face, elegant hands with perfect fingernails (Lily thought they looked like pianists hands, they were so lovely) and warm, brown eyes.

"I'll be right out," Lily called back.

She quickly toweled off, wrapped the towel around her body and rummaged through her saved purse for a hair band. She pulled her hair into a ponytail at the back of her head and went into the bedroom where she saw Laura standing at the bed, which now had a half a dozen shiny boxes resting on it.

Lily stopped and stared.

Laura explained, "I called a few shops. Since you're staying, you need a few things, of course. I hope you don't mind but I checked the labels on your clothes and found your size."

How long was I in the bath? Lily thought incredulously as she stared at the boxes.

"I can't," Lily resisted.

"You can, you will, you must," Laura returned in a mother's voice that would not be denied. Lily had heard that voice before. Her own mother used it on her often. Laura lifted the lid off a box and pulled out a silvery blue silk robe with long flowing sleeves like a Japanese kimono and ordered, "Put this on."

Lily let out a soft laugh and then exclaimed, "I can't face the police in a robe!"

"They only have a few questions. I told them you're in no state to be given the third degree," she stated smartly then ripped the lid off another box and pulled out a pair of pristine white satin underwear edged in delicate lace. "If it'll make you feel better, wear these . . . and . . . this." She found and shook the matching bra at Lily.

Lily couldn't help herself. As rude as it was (and she knew it was rude), she continued to stare.

Two hours ago she'd been walking down a London street intent on doing a bit of window-shopping as her meager finances didn't allow much more. She had several days off from work at Maxine's store and didn't fancy working on her house, scraping, painting, priming or hauling herself under a sink with a plumber's manual to try to fix a pipe. She'd come to London for a little day break, to go to a few museums that were free admission and to do some shopping.

Now she'd entered Fantasy Land.

"Laura you . . . honestly, really, I just can't."

Laura moved toward her, pressed her palm against Lily's face like Lily's mom did sometimes in her tender moments (of which there were many) and looked into Lily's eyes.

"Don't keep them waiting, my dear. The sooner you get this over with the sooner we can all enjoy our evening."

On that she exited the room and Lily, because of the motherly touch that Laura had given her (such a familiar touch), swiftly donned the undies, the robe and just stopped herself from running to the bathroom to grab another bath sheet and wrap that around her as well.

She gingerly walked out of the room. The bath had helped as had the pills but she most definitely felt like she'd been flipped over someone's shoulder onto a concrete sidewalk.

Lily didn't know what she was thinking charging after a purse snatcher except it was an expensive designer purse that she could never have afforded under normal circumstances. She'd found it while trolling through a vintage clothing store and she'd bought it for a song. She'd never be able to replace it.

Regardless of that, her actions were reckless. She could have been hurt or harmed in some other way if he'd had a knife or another weapon.

Her parents, if they ever heard of this, would kill her. Fazire would start floating and look down his genie nose and wag his genie finger at her. She could never tell them.

Holding onto the banister, she carefully descended the stairs. She kept her body even stiffer than it felt so as not to jar any of the aches and pains that threatened. Her head was throbbing where it had hit the wall, not the pounding pain of one of her intermittent migraines but not pleasurable either.

She was concentrating on her feet hitting each of the dove-gray carpet-runnered stairs. She was also assessing her pedicure, mentally telling herself that, even in England, as it was May, it was time to move away from the deep wine color of winter and find something else like a pearly pink. Her foot hit the parquet floor of the entryway and it was then she became aware that she wasn't alone.

Her head snapped up and there he was.

Nathaniel.

He was watching her as any romance novel hero would watch the heroine. With one shoulder leaned against the wall and his arms crossed on his chest.

And he was utterly beautiful in a raw, powerful, immensely masculine way.

They didn't, however, stare at each other with blissful, love-induced wonder. Or at least he didn't stare at her that way. She, unfortunately, was more than likely staring at him that way, to her horror. He was watching her with narrowed scrutinizing eyes. Eyes that didn't miss a thing.

Not . . . one . . . thing.

"How are you feeling?" he asked, his voice deep and strong and sending tingles across her skin.

"Fine," she lied and tried for a jaunty smile.

His face darkened. Obviously the jaunty smile didn't work.

"Liar," he said softly, dangerously, and he looked like he wanted to commit a violent act. Something like what he did to the thug, ferociously slamming him against the building like the thief had slammed her, exacting her retribution for her. The very thought of that memory chased a thrill up her spine.

"I *will* be fine . . ." she hesitated, doing a mental assessment of her aching body, "eventually."

He watched her for a moment, his eyes sweeping the length of her, that awful look on his face. She blushed at his gaze and found she was frightened of him just a little bit. He looked sophisticated and urbane on the outside, wearing that suit so casually as if he was in jeans and a t-shirt. Somewhere, though, somewhere very close to the surface, he was anything but sophisticated and urbane.

He broke into her thoughts. "The police are in the drawing room."

Lily was relatively certain she'd never been in a drawing room before or not one in a house where people actually lived. She didn't know people who had drawing rooms.

He pulled away from the wall and she found her body stiffening in weird preparation for something as he came toward her, but he just walked by her.

With no choice, she followed.

He entered a room and she came in after him. In the room were Laura, Victor and two police officers.

"Here she is," Laura announced, smiling at Lily encouragingly.

The room was lovely, decorated in soft pale greens, accented with white cornices and stately yet comfy-looking furniture. Nathaniel moved to stand behind and beside a high-backed chair. He glanced at Lily and then down at the chair and she understood somehow that he wanted her . . . no, was *telling* her to sit in the chair.

She did what she was mutely told.

The interview, as Laura promised, took less than ten minutes. They asked questions, they took notes and Laura and Victor watched her with kind, parental eyes. Not as if she'd met them hours before but as if she had been under their guardianship and devoted care since birth.

However this was not why the interview was so short.

Although she did not see him, she knew that Nathaniel stood behind her the entire time. And she knew this because she felt him there. He did not move a muscle or make a noise until the police seemed to be checking facts and asking the same questions over again.

Then in a tone that even General Patton would have calmly and unresistingly obeyed, he said, "You have enough."

They didn't argue or even demur. Immediately one of them simply said, "Right, Mr. McAllister."

They nodded at Nathaniel, and Lily found she now had his last name, a name of which she approved.

McAllister.

"Mr. and Mrs. Roberts." The police nodded at Laura and Victor.

The realization dawned that Nathaniel and the Roberts did not share the same surname and Lily wondered at Nathaniel's relationship with Laura and Victor because he obviously wasn't blood as she thought. He didn't look like either Laura or Victor but Lily thought for certain the relationship was deep enough for blood ties.

Maybe he was a favored nephew.

"We're off," the policeman finished.

They did not give Lily a card, ask her to call them if she remembered anything else, they just left.

Before anyone could say anything, a boyishly good-looking, not as tall as Nathaniel but still tall, brown-haired man walked in.

"What's this? First the anniversary celebration is off, now the police are at the house. What? Has Nate's checkered past finally caught up with us?"

Then he stopped dead and stared at Lily for some reason in open-mouthed surprise.

She didn't think much about this new man's open-mouthed surprise. She instead found herself thinking she did not at all consider it was surprising that Nathaniel had a checkered past.

"My God," the man breathed bringing Lily's thoughts back into the room.

"This," Victor stated as introduction to Lily, "is my son, Jeffrey."

Jeffrey came forward, extending his hand and told her, "Everyone but Mum and Dad call me Jeff."

She lifted her hand to shake his but he turned it, bent at the waist and brought it to his mouth, brushing his lips against her knuckles.

His eyes came to hers.

"And who are you?" he asked, and she thought his tone was flirtatious although she didn't have a great deal of experience with flirtatious. Or at least for the past four years or so she naively hadn't noticed it relentlessly coming her way.

"I'm Lily Jacobs," she answered.

"No, you're not Lily Jacobs. You are an angel sent from heaven," he surprised her by saying quietly, definitely flirtatiously, finally dropping her hand after holding it longer than necessary.

As he straightened, Lily noticed the entire room changed and seemed even to shift at his words. The air became so thick it could be cut with a knife. Victor tensed and his eyes flew to where Nathaniel was still standing at the back of her chair. Laura slowly stood and her eyes slid to Lily, her hand moving to her throat in a strange gesture of imminent peril. And Lily could actually feel something dangerous emanating from behind her.

Lily bravely ignored whatever was happening and her eyes held Laura's because they seemed the safest.

"What anniversary celebration?" she asked.

Laura started to answer, "It's nothing, my dear—"

Jeff was moving to the fireplace and he interrupted his mother, "It's not nothing. I wouldn't say your thirtieth wedding anniversary is nothing." He turned and blithely leaned an elbow on the mantel.

Lily gasped and opened her mouth to speak. She couldn't believe that they'd cancelled their anniversary for her but Jeff wasn't finished.

His eyes moved to Nathaniel and when they did they were calculating.

"By the way, Nate, Georgia called. She's pretty pissed off about something. Likely best if you put that damned ring on her finger, finally. That'll bring her to heel."

Lily closed her mouth with a snap.

He had a girlfriend, a girlfriend that sounded very close to being a fiancée.

Of course.

Of course, of course, of course.

She knew it couldn't be real. He would never have even looked at her anyway, not plain, small-town Indiana girl Lily Jacobs. Even with her wish from Fazire, she'd never get a glorious man like Nathaniel McAllister.

Never.

"I hope you didn't cancel your anniversary for me," Lily covered her disappointment with words.

Laura's eyes, which were not so kind at the moment but looked rather nettled, moved away from her son to Lily and immediately softened again.

"We've only postponed it until tomorrow."

"Oh no! You must carry on," Lily cried.

"It's all been sorted, Lily. Not to worry," Victor barged in to the short, now dismissed discussion and then started purposefully toward the door saying, "Jeffrey, I'd like a word with you."

"Oh for fuck's sake, what have I done now?" Jeffrey muttered not-so-under his breath and Laura's eyes turned back to annoyed. "I see, my dear brother, he doesn't want a word with *you*," Jeff finished, eyes to Nathaniel looking strangely like a bratty little boy.

Nathaniel didn't utter a word, which seemed to anger Jeff more.

But Lily was wondering how Nathaniel was his brother. The brother thing made sense in the way Victor treated Nathaniel and Laura looked at him. But they didn't share the same last name and they didn't look a thing alike.

When Nathaniel was obviously not going to be lowered into a useless fight about what appeared to be nothing, Jeff started to slink away but stopped when he reached Lily.

"I don't know who you are but I hope to see more of you." He smiled, his boyish good looks and good humor restored, and he seemed quite charming again.

She smiled back tentatively but somehow Lily found that he made her uncomfortable. For the first time in Lily's life she took a near immediate dislike to someone.

After he left the room, Lily turned back to Laura.

"I feel terrible. Your anniversary—" she started.

"Really, Lily, it's no trouble. I'm actually relieved. We can have a nice quiet night just the two of us. I'd rather that anyway. I'm sure Nathaniel can entertain you while Victor and I go out to a dinner à deux."

Laura raised hopeful eyes to Nathaniel, and even though she didn't want to, Lily turned in her chair to look at him too.

Gone was the suppressed violence. In its place was bland unconcern.

"I should see to Georgia." He'd been leaning his weight on his hand on the back of her chair and with his words, he pushed away.

"I'm sure Georgia would understand. We have a guest in the house," Laura replied.

Nathaniel approached Laura, and Lily watched in fascination as he stopped in front of her and kissed her forehead in a familiar, loving way.

"I don't live here anymore, remember?" His voice was light, even teasing, and Lily felt her insides melt (just a little).

"I suppose Jeffrey will find *something* for him and Lily to do," Laura said this like a dare and Lily didn't know what to make of that.

"I'm sure he will," Nathaniel muttered, turned his dark eyes, *impossibly* dark eyes, to Lily and said in his deep voice, "Lily."

Even as his voice sounding her name stole over her skin like a soft touch, he strode, just like his father, purposefully from the room.

And Lily could swear she heard Laura say the word, "damn," under her breath.

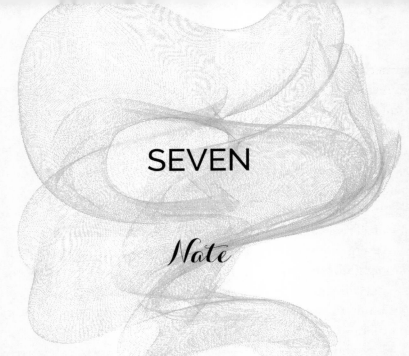

SEVEN

Nate

"I CAN'T BELIEVE I'M doing this." Georgia's voice was bitter and angry. "I can't believe I agreed to attend your parent's anniversary party with you after you just broke up with me. Tell me again why I'm doing this?"

Nate maneuvered the Maserati into a parking spot, pulled up the emergency brake and shut down the car. Then he turned to Georgia, resting his forearm on the steering wheel.

"Out of respect for my parents," he answered what he thought was obviously.

His words were short, his patience was fraying. She'd been carrying on since they left his flat and Nate vowed never again to get entangled with a spoiled-rotten, filthy-rich bitch.

"Well I've changed my mind," she returned sharply. "I'm not going to do it."

He turned from her. "Then I'm sure you'll find your own way home."

She gasped in outraged shock as if there weren't hundreds of taxis in London that would take her safely home, and just like that, Nate was finished with her.

He exited the car and didn't bother to help her alight as he normally would, a gentlemanly courtesy Laura had taught him years before. Then he walked to his parent's home. He heard her high heels clicking on the pavement double time to keep up with his long strides. He didn't knock because he didn't have to, it was his home even though after all these years he still found that fact difficult to believe, and he strolled into the house.

He heard party sounds immediately, the low murmur of conversation and soft laughter.

Lily, he knew, was there somewhere.

Laura had called Nate to tell him she'd convinced Lily to stay another night and attend the party. His mother explained that Lily had woken stiff and sore and they'd called the physician straight away. Lily, Laura assured him, still had a clean bill of health but needed time to recuperate which Laura, being Laura, was determined to give her. Nate also had the feeling that Laura was instilling a bit of drama into the situation in order to keep Lily there, considering, after she told him the story of Lily's pain and suffering, she announced they were going out shopping.

Nate wondered how Lily and Jeff had spent their evening last night. He very much didn't like the idea of a "Lily and Jeff" but he felt it was far more appropriate than a "Lily and Nate."

Nate knew who he was, what he was and where he came from. He had no qualms at taking the cosmopolitan, seen-it-all, done-it-all Georgia to his bed.

However the likes of Lily Jacobs, with her sweet, low voice, perfect, untouchable skin and trusting eyes was not for the likes of Nate.

Nate McAllister didn't know his father. His mother was a drunk, a drug addict and, for all intents and purposes, a whore. She'd been murdered by one of her many drug-addled lovers in a grimy, dingy flat in a grimy, dingy neighborhood. Nate started stealing before his age hit double digits and his first mode of employment had been working for a gangster who was no longer, but it didn't change the fact that Nate had participated in a life of crime before he'd even entered his teens.

Lily Jacobs was too good for him.

Nate knew this straight to his soul.

"Nate!" It was Danielle, his adoptive sister, looking lush in a black dress that, as usual, showed way too much flesh.

She rushed to him and gave him an overfriendly, overlong and not at all sisterly hug.

"I hear you played the hero yesterday," she remarked as she leaned away from him, keeping her hands on his shoulders and her eyes, Laura's eyes but without the warmth, peered closely at him.

He didn't answer.

"She's still here, the American," Danielle informed him and disengaged when he didn't so much as touch her. "You should see what she's wearing. She and Mum took off somewhere this afternoon, I think Covent Garden or Notting Hill, who knows? Came back from shopping with loads of bags. It's embarrassing, Mum shopping in Notting Hill at her age. Oh, hi Georgia."

Georgia had arrived and stopped beside Nate, her face a mask of anger.

Danielle, ever-assessing, looked closely at Georgia then back at Nate, who in turn looked indifferent. A sly, satisfied smile crept across Danielle's face making her pretty features a lot less pretty.

"Everything okay?" Danielle asked with feigned concern, knowing the answer.

She'd been watching his relationships closely for years. She knew Georgia's time was at an end.

"Fine," Georgia answered curtly, knowing for a long time that Danielle considered herself competition for Nate's affection. "What are you talking about?"

Danielle crossed her arms, which forced a goodly amount of cleavage to spill out the top of her strapless dress.

"Well, apparently Nate saved some American woman from a purse snatcher. She got tossed around a bit and Mum and Dad are doing the nursemaid thing."

Quickly moving from adversary to ally with Georgia against a new foe—as any woman, especially an attractive one and *definitely* a stunning one was considered a foe by both Danielle and Georgia—Danielle went on.

"You should hear her talk. Half the time I don't know what she's saying, she's got such a country twang. Says she's from *Indiana*." Danielle said the word "Indiana' like it tasted foul. "Definitely one of those hillbillies. Mum thinks she's adorable. I personally don't see it."

Nate found himself annoyed . . . no, *immensely* annoyed at Danielle's words.

Lily definitely had an accent that wasn't stereotypically American southern but certainly had an endearing, countrified lilt. Nevertheless, it was not difficult in the slightest to understand her and she didn't carry herself in any way like a hillbilly. In fact, the very idea was ludicrous.

"I need a drink," he announced, because suddenly he did and badly.

Danielle actually batted her eyelashes at him. "Me too, be a darling and get me one, will you?"

He clenched his jaw at the sight. She was his sister for God's sake. The concept of anything else was simply vile.

As he'd learned to do from years of practice, he ignored her and entered the drawing room.

And there he saw Lily immediately.

She was standing by the fireplace next to Jeff, looking up at Nate's brother slightly, with high heels she was nearly his height, and smiling vaguely.

Her dress was not at all embarrassing.

It was not couture but it was beautiful and fit her like it was made for her. It was apple green silk and had a low, deep V at the front showing just a hint, but not a flagrant display, of cleavage. It had a thin ruffle along the neckline, the ruffle seemingly being the only thing that held the dress to her graceful shoulders. It skimmed her voluptuous body perfectly to fall in a straight line to just above her knees.

She wore not a single piece of jewelry, not even earrings, and she didn't need to. Her sparkling eyes and shining hair that had been swept up away from her face and off her neck, were the only accompaniment the dress required. Her feet were encased in high-heeled sandals a deeper green than the dress, the heel spiked with a daring strap around the ankles and two thin crossed straps around her toes. Toes, he noticed with his usual sharp eye for detail, which were no longer painted the deep wine of yesterday but now a pearly, iridescent pink.

She looked, regardless of the friendly smile, like a serene, unobtainable princess.

She also, Nate noted with firm detachment, looked good with Jeff.

They made an excellent couple. And Jeff quite obviously felt the same.

"Hello, my dearest." Silently, Laura was at his side, touching his arm, and he turned to her to bend low to allow her to give him a kiss on his smoothly-shaven cheek.

He looked at the woman who had become his mother, the only woman who had been a true mother to him and he smiled with genuine pleasure at her company.

"Having a good time?" he inquired.

"I hate this," Laura announced honestly. She was an excellent hostess, she was very good at socializing but she much preferred to be in the company of her family or small gatherings of close friends than having a huge party. "But, Danielle was intent on making this a big deal so . . ."

Nate read the rest of her statement. What Danielle wanted both Laura and Victor, and now Jeff, gave to her. It was far easier than the tantrum that would result if they did not. Nate seemed to be the only member of the family who could say no to Danielle.

And he did it often.

"How's Lily?" Nate found himself asking, and at the sweet, knowing smile that twitched on his mother's lips, he wished he had not. It had become very clear that both his parents had decided to play matchmaker.

"She's better, I think, though I wouldn't know. She's determined to hide any stiffness or soreness. She was more distressed at my distress this morning when I found out she could barely move to get out of bed than at any pain she was feeling. Regardless of it all, she and I have had the best day." She hesitated then leaned closer, saying in a quiet voice, "Nathaniel, it's very strange but I feel like I've known her an age instead of a day. She's so open, so sweet. You should hear some of the stories she tells about her family in Indiana. They're hilarious. *She's* hilarious."

Nate continued to smile into Laura's dancing eyes then turned back to regard Lily.

He had been to America on business on several occasions though he'd never been to Indiana. He wondered at her family. She was quite clearly from money. That purse she fought so hard to keep cost a small fortune. He knew, he'd paid for one for Laura for Christmas the previous year. Not to mention everything about Lily screamed class and breeding.

"How long is she here?" he asked, not shifting his gaze from Lily.

"I'm trying to get her to stay another day and night just to be certain she's all right. She's very intent on going home," Laura answered.

Nate was surprised at this response.

"Is her holiday finished then?" he queried.

"I'm sorry?" Laura queried in return.

He reluctantly stopped watching Lily, who was now talking to both Jeff and Georgia's father, and Georgia's father seemed equally as smitten with her as everyone else. It wasn't surprising, she'd said something that made both men throw their heads back and laugh.

Nate turned to Laura. "Her holiday, is she wanting to get back to Indiana?"

Laura looked confused for a moment then shook her head. "No, no. Lily lives here in England. Some seaside town in Somerset. She's been here for years, came here for university, Oxford, and decided to stay."

An American at Oxford who decided to stay, Nate thought.

Definitely money.

This knowledge cemented his resolution to steer clear of her. He could win her, of course, but if she ever discovered his background she'd turn her cute but cultured nose up at him.

And that he could not abide.

"Jeff seems taken with her," he noted to Laura, his resolution making his tone sound unconcerned, and his mother's knowing face turned instantly to dismay.

"Yes," she agreed quietly and Nate could even hear the disappointment in her voice.

"They make a handsome couple," he remarked absently as he turned away from Lily, pushed her out of his mind and thought instead about a drink, a stiff one. "I hope something comes of it for you especially, if you like her so well," Nate finished then bent and kissed Laura's cheek fondly before he departed her now disappointed company to find himself a drink.

For the next two hours as the party became a crush (no one missed a Roberts party, even if it was postponed for a day, Victor was famously free with his bar), Nate didn't even have to try to avoid Lily. He was often sought out at these events, business acquaintances and women both pressing for his attention.

After he felt he'd done his duty to his parents, he decided to step outside for some peace and quiet and a cigarette. Laura hated his smoking, thus he did not do it in the house, and Victor tried to get him to switch to cigars, which was what Victor smoked, but also not in the house. But Nate felt it somehow necessary to hold on to his vice, felt it said something about him, about who he was. And at least it was legal.

He made his way to the front door and opened it but froze when he saw Lily sitting on the front step.

He had not seen the back of her dress, which was cut in a low, ruffle-edged V exposing her spine past her waist in a way that seemed both vulnerable and seductive. Her hair was pulled back in a messy chignon, haphazardly but stylishly pinned in place at the back of her head and tendrils of red-gold hair fell about her neck, face and delicate jaw.

She twisted around at his arrival and he saw her wince at the movement.

His lips thinned at the sight of her pain and he thought, not for the first time, that he should never have stopped squeezing that thief's throat.

Her face registered some emotion at seeing him, something he could not read, something that seemed strangely melancholy.

Then he watched as she tried to hide it, not completely successfully, and greeted him with a casual, "Hey."

"Lily," he greeted back, vaguely annoyed.

He could not return to the house and close the door. It wouldn't only have been impolite but also shown too clearly he was avoiding her. Therefore, he walked out onto the front stoop and shut the door behind him. He stood next to her and leaned his hip against the glossy black, wrought iron railing.

He pulled the pack of cigarettes out of his inside jacket pocket and held them up to her.

"Do you mind?"

She'd watched him the whole time, her incredible eyes never leaving him. Then they dropped to the cigarettes and something flashed in them.

"You shouldn't smoke," she said in a quiet but disapproving tone.

"You sound like Laura," he told her.

"If I do then Laura's right," she returned, exhibiting a little bit of the spirit he'd been introduced to during her mad dash toward the purse snatcher the day before.

At her words, he moved to put the cigarettes back in his pocket but she shook her head and looked away.

"No, no, go ahead. Really, I don't mind," she lied.

Even though, or probably because he knew she wouldn't like it, he lit a cigarette with the gold lighter Victor had given him while she settled back in the position he'd first seen her in. Leaning forward and resting her forearms across her knees, her hands grasping the insides of her elbows.

"Where's Jeff?" Something compelled him to ask even though he couldn't have cared less.

Her shoulders moved up in a careful shrug but she didn't answer.

She continued her avid contemplation of the steps while he quietly smoked and continued his avid contemplation of the flawless skin of her bowed back. He wondered what that skin felt like, tasted like, and lastly, he wondered at her strange mood.

"I didn't thank you," she said to the steps, interrupting his thoughts.

"Pardon?"

She twisted again, just her head, and lifted her eyes to him.

"For yesterday, for saving my . . . well, me . . . from the purse snatcher. I didn't say thank you."

He had no response so he didn't make one.

"Thank you," she whispered.

He lifted his chin slightly in acknowledgement of her gratitude and fought back his pleasant reaction to her quiet words.

"It was very heroic," she told him.

"It was hardly heroic," he replied dismissively.

This put a crack in her contemplative mood and the corners of her lips moved up marginally.

"Considering there were approximately three thousand witnesses and not a single one lifted a finger to help, I'd say it was heroic."

"I'd say three thousand is a bit of an exaggeration," he returned, his tone light and faintly teasing. He found he was completely incapable of not responding to her small smile.

His words garnered him a full one at the same time her eyes brightened and he was momentarily transfixed.

"Is it an exaggeration? It *felt* like three thousand people," she noted and leaned back, putting her hands behind her on the stoop and casually crossing her legs. The hem of her skirt rode up her knee exposing the barest hint of thigh and Nate felt his body heat at the sight of it. "I felt like a street performer. Like you and I should have passed the hat around after we were done. I could swear some of them even took pictures."

He felt his own lips twitching as her mood melted and she introduced him to her dry humor.

"They did," he informed her.

She shook her head and laughed softly, a sound he liked so much, it felt almost as if it was a physical touch.

"People," she muttered, the word was loaded with meaning and Nate found it adorable.

She likely had absolutely no idea what people were capable of, what depths they could sink to. And he wished, uncharacteristically rather fervently, that she never discovered that awful fact.

She sighed deeply and moved her head to gaze across the street.

"Even though I don't know but a few souls in there, I should go back in," she said.

"Yes," he agreed.

They definitely should go back in.

One more minute out here alone with her and he was going to forget his firm resolution to steer clear of her. He was going to forget a lot of things. Things he'd not allowed himself to forget for sixteen years.

He flicked his cigarette into the gutter and he noticed her body immediately stilled at this act.

Then she did something extraordinary.

"You just littered!" she accused hotly, jumping gracefully to her feet, glaring at the smoldering cigarette butt like it was about to explode and take out half of the street in a blaze of fiery destruction when it did.

Her glare turned to him.

He hadn't a word to say in response. She was, of course, right.

She was also somehow even more imposingly beautiful when she was angry.

"Fazire says you shouldn't litter. He says humans litter too much."

While talking, she had turned and was stomping down the steps in agitation.

Nate watched in stupefied fascination as she marched straight to his cigarette end, and leaning down slowly she snatched it out of the gutter and held it between her thumb and forefinger like it was abhorrent. Which, in her hands, it was.

"He says humans should take better care of where they live or we won't have it very long." She leaned forward and smashed it out against one of the steps, giving him a tantalizing glimpse at more of her cleavage.

"Who's Fazire?" Nate asked and watched as she straightened.

He saw the flush of ire pinking her cheeks and he found his resolution of earlier this evening slipping another hefty notch after the notch it had slipped while seeing her cleavage, the other one it had slipped upon witnessing her smile and the *other* one it had slipped upon hearing her say "thank you."

She was looking around for somewhere to deposit the cigarette.

"He's a family friend. He helped raise me," she explained distractedly.

"Lily, give it to me," Nate said softly and her eyes came to him and focused.

He'd stretched out his hand and she walked up the steps, stopped two down from the top where he stood and deposited the remains of the cigarette in his palm.

After her rather vain attempt to save the earth by cleaning up his lone cigarette end, she seemed to realize belatedly how bizarre her behavior and her words were. This realization caused her to look hilariously mortified.

"I think," she whispered, putting her eyes on anything but him, "that might have been a little rude." She finished this as if rudeness was the worst of sins.

"No more rude than my thoughtless participation in the destruction of the planet," he drawled, definitely teasing this time.

Her eyes flew to his and at one look at him her chagrin instantly faded and she laughed, not soft or low, but with great feeling and it was so catching, he found himself grinning at her.

And in that moment, his resolution was completely forgotten.

"Yes, true." She was no longer laughing but her eyes were still dancing. "You are definitely ruder than me. You should feel ashamed, Nate, very ashamed."

He asked before he could stop himself, before he could start thinking or remembering all the reasons why he should not, "Are you staying tomorrow?"

"I'm sorry?" She tilted her head quizzically, her gorgeous eyes still smiling.

"Tomorrow. Are you staying with Laura and Victor another day?"

"I . . ." she hesitated, watching him, "I don't think so. I've taken too much advantage as it is. Your um . . . parents are very kind but fish and guests stink after three days."

"What?" He no longer had to stop himself from thinking because all he *could* think was that he had no idea what she was talking about.

"Something my grandmother used to say, fish and guests stink after three days. Her way of saying not to wear out your welcome when you're a guest." She ascended the last two steps, stood in front of him and tilted her head up to look at him. "What I'm saying is that it's time for me to go home."

"You've only been here two days," he informed her helpfully, smiling into her upturned face.

Something changed in hers as she caught his smile and for some reason this caused another blush to creep into her cheeks.

"The way I figure it is, I didn't even know Laura and Victor when I arrived so that has to shave off at least a day, maybe two. So I'm past my expiration date." She gave him her quirky grin and he had to concentrate all his effort on not snatching her into his arms.

She was close, not unseemly close but close enough she filled his vision, he could feel the warmth from her body, smell her subtle perfume.

He straightened from his lounge against the banister. This brought them only inches closer but enough so that the once decorous distance was now not.

"Stay another day," he urged, his voice lower in timbre as well as coaxing.

Her body gave an almost imperceptible jerk and she had to tilt her head back further to look at him.

"Why?" she whispered, her eyes adorably bewildered.

He moved closer and her head tilted back more. This was how she would look before he kissed her, he knew, and the thought shot through him like a bullet.

She seemed frozen, rooted to the spot. He lifted the hand that was not carrying her litter-saving cigarette and captured a tendril of her hair that had escaped at her neck. He twisted it around his finger and felt its softness.

"So I can take you to dinner tomorrow night," he replied quietly.

It was then Nate realized she wasn't breathing.

There was something about her that made him understand he was in complete and total control of her. The way she was looking into his eyes, she was lost in him. She was, quite simply, his to do with as he pleased. She communicated this with only a look, not uttering a single word.

And this knowledge shook him. That this perfect, pristine, untouchable creature could be lost in Nate McAllister, the boy from the wrong side of town, the son of a whore. He had the unspeakable but heady desire to shout his satisfaction and the equally strong desire to bury himself in her, bury his tongue in her mouth, bury himself deep inside her, claim her, possess her, do something violent and long lasting that made her truly his.

"What about your fiancée?" she breathed.

"I don't have a fiancée."

"Your girlfriend then . . . what's her name, Georgia?"

"Georgia and I are no longer together."

After he spoke, without hesitation she said, "Okay."

He released her hair, lifted his hand and ran his finger down the soft skin of her hairline, right in front of her ear, down to the spot where her jaw met her neck.

Her lips trembled.

"Okay, what?" he asked softly.

"I'll stay another night," she answered, her voice just as soft.

Nate smiled.

Lily sighed.

EIGHT

Lily

"NATHANIEL'S HERE, LILY."

Lily jumped.

Victor had peeked his brown head around the door of the guest bedroom, and after one look at her, he started smiling.

He opened the door fully and straightened in its frame. "You look lovely."

"I do?" Her voice was uncertain and maybe a little frightened.

"Yes, Lily, you do."

"I . . ." She didn't know what to say, she didn't consider herself lovely. She'd never *been* lovely. She had no idea that she *was* lovely.

In fact, she had no idea why Nate had asked her out in the first place. Temporary insanity, she decided. Or more likely thinking *she* was suffering from it and feeling sorry for her after she went off half-cocked at his innocent flicking of a cigarette butt. Thousands of people flicked thousands of cigarette butts a day. She acted like he'd just gone on a murder spree. The thought of it made her nearly expire from mortification.

But she was not going to look a gift horse, or in this case Fazire's magical genie horse, in the mouth, as the whole reason Nate asked her out had to be Fazire's magic.

The only thing she could think to say to Victor was, "Thank you."

Victor inclined his head and she could swear he was laughing at her, not, however, unkindly.

This was the weirdest situation she'd ever been in in her whole entire life.

Not that she had been in very many weird situations. She'd lived a pretty sheltered life.

That was, of course, if you didn't count the fact that one of the "adults" participating in her upbringing was a real life genie. This something she didn't count because, as it was all she'd ever known, she found it the most natural thing in the world.

But there she was, staying with people she barely knew although she felt like she'd known them forever. She was taking advantage of their kindness although her mother and especially her father, who thought politeness and good manners were practically more important than oxygen, taught her not to take advantage of anyone. And she was going out on a date with their son, although somehow it seemed that she was their daughter and they were unbelievably proud she was going out on a date with the tall, dark, handsome, popular captain of the football team.

Unsure of what to do, Lily just stood there.

She'd never been on a date in her life.

She'd dressed in one of the outfits she'd bought the day before while out shopping with Laura. She couldn't afford it but she adored it so she charged it as well as everything else she bought yesterday. If her mother knew she was using her credit cards on anything but necessities, Becky would have a brain hemorrhage.

She wore a straight, pencil skirt in the palest pink that was boldly patterned around the hem in vermillion and orange. She topped it with a tight-fitting, pink cotton camisole and a lightweight cotton vermillion cardigan that she left open at the front. Laura had loaned her a pair of her shoes (what Lily didn't know was that they were Danielle's and if she had known she wouldn't have worn them, she'd had the same reaction to Danielle as she'd had to Jeffrey), red, spike-heeled slingbacks.

She looked straight from the fifties without the scarf. A Pink Lady with even more attitude.

She felt like an idiot.

She had absolutely no idea she looked stunningly chic.

She picked up the small, sleek, matching red bag Laura had loaned her.

"Is everything all right?" Victor was watching her closely.

"I . . ." she started again and stopped then she looked at him hopelessly. She didn't know him as far as she could throw him but somehow she trusted him enough to tell him, "Victor, I don't know what to do."

Her voice was so quiet she was surprised he heard her. But he did and he walked into the room.

"What do you mean?" He looked slightly bemused and his usually very controlled face showed it.

She tucked the bag under her arm and brought her hands up, her fingers fidgeting, and she studied her manicure.

"I've never been on a date," she confided to her hands, her voice even softer.

"Bloody hell," Victor cursed. "You must be joking."

Her head came up and her hands went out. "Do I look like I'm joking?"

She meant her appearance, what she considered her bizarre Pink Lady outfit, just *her*. She was—she knew from all the teasing at school, years and years of teasing—no raving beauty and she never would be. She'd lost weight, she wasn't blind. She could see herself in the mirror. She could also read a clothing label. But regardless of that, she'd *never* gained any confidence.

"How old are you?" Victor's eyes had narrowed.

"Twenty-two."

"Bloody hell," he repeated.

"That isn't helping," she tried to joke but she sounded as scared as she was.

"You must have grown up in a convent school, am I right?"

She was surprised at this response but answered honestly, "No, just a small town in Indiana."

He came forward.

"Same thing," he said dismissively. His hand went to the small of her back and he guided her resisting body firmly to the door. "You just go downstairs, smile at Nathaniel and after that, I promise, he'll take care of the rest."

She relaxed enough to let him guide her down the hall. "Why do you call him Nathaniel when everyone else calls him Nate?"

There had been much talk of Nate. It seemed Nate was a popular topic of conversation with just about everyone. Her first night with Jeffrey, who Lily thought might not like Nate very much. The next day when she met Danielle who talked about Nate quite a lot and liked him a *whole* lot more than their brother. At the party last night where everyone mostly wanted to know where Nate was in order to talk to him. And all day that day, a day she spent with Laura and Danielle out to lunch and shopping in stores where she couldn't even afford to buy a hair clip.

Lily was trying to keep her mind on other things, anything other than her date with the man of her dreams, the man of her most fervent wishes, the man she'd been reading about in her romance novels for years. A man come alive and now, taking her out to dinner.

But try as she might, she couldn't stop herself from asking about him.

"Nathaniel is the name of a gentleman, a genius, a man of means and power. Nate is just a name. And my Nathaniel is a *Nathaniel*." Victor said it with such pride that Lily couldn't stop herself from turning and smiling at him.

"You know, I think you're right," she told him and Victor beamed his approval at her words.

"He prefers Nate, to my and Laura's everlasting annoyance," Victor confided in a mock-whisper.

They were walking down the stairs by this time and she tilted her head back and laughed at his comment. And she found at that moment that she very much liked this intense man. He reminded her of her father. And therefore, being Lily Jacobs, she told him so (in a manner).

"You're a very kind man, Victor, thank you for all the kindness that you've shown me."

He stopped nearly to the bottom of the stairs, abruptly and in deep surprise. He turned to stare at her as if her words were audacious.

"I . . ." It was his turn to stammer and she found herself uncomfortable with his loss of control. He seemed a man who needed to be in control at all times.

She was however, confused. He had to know he was kind, for goodness sake. It wasn't as if she told him he was Superman and she thought he could catch bullets with his teeth.

He found his control and she was happy for that, as he seemed to need it, seemed to wear it like armor.

Then he remarked, "I must say, Lily, I'm delighted your purse was snatched."

"*What?*" she cried, somewhat loudly on an effervescent giggle.

"If it hadn't been, we may never have met you," he explained, taking her hand and patting it in a fatherly gesture that seemed entirely out of character for him.

"What's going on?" Jeffrey was slouching against the wall of the entry, his arms crossed on his chest, his face registering his unhappiness.

Lily and Victor finished descending the stairs and at the sight of Jeff, Lily felt a twinge of guilt she didn't quite understand. She also noted that there was a difference to how Jeffrey stood with his shoulder against the wall than how Nate did it. Jeff's was an insouciant *slouch* while Nate's was a predatory *lean*.

"Lily and I were sharing a private moment," Victor stated, his voice somehow shut off.

"Lily seems to be amassing a fair few private moments with members of the family in a very short period of time," Jeff commented.

Something about his words stung, and the way he said them made it stunningly clear that was his intention.

Victor's face turned to stone as he stared at his son.

"Oh Lily, you look lovely!" Laura was coming out of the drawing room no doubt heralded by Lily's near-shout and thankfully broke the odd tense moment. She was followed by Nate, and at the sight of him, Jeff's residual sting faded away and Lily caught her breath.

It was the first time she'd seen him when he wasn't wearing a suit. Instead he was wearing a pair of faded jeans, a black V-neck sweater and black boots.

And he looked absolutely beautiful.

"It's going to be hard for her to get on your bike in that getup." Jeff's voice had gone from glum and contentious to jovial and vaguely snotty.

"Bike?" Lily murmured, confused, her awe at the sight of Nate melting.

"You can take the Jag," Victor offered.

"You rode here on a bike?"

She stared at Nate. The very thought of Nate on a bike was preposterous. Romantic heroes didn't pedal around on bikes. It was, of course, London where bicycles were likely the best and easiest transport, but she just couldn't credit it and she found it somewhat disappointing, even though she knew that was not very nice.

"The car, unfortunately, was scheduled to go in for a service. We'll take a taxi," Nate explained.

"Bike?" Lily repeated, still at a loss.

Jeff pushed away from the wall.

"Yeah, his Ducati. Nate likes to go fast, live dangerously, that kind of thing." This was said in a way that was cutting, but it seemed there was jealousy underlying his tone.

"What's a Ducati?" Lily turned to Victor, still bemused but Laura answered her.

"A motorcycle, my dear, and he shouldn't ride it. It's dangerous. I keep telling him he's going to kill himself, racing around on a motorcycle and in that blasted sports car, but does he listen to his mother? No, he most certainly does not."

Her eyes flew to Nate with delight.

A motorcycle!

Lily completely dismissed the idea of a man like Nate, a man who looked like Nate, a man who acted like Nate, a man who rode a motorcycle (like Nate), listening to his mother ever.

All she could think about was his motorcycle.

Her father had a motorcycle. He used to take her out on it all the time because she'd beg him to do it. She loved it, loved being out in the open air. She loved the speed, the danger (though there was no real danger, Will was always very careful and never took chances, but she could pretend).

Therefore she cried excitedly, "I *love* motorcycles!"

She had been telling herself all day to be cool, calm and collected. To act the sophisticate, as she was sure Nate was used to, not to let on she was just a small-town girl, which she was sure would bore Nate to death.

But, *a motorcycle!*

She had no idea that she looked exactly, enticingly, alluringly as excited as she sounded.

She turned shining eyes to Nate and asked, "Can we take your motorcycle?"

Nate, who she saw, and Jeff, who she did not see, were both staring at her, lost in her look of delight and abandoned desire.

Nate forced himself out of his daze first.

He walked towards her, a grin playing about his sensual lips.

"I'd say your skirt is not conducive to a ride on the bike."

Without a hint of artifice or any idea of the reaction her words would cause, she waved her hand casually in front of her and said, "Don't worry, I'll pull it up."

Victor cleared his throat.

Laura dropped her head and smiled at the floor.

Jeff's (she did not see) mouth fell open and immediately (also Lily did not know) he decided silently that he hated Nate even more.

Nate's eyes warmed in a way that made Lily's belly do a funny flutter.

"Do you have an extra helmet?" she asked, doggedly pursuing her opportunity of a ride on his bike just as she doggedly ignored the strange flutter in her belly.

"I keep one here, yes," his deep voice answered.

"That settles it," she announced, clapped her hands in front of her and linked her fingers, staring up at him with glee.

"Lily." His tone said he was going to refuse her and she leaned toward him.

"Nate, please? My dad has a cycle." She pronounced this "sickle" as many people in Indiana did the same. "He used to take me out all the time. I'm a good rider, you'll see. I won't be distracting at all. I promise."

Her words were said in all innocence and amusement flickered in Nate's eyes just as Jeff muttered, "That would be impossible."

She turned to Jeff.

"No really," she said on a huff. "I'm a very good passenger, Dad said so." She turned back to Nate.

He was watching her as if she was the most fascinating creature ever born.

Somehow at the same time he also had an expression that clearly said he was going to say no.

"Please," she begged on a whisper, and Nate's eyes flickered again, and again her belly did a funny thing that felt just like a somersault.

"For God's sake, Nathaniel, take her out on the bike," Victor broke in, giving in in his usual manner as he'd been doing with his children since they were born.

"No!" Laura cut in. "Lily, you're wearing *a skirt*," she noted unnecessarily.

Lily just kept looking at Nate imploringly.

"You really want to ride, don't you?" Nate asked softly.

She nodded her head happily, sensing rather than knowing she was going to get her way.

"We'll ride," Nate decided.

"Yay!" Lily shouted, clapping her hands in front of her, completely lost in her reaction and she would think later she likely looked like a childish fool, not realizing how compelling her exuberance was.

"Fucking hell," Jeff cursed not so under his breath.

"That's enough, Jeffrey," Victor clipped.

Lily ignored them. She wasn't going to give Nate time to change his mind so she asked, "Where's the helmet?"

"I'll get it," Laura, giving in with dignified but somewhat ill-grace, said.

"I'll get my jacket," Nate followed his mother, and as she went toward the kitchen, he turned into the drawing room.

Victor extended his arm, a cheeky grin on his face. "And *I'll* introduce you to the Ducati."

"Okay," Lily breathed, her eyes shining.

Victor took her to the bike, which was a kind she'd never seen before (a *lot* nicer than the one her father owned), and she loved it the moment she clapped eyes on it.

Nate joined them moments later.

Jeff had disappeared.

"Wear this," Nate said, shaking out a black, leather jacket.

"Oh no, you wear it," Lily replied, finding herself shy at the thought of donning a piece of his clothing.

"Lily, something happens, the leather is at least a modicum of protection. Lord knows, the rest of you won't be protected," Nate explained, amusement and annoyance struggling for control of his voice.

"Are you going to crash?" she asked, tilting her head.

"No," he replied, a grin twitching his beautiful lips.

Amusement was winning, she was pleased to note.

"Have you ever crashed before?"

His dark eyes moved to his father and Victor chuckled.

"Just put the coat on, Lily," Nate ordered in a tone not to be disobeyed.

She ignored it. "You *have* crashed."

Nate didn't answer. Victor's chuckle turned into soft laughter.

"I'll wear the jacket," she decided prudently.

"Good idea," Nate muttered, opening it for her and she turned her back to him and put her arms through the sleeves.

It swam on her but she didn't care. Something about having it on felt nice.

He turned her around with his hands at her shoulders and she felt them there like they'd stay there (or like she wanted them to stay there) for the rest of her life. Then they were gone and she was facing him again. He surprised her by zipping it smartly up all the way to her chin.

She immediately regretted allowing herself to be pushed into wearing the jacket.

Now she *really* looked like a Pink Lady, wearing a huge leather motorcycle jacket.

Her regret melted as she lifted her eyes to Nate's. He was looking down at her wearing his jacket and even Lily, with no experience whatsoever, realized the look in his eye was something intensely possessive, untamed and very, very dangerous, but in a *good* way.

She gulped.

"Here's the helmet." Laura had arrived on the scene.

With great spirit, deciding instead to focus on her unexpected treat, she took the helmet from Laura, giving her a throwaway smile. Lily pulled back her hair and expertly donned the helmet while Nate pulled on his own and threw his muscled leg over the bike and Lily noticed, not at all distractedly, how his jeans tightened against the muscles of his thigh when he did this.

His visor was down and he turned his head to her. She didn't hesitate just in case he changed his mind at the last moment. While he watched, Lily wriggled her skirt up, shaking her hips and bouncing on alternately bent knees. When she had it up to her hips, enough to straddle the motorcycle, she slung her leg around the bike and settled into position behind Nate. She gave a jaunty wave to Laura and Victor and without even thinking she wrapped her arms around Nate's waist just like she'd do with her dad.

"I'm ready!" she shouted and her voice both ricocheted around in her helmet and was muted by it.

Nate gave a short nod, started the bike with practiced movements, movements that never affected her when her dad did it but seemed, somehow, *impossibly* male when Nate did.

They took off.

And her arms, wrapped loosely around his waist, tightened.

Because Nate didn't ride like Will did.

Nate rode fast and Nate rode hard.

As they rode, her tightened arms tightened even further until she was pressed against his back, the tops of her thighs pressed under the bottoms of his and her nether-regions were pressed against his backside.

She didn't care. She gloried in it.

She was riding with Nate and that was all that mattered.

She rested her chin on his shoulder and she loved every minute of it.

They arrived at where they were going and Nate stopped the bike and settled it on its stand as Lily hopped off and wriggled her skirt back down. When she straightened her body, Nate was also off the bike. She could tell he was watching her through his dark visor and his hands were lifted to take off his helmet. She tore off her own helmet, shaking her head to clear her hair from her face.

"That was great!" she cried, still lost in the thrill of the ride. She had no idea her smile was shining on her face and her eyes were bright and carefree.

And then something happened that she would never have guessed, never have planned for, never have dreamed, not even wished for and never would have known would ever, in a million years, happen.

With his helmet dangling from the fingers of one of his hands, Nate's other arm snaked out, hooked around her waist and pulled her forward with a controlled violence that stole her breath.

She slammed against the wall of his body.

His mouth came down on hers.

Hard.

At this, she made a little surprised sound which came from the back of her throat.

As she felt his body heat seep through the leather, her breasts crushed pleasantly against his hard chest, she relaxed into him. Her lips relaxed, her hand lifted to rest on his shoulder and she pressed herself against him as her belly did somersault after somersault after . . .

His head came up just as abruptly as it went down.

It was the first time she'd ever been kissed and she couldn't breathe.

"After dinner, we're going back to my flat," Nate stated in a voice that caused shivers to go down her spine and all along her skin.

She didn't even think to refuse him, she simply nodded mutely.

He tugged the helmet out of her hand and, both helmets in one of his, her hand held firmly in his other, he guided her to the restaurant.

And finally, on a great whoosh, she let out her breath.

"LET'S WALK."

Lily was standing out on the sidewalk gazing up at Nate.

The sun was still lighting the sky and even after all her years there, she couldn't get used to the long summer days in England.

They'd had a lovely, delicious dinner with her doing most of the talking. Nate didn't say much and anyway, she was nervous, *very* nervous, mainly because of the idea of going back to his flat after dinner but also because of the way he kept looking at her.

"To the flat?" Nate asked, looking down at her, his handsome face relaxed, a smile playing about his lips.

"No, just a walk. I feel the need to stretch my legs." She used the words Sarah often said after a meal and she tugged at his hand, a strong, long-fingered hand that was holding hers.

She'd already noticed his hands, powerfully veined and well-formed with tapered fingers. Lily rather liked his hands but then again, Lily rather liked everything about him.

"Come on," she urged.

She started walking and felt resistance on her arm when he didn't and looked back. She gave a little, inviting jerk of her head and an encouraging smile.

Nate relented and started moving forward.

The smile she directed at him deepened.

He immediately stopped, tugged on her arm and she stumbled backwards, whirled and fell into him.

His arm closed around her and he bent his head and brushed her lips with his.

Even though it was feather-light, she stared up at him dazed and, she noticed vaguely, her knees were going weak.

He seemed satisfied by something then said, *"Now* we can walk."

She shook herself out of her daze and fell into step beside him.

"I'll hold one of the helmets," Lily offered.

"I've got it," Nate returned.

"No, really—"

"Lily, I've got it." His voice sounded like he was trying not to laugh.

"Okay," she gave in, somewhat disgruntled that he found her funny when she wasn't trying to be.

They walked hand-in-hand down the sidewalk until suddenly they reached Hyde Park.

Lily knew London well, had been there many times but Hyde Park (which she *loved*), regardless of its enormity, always seemed to creep up and surprise her.

"Let's walk in the park." She changed direction not waiting for him to answer or refuse her and entered the park. To her astonishment, he followed without argument.

They walked more and she realized that she had never been so content, so happy, not in her entire life.

And she'd had led a contented (mostly), happy (mostly) life.

She sighed with pleasure.

After a while she felt conversation was in order. Not because she was uncomfortable but because she was curious.

"Are Laura and Victor your parents?"

She was timid at asking him questions. She'd tried a couple at dinner and he hadn't been very forthcoming with answers. He'd answered, of course, but he went into no detail and seemed to prefer, vastly, getting her to talk about herself.

Nate answered, "In a way."

She looked at him out of the sides of her eyes.

"How can they be your parents *in a way*?"

She thought he wouldn't answer her but he did. "They adopted me when I was twelve."

Reflexively, her hand tightened in his with this knowledge.

All sorts of thoughts raced through her head as to why he was available at the age of twelve to be adopted, none of them near as bad, although her heart broke at them, as what had actually happened.

"Are they family?" she asked quietly.

"How do you mean?"

She could tell by his tone that he was distracted and was thinking of something else, and if she knew *what* he was thinking, she might have run screaming from the park.

Or possibly thrown herself at him.

She walked, and always had done, watching the ground. He walked, she noted with another sidelong glance, facing straight ahead, confident and self-assured.

She found this rather affecting.

"Laura and Victor. Is one of them family? An aunt, an uncle?" she explained, thinking of his parents and how they so obviously loved him and were equally obviously proud of him, yet he didn't call them "Mum" or "Dad."

"No relation." His answer was short and didn't invite further questions.

They walked deeper into the park.

He didn't want to talk about it, she knew. But she needed to talk about it.

He was, quite simply, hers. She'd wished for him. He didn't know it, even she didn't really know it at that moment, she would only really know it later, but he was the love of her life.

For these reasons she carried on.

"What happened to your folks?" she inquired, her voice soft.

This time, his hand tightened reflexively and she didn't know what to make of it except that it couldn't mean anything good.

He stopped walking.

She did as well, turned to him and tilted her head up to look into his eyes.

"Lily," he said quietly and looked down at her.

She liked the way he said her name, it sounded good on his lips. His eyes, so dark (she didn't know how, if they were gray or if they were blue), were intense.

Nate kept talking. "I never knew my father. My mother was murdered."

Her eyes rounded in shock and her hand shot to her mouth, her fingers pressing against her lips. He said it tersely as if it was torn from him. As if he'd never said those words to anyone in his life.

"Nate," she breathed against her fingers and she injected so much feeling in his name that she was surprised it didn't come alive and hover in the air.

He carried on, still watching her, assessing her reaction.

"I knew Victor. He took me in and he and Laura adopted me. End of story."

And that it was for he turned and headed back the way they came.

The walk was over.

"Why didn't you take their name?" Something made her whisper. It was none of her business and everything about him said so.

"I never want to forget who I am," he replied, though his answer made little sense to her.

"And who are you?" she asked, curiosity getting the better of her.

And this curiosity took her irrevocably *out* of the safe, protected, sheltered bubble she'd resided in her whole life.

He stopped, halted her with a tug on her hand and turned to face her. Then his arm slid about her waist and brought her toward him until her body hit the heat of his. His head bent, she thought he was going to kiss her again and she held her breath in anticipation.

But instead he said more words to her than he'd ever said before in their short acquaintance.

And they were very, *very* shocking.

And very, *very* effective.

"I'm the man who's going to put your lush body on the back of his bike and take you to my flat. Then I'm going to take every piece of that lovely outfit off that lush body. Then I'm going to take you to my bed and I'm going to memorize, slowly, every inch of your skin. And finally, I'm going to watch you come while I'm inside you. That's who I am."

Her mouth had dropped open.

She hadn't been spoken to like that in her whole entire life. She didn't even imagine anyone spoke to anyone like that. And she hadn't been naked in front of anyone, not another living soul since, well, since she could remember.

"Lily?" Nate called.

If there was a time when she should run, hide, escape, that was it.

But Lily wasn't even thinking of escape because she was too busy staring at him in dumbfounded awe.

She realized he was waiting for her to answer.

"Yes?" she whispered.

It was then he bent his head to kiss her.

This kiss was not hard and reactionary. This kiss was not feather-light. This kiss was something else.

His lips settled on hers firmly as his arm tightened about her waist, pulling her deeper into his body. His tongue came out and touched her lips, and not really knowing what to do but thinking her best bet was to open her lips (slightly), she did so.

He took advantage, his tongue sweeping in her mouth and at the touch of it, the feel of it, the taste of it, her belly stopped all pretense at somersaults and launched right into several back handsprings and, she was pretty certain, a forward pike.

She moaned (she couldn't help it, it felt so good and she felt his kiss not just in her belly but *everywhere*) and her arms went around his shoulders, her fingers sifting into the crisp, soft hair at his nape.

She heard from what seemed a great distance the helmets hitting the ground and his other arm came around her and crushed her to his body. One hand slid down over her bottom.

She moaned again (she couldn't help it, his hand on her bottom felt so . . . very . . . *nice* and what she felt of him straining against her front was even *nicer*).

His tongue played with hers, danced with hers, dueled with hers and she matched him, mimicking his actions, going on instinct, not able to wrap her mind around a single thought. She pressed her hips against his, wriggling them for good measure and to get better purchase because she *liked* what she felt, and she slid her fingers deeper into his hair, holding his head to hers.

It was his turn to groan and she absorbed it in her mouth, realizing with knees going weak, how he felt when he absorbed hers.

It was luscious.

He lifted his head, or rather ripped his lips from hers in what appeared to be a great effort.

Then he murmured, "Fucking hell, you're magnificent."

It might not have been a compliment every girl who'd been addicted to romance novels for a decade desired to hear but it worked really well on Lily.

"We're going home." His voice was both determined and urgent.

Lily nodded.

Their stroll back to the bike was more like a race. In fact, halfway there she pulled her hand free and stopped while he looked back at her impatiently. She didn't say a word, just bent over, slipped off her shoes and held them dangling from their straps in her fingers.

When she straightened, she tilted her head and smiled a quirky smile at him.

And then she ran all the way back to his bike.

Nate did not run. He strode purposefully with long-legged, ground-eating strides and he watched her as she ran.

And even though he didn't run, he made it to the bike mere moments after she did.

And then they went home.

NINE

Nate, Lily and the Conception of Tash

NATE NEARLY KILLED THEM on the way home.

It was sheer, erotic torture having her sweet body pressed against him after that kiss.

Once there, thankfully safely, Lily alighted from the bike first but he didn't wait for her to take off her helmet. He grabbed her hand and dragged her behind him, using his free one to tear his helmet off as he strode into the building, completely ignoring the doorman who called out a greeting.

She struggled to keep up and struggled with her helmet but managed to pull it free at the elevator. Just like she did before, she tossed her head and her shining, gold-red hair flew free about her face and tumbled down her back as she tugged it off,

She immediately tilted her head up to him.

She looked scared and excited and he found he liked that look on her face.

Very much.

The elevator came, its doors opened and he shoved her roughly in-side. He followed her, tagged the button for his floor, and as they ascended, he pushed her against the wall and pressed against her.

The minute his lips met hers, she moaned and at the sexy, little sound, he fought to control the impulse to tear her clothes from her body in the elevator.

She opened her mouth and he took immediate advantage. She still tasted like wine and the rich chocolate dessert she'd ordered and eaten with abandoned relish, this being a first for him. Most women flatly refused dessert or even acknowledged that they desired it.

Her arms wrapped around his waist under the jacket he was too impatient to force her to wear on the way home and he wondered how she could bear to touch him. He felt like a fever had overcome him and he was certain a single touch would sear her skin.

The elevator doors opened and he wasted no time. He dragged his mouth from hers, grasped her hand and advanced down the hall. She had to run to keep up with him, and when he halted abruptly at his door, she couldn't stop herself and ran into him.

This caused her to giggle as she righted herself and his head swung to look at her as he dropped her hand to put the key in the lock.

She smiled her quirky, effective smile and said, "We're rather in a hurry, aren't we?"

He shoved open the door. "Damned right."

He grabbed her hand and pulled her in.

He threw his helmet in the vague direction of the couch, ripped hers from her hand, not noticing she was glancing about inquisitively, and sent it flying in the same direction. Then his hand locked on hers again and he headed for the bedroom.

"Nate," she said behind him.

He didn't answer and his step didn't falter.

"Nate," she called, louder this time with her hand tugging at his.

He heard her but he still didn't respond nor did he release her hand. He walked into his bedroom, straight to the side of the bed.

There he stopped.

"Nate."

His hands went right to her cardigan as his eyes locked on hers.

"You know, Lily," his voice was deeper than normal, and harsh, as he pulled the jumper from her body, "you get in that bed with me and it's anything like what I felt the first time I laid eyes on you, anything like when you first touched me, *anything* like that kiss in the park, I'm never letting you go. Do you understand me?"

His words were irrational, even insane.

But he never dreamed he'd have a woman like Lily.

Never in his wildest imaginings (of which there weren't many, Nate was not a man prone to wild imaginings), his most fervent desires, even if he'd had a wish, even a single wish from a genie out of a bottle, he would never have expected to have a woman like Lily.

Not while growing up and sleeping in sheets that were never cleaned. Stealing food so he could eat. Watching his mother insert needles in her veins.

Never had he expected someone as regal, as magnificent, as Lily.

Lily, a woman who liked to walk in the park while holding hands. A woman who loved—with unsurpassed glee—to ride on the back of a motorcycle. A woman who would chase courageously after a purse thief and throw herself on his back. A woman who could win over Laura, which wasn't hard, Laura had a soft heart, and Victor, who most certainly did not have a soft heart, both in a matter of hours.

Nate never expected a woman like that, like Lily, to so much as look at him. At least, not the way she looked at him.

As if he was conqueror of nations, creator of worlds.

As she was looking at him now, her face wreathed in awe.

"Do you understand me?" His voice went beyond harsh. It was as rough as sandpaper.

"I . . . think . . . so."

That was enough for him.

"Good." His hands went to the hem of her camisole and he whipped it over her head, forcing her arms up with it.

She gasped. She wasn't wearing a bra and her own hands went to cover her breasts.

"No." He grabbed her wrists and forced her hands behind her back, his mouth coming down on hers in a wild, bruising, wet kiss.

When he felt the struggle leave her wrists as she relaxed into the kiss, he released them and her and stepped back just enough to rip off his jacket and jumper.

This time she stared at his chest in awe.

"Christ, Lily," he swore when he caught her look and his hands found the zipper at the back of her skirt, looking down with near the same reverence at her amazing, full breasts.

He yanked the zipper down and his hands slid up her back, pushing brutally against it, forcing it to arch, forcing her to bare herself more fully to his gaze. Then, completely unable to stop himself and not wishing to anyway, he bent his head and closed his mouth around her nipple.

Her breath caught, he heard it, then it released and came out in frantic pants as his tongue swirled around her hardening nipple.

"What are you doing to me?" she breathed in wonder, her hands sliding into his hair.

He didn't answer. He did the same thing to her other nipple until he felt her legs buckle and he had to support her weight as he felt tremors flow freely through her.

He lifted his head and left her standing there as he sat on the bed, tugged off his boots and then followed his jeans.

She looked at him, her eyes wide and fearful as if she'd never seen a male form before in her life.

This didn't register on him. He pushed her back on the bed so that she was lying across it and before she even settled, he leaned over her and yanked her loosened skirt down her legs.

"Nate," she whispered, her hands cradling her belly protectively but he didn't note this gesture's meaning. He simply did the same with her panties.

"Nate!"

"What?" he growled, his hands at her bottom, lifting her up and depositing her deeper in the bed.

"I need to tell you something." She was still breathing heavily, the midnight blue had moved deeper into her irises but the pure blue was still there.

He spread her legs and settled between them.

"Talk fast," he said against her mouth but didn't allow her to say a word.

He kissed her.

And it was *everything* the kiss in the park had been.

She was beyond magnificent. She was beyond description.

His hand went between their bodies. She had to be ready for him. If she wasn't this entire scene was going to become very uncomfortable.

She was ready, wet and slippery, and when he slid his finger inside her, unbelievably tight.

She gasped against his mouth, sucking his tongue deeper inside as his thumb found her. He started circling his thumb at the same time he moved his finger in and out.

When he did, she rode his hand hard, now kissing *him*.

Her hands were everywhere, trailing hotly against his skin, begging him through touch to give her the release he was building.

"What did you need to tell me?" His mouth was still at hers. Her hips were still moving insistently against his hand. He was more than ready for her. He couldn't wait much longer.

"What?" she asked in distraction and then gasped as his thumb pressed harder and swirled. "Oh *God*," she moaned, her face flushed beautifully, her neck arched regally and he knew she was there.

Right there.

His fingers moved away, both his hands found her hips and he positioned himself expertly.

"Lily, look at me."

Her chin dipped down and she tried to focus on him. Her gorgeous hair was spread across his bed, her blue eyes were dazed, her full mouth was swollen. She was on the edge of climax.

He'd done that to her, he'd made her look so fucking, unbelievably beautiful.

And as that knowledge scored through him, Nate drove into her.

And she screamed.

THE PAIN, MINGLED SO FIERCELY with the pleasure, tore through her like a blade.

Nate's entire body stilled.

He was still deeply embedded inside her and she closed her eyes in humiliation.

Now he would know that she'd never been touched. Now the shine would go off her wish and he'd see her as she truly was and whatever was driving him to his behavior would fade away.

"Lily?" he called gently.

She turned her head to the side. The pain was receding. It had been sharp but her cry was mostly of surprise. She was so close to something, something resplendent, and it all flew away when the pain came.

"Lily, look at me."

She shook her head.

She didn't want to open her eyes, didn't want to see anything in his but the way he looked at her that night. She didn't want to see the revulsion, didn't want to feel him pulling away.

Although he wasn't pulling away. He was still deep inside her and not moving a muscle.

"Darling, look at me."

In surprise at the endearment, her eyes opened, her head righted and she did as she was told.

She wouldn't have been more surprised at what she saw on his handsome face if every living past president of the United States of America barged in and did the can-can.

He was smiling one of his glamorous smiles. This one chockfull of deep satisfaction.

"No one's ever touched you, have they?" he asked.

She shook her head.

He went on, "It's only been me."

This wasn't a question but regardless, this time she nodded her head.

If anything, his smile became more arrogant, more self-satisfied.

"Why are you smiling?" she whispered, not courageous enough to use her full voice and wondering if maybe he'd gone a little mad.

His hands moved from her hips to her face and they framed it.

"Because, darling Lily, no one has ever touched you," he explained, his voice a contented, velvet purr that seemed to slide delightfully against her skin.

"Is that good?" she asked tentatively.

This, for some unknown reason, made his body shake with laughter and she felt it *everywhere*.

When his eyes focused on hers again, they were shining with a light she'd never seen in anyone's eyes ever before.

Her whole body started to warm again.

"Oh yes," he answered softly then brushed his lips against hers before he said there, "That's good."

"Okay," she allowed. "I was trying to tell you before—"

"I know." He moved slowly, watching her closely as he slid out of her just the barest inch. When she didn't flinch, in fact she thought it felt rather nice, he slid gently back in and that *definitely* felt nice.

"I was worried I wouldn't do it right," she confided when he slid back out, further this time, and her lips pursed a little at losing him. She liked the feel of him inside.

He was watching her lips and his *impossibly* dark eyes darkened completely to black.

"You were definitely doing it right," he informed her, his voice filled with meaning but his lips were twitching as if he wanted to laugh and was stopping himself.

He carefully slid back in and her mouth parted into an "o" of sweet wonder at the delicious feel of him.

It took a moment to realize his body was again shaking with laughter.

"Quit laughing at me," she reprimanded him and he executed another smooth stroke.

His mouth touched hers and he said there, "I can't help it."

"You can!" she demanded and he pulled out fully and she thought he was going away but then he came back, faster this time and she lost her not-yet-fully-formed anger and gasped in pleasure as the sensations came back.

She bit her lip, he watched her do it and he lost his caution and lapsed into a heady, belly-somersault-inducing rhythm.

"That feels quite nice," she whispered, although it felt more than nice. It felt lovely. It felt delightful.

It felt magic.

"It feels fucking unbelievable," his voice growled into her ear and tingles slid up from her belly like champagne bubbles.

"It does?" she was still whispering, moving her hips up to meet him and finding that deepened his thrusts magnificently. She caught her breath and decided immediately to do that each time.

His tongue was at the skin just beneath her ear, and she felt her belly fluttering, her skin tingling and a lovely tickling spread from her ear to everywhere.

"You're so tight, so wet, Lily, the sweetest I've ever had."

He was going faster and she was climbing higher, going to that place he took her before. His words touched her at her core and she felt herself quiver in places she didn't even know existed.

"Nate," she breathed as his hand went between them and touched her *there* again, "God, Nate!" This was not said on a breath but an explosion, her hands crawling over his skin, memorizing the hard muscles of his back as he said he'd memorize her.

He thrust in and out, filling her completely as his fingers did their magic and she lifted her hips, matching his thrusts, feeling it build. It was almost unbearable, exquisite torture.

He was right, it *was* sweet and beautiful, and she let him ride her like she rode his hand, desperate for it, her body crying out for it, the tension at waiting for it seemed to clench every muscle she possessed.

"Let go, darling." At his murmured words dancing deliciously in her ear, she did as she was told, not even knowing she was holding on.

She cried out as it overwhelmed her, planting her heels in the bed to press up against him. While the fire engulfed her, the waves of pleasure undulated deliciously up and out and all around from between her legs, he stopped all attempts at gentle, his hand moving from between them back to her hips. He held them steady as he slammed into her again and again and she gloried in the pounding.

She lifted her head, so beyond timidity it wasn't funny, completely overtaken by insistent, heady, pulsating passion. Her hands slid into his hair, guiding his face to hers and she kissed him, open-mouthed. His tongue invaded her mouth like his body was invading between her legs. She coaxed it, goaded it, welcomed it, and when he finished, she accepted his luscious, deep groan against her tongue like it was a precious gift.

NATE LIKED TO SLEEP ALONE.

He rarely brought a woman back to his flat. It was too difficult to get rid of them once he was finished with them. If he went to their flat, he could leave whenever he was finished.

He'd moved into this flat years ago but he'd recently purchased a large apartment closer to the office in an even nicer neighborhood and he was moving to it in just a few weeks.

He lay on his back in the bed, the sheet casually thrown over his lower body, listening to Lily moving about quietly in the bathroom but giving her privacy.

And as he lay there, he thought of his new apartment, a purchase he had made with investment on his mind. And he thought of Lily in that apartment and nothing about investments entered his mind.

Nate also thought of Lily in the enormous new bed that was being custom built to go in that apartment and the idea of sleeping alone never entered his mind.

He rolled on this side, grabbed his phone and dialed his parents' number. Laura, he knew, might get worried.

Luckily, Jeff, Laura nor Danielle answered. His brother and sister, unlike Nate, had never moved out. They had never paid rent, as Nate had done on his first flat, or a mortgage, like he'd done on this one, nor had they bought a bag of groceries or anything that came close to self-sufficiency.

Instead, Victor answered.

"Lily isn't coming back tonight," Nate informed him.

"I figured as much," Victor replied, not even attempting to keep the prideful chuckle out of his voice.

"She isn't coming back tomorrow either."

"Going back to Somerset?"

"No," Nate answered shortly.

"I figured that too."

Nate tried not to be annoyed at his father's know-it-all attitude. To-night was a good night. It was the best night of his life. He didn't much feel like being annoyed.

"Son, when you make your mind up about something you usually don't fuck around. Never have, likely never will. I saw you looking at that girl outside Harrods. Frankly, I'm a little surprised it took three days."

Nate decided to end the conversation. "Goodnight, Victor."

The amusement never left his father's voice when he returned, "'Night Nathaniel."

"Who are you talking to?" Lily was standing in the doorway to the bathroom.

As the sun was finally down, Nate had turned on the lights at either side of the bed.

She had a white towel wrapped around her body and she was rubbing the balls of one of her feet against the top of another one.

"Victor," he answered, watching her, making every effort, and it took a lot of effort, to stop himself from hurtling out of the bed and dragging her back.

She looked absolutely adorable.

And she was his, only his, no one else's, just his.

She was the only good and decent thing in his life that had been just his.

She interrupted his pleasant reverie. "I knew that, I heard you say your dad's name. I meant to ask why?"

"I told him you weren't coming back tonight."

Her eyes rounded in shock, she took a quick step forward and halted. "You did *what?*"

"You're staying with me tonight," he told her.

"I can't *stay* with you. I can't *not* go back. If I don't go back they'll know what we're doing, what we did, I mean, what we've *done!*"

He didn't respond mainly because she was correct.

She shot into the room and started to grab her clothes from the floor.

"I have to go back," she announced, bending double to put on her underwear, the rest of her outfit tucked under her arm. "They put a roof over my head. I mean, you're their *son*."

"Lily, come to bed."

She whirled on him at the same time attempting to pull the camisole on over the towel.

"No! You have to take me back."

"I'm not taking you back."

She had the camisole on, ripped the towel off and threw it on the bed. This sent the clothes under her arm flying but she grabbed the skirt as it fell. Then she shook it out and was clearly about to put it on and ignore him completely.

"Lily, if you put on that lovely skirt, I'll just take it off again."

"They'll think I'm a brazen hussy," she mumbled, deep in the throes of agitation.

He wanted to laugh but sensed this was not the time. Instead he threw the covers off the bed and, naked, approached her.

She was still trying to put the skirt on, bent double again and hopping around, clumsy in her turmoil. She was also muttering to herself.

"My mother would just *die* of mortification and my *grandmother*! Oh, I don't even want to *think*. She would have disowned me. She's probably *twirling* in her *grave*."

"Lily." He put his hand on her back and she jerked up, tangled her leg in the skirt and started to fall backwards.

His hands shot out, he caught her and pulled her against his body.

She talked about her family a great deal, nearly all the time. At dinner she told him stories of her mother, father, grandmother and some man with the strange name Fazire who she obviously adored. Every time she spoke of them, her eyes would light with love. He'd never seen anything like it, never experienced that kind of devotion, never let his heart melt enough to realize he had it from Laura and Victor.

And he wanted it, but from Lily.

"Nate, you *must* take me back to your parents," she pleaded, her eyes meeting his. "I *like* them. I don't want them to think I'm . . . I'm . . . *wanton*." She was underlining her words with great regularity and Nate had to bite back his laughter.

"They won't think your wanton." He could barely say the word without laughing. He definitely was smiling.

Her eyes rounded further then they narrowed dangerously.

"You think this is funny," she accused.

He bent his head to kiss her but she arched against his arm at her waist and dodged him. His hand went between her shoulder blades and forced her closer.

"It *is* funny," he told her.

"It . . . is . . . not." She enunciated every word carefully and he found, to his surprise, he liked her when she was angry.

When his mother was angry she became mean and spiteful and said hideous things. Danielle was exactly the same. Laura rarely became angry.

Lily was entirely different. Lily was spirited and hilarious and Nate knew somehow that she couldn't be spiteful if she had to do it to save her own life.

"Lily, calm down and listen to me."

"*I am calm!*" she shouted not the least bit calmly, her outburst surprising even her and that subdued her. She bit her lip and her eyes slid sideways. Then she sighed before admitting, "Okay, maybe I'm *not* calm."

Finally she stopped moving enough for him to kiss her and he brushed his lips lightly against hers.

When he had her attention he asked, "Do you remember what I said when we came into this room?"

She thought for a second and nodded.

"What did I say?" he asked.

"Well . . ." she hedged.

He pulled her closer and reminded her even though he knew she hadn't forgotten, "I told you, if you got in that bed with me, I was never letting you go."

She stared at him, her eyes filled with wonder and all traces of anger simply ebbed away.

"Do you remember me saying that?" he pushed.

She nodded.

"Do you remember you agreed?"

She nodded again.

"Did you get into bed with me?"

"Well, you kind of threw me into the bed, or sort of . . . *pushed* me."

At that, he finally allowed himself to let out a sharp bark of laughter. She was just too much.

Once he had himself under control, he realized she'd relaxed against him and her body had become pliant.

His tone gentled. "Fair enough. So, once I threw you in, did you leave?"

She shook her head.

"Do you want to leave now?"

She stared at him a moment and he held his breath.

Then she sighed and shook her head again.

He let out his breath, his relief so great he had trouble coping with it. So he set it aside and slid his hands under the camisole.

"Now, let's get you out of these clothes and back into bed."

He pulled the camisole up again but this time her arms came up of their own volition.

"Nate?" Lily called as he tossed her camisole aside.

He was gliding his hands across the smooth skin of her back and staring at the flawless skin of her shoulders.

"Mm?"

"Nothing."

His eyes found hers and they were uncertain. He misread her mind and bent to brush his lips against hers again.

"Come to bed."

She sighed again and nodded.

LILY HAD ALWAYS SLEPT ALONE.

Except a few times at sleepovers with her best friend from grade school, Colleen. Colleen had a big double bed and they'd slept there together.

That was it, her entire experience of sleeping with another human being.

Therefore she had no idea how to sleep with a man.

She was pressed against Nate's side, his arm underneath and wrapped around her, his fingers stroking her hip.

When he took her clothes off (again) and took her to bed, he made love to her again.

Well, not exactly, as he didn't come inside her even when she asked him to. He told her he didn't want to hurt her. Instead, he did things to her with his hands and his mouth and took her to that beautiful place while he watched.

She would have been immensely embarrassed by this but once she'd had her body and pulse under control, she looked at him and he was looking at her as if she'd just announced she'd cured cancer. She couldn't be embarrassed when he looked at her like *that*.

And then he'd pulled the covers over them and tucked her against his side and seemed, as she was finding was usual with Nate, to be quite happy in complete silence.

Lily was not happy.

Lily was thinking about what she'd promised and what that meant.

"Um . . . Nate?" she said against his shoulder where her head was laying and she had an unobstructed view of the wall of his chest.

She liked his chest. It was strong and broad and muscular. She liked it just as much as his hands and *now* she had even more reasons to like his hands, even love them.

"Mm?" This was a low rumble that seemed to come from somewhere deep inside him. She found she liked that too.

"What does not letting me go mean, um . . . exactly?"

His fingers stopped their lazy stroking at her hip and his hand flattened, his fingertips digging into her.

"It means you aren't going anywhere." His voice sounded somehow tight.

"Tonight?" she asked, deciding it best to ignore his strange tone.

"Tonight, tomorrow night, the next night, the next week." He stopped, but only because he was finished talking not because what came after next week wasn't included in his statement.

This idea warmed her very soul but she *was* a practical Indiana girl. There were other things to consider.

"But I live in Somerset," she told him.

"Now, you live here," he returned as if it was as easy as that.

Her body jerked in stunned surprise at his announcement and she lifted herself to her elbow, reaching down at the same time to grab the sheet and pull it up to her chest. *He* was blithely unconcerned with his (rather wonderful) nakedness but *she* was not.

She stared down at him. After one date he expected her to move in with him?

"I own a house in Somerset," she explained.

His eyes moved to hers and they were unreadable. "We'll visit on the weekends."

She gasped.

"But I have a job in Somerset!" she informed him.

"Resign. You no longer have to work."

She gasped again, this one even more shocked than the last.

"I've been working since I was thirteen years old!"

Something shifted in his eyes as she glared at him and she realized that she'd surprised him somehow.

She had indeed been working since she was thirteen. Neither her parents nor her grandmother thought idle children were a good thing. She had a paper route that she did every morning, not to mention she'd gone to work at one of her father's friend's golf courses, picking up the balls on the driving range all day Saturday. When she was able to work legally, she'd found a job at a fast food restaurant for a year. At Oxford she definitely had to work and pulled pints at a local pub.

She didn't tell Nate any of that nor did she let him comment but continued to speak.

"I don't know how *not* to work. I wouldn't know what to do. What will I do?"

He came up on his elbow and faced her, his hand moving the hair from her neck to behind her back.

"You can shop, go out to lunch with Laura. She'd love it." His voice was soft and his eyes were on her mouth and he obviously thought this was a satisfactory answer.

As much as she liked shopping, she couldn't do it every day. It wouldn't be fun if she could do it every day. And she had a mortgage, she had credit card bills, she had to work.

"I need a job," she told him determinedly.

His head was descending.

"Then get a job," he said against her lips. He was pressing her back on the bed and she didn't resist. She couldn't have even if she wanted to, which she didn't. He came over her and then he kissed her. Her belly was warming up for a full-blown gymnastic extravaganza, she could feel it.

"Nate . . ." she began, this time far less fervently as her voice was quivering.

But finally he took her seriously.

He lifted his head, his voice was low and determined and his eyes were completely black.

"Lily, I'll take care of you. Always. Whatever you want, just ask and I'll get it for you. You'll never need for anything, want for anything, not while you're with me. I'll take care of everything."

Then, the subject closed, he kissed her again, and when he did all thoughts of jobs, mortgages and credit card bills swiftly exited her mind.

Much later she learned how to sleep with someone. Nate pulled her back against his front, wrapped his arm tightly around her waist and buried his face in her hair.

Lily fell asleep thinking it felt rather nice.

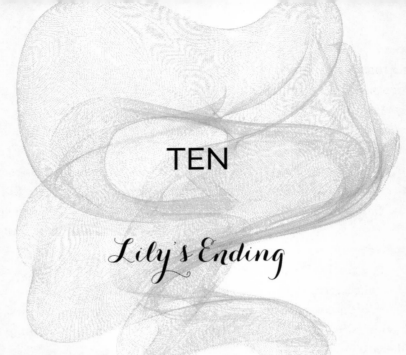

TEN

Lily's Ending

LILY WAS WORRIED.

How she could be happier, more contented and at peace than she'd ever been in her whole life, and be so damned worried all at the same time, she did not know.

Things with Nate were wonderful . . . no, splendid . . . no, *magnificent*. Well, most of the time.

He worked quite a bit. Even at his age (he was only twenty-eight!), he was the Executive Vice President of two divisions of his father's company and he took his job for his father very seriously. Dead seriously. It was almost like he owed his life to that job. Nate left before Lily woke up every morning (and Lily was an early riser) and didn't come home until after eight o'clock every evening.

Sometimes she'd have dinner ready when he'd come home. Other times he'd call her during the day to tell her he was going to take her out to some fabulous restaurant (so fabulous, Nate was significantly taxing the limits of her wardrobe). Twice they'd been to Victor and Laura's for dinner.

Every night he'd make love to her (and mornings besides), most nights more than once and each time was better than the last.

She'd gone back to Clevedon the second morning after their first night together. She'd told him she had to give Maxine notice and work that notice out at the store. He hadn't been happy but she'd put her foot down telling him the truth, that her mother and father would never forgive her if she just quit a job and didn't work out her notice. It was bad form. Eventually, sensing how important it was to Lily because she repeated it, over and over, in a louder and louder voice, he gave in. It was the only time he didn't go to work early. Instead he took her to the train and kissed her on the platform, kissed her in a way that made her not want to go.

"I've changed my mind, I'm not going," she whispered against his lips.

He'd smiled against hers and she had to admit, she really liked it when he did that.

"Now," he murmured also against her lips and she really liked that too, "I don't mind that you're going." He kissed her lightly and finished. "I'll see you at the weekend."

Maxine, at first, had not been happy.

"I'm never giving you time off again!" she'd yelled (Maxine was somewhat dramatic so Lily was used to her yelling).

"But Maxine, I just quit," Lily had replied gently and sensibly.

"Tell me about him. What's he done to you?" Maxine demanded to know.

Maxine had never known Lily Jacobs to even look at a man, much less date, much less drop everything in her life to move to London for some bloke she'd known three days.

Lily told the story, the *full* story, leaving nothing out. She would have left out the sex parts but Maxine was insistent that she wanted it all.

When she was finished, Maxine contradicted herself.

"You're not working out your notice. Get back to this man, get back to him *immediately!*"

"But, the store . . ." Lily resisted.

She loved Maxine and she loved that store and she would miss it. It was hidden down a cobbled alley, had a front window that was just two feet up from the cobbles, the window filled mostly with a window box chockfull of dazzling flowers. Both sides of the old, tiny front door were flanked with enormous, gleaming, cobalt-blue flowerpots that also blazed with color and trailed luscious greenery. The shop was crammed with fun, funky clothes and jewelry made by local artists.

But best of all, it was filled every day with Maxine who was what her grandmother would call "a character."

Maxine went on with her drama, "Blast the store, it'll survive. We've been talking for an hour and one customer came in and didn't buy a thing." Then she'd leaned in, her violet eyes dancing (Lily fancied that Maxine looked a little like Elizabeth Taylor, violet eyes and dark, dark hair, but it must be noted, not unkindly, Maxine was an Elizabeth Taylor in her chubby, older years). "Most girls *never* find a man like that, Lily. You hold on, you hold on for dear life."

Maxine, Lily knew, read romance novels too. Lots of them.

So Lily had called Nate's answering machine, left a message and told him she'd be home two weeks earlier than expected. She went to her ramshackle house and did what she needed to do, packing a couple of bags. Nate had told her they'd be back and frequently so she'd have plenty of time to get more of her things. She felt funny leaving her house, but it wasn't going to grow legs and walk away whereas Nate already had legs and she never wanted to give him a reason to walk away. And after a while, after she knew Nate better, they'd come to a different arrangement.

But now he wanted her in London. He wanted her with him and he was wonderful, handsome and smart. He was a fantastic kisser and even better with his hands and other parts of his anatomy and he thought she was funny.

And he looked at her like, well, like she was beautiful.

He was everything she'd ever wished she would have, everything she wished for Fazire to give her.

And she was going to hold on to him for dear life.

THE FIRST WEEK WITH NATE had been fantastic.

The only thing marring it was dinner at Laura and Victor's. Jeff and Danielle had been in attendance, and even though Victor and Laura seemed pleased that Nate and Lily were together (not exactly pleased so much as over the moon), Nate's siblings did not.

Danielle said catty things about Lily's outfit and her accent, things which made Victor's lips thin and Laura blush with ire.

But it was Nate who said, "Danielle, enough," in a way that everyone at the table knew it was *enough* and Danielle stopped immediately, if rather mutinously.

Then, if that wasn't bad enough, after dinner when Lily had been coming back from the powder room, Jeff was waiting for her. He cornered her as in literally *cornered her*, against the wall in a corner, blocking her path with his body so she couldn't get out.

"I can't believe you chose him, Lily. I can't believe it. Do you know who he *is*?" Jeff was talking low and fast and looking at her as if she was a juicy steak and he was a rabid dog.

He was also scaring her half to death.

"Jeff—"

"I don't mind that you've slept with him. I don't care that he had his filthy hands on you. You and I can start again."

She stared at him open-mouthed and speechless.

She didn't know they'd started at all.

He unfortunately kept speaking. "But once you know who he is, *what* he is, where he came from . . . Lily, you have to know."

Lily interrupted him, saying, "I choose Nate."

She wanted to get away from him, *needed* to get away. He was revolting, vile and now, frightening in his hatred. She didn't know what he was talking about and she didn't care. Lily realized she'd been right the first time she met him. There was nothing to like about him at all. He was talking about his brother, for goodness sake.

"Lily, once I tell you—" he went on, moving closer to her and lifting his hand like he was going to touch her.

"I choose Nate!" she snapped, not wanting him to touch her, angry at his cornering her and angry that a man such as Nate would be strapped with a spoiled, snotty, adopted brother like Jeff. Further she was angry that Laura and Victor had such a son. "Step away," she demanded.

"Lily," he said her name like a plea.

"Step away!" she repeated.

"She said, step away."

This came in a deep, lethal voice from behind Jeff, and Jeff jerked his head around just as Lily's gaze shifted over Jeff's shoulder and they both saw Nate.

He was standing down the hall not five paces away, his legs were planted apart and his arms were crossed on his chest. This was not a casual stance, this was a frightening one.

He was poised to strike.

And his face was horrible, even murderous, as he scowled at his brother.

Jeff didn't move and he had his hand on the wall by Lily's head. She ducked under his arm and fairly ran down the hall to Nate.

His stance didn't shift but his arms came uncrossed. The moment she was in reaching distance, one shot out and pulled her against the side of his hard body.

She didn't resist. She plastered herself there and lifted her hand to rest on his chest. For some reason she was breathing heavily.

Jeff and Nate stared at each other for what seemed like eternity to Lily.

Then Jeff said, "You should tell her, you know."

Nate didn't respond.

"You don't tell her, I will," Jeff threatened.

Nate, again, didn't respond.

Jeff's eyes turned Lily. "He's adopted. He isn't a member of this family at all."

Lily could not even believe that Nate's adoption was what all this was about. Her anger turned to a rage so strong she was beside herself.

Lily leaned towards Jeff but didn't leave Nate's side.

"I know. He already *told* me." She was pleased her voice was strong and even.

"I bet he didn't tell you everything," Jeff retorted, and he was a grown man but he still sounded like a brat.

She was pretty certain he meant about Nate's mother being murdered. But she wasn't going to mention that again. The last and only time Nate talked of it, she knew it was painful, as it would be.

So instead, she said, with all the loyalty that was born and bred in her as the granddaughter of Sarah and daughter of Will and Rebecca, and with a lifetime of living amongst the people of the fine state of Indiana (which Danielle had also attacked at dinner, comments at which Lily was still smarting), "I know all I need to know."

At Lily's words, Nate's arm tightened about her waist and she tilted her head to look up to him.

"I want to go," Lily demanded.

Nate dipped his chin to look down and his eyes were glittering with something she couldn't read. They left Jeff where he was standing and Nate guided her to the drawing room where the rest were sitting and having coffee.

One look at Lily's pale, stricken face sent Victor out of his chair. Laura's own face paled. Danielle looked on assessing the looming situation with what appeared to be delight.

"What's happened?" Victor asked.

"We're leaving," Nate answered.

"Lily, you look like you've seen a ghost. Nathaniel, bring her into the room, I'll get her a drink," Laura said, slowly coming out of her chair.

"We're leaving," Nate repeated implacably.

"What happened?" Victor inquired again, this time his voice a demand.

"Where's Jeff?" Danielle asked sweetly.

Both Victor and Laura's eyes flew to Lily's face and they must have read the truth there because Victor viciously cursed and not under his breath.

"Nathaniel." It was Laura's turn to have her voice turn into a plea and Lily's heart went out to her. How her two children could have come from her sweet body was a mystery.

"I'll call you later," Nate replied and that was that, no good-byes, nothing.

They left.

In his sleek, purring Maserati on the way home, Lily found that, although he clearly did not want to talk about it, she could not stand it. And anyway, she was angry.

"I'm sorry to say this about your very own brother, Nate, but I just do *not* like Jeff."

Nate was silent.

Lily went on, "The first moment I met him, I didn't like him and that's never happened to me before."

Nate remained silent.

Lily continued, "I just cannot *believe* he spoke that way. What's the matter with him?"

Nate kept his silence.

As Lily had allowed her anger loose, she found it didn't last long, especially without Nate's participation, and she lapsed into silence as well.

It wasn't until they were in his flat and Nate was preparing himself what appeared to be a very large, very stiff drink (he didn't offer her one, by this time he knew she didn't drink very much), that she spoke again.

"How much did you see before you arrived?"

To her surprise he answered her with, "All of it."

Lily stared at him.

"You saw him corner me?" she asked, aghast.

He threw back the drink in one gulp. No matter how large it was, he still drained the glass.

"Why didn't you do something?" she demanded.

She was standing behind one of two leather couches that faced each other in his living room and ran perpendicular to a fireplace. Her body was stiff as a board.

This was not romantic hero stuff. Romantic heroes wouldn't let their heroines get cornered by bratty adopted brothers and not lift a finger.

"I wanted to see what you'd do," Nate replied.

She had no response to that. She simply kept staring. She thought perhaps she hadn't heard him correctly.

He wasn't looking at her. He was pouring himself another drink.

Surprisingly, he broke their tense silence. "You haven't asked about what he said." His eyes came to her and his were completely blank.

"What?" She was still recovering from the knowledge that he'd let Jeff corner her.

"You haven't asked me to explain what he said."

Lily stared at him harder, if it could be credited, and then threw her hands out in agitation, blowing a breath out to underline just how annoyed she was.

Then she started pacing.

"You already told me what you want me to know. It wasn't any of my business in the first place, but you told me. If there's more, you'll tell me when you're ready. Nothing you say or he could say would change how I feel about you—"

She stopped talking because she heard his heavy crystal glass slam down against the top of the chest where he kept his liquor, and Lily, who had her back to him and was in mid-pace, whirled around.

He was stalking straight toward her.

His face was filled with . . .

She stared in awe.

Now Nate was staring at her like she was a juicy steak and he wasn't a rabid dog but a starving man offered a feast, a feast that was Lily.

"What's the matter?" she asked.

He kept coming.

She started backing up then faster as he was gaining quickly.

"Nate, what's wrong?"

He didn't explain but when he caught her and dragged her to his bedroom, he didn't push her onto the bed, he threw her on it. Without a further word, he made love to her in a way he'd never done before. It was fierce and violent and possessive. When she was nearly ready to climax, he stopped it, stopped her and made her say his name over and over and over again before he finally let her finish.

It was glorious and, she felt intuitively, it was somehow immensely important.

Although Lily reveled in the former, she didn't quite understand the latter.

THE NEXT TIME THEY WENT to Victor and Laura's house for dinner neither Jeff nor Danielle were in attendance, and Lily found that a small blessing.

Lily had tried to find a job but wasn't having much luck. Maxine was forwarding her mail and her mortgage was due, her bills were due and she didn't have enough money to pay them.

What she wanted most in the world was to be a writer, to live her life sitting at her computer and telling her stories. She didn't bring her computer with her from Clevedon because she figured they'd move that later, and when she confided to Nate her dreams of being a novelist, sleepily after he'd made love to her one evening, he'd told her not to worry about getting a job and just concentrate on writing.

Easy for him to say, he didn't have bills mounting up and no money coming in.

He'd told her he'd take care of everything but Lily couldn't ask him for money. She wasn't like that, and further, wasn't raised like that. She'd have to find a way to take care of her own problems.

However, Nate, she was finding, was a very perceptive man. He knew as the second week slid along that something was bothering her and he asked her about it.

Lily lied. She hated it but she had to do it. She didn't want anything, outside of his awful siblings, to mar their idyllic life. She was embarrassed she'd put herself in this position, especially the credit cards. The amounts weren't astronomical but they were when you didn't have any money.

So she doubled her efforts to find a job, *any* job.

Late the second week, she'd gone out to lunch with Laura, and Laura realized something was wrong straight away.

"It's just something I need to sort out," Lily had responded when Laura asked.

"Is it Nathaniel?" Laura queried, her eyes gentle.

"No! Of course not, everything is fine, great, *wonderful* with Nate."

Laura smiled then the smile wavered. "Is it Jeff?"

Without hesitation Lily grabbed the woman's hand, squeezed it with reassurance and just shook her head. They didn't need to talk about Jeff, ever.

Laura's smile strengthened again and she said, "Whatever it is, just tell Nathaniel. He'll sort it out. He's good at that kind of thing."

She said it in a way that meant he was good at *every* kind of thing. And Lily couldn't help herself, she hugged the other woman and Laura returned the hug with a strength that astonished her.

Laura may have raised two terrible children but surprisingly, she was an excellent mother to the one she did not bear.

That night in bed (unless they were at the dining room table, a restaurant or at Victor and Laura's, they seemed always to be in bed, though Lily wasn't complaining), pressed up against Nate's side, her arm wrapped around his stomach, she'd asked, "Do you think we were a bit hasty?"

It was a silly question, obviously they *were* a bit hasty. They'd barely known each other and moved in together. Or he'd demanded she move in with him and she'd done it.

Nate still didn't talk very much. He didn't share very much at all.

Lily didn't mind this. He did the same with his family, it wasn't just her. He listened and laughed when she told stories about her family and Fazire and growing up in Indiana. But most of the time he was working. Most of the other time, they were making love. Any other time there was left over they were eating so they could have the strength to make love. Talking wasn't exactly their strong suit.

Now she had significant money troubles and didn't know him enough to know how to broach it with him, ask for his help.

It wasn't that she didn't trust him. It was that she didn't want to take advantage of him.

He was already housing her and feeding her in great style. His flat was fantastic. She knew a bit about London real estate and it had to cost a mint. Not to mention he had groceries delivered and they were from a very posh store, *and* he had a housekeeper that came in once a week to clean and do the laundry.

Lily was certainly not going to ask him to pay her mortgage. She'd considered asking him to find her a job at Victor's company but that was just too weird.

She'd bought her house as a screaming deal because it was so run down it was barely worth what she paid for it. But even if it wasn't much, it was *still* a mortgage.

She stopped her careening thoughts and sighed, loudly.

Then she realized Nate hadn't answered.

"Nate?" she prompted.

It was his turn to sigh.

Then he asked, "Hasty with what?"

"Me moving in," she told his chest.

"Lily, what's on your mind?"

Her head came up, she looked at him and he dipped his chin to stare her straight in the eyes. He did that all the time, stared straight in her eyes. He was not a man who was incapable of a direct look. She liked that about him too and her father would *definitely* like that about him. Her dad always said, "Never trust a man who won't look you in the eye."

"What do you mean?" she asked.

To her surprise, he answered her earlier question. "Yes, it was hasty. It was rushed. It was fast. But it wasn't wrong. You know this is good. I know this is good. That isn't your question. Therefore I'd like to know what *is* your question."

She smiled at him, she couldn't help herself. He was *very* astute. Nate seemed to get down, rather easily, to the meat of the matter. It wasn't the first time she noticed it.

"Now she's trying to distract me with a smile," he told the room in a harassed tone and she giggled at him, put her cheek to his chest and hugged his waist.

"It's nothing. It doesn't matter," she whispered.

And it didn't. She'd figure it out. She always did. All that mattered was him and that they were together. If she needed to, as a *very* last resort, she could always ask for her last wish from Fazire.

"Lily."

She slid her head up his chest and looked at the underside of his strong jaw.

"Yes?"

"You know you can tell me anything, yes?"

She didn't answer but she nodded her head and his hand tightened where it was resting on her hip.

She sighed.

She would figure it out and everything would be fine.

THE NEXT DAY THE MAIL came including Maxine's bunch of forwarded post. It held the notice that an article she'd submitted to a magazine
was to be published. It also included a check. It wasn't a great deal of
money but it would cover her mortgage and the minimum payments on
all her cards.

Lily was ecstatic.

"I knew everything would be all right!" she told the living room and
whirled around with her excitement.

The phone rang in mid-whirl and she grabbed it, beside herself with
happiness.

It was, to her shock and delight, Fazire.

"Fazire, oh Fazire, I'm so glad you called. I can't wait—" she began.
But he interrupted her.

"Lily-child," he said in a voice she'd never heard from the usually
happy-go-lucky or sometimes pompous know-it-all Fazire.

Her body froze at his tone, and when she heard what he had to say,
it became rock solid.

"I'll be there right away," she assured her dear friend when he quit
talking.

She hung up and stood frozen for what could have been a minute,
it could have been an hour.

Then she flew into action.

She called Nate's office but his secretary was not answering and Lily
didn't want to leave a message, especially not *this* message. She called the
airline, maxed out her credit card and got a ticket. She packed everything
she owned because she didn't have much at Nate's and she'd likely need
all she had.

Then she called Laura, and to her great misfortune Danielle answered and told Lily that Laura wasn't home.

"Can you ask her to phone me the minute she gets in? I'm leaving
Nate's in an hour." She pulled in a breath and begged, "Danielle, I really
need you to do this. It's urgent."

"No problem. I can take a message, you know," Danielle retorted
acidly.

Lily expressed her gratitude, suppressed her misgivings and

swallowed down her tears.

She put the phone down, picked it right back up and called Nate again.

Still no answer on his work phone. He had no direct line, everyone went through his secretary, and she called again three times, no answer each time.

She called Maxine and told her what had happened but didn't stay on the phone for long just in case Nate or Laura called.

As the time slid by, Lily was becoming frantic. Laura didn't call, Lily couldn't get through to Nate and she had to get to Indiana immediately. She had to get to Fazire. He wouldn't know what to do. He wasn't even human. He was all alone in that rambling limestone house for the first time without his Becky.

She gulped down the emotion that swelled in her throat at the thought of her mother, which led to thoughts of her father, and she wrote a note to Nate. She was just signing it when the intercom rang, announcing someone was downstairs waiting to be let in.

Hoping it was Laura for a surprise visit, Lily flew to the intercom.

Seeing as it was the absolutely most unlucky day of her life—and that was an understatement—it was Jeff.

Lily's heart plummeted.

"Lily, don't hang up!" Jeff cried urgently. "I'm here to apologize. Promise. I was out of line."

She hesitated, stared at the phone across the room for a moment, begging it to ring.

It didn't.

Her last chance was telling Jeff. He at least seemed to like her, unlike Danielle, and he was there to apologize. Maybe he wasn't the jerk she thought he was.

"Come on up, Jeff," she said and buzzed him in.

She had to leave in five minutes. She had her bags packed and at the door and while she was waiting for Jeff, she called the doorman to hail a cab for Heathrow.

There was a knock on the door and Lily moved to it to let him in. Jeff saw her bags immediately and his head snapped from them to her, his eyes alight.

She was too wired to notice, trying to fight the tears crawling up her throat and her frenzy at needing to get word to Nate or Laura.

"What's happened Lily?" he asked softly.

She stared at him and then it happened. The dam broke. She could hold it back no longer.

She burst into tears.

He pulled her into his arms and stroked her back.

"Tell me, Lily, tell me what he's done," he whispered encouragingly.

She just shook her head and said in a broken voice, "It's not Nate. It's my parents. They died in a plane crash yesterday. Both of them."

His arms tightened.

"Oh, Lily," Jeff murmured and she could swear he actually sounded upset for her.

She pulled away, dashing her hands on her tearstained cheeks.

"I have to go," she announced urgently and looked at her watch. "Now!" she cried in panic. "I haven't been able to get hold of Nate or your mother. Jeff, you must phone Nate. Tell him. You must. Please. Tell him I'll call him later, in a few days. Promise me."

His hand reached up and touched her cheek where a tear was sliding down.

"I promise," he whispered.

She threw her arms around him and hugged him tight. "Thank you."

Then she grabbed her bags and tore out the door to go home.

To Fazire.

JEFF WATCHED THE DOOR SLAM behind Lily and saw the note on the table.

He calmly walked over and read it.

He thought, vaguely, that it was rather sad.

Then he bunched it in a ball and put it in his pocket.

Nate, he knew, was moving in a few days.

Lily just told him she wouldn't call for a few days.

There wasn't much time.

He walked through his brother's posh flat and searched for anything that she may have left behind.

He found a bottle of perfume on a bureau, a pair of earrings on the bedside table and a lone nightgown, the only thing in an otherwise empty drawer.

That was it.

He shoved these in a trash bag, carried them out of the flat and deposited them in the first dustbin he found.

Then he called his sister.

ELEVEN

Nate's "Death"

"I THINK WE SHOULD do it."

Nate was at his desk and Victor was sitting across from him. They were going over some figures for a proposed deal that Victor very much wanted to do.

Nate was staring out the window and wondering what was wrong with Lily.

She was guarded, she was being secretive and there was something she wasn't telling him.

He didn't want to push her. After Jeff cornered her, she could have forced Nate to bare his soul about his past but she told him she'd wait until he was ready. Although he wanted to force her to share with him whatever was bothering her, he thought it best to take her cue and wait until she was ready to share.

Nate had no idea how to behave in a healthy relationship. He could easily cope with dysfunction, indifference, malice and greed, but he was hopelessly out of his depth with Lily.

He knew she wanted more from him but it was something he couldn't give. He didn't want to do anything that would make her turn away, make the shining light that blazed in her eyes whenever she looked at him even dim, much less go away.

He had stood behind Lily and Jeff listening to Lily choose him, feeling for the first time in his life a fierce pride in himself that this magnificent creature would want him, would *choose* him. At the same time he wished for Jeff to tell her, tell her whatever it was he knew, tell her so it would be out in the open.

Jeff didn't do it, which was both a continued burden at the same time it was an immense relief.

Nate even entertained thoughts of packing her up, taking her away, going back to Indiana with her and leaving his past behind forever. He didn't want to hang on to who he was anymore. He didn't want it to destroy his life and what he hoped to build with Lily.

But he couldn't do that, he could never leave. He owed everything he was to Victor and Laura and that came with Jeff and Danielle.

Nate was existing on borrowed time when it came to Lily.

Therefore, as always, he had a plan.

"Nathaniel?"

Nate's head jerked around to look at his father and Victor lifted up the papers they were supposed to be going over as a reminder to his distracted son.

"No," Nate stated flatly.

"You don't want to do it?" Victor asked in disbelief.

"It's too much of a risk."

"Ho, ho, hoooo . . ." His father drew out his last "ho" grandly. "You're getting soft." He stared knowingly at Nate, and Nate knew he meant Lily.

"Not soft, Victor. That deal's a train wreck," Nate responded calmly.

"Two weeks ago, you would have been all over this," Victor volleyed.

"Two weeks ago, those papers were on my desk. I read through them and tossed them in the bin," Nate returned.

Victor's eyes rounded. "Jeff brought this to me two days ago."

"Jeff wants the deal and I also told Jeff no."

No more needed to be said about Jeff or the deal. Jeff had lost the company enough money making foolish decisions, not taking advice and not thinking things through.

Nate, however, had been the driving force behind their success and both Victor and Jeff knew it. Victor was always a ruthless risk taker but it was Nate who assessed their options and advised the route. Victor always took Nate's advice. Nate, in turn, had never been wrong and Victor had never been sorry.

Furthermore, Jeff was a sore subject for Nate especially after that dinner and Victor knew that as well. Knew it well enough to make certain that Nate didn't see Jeff anywhere, not at the house or at the office.

Victor threw the dismissed papers on Nate's desk and sat back.

"So, no deal. Let's talk about something else. How's Lily?"

The phone rang in his outer office and no one answered it. His secretary was out sick and HR was having troubles getting a temp to replace her.

Nate ignored it and told his father, "She's fine."

"You gonna marry her?" Victor asked.

At this blunt query, Nate decided to turn his attention to the window again.

"Son, I asked you a question," Victor said quietly but kindly. He was never menacing to Nate, as he still could be, very much so. Firstly, Nate wouldn't respond to it. Secondly, Victor held Nate in too much esteem. Thirdly, Nate was not the type of man who could be menaced.

"I think Lily needs things to slow down," Nate finally answered.

"Take my advice," Victor said and Nate's eyes shifted to him again, "Get the girl pregnant. It worked for me with Laura."

After saying this, he grinned cheekily.

Nate nearly flinched at his words but he stopped himself.

"Victor, you've been married thirty years and Jeff's twenty-eight."

Nate didn't believe his father and thought he was being purposefully shocking to get his point across.

"She lost it. It was a boy," Victor announced and Nate stared in stunned surprise as Victor's jaw clenched. Nate had never heard this story. "She says it took her fourteen years to get him back."

At these quiet words, Nate felt like Victor had punched him in the gut. He didn't let on to this extreme reaction. He just nodded once to his father.

The mood already turned, Victor decided to go with it.

"Laura was the best thing that happened to me. I was a thug, worse, and I had no business being with her. I knew it, Nathaniel, right to my bones. But nothing was going to stop me from having her, nothing. It wasn't the right thing to do, fuck, wasn't even the nice thing to do, but I did it. I got her pregnant and I did it on purpose. I'd have done anything to bind her to me."

Nate kept his silence and kept his outward calm but his father's words were slamming into him like hammers.

"You and me, son, we're a lot alike. I don't know the way you process things because you're a helluva lot smarter than me, but I know how you think."

Nate turned his attention back to the window.

"Lily was a virgin," he told his father.

"I know," Victor replied.

Nate's body stilled at this comment. Victor somehow always seemed to know everything.

Even though Nate didn't ask, Victor went on to explain, "She confided in me you were her first date."

Nate's eyes turned again to his father at *that* bit of news. He could barely credit it.

As usual Victor seemed to know what Nate was thinking even though he hadn't said a word. "I know, shocked me too but I swear she wasn't lying. She was nervous as a cat."

This made Nate smile.

Victor went on, "Lucky you had a motorcycle. That broke the ice." With that, Victor again grinned at him.

Uncharacteristically, Nate decided a confidence was in order and he shared his plan.

"She hasn't brought up the subject of birth control."

Victor watched him closely. "I reckon you haven't been seeing to it." Nate shook his head. This he also did once.

Victor beamed. "We think alike, you and me, always have."

As Victor had said, it wasn't the right thing to do and it certainly wasn't a nice thing to do but Nate didn't care. If he thought she was likely to leave him, he would have chained her to the bed. Making her pregnant would bind her to him for life. He knew that and he wanted it and he was going to do it.

If she was pregnant, she wouldn't leave him. Family meant more to her than anything in the world. She made that perfectly clear, not only in the way she spoke of her own but in the way she treated his.

When she found out about him, whether he told her or Jeff told her or Victor or Laura let something slip, she wouldn't be able to leave. She could move out now, divorce him if they were married, but she'd never break up a family. He, like his father, knew this to his very bones.

The phone rang again in the outer office.

"You gonna get that?" Victor asked, getting up from his chair.

"I've work to do. I want to be home early tonight."

"Don't blame you," Victor muttered, lifted his hand casually in fare-well and left.

Nate went to work.

He did this having no idea his life, for the second time in as many weeks, was about to be rocked to its very foundations.

NATE DID GET HOME EARLY. He'd been meaning to tell Lily they were moving and had never gotten around to it. They always had much better things to do.

The movers would be there the next day to start packing and would be moving them the day after that. He wanted to talk to Lily about having them move whatever she needed from her house in Somerset.

However, he arrived home to an empty flat.

He hadn't called her to tell her he was coming home early and ex-pected she'd gone out somewhere. She was nearly obsessed with the idea of finding a job. Or she could be with Laura.

He picked up the phone and dialed his mother.

"Nathaniel, my dearest, I'm so glad you called. Would you and Lily like to come over for dinner next week?"

Nate was walking into the bedroom to change clothes and he stopped.

Then he froze.

"Nathaniel?" Laura called when he didn't respond.

"Sorry, Laura, I'll ring you back," Nate murmured.

He pressed the button without listening to her good-bye and stared around the room.

Lily's cosmetics were not messily piled on the bureau. He could smell her perfume but the bottle was gone.

He walked to the bathroom.

Her toothbrush and all the other bottles and jars (and Nate had noted there were a great number of them, the sight of this, he found to his surprise, made him feel an unusual sense of contentment) were gone.

He went back to the bedroom and pulled out one of the drawers she'd moved into.

It was empty.

He pulled out another one.

It too was empty.

He walked back into the living room and saw some mail on a table. She'd had another mess of post forwarded from her friend Maxine. It was all still there opened, but left.

Nate noticed her mortgage was overdue as were two credit cards. Nate found this surprising and wondered, vaguely, why she hadn't given them to him. He'd told her he'd take care of it, take care of everything. There was absolutely no reason her bills should be overdue.

There was also a letter written in a neat slightly creative handwriting. Her mother, telling Lily of the "latest antics" of Fazire and her excitement at their imminent holiday to Hawaii.

He got himself a drink, sat on the couch and waited.

After darkness had fallen, he smoked and drank more, a good deal more. He hadn't had a cigarette since that night outside the front door of his parent's home. Hadn't even wanted one but he wanted one then.

She didn't come home. She didn't call.

Not that night, not the next.

The movers moved him, and on that day he went to the address on her mortgage bill.

The town where she lived was smart and he could tell it was expensive by the number of BMWs, Mercedes and Jaguars parked in the drives.

Her house was right on the seafront, he could see from its position that there was a view of the Victorian pier from the back windows. He noted with detachment that it was a very fine piece of real estate, an excellent location. It was a terraced house, three stories at street level but likely another one set in the cliff. It was a lot of house for just Lily. It was also rather stately even if it looked from the outside a bit rundown. She'd planted two enormous terracotta planters with a wealth of flowers and they sat on either side of the front door.

He knocked, looking to his left into a sunroom that sat at the front of the house. It had mosaic tiled floors and wicker furniture in it with gaily printed cushions inviting you to sit. He was not in the mood to notice the furniture was not new and rather battered. He was not in the mood because no one answered. The house looked deserted.

Then he heard, "Are you looking for Lily?"

A neighbor had come out to walk her dog and Nate turned to the old lady. "Yes, is she here?"

"Nope, moved. Moved back home I heard. Just up and left. Gone back to America. Surprised me, she seemed a solid sort of girl. But there you go. You never know people."

She kept walking her little dog and Nate watched her move down the small street Lily's house was on. He watched her hit the wider pavement that edged the larger road that was the turn off to Lily's street. He watched her as she disappeared down the steep hill toward the pier.

Then he got in his car and drove back to London.

THREE DAYS AFTER LILY LEFT, Nate moved into his new apartment, the same day he disconnected his old phone.

His secretary took a leave of absence due to an unexpected extended illness.

His temporary secretary had never heard of Lily Jacobs. When she took the calls from the woman, she lost most of the messages under a pile of ones marked urgent (nearly all calls to Nate McAllister seemed to be urgent and the secretary simply couldn't cope). She lost a lot of messages in the two weeks Nate put up with her, none of them nearly as urgent as the ones from Lily.

The ones Nate's temp didn't lose, Jeff stole.

Danielle was awash with delight at the strange abrupt exit of Lily.

So much so, weeks later, she made her last, desperate attempt at capturing his heart by seducing his body.

He'd been so revolted, he'd told her, in more words than he would normally use, exactly what he thought of her.

Unbeknownst to him, five minutes after he pulled his Maserati out from in front of his parent's house after this somewhat dramatic scene, Lily had walked up the stoop for the last time with her beloved Fazire. It was *very* unfortunate timing as, at that moment Lily was *the last* person on earth Danielle Roberts wanted to see. And anyway, Danielle and her brother had prepared well for this moment.

Victor and Laura were, at first, confused then worried then they both became angry at Lily's unexplained departure. Surprisingly, for the first time in Nate's life, he saw Laura's anger turn to rage and it didn't blow itself out in a matter of minutes. She seemed to nurse it for days, weeks, even, if Lily's name ever came up in conversation (usually by Jeff), years.

Jeff was also quite happy and very smug about Lily's departure. He knew something. Nate understood this by the way Jeff acted. At first he was cagey and jumpy as if he expected whatever he did to backfire, which happened often with Jeff. But when it didn't, the smugness was complete and it, too, lasted for years.

Nate knew that Jeff told Lily about his past life, how his relationship started with Jeff's father and she ran. She had told him that nothing Jeff could say would change how she felt about him but she had lied.

Nate was well acquainted with people who lied. This didn't surprise him one bit. A glorious, twenty-two-year-old virgin from Indiana, who probably lived in a palatial home that looked like a plantation (at least this was where Nate saw her in his mind whenever he thought about her, which was a great deal for the first few months, but later as a well-honed defense mechanism, not at all, or at least, not during daylight hours) and had been cosseted and sheltered all her life, confronted with what Nate was . . .

She was probably still showering to wash away the filth of him.

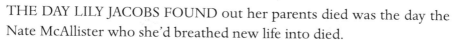

THE DAY LILY JACOBS FOUND out her parents died was the day the Nate McAllister who she'd breathed new life into died.

He found new women, none of them a single thing like Lily. His father became Chairman of the Board while Nate took over as CEO. He bought an enormous penthouse apartment and commissioned an even bigger bed.

And he slept in it, in the rare times he slept at home, alone (or at least, most of the time).

Part Four

TWELVE

Laura & Lily

Eight years later, Nate is thirty-six,
Lily is thirty and it's early in the month of May . . .

LAURA ROBERTS WAS WALKING through Hyde Park.

She liked to walk, did it often, it kept her legs shapely (that's what Victor told her at least). It kept her fit. It kept her young.

Hyde Park was her favorite place to walk with the Serpentine running through, all the trees, the different monuments and statues here and there, Diana's Memorial, Speaker's Corner, the people riding horses, and there were so many dogs being walked and babies in prams. There was always something to see and it was never the same.

That sunny, beautiful, warm day, for instance, Laura saw a man who looked like he was wearing black kohl all around his dark eyes. He had hair nearly as black as Nathaniel's but without the blue sheen, darkly-tanned skin, a protruding belly and a pointed, black goatee.

He looked almost, Laura thought fancifully, like a genie but in regular people's clothes.

She watched as he stopped and planted his feet wide apart and crossed his arms, his face mock fierce with annoyance, just like Yul Brynner in *The King and I*. This made him look *exactly* like a genie.

With curiosity to discover what was annoying him, Laura turned her gaze to where the genie-man was scowling.

And then her entire frame froze.

Lily.

Laura couldn't believe her eyes and blinked twice to see if it cleared her vision or if perhaps the woman she saw was someone else that looked like Lily but was not and Laura's mind was simply playing terrible, horrible tricks on her.

But it *was* Lily.

She looked nearly the same, except thinner. She was wearing a pair of very faded Levi's and an even more faded t-shirt that said "Chicago Cubs" on it. She was running toward the genie-man and smiling that same, strange, quirky but beautiful Lily smile.

Except different.

Laura regarded more closely the woman who had broken her Nathaniel's heart.

She looked pale, slightly drawn and even tired.

The Lily Light she thought she knew so well was gone.

Life, Laura saw and felt an atypical satisfaction at seeing, had not treated Lily Jacobs very well.

Laura decided immediately to put Lily out of her mind. She would, of course, tell Victor about this but she'd never breathe a word to Nathaniel. Her son had never let on to how shattered he was at Lily's unexplained departure, but Laura, as any mother would, knew.

Lily Jacobs was truly the only person in the world that Laura Roberts hated. Laura knew all about Nathaniel's past, Victor had told her. That Lily would bring such life and light to him, make him actually *laugh* (a lot), make him so *happy* and then tear it away without an explanation or even a good-bye . . .

Well, she was simply not worth Laura's regard and she definitely wasn't worth her kindness.

Laura started walking again in hopes she'd get away before Lily saw her. She couldn't abide speaking to her *not*, she imagined, that Lily would ever approach her if she had a single decent bone in her body.

Then she heard the still familiar voice call, "Tash! Stop dawdling, baby doll."

Laura's head came up and she froze again.

Running toward Lily and the strange genie-man was a little girl.
Nathaniel's little girl.

Laura knew it immediately. It was stamped all over the child.

The same blue-black hair, the same (even at that distance Laura could tell, she *was* Nathaniel's mother after all) darker than dark eyes, the same bone structure, the same long-legged, long-waisted body, except feminine and in child-like form.

Indeed, there was no mistaking it. No denying it.

The child was Nathaniel McAllister's child.

Laura watched in stunned, frozen silence as the little girl ran toward Lily and threw her arms around her mother. Lily bent to kiss the top of her head and was talking to her, smiling down on her. This smile was not tired and drawn. It lit up her face, just like the old Lily.

Laura couldn't believe it. She didn't know what to do. She wanted to scream, to run forward and snatch the child from her mother's arms.

Lily straightened from the girl, turning to lead them in the opposite direction and then Lily saw her.

Her pale face, if it could be credited, drained of color. Her mouth dropped open, and she too, froze.

Moments later, Laura watched, her astonishment deepening, as Lily's stupor cleared and her face melted into a look of such abandoned happiness, such love that it turned Laura's stomach.

And Laura looked at Lily with every shred of hatred she had for the woman, turned on her heel and ran.

"MY GOD, FAZIRE, MY GOD. Did you *see* the way she looked at me?"

Fazire was levitating. He did this in agitation now, she knew, not just when he was practicing or when he wanted to make a point.

He didn't respond. He couldn't have, Lily kept talking.

"She saw Tash. She knows. I told you I should have gone to them ages ago. Now it's too late. Now . . ."

She stopped talking and started pacing. Or more to the point started pacing more frantically.

Lily had been wanting to go to the Roberts's home for years. Natasha was their grandchild. They would want to know she existed. Even if it would be painful after Nate's death (this, she decided in her fevered imaginings, happened on his motorcycle or in his Maserati, but she didn't know, never *wanted* to know).

Something always got in the way. The store, the house, Tash getting sick, Lily having a migraine (they came far more frequently now, stress, the doctor told her), not enough money for the train tickets (there was never enough money), the phones got cut off, laundry, cleaning, grocery shopping, the car needing fixed (the car always needed fixed).

She should have written but how do you say *that* in a letter?

It was something you had to do in person.

And Lily was so sick at first, the pregnancy had not gone well and by the time she and Fazire decided to cast their lot in Clevedon, she was practically bedridden. By the end of the pregnancy, she was forcefully bedridden.

And the birth had not been good. It took her a year to recuperate. By that time the debts had mounted, the bills were all overdue and she'd nearly asked her last wish of Fazire. But Maxine had saved the day. Maxine and Grammy Sarah's beautiful limestone house with its Italian marble windowsills and its ten acres.

While Lily was ill, she'd had time to think. She started wondering why Laura and Victor didn't contact *her*. Why they let it be Danielle who told her that Nate had died. Why, when Lily knew that they knew she also lost her parents at the same time, had they not come to her knowing the enormity of her loss?

Even not knowing about Tash, Lily was absolutely certain that they knew she loved Nate and she'd need to grieve with them when her vital, handsome dream man was swept away.

She didn't understand and thought, maybe, she had misjudged them. In her darkest moments (of which there were many), she realized they *had* raised Jeffrey and Danielle. Perhaps they *were* just like their two children by blood.

Eventually time just flew, as time does, and it became too late.

This was the first time Lily had been to London in eight years. *Eight years.* They had a dingy hotel room in a not-so-good part of town. It was all they could afford.

It didn't matter. They only had to sleep in it. The rest of the time Lily was supposed to be showing them all her favorite places in London and that included where she and Nate had taken their walk in Hyde Park.

Lily's daughter knew all about her father.

Every detail Lily could remember, and that was most of them, were told to Tash in the grandest stories Lily had ever created. And as the years slid by, Lily even made up details just to keep Nate alive in some way for their darling daughter.

"I have to go to her," Lily fretted.

Fazire looked down his nose at her and crossed his arms.

He, personally, did not think much of these Roberts people. Every time they looked at his Lily-child they did it with hate, which was *precisely* why he consistently tried to talk her out of telling them about Tash and would distract her when she got down to the business of writing or phoning them.

If they knew about Tash, he couldn't imagine what they'd do.

And obviously today's events stated he had, as usual, been *absolutely* correct.

"I do not think that is wise," he declared.

"I *have* to, Tash is her grandchild!" Lily cried.

"What are you talking about?"

Tash had come out of the bathroom and was looking at them curiously.

Lily looked at her beautiful daughter who had not a shred of her or Becky, Will or Sarah, but was absolutely all Nate.

Tash Jacobs was a bright child, fearfully bright. A genius her teacher's said, which was another reason Lily had no money. Anything extra she was setting aside in hopes of getting Tash into a special school for gifted children.

This, Fazire believed, came from Lily. This, Lily *knew*, came from Nate. Tash had exactly the same way of cutting to the meat of the matter as Nate had.

On this thought, Lily made her decision.

She smiled at her daughter. "Mummy needs to go see some friends. She'll be back soon."

"Lily—" Fazire said in a dire, warning tone.

Lily looked at him with determination. "I'll be back soon."

And before her genie could speak another word, she was off.

"YOU ARE . . . fucking . . . *kidding me.*"

Laura did not like it when Victor cursed.

However, if there ever was a time to curse, now was that time.

As luck would have it (or not, depending on how you looked at it), Nate had come home with Victor. So Laura thought she might as well tell them both at the same time. Nate had to know anyway and it might as well come from his mother. And by the look of things, Victor would not have imparted the information nearly as thoughtfully as Laura did.

Victor looked like he was about to hit the roof.

Nathaniel, sitting opposite Laura with one ankle resting casually atop the opposite knee, looked like he could happily commit murder.

However he would do it in a very cool, very controlled manner.

One look at her son and Laura began to feel a creeping concern.

And it all had to do with that joyous look.

Lily had been happy to see her.

That may have been an act, of course. Moments before she'd looked horrified, but Laura, well, Laura was beginning to have her doubts.

Why was Lily happy to see her? Especially considering the daughter she'd hid from them all for (Laura counted back then couldn't wrap her mind around it and just guessed) eight years was standing right there, the very vision of Nathaniel.

"I'm going to hunt that bitch down and I'm going to wring her white, hillbilly neck," Victor threatened.

"Victor, calm down," Laura soothed.

"I will not calm down! That's my goddamned grandchild!" he shouted so loudly the windows shook.

"What's happening?"

Laura closed her eyes in despair.

This they did *not* need.

Danielle had taken that moment to walk into the room.

Her daughter had finally moved out, was living with a man that neither Victor nor Laura cared for but who all of them thought suited her. Nevertheless, she came home regularly and seemed to do it with an uncanny sense of when Nathaniel was there.

"Your mother has seen Lily," Victor informed his daughter and Laura's eyes flew open.

"Victor!"

Laura didn't think it was wise to bring Danielle into this drama. It wasn't ever wise to bring Danielle into any drama. She created enough dramas on her own.

"Who?" Danielle had gone to sit on the arm of the chair where Nathaniel was sitting.

Her son went momentarily still and then immediately stood and crossed the room. As usual, he made himself perfectly clear without uttering a single word.

"Lily, Lily, *Lily!*" Victor shouted, incensed. "That girl from backwater Indiana who left Nathaniel."

Danielle's eyes rounded and Laura, again with Mother Vision, noted that she looked somehow frightened.

At this point the doorbell rang.

"I'll get it," Danielle jumped up eagerly. Too eagerly.

"No! I'll bloody well get it," Victor shouted even though this was completely unnecessary.

Danielle shakily sat back down.

Laura dismissed her daughter, she'd deal with her later, and turned to look up at Nathaniel. He'd schooled his features but Laura saw they were still tight with anger *and* disbelief.

"You haven't said a word," she informed him.

"Nate *never* says a word," Danielle mumbled and Laura had just enough time to shoot her daughter a killing look before the explosion came from the front hall.

"*You've got a fucking nerve!*" Everyone heard Victor shout and in moments they all rushed into the hall.

Nathaniel's legs being longest and he being the swiftest meant he exited the room first. Danielle followed with Laura coming up the rear.

When Laura skidded to a halt in the entryway, she could not believe her eyes.

Victor had Lily in a death grip, both of his big hands wrapped around her upper arms and he held her imprisoned. She was staring up at him in complete shock.

"Victor, let her go!" Laura cried.

Lily's head turned toward Laura's voice.

And she saw Nathaniel.

And then something happened that Laura would never have guessed.

Lily's eyes rounded. The expression on her face immediately went funny, her mouth fell slack and every muscle in her body visibly tensed.

And then her lips came back together and she said, or mouthed as no sound came out, "Oh my God."

Laura watched as Lily's face started to melt. It melted like it had when Lily had seen her in the park but this time it wasn't an abandoned happiness.

It started to be absolutely glorious.

But it stopped when Victor gave her a vicious shake and her head snapped back.

"Victor! I said to let her go," Laura tried again.

He did immediately and she stumbled back and had to throw her arms out to stop herself from careening backwards out the front door. She just managed to catch herself on the doorjamb.

"You bitch!" Victor yelled. "You take your silly, hick self out of my goddamned house and you better get yourself a damn fine lawyer because we're getting that child. You've had her for eight years and we're going to have her for the next eight!"

Lily's head jerked up and she stared at Victor in shock.

"Wh-what?" she breathed in a barely-there voice.

Laura noted that Nathaniel had crossed his arms on his chest and was watching this drama like it was being staged for his personal amusement.

And he found it lacking.

Lily's eyes flicked from Victor to Nathaniel and her pale face became bloodless when her eyes locked on Laura's adopted son.

Then she spied Danielle and something seeped into her face. Something that was simply awful to see.

"You told me he was dead," she whispered.

"Out!" Victor shouted, stepped forward and shoved her out the door with a hand on her chest. She went back several steps and Victor slammed the door in her face.

"Victor!" Laura screamed and ran to the door.

Something was wrong. Something was very wrong. She knew it. She sensed it. Her heart was racing and she became panicked. She *had* to get to Lily.

She clawed at the handle but Victor pulled her away.

"We have to hear what she has to say!" Laura yelled at her husband, yanked her arm free and jerked the door open.

And saw nothing but Lily running away.

Running for her very life.

THIRTEEN

Lily

"THEY'RE HERE," JANE CALLED.

"Make them wait," Alistair Hobbs replied.

Lily was looking out the window of Alistair's conference room and ignoring this exchange between Alistair and his assistant, Jane.

Alistair Hobbs was a friend of a friend of Maxine's. He was tall, slender and had ginger hair and eyebrows. In a vague way (as usual when it came to these sorts of things), Lily noted he was quite good-looking. Lily had met him at Maxine's store, seen him in the market several times and they'd chatted. He'd asked her out once but she'd said no.

Lily never went out, ever. She didn't have the time *nor* the inclination.

Alistair didn't seem to take offense to this. Regardless of his profession, he was a very nice man.

Maxine took offense to it. She thought Alistair was the bomb.

Now, as Lily was his client, it was a moot point. Alistair couldn't ask her out again because he was her lawyer.

Or, at least he couldn't ask her out for a while.

She couldn't afford him, of course. She couldn't afford much of anything. She certainly couldn't afford to go head to head with Nate and the entire Roberts clan in a custody battle for Tash. Lily had no idea how rich they were but she knew from their homes, cars and clothes they had a *lot* more money than she did.

Lily, Fazire and Tash had no sooner got home to Somerset when Victor was good at his word and she received a letter, hand-delivered, from their attorneys.

Nate, alive and well, kicking and breathing and apparently angry, was going for full custody although *Lily* had no idea why *Nate* should be angry. *Lily* didn't get her sister (had she had one) to brush off her unwanted boyfriend by telling him *she* was dead.

The letter said he wanted full and complete custody.

Nate was going to try and take her daughter from her.

Lily couldn't believe it. Couldn't believe Nate was even alive much less he would do something so vicious and cruel.

Granted, he had a daughter he knew nothing about for the first seven years of her life but that wasn't Lily's fault.

It had been only days since that humiliating scene in the Roberts's entryway with Victor. The living, breathing Nate staring on like . . . like . . . she didn't know what it was like. Like she was a creepy crawly and he was watching Victor scrunch her under his shoe.

Lily couldn't figure it out, couldn't manage to put even two of her thoughts together much less the number of thoughts it would take to figure out this mess.

Why?

Why, why, why?

She closed her eyes.

She knew why.

He had been finished with her. Just as he'd finished with his girlfriend Georgia. One second an item and talk of an engagement ring. The next second they were over.

Lily had to admit she was surprised they'd lasted as long as they did. Lily was not exactly in Nate's league. She was an inexperienced virgin for one. For another she wasn't beautiful and slim. And another, she was a sheltered Indiana girl and not a droll, cosmopolitan sophisticate.

She must have gotten very boring very quickly.

Well, obviously she had.

When he heard the story, Fazire had been enraged. He was beside himself and Fazire beside himself was a sight to see.

He channeled all his genie friends in hopes of a wayward wish so he could turn Nate, Victor and the entire Roberts family into vermin and he was going to do it, he assured her, floating barely inches from the ceiling.

Fortunately or unfortunately, depending on how you looked at it, there weren't any wayward wishes to be had. There never were. Lily's family was the first in Genie History to hang on to their wishes *and* their genie.

And Lily wasn't going to use her last wish for *that*.

She had bigger battles on her hands. Much bigger battles.

"Lily," Alistair said softly.

Her eyes opened, her head shot up to look at him and he was smiling at her kindly.

"You know the plan?"

Lily nodded.

She knew the plan. She knew the plan but she hated the plan. She hated it with a passion.

But she'd do anything to keep Tash. Anything to keep her precious daughter.

Anything.

Alistair knew everything, her whole, sad, stupid, gullible story. Lily had told him every humiliating detail of her meeting with Nate and her life for the last eight years. Her difficult pregnancy, the bills, the state of her house when they'd moved there, not fit for Fazire and Lily much less a baby. She'd told him about the second jobs she had to get to put in decent wiring and plumbing. Lily herself doing most of the other work on the house. Lily's saving up for Tash's special school.

Everything.

When she was finished talking, Alistair stared at her a moment with a funny look on his face. Then he picked up a glass paperweight on his desk and threw it across the room. Lily wasn't certain that was professional lawyer-type behavior but she'd let it slide.

"Send them in," Alistair called to his assistant and then turned back to Lily. "Don't say anything, Lily. Just leave it to me."

Lily nodded again.

She had thought about it in her rational moments, of which there were few, and she didn't mind letting Nate have visitation rights, though she wasn't keen on Tash spending a great amount of time with Danielle or Victor or, indeed, Jeff. However, Tash needed a father and never expected to have one and didn't even know she *did* have one . . . yet.

For Tash this would be a boon from the gods. Lily had been telling her daughter stories about Nate since she was born. Huge, lavish, adoring, heartsick stories that made Nate seem like any prince in any fairytale. Tash was going to be overjoyed when she heard Nate was alive. Tash thought Nate had been a superhero, the leader of the free world and a saint all rolled into one.

This was indeed a boon that neither of them ever expected. A boon that Lily would have wished for if Fazire would have done it, which, he informed her, he would not. Indeed, she did wish for it, prayed for it, begged for it, cried for it nearly every day for years and years.

When she'd seen Nate standing, breathing, *living*, she'd thought every dream she had of his return from the dead had come real. It had been the most glorious moment of her life.

For about two seconds.

Then it became every nightmare.

And then it got worse.

Now she was going to have to humiliate herself again. Have her whole sordid story and naïve stupidity laid out for all to see.

All for Tash, her perfect, sweet, brilliant, beautiful Tash. Tash, who Lily had clung to in those dark days. Tash who looked just like Nate, a fact Lily used to think was a treasure, a precious gift. Tash, who was the only person besides Fazire (in his less annoying moments), who could truly make Lily smile anymore.

Tash was the only beautiful thing that had come out of eight hard, dead years.

Alistair put his hand on her arm and squeezed reassuringly.

Lily winced carefully so he would not see her doing it. The deep, angry bruises that Victor had given her were still there. She did not tell Alistair about the bruises. After the paperweight incident she thought that omission was sensible.

"You don't have to worry, we have them Lily," he promised in a whisper.

"Hobbs," a voice said from behind them and Lily turned her head to look.

Jane was leading in four men, two of them she knew.

She held her breath in surprise and fear.

Victor was there, wearing a face that was a mask of fury. And Victor's fury was a scary thing. This she knew now all too well.

Nate was also there, wearing a well-tailored, unbelievably expensive-looking suit. He was no less tall, no less handsome. The years had only deepened his impossibly good looks until they were nearly *unbearably* good looks. He was looking at her, or more to the point at Alistair's hand on her arm, with a look that could only be described as contempt.

If her heart had not already turned to stone, it would have at that look.

Instead, it pulverized.

It was then Lily became numb. Nothing worse could happen to her, not after losing her grandmother then both her parents then, she thought, Nate and her dreams of a bright future as a bestselling novelist, living with her dreamy romantic hero husband and creating a family together. Finally, Tash coming and it being so very hard after that. So, very, very hard.

Numb, she thought in a vague way, was a good way to be.

Alistair led her to her seat. Alistair had explained the drill. Jane would be courteously getting drinks, lulling them into a sense of security before Alistair unleashed his plan.

Automatically, Lily stated her preference for coffee to Jane and Lily was so removed from the scene she was surprised when she was served her drink.

She didn't touch it.

Alistair had arranged for the informal meeting to happen at his offices in Bristol. He'd been pleased to win that small battle but Lily didn't care. Though she was happy not to have the added expense of going to London.

She'd go to Sri Lanka if it meant keeping Tash.

Lily had dressed carefully in an outfit that Maxine bought her.

Maxine had done a great deal in the eight years that had passed. She'd given Lily back her job. She'd taken care of Lily when she was recuperating after Tash's birth. She held Lily's hair back when she vomited in the throes of one of her excruciating migraines.

Lily owed Maxine a lot and more than just her lovely outfit.

It was a tan suit with a straight skirt that hit her just above the knees and had a deep slit up the back and a safari jacket belted at the waist. She wore a scarf patterned in tan and shocking orange jauntily tied at her throat (tied by Maxine who did everything jauntily). This was accompanied by a pair of tan, high-heeled pumps with a shock of patent leather orange at the pointed toe.

"You'll knock 'em dead," Maxine had told her upon looking at Lily in her suit.

Lily was too scared to care who she knocked. Fear was the only emotion she had anymore, fear and humiliation. The rest was just . . . dead. As dead as she thought Nate was. As dead as everything she ever felt for him.

And she had felt *everything* for him.

"Can we begin?" one of Nate's solicitors was asking, and Lily, who had been staring at her hands, felt her head come up as if it had a mind of its own (which of course it did, but normally Lily controlled it, now nearly everything in her life was out of her control).

She saw Nate coolly staring at her from across the table, again as if she was an insect and he was biologist getting ready to pin her to a board.

Strangely she had no reaction to this. She was beyond reacting.

He hadn't said a word to her, not a single word.

This wasn't unusual for Nate but perhaps he could have at least said a *single* word. Though, from the look in his eyes, she wasn't sure she wanted to hear what that word might be.

Lily's eyes swept down the table.

His two solicitors sat side by side. Alistair said this was all just show but the fact that Lily could barely afford one and Nate could blithely bring two scared her socks off.

Victor sat to Nate's left and glowered at her with a hatred that eclipsed that of Danielle and even Laura, who Lily would never have thought had it in her, but apparently she did.

Lily decided to look back down at her hands. She figured that was her safest line of sight at the present moment.

"Firstly, I'd like to say thank you for accepting this informal meeting. We're here to discuss a visitation schedule for Natasha Roberts McAllister Jacobs," Alistair announced somewhat grandly.

At Tash's full name being read out, something immediately shifted in the room. Lily felt it but was too numb to register it. Instead, she lifted her head to watch Alistair as he spoke.

"We're not here to discuss visitation. We're here to discuss custody. As you know, Mr. McAllister wants full custody of the child," Nate's solicitor pointed out.

"Obviously my client isn't warming to that idea," Alistair retorted and Lily didn't move her eyes from him.

"For seven years, since the girl's birth, Ms. Jacobs kept knowledge of the child from that child's father. My client obviously doesn't warm to *that* idea," Nate's solicitor returned.

"She could hardly tell him she'd given birth when she thought he was dead," Alistair parried swiftly.

Another shift came about the room and Lily's head dropped again to stare at her manicure. She needed one, she decided distractedly. Of course she could never afford one but that didn't change the fact that she needed one.

"That's preposterous. It's quite apparent that Mr. McAllister is alive as he's sitting at this very table," Nate's solicitor shot back.

Alistair retorted smoothly and immediately, "Yes, of course, she knows that *now* but she only discovered that fact a few days ago."

"This is an interesting defense," Nate's other lawyer decided at this point to throw in his lot and he did so sarcastically.

"I agree. It *is* most interesting," Alistair commented absently all the while sorting through his papers lying on the table as if trying to find something. "Let me see. Yes," his head came up, "here it is," he said even though he wasn't looking at a single sheet of paper.

Then he launched into "the plan."

"Our story begins eight years ago when Ms. Jacobs was living in

London with Mr. McAllister. However, she had to leave the country urgently due to a family emergency."

"Considering the 'he-was-dead' defense, I'm sure *this* will be hugely entertaining." Lily didn't see it but she heard the scoffing behind Nate's attorney's tone. That would be attorney number two or Sarcastic Attorney.

Her startled eyes moved to the man who, she noted distractedly, was staring at her with extreme distaste.

"Well, I'm not sure one would describe losing both of one's parents in a plane crash as 'entertaining,'" Alistair noted blandly.

It was at this comment that the room didn't shift. It tilted on its axis and the tilt was caused by Nate. Lily felt it, felt it so surely that her eyes slid to him of their own accord.

He was no longer staring at her coolly, leaning back in his chair arrogantly. His face had paled, he'd leaned forward and he was staring at her anything *but* coolly.

And the power of his intensity rocked the room.

Lily immediately looked away.

Alistair continued, "Ms. Jacobs informs me that the minute she heard the news, she tried frantically to get in touch with Mr. McAllister but no one was answering at his office. She left an urgent message with Mr. McAllister's sister, a Ms. Danielle Roberts, to have Mr. McAllister's mother return her call. However, Mrs. Laura Roberts did not return Ms. Jacobs's call before Lily was forced to leave to catch her plane. Ms. Jacobs wrote and left a note but was assured by Mr. McAllister's *brother*, a Mr. Jeffrey Roberts who had stopped by for a visit, that *he* would get the news to Mr. McAllister."

"There was no note." This was Victor, Lily knew, and she watched as Alistair turned his head to her in question at his stated fact.

Lily nodded once.

"There was a note," Alistair affirmed stoutly.

"There was no goddamned note," Victor snapped and Lily looked at him.

He, too, was white as a sheet and he didn't look furious anymore. He looked upset and confused and in so being trying to bluster out of it.

Victor carried on, "And anyway, when she got back, she could have come to the house. We haven't moved. We live in the same damn—"

Alistair smoothly cut in.

"I'm glad you brought that up, Mr. Roberts, for Lily *did* go to your home. She realized, while home in Indiana dealing with the business of her parents' tragic death, that she was pregnant. From Indiana she called Mr. McAllister at his home and at his office on several occasions. His home phone was disconnected. The messages left at his office were not returned. When Ms. Jacobs came back to England to return to Mr. McAllister, she was informed he no longer lived at the flat in which she resided with him. She went immediately to *your* house and was told by your daughter that Mr. McAllister was dead."

Lily's eyes flicked to Nate to see his response to this news.

He was definitely way beyond cool, composed and arrogant. Cool, composed and arrogant were all a fleeting memory.

"This is ridiculous. She could have come back. She could have talked to someone else. Why on earth would Danielle Roberts tell—" Nate's attorney burst out.

"Why indeed?" Alistair broke in. "Nevertheless, it's a moot point because Lily couldn't come back. The pregnancy was complicated. Ms. Jacobs had difficulties and nearly lost the baby twice. She was not allowed to travel and forced to stay in bed for the last three months of her pregnancy."

"After that—" the solicitor interrupted.

"After that, Lily was recuperating and then dealing with significant financial hardships. The birth was described to me by Lily and also by her obstetrician, who I spoke to myself yesterday. The doctor, in his own words, remembers what he describes as that 'hideous day' like it was yesterday. The labor, intense and excruciating, lasted for days. In the end, in extreme distress at the length of the labor, the baby nearly died. Lily *did* die. She was flatline for two minutes and thirty-eight—"

Alistair didn't get the opportunity to finish his grand statement because Nate surged out of his chair so fast it flew on its wheels and shot across the room, slamming into the wall.

"Mr. McAllister . . ." Alistair said warningly but Nate was coming swiftly around the table.

Coming at *her*.

At this sight, Lily, too, jumped out of her chair in a panic—her numbness not *that* complete—and backed away in self-defense as Nate came at her, came at her with purposeful, long strides.

She backed up jerkily, one hand behind her, one hand in front, retreating until she hit the wall. Before she knew what he was about, his hard chest came up against her hand, pushing it back and his body pressed against hers.

Terrified and confused at this sudden change, she looked to the right and to the left, anywhere for escape, anywhere but at Nate.

And to her shock, his hands caught her face, resting one on either side, gently trying to force her to look into his impossibly dark eyes.

"I didn't know," he whispered and the absolute ache dripping from his first words said to her since she found out he was alive cut through her thin shield of numbness like a razor.

She attempted to pull her face free but his hands tightened.

"Lily, I didn't know," he repeated, and she caught his eyes and they were glittering dark with something that she couldn't read. Something hideously painful and she had to get away from it. Was desperate to get away from it.

She needed to flee.

She tried to look over his shoulder but he was too tall, too close. Things were happening in the room, there was urgent talk, maybe even a tussle. But all she could see was Nate.

"Look at me," he demanded.

She frantically shook her head against his hands.

"Lily, look at me."

At his soft, gentle words, she couldn't stop herself. She looked at him. She looked into his impossibly handsome face.

And then, for the first time since she knew he was alive, she spoke to him. She said the words she'd been saying in her head for days.

"You told me you'd never let me go," she whispered, but it was an accusation.

His eyes closed and the pain in them swept over his entire face and settled there like it would never, ever leave.

Then he shocked her again. He dropped his forehead to hers and kept his hands on her.

Something out of her control made her continue.

"You told me," she said in a shaky voice, "you'd always take care of me."

He opened his eyes and stared into hers. He was so close that if she moved the lower half of her face forward, less than an inch, she would have been kissing him.

"You didn't take care of me," she murmured, stating the obvious.

"Mr. McAllister, step away from my client!" Alistair demanded from somewhere close.

Nate didn't move, not a single muscle.

"Mr. McAllister!" Alistair snapped.

"Let him be!" Victor shouted fiercely and then, "Let them be," he said this last in a voice that, Lily noted dazedly, was utterly broken.

Alistair was not to be denied. "Mr. McAllister!"

Nate ignored him, his eyes drilling into hers.

She couldn't bear it a second longer. She couldn't shift moods this easily. Something was happening but she had no idea what it was. She had so little fight left in her and she had to concentrate. She wasn't strong enough, in that moment with Nate's hands on her, his warm body pressed against hers just like she'd been wishing for years, his forehead resting on hers. She simply couldn't bear it.

"Nate," Lily said softly, beseechingly, "let me go."

He ignored her too, for a moment.

Then, just as abruptly as he pursued her, he did as he was asked and let her go.

And just as swiftly, he walked back to his chair, righted it to the table and sat down.

After a moment of stunned silence where everyone seemed immobile, the entire assemblage did the same though not nearly as quickly.

Nate watched Lily as she slowly, shakily walked back across the room and resumed the seat Alistair was holding for her.

"Are you quite all right?" Alistair asked once he'd also sat down and was leaning into her, peering at her, his own face beyond angry, and she was glad there were no paperweights in the room or there would have been hell to pay.

She nodded, undone by the whole scene and wanting nothing more than to leave. To go back home, to Tash and Fazire, and recoup, recharge and fight some other day.

Worse still, her head was beginning to ache and she felt more than slightly queasy and she had the terrible feeling that a migraine was coming over her.

"Let's just get this over with," she begged, her voice so small it was tiny.

She had no idea her voice betrayed to the two men in the room she knew a very short time many years ago, one she had come to care about deeply, one she had adored more than life, that she was now just a mere shadow of the former Lily Jacobs.

At her words, Alistair fully lost his temper and his head jerked around toward the others.

"Right. Then. I suppose after *that* scene I don't have to go into detail about the financial situation all that left Ms. Jacobs in. There was not a great deal of wealth in her family, Lily had attended Oxford on a scholarship and had been working in pubs and shops since her arrival in England. Due to the pregnancy, she was unable to work, had a mortgage that went unpaid for months and was nearly thrown out of her home. She was not entitled to National Health Service so the birth and subsequent hospitalization were all private and cost a fortune. She was forced, even though she didn't wish it, to sell her family home in Indiana, but death duties and a bad exchange rate meant that money was practically gone before it got to the country. She—"

Nate's solicitor interrupted Alistair wearily, sensing they'd lost the upper hand they'd been so certain of when they'd entered the room, "Just tell us what you want."

Alistair didn't hesitate. "We want five hundred thousand pounds for back child maintenance for the last seven years. We want two thousand pounds a month starting now. Mr. McAllister can see his daughter one weekend a month, two weeks during summer holidays and alternating school holidays. Ms. Jacobs wants Natasha every Christmas. The first meeting of Mr. McAllister and Natasha will be supervised by either

Maxine Grant or Lily's long-time family friend, Fazire."

Alistair was on a roll, he was asking for more than they agreed. If Lily wasn't already wound up by all that had happened, she would have spun like a top at what he was currently demanding.

But he was interrupted.

"Give it to her." This was Nate's deep voice cutting in and Lily's head jerked to him.

He was staring at her. Staring at her so intensely she felt his eyes like they were a physical touch on her skin.

"I'm sorry?" Alistair asked, nonplussed at being disturbed in his postulation.

"Give it to her. Have the money transferred to her account by the end of the day." As he said this, Nate's head moved to look at his solicitor and it was clear it was an order.

"But, Mr. McAllister—" his solicitor began.

"The five hundred thousand?" Alistair was, Lily saw, thrilled.

"A million," Lily's head jerked back to Nate and her mouth dropped open in shock.

"A million pounds?" Alistair was nearly bouncing in his chair.

"Yes, a million pounds . . ." Nate stated and Alistair was about to shoot to the moon when Nate continued, "for each year Natasha has been alive."

Lily blinked, her shock so profound a stampede of buffaloes could have stormed through the room and she wouldn't have moved. If Alistair had done a back flip out of his seat, Lily would not have been surprised.

"Seven million pounds?" Alistair was now, simply, agog.

Lily didn't know anyone who had seven million pounds much less could transfer it into another bank account "by the end of the day."

"Yes," Nate said flatly.

Lily couldn't look at Nate. Her eyes moved to Victor and he was staring at her in a way, in a way . . .

In the way he used to look at her.

She had no time to process Victor's look as Alistair pressed, "Do you agree to the visitation schedule?"

"No," Nate noted implacably.

Lily, already stunned, became so still a single touch would have sent a crack running through her body.

She had known it was too good to be true.

"I'm sorry?" Alistair parroted his earlier question.

"I want full custody," Nate declared.

It was Lily's turn to shoot out of her chair. At his words, all the shock and numbness fled and the fight came crashing back into her.

"What?" she shrieked.

Nate rose too, albeit slowly. He faced her, his eyes looking directly into hers, the expression on his face carefully controlled.

"I want full custody of my daughter," he told her calmly.

"You can't have it!" Lily shouted, not at all calmly and forgetting her promise to Alistair not to say anything.

"She's moving to London to live with me," Nate stated.

"No!" Lily yelled.

Nate went on, "And you are too."

"What?" This time it came out as a high-pitched scream.

"What?" Alistair shouted, also jumping up from his chair.

Victor, not to be left seated, also got up.

Eyes never leaving Lily, Nate announced, "You're moving to London."

"I am not," Lily returned.

"You and Natasha are moving in with me. You and I are getting married in two months."

"What?" Lily shrieked.

"This is *insane*," Alistair threw in.

Nate's gaze sliced to Alistair and he repeated, "Lily and I will be married. She and Natasha are moving to London, moving in *with me*."

Lily leaned forward and put her hands on the table.

This was too much, just too damned much. She'd had *enough*.

"You forget, I tried that before and it . . . did . . . not . . . work!" Lily flung at him.

Nate's carefully controlled face flinched.

"Lily—" Victor said softly.

She interrupted whatever Victor was going to say, "No! No, no, *no!*"

Lily pushed away from the conference table and looked at Alistair. "I'm leaving," she declared flatly.

Alistair was visibly grinding his teeth. If there was a paperweight close by, at that moment she would have gladly handed it to him and showed him where to aim.

He stopped grinding long enough to grunt, "Go."

She grabbed her bag where it was sitting on the table, whirled and headed smartly for the door, not looking back.

She was brought to an abrupt halt with a strong hand on her upper arm.

She winced uncontrollably in pain when the hard fingers closed around her bruised arm, and she turned and looked at the familiar, strong, long-fingered hand then at Nate who was standing behind her.

He watched her wince at his touch and something anguished flashed through his eyes.

"Take your hand off my client." Alistair, seething, was walking swiftly toward them.

Nate ignored him.

"I want to meet my daughter," he told Lily.

"Fine," Lily snapped, wanting nothing but escape.

Her head was beginning to pound.

"I want to meet her tomorrow," Nate demanded.

"Fine!" Lily clipped.

"I want you there," he pushed.

"*Fine!*"

"Lily, don't say another word," Alistair warned from beside them.

"You'll be there tomorrow," Nate ordered, it should have been a query but it was a command.

"Yes!" she cried.

She would have said anything to get away.

She wrenched her arm free as Alistair said her name sharply in frustration.

She didn't pay attention.

She turned from Nate and ran away as fast as her high heels would carry her.

FOURTEEN

Nate & Victor, Nate & Laura

FOR THE FIRST FIFTEEN minutes of the ride back to London, the two passengers in the back of the Rolls-Royce were completely silent, each lost in their own tormented thoughts.

Then the silence was broken.

"Nathaniel—" Victor began.

"Don't," Nate's voice cracked like a whip.

Victor held his breath for a moment.

There was not a single man on earth he would allow to speak to him that way.

Except Nathaniel.

Especially now.

Victor sighed, looked out the window and instead of seeing the rolling pastureland, his vision filled with Lily.

Jesus, fucking, God, he thought.

Laura couldn't tell him not to curse so blasphemously in his thoughts, and more than likely if she'd witnessed the nightmare in that conference room, she'd have a few curses of her own.

The minute Victor walked into the room, seeing Lily so close and cozy with her lawyer, looking so beautiful, stylish and serene, he'd wanted to tear her head off.

Ten minutes later he'd had the crazy, sudden, unprecedented urge to get down on his knees and beg her forgiveness.

She'd named her child Natasha, for Nathaniel.

She'd named her child after *him*, Victor. She'd given her baby, *Nathaniel's* baby, Victor's surname as a middle name

And she'd nearly died doing it.

And after ten minutes more, Victor had been too broken to know *what* to do and that was a feeling he'd not felt for decades.

He was broken because she was broken. Broken because the bright, vivacious girl who had walked innocently into his home eight years before had been all but destroyed.

That suit she wore was camouflage, making it not so easy to see all that had been the glorious Lily was lost. The longer the attorneys talked the more she retreated, the further she got from them, from anyone and especially from Nate. She was so thin, so pale, she actually looked at the end in physical pain.

All because of Victor's two spoiled-rotten, dead-rotten children.

He was to blame for this.

Victor.

His past sins had come home to roost.

"Nathaniel, we have to talk," he tried again.

Nate's head slowly turned from the window he was staring unseeingly out of and his eyes focused on Victor. At the look in his son's eyes, Victor immediately had nothing to say.

But Nate spoke.

"Eight years," he said.

Victor closed his eyes in pain.

"They cost us eight years." Victor heard Nathaniel say.

Victor opened his eyes again.

"I'll take care of Danielle and Jeffrey," he vowed.

And he most definitely would.

A muscle in Nate's jaw jumped, and he turned his head back to his contemplation of the scenery.

Victor went on, "Son, I swear to you, they'll wish they were never born."

And he meant it. They were his children by blood but they were his children no more.

Neither Nate nor Victor for a second questioned that Jeff and Danielle had done exactly what Lily's attorney had said they'd done. The whole time Laura ranted and raved and Victor cursed and shouted after Lily disappeared, they didn't say a word.

It wasn't as if Lily had a great offer to go shopping in Milan that she couldn't resist and that's why she left Nate. She was at home in Indiana grieving the loss of *both* of her parents. Then, at twenty-two years of age, grieving, also pregnant, she came back to Nate only to be told he was dead.

And his children knew and neither of them said one single word.

Not only that, they'd participated in this terrible deception. Jeff likely took the note and Danielle . . .

Victor shook off his thoughts. He'd deal with them later.

"What are you going to do?" Victor asked.

Nate sat silent.

Victor continued. "Nathaniel, you saw her. She's—"

"I saw her," Nate bit off, his voice eloquently stating, without a great many words, exactly what he'd seen and exactly how it affected him.

"You have to . . ." Victor started but didn't finish.

How did one go about piecing together a shattered person?

Victor thought that Nathaniel could do anything he put his mind to doing. He believed this with everything he was.

However, this was going to be his son's mightiest challenge.

"What are you going to do?" Victor asked again.

Nate took in a deep breath and slowly let it out.

He turned to Victor and looked him directly in the eyes.

"I'm going to put my family back together."

NATE STOOD AT THE FLOOR-TO-CEILING windows that made up the entire wall to the vast living room in his penthouse apartment.

As he drank from a tumbler that was filled with two cubes of ice and a lot of vodka and smoked what would be one of his final cigarettes

(Lily didn't like his smoking and he was not about to smoke in front of his seven-year-old daughter), he watched the sun set on London.

Lily had come back to him.

He tried to make this his only thought. Any of the others that were determined to crowd in his head were too painful to bear.

Like her pale, lifeless face, her fidgeting hands, her once curvaceous, now nearly-too-thin body.

Like the fact that his brother and sister had connived, lied and stole away eight years of their happiness.

Like her horrible voice saying, *"Let's just get this over with."*

Like her haunted look when Nate's attorney had suggested that the news of her parent's death would be "entertaining."

Like her flinching at feeling his hand on her arm.

Like her once expressive eyes now blank and looking through him like he wasn't there.

Like the fact that he'd purposefully, with great relish, got her pregnant, which nearly caused her to die.

Like her telling him, *"You told me you'd always take care of me."*

Like the fact that he made promises to her, promises he didn't keep, promises he didn't even attempt to keep.

Like her whispering, *"You told me you'd never let me go."*

On this final thought, he turned swiftly from the window and threw the tumbler of vodka across the room so savagely his arm was a blur. The tumbler exploded on the wall well across the room, dead center of an exorbitantly expensive painting.

And then he heard a small, fearful noise and his head came around.

Laura was standing just inside the front door.

She was wearing a stylish dove-gray skirt and a soft-blue blouse. Both of these were crinkled and in disarray. Her face showed she'd been crying. It was mottled and red, her makeup smudged and worn.

She looked ravaged.

Nate turned fully to her. "How did you get here?"

"I have a key," she explained unnecessarily for of course he knew she had a key.

"That's not what I meant. Tell me you didn't drive in that state."

She didn't answer for a moment and they stood there, mother and son, the colossal expanse of his living room separating them physically. Something else entirely separating them emotionally.

Then she smiled but it was a terrible, sad smile.

"Of course, my Nathaniel, after what happened to you today, you'd worry about me driving." She shook her head. "I took a taxi."

Nathaniel made no response. Instead he leaned toward a table near him and put out his cigarette in a crystal ashtray.

Laura kept watching him as she said softly, "Victor called the children to the house. He's disowned them. He sacked Jeffrey. He cut off Danielle's allowance. They both only have their trust funds of which, Victor tells me, they've already used a significant portion."

Nathaniel kept his silence. There was nothing to say except that it was all too late, and everyone knew that fact quite painfully well enough already.

"He did this with my blessing," she whispered. "I can't say, I can't explain how sorry . . ."

She didn't finish and he watched her swallow convulsively, fighting back the tears.

"I now have only one son," she finished, her voice aching.

The pain on her face was wretched, unlike anything Nate had ever seen before. She was watching him closely, waiting for a reaction but he didn't move.

She seemed to come to some conclusion. She nodded slowly and then started to turn to leave.

That was when Nate spoke. "And a granddaughter."

Her head snapped around and she stared at her son.

Nate went on, "And, if I can convince her, a daughter-in-law."

"Oh, Nate." She used his shortened name for the first time in their acquaintance and flew across the room, throwing herself at him and bursting into tears. "I'm a terrible mother," she wailed as his arms closed around her. "Terrible."

Nate held her more tightly.

"You aren't a terrible mother," he murmured.

"I lost the first one, my first baby boy." She raised her tearful eyes to him. "I promised God if I had any babies, I'd do anything. I'd make them so happy. I'd give them everything they wanted. And look! Look what I created!"

She buried her face in his chest and Nate dropped his cheek to rest on the top of her head.

There was nothing to say to take away her pain, no words that would assuage her guilt. So he offered her none.

Against his chest, she muttered, "I knew it when it was too late. I knew I'd ruined them but there was nothing I could do. Then God gave me a second chance," she lifted her head, dislodging his and he stared down at her. "You."

"Laura . . ." At that, he didn't know what to say.

"I want to come with you tomorrow."

Nate knew exactly what he was going to say to that.

"Laura, no."

Her arms squeezed him tightly. "You can't go there alone. I won't let you go alone. And I have to face Lily. I have to . . ." She stopped then immediately started again, "I want to meet my granddaughter."

Nate shook his head. "Lily isn't—"

"I know," she interrupted, her warm eyes beginning to fill with fresh tears. "Victor told me. Nathaniel, she has to know we . . ." Laura hesitated and then went on, "she has to know she isn't alone anymore."

"I don't think—"

"*Please*," she begged. "I have to do *something*," she said this last with desperation.

Nate started to relent because he knew that feeling. He felt that feeling himself when he'd heard she'd died while having his child. The child he'd intentionally planted inside her and then left her to bear on her own.

Without thinking, Nate had come out of his chair and his intention had been to pick Lily up and carry her out of the room. Carry her someplace safe where he could spend every ounce of energy, every pound he'd earned, every day of the rest of his life if it was required to bring back her joy. Bring back the girl who'd clapped and shouted her delight at a ride on a motorcycle, the girl who'd trusted him so easily with her body and her heart, the girl who'd looked at him with awe.

"Please," Laura asked, taking him out of his dark thoughts.

Nate used his thumb to wipe away a tear on his mother's cheek.

"She's not the same," he warned.

Her face lit. It wasn't a glowing light but there was hope.

It was the first hopeful thing he'd seen that day. Perhaps the first hopeful thing he'd seen in eight years.

"You have to be prepared, Laura, she's not the Lily you knew." Nate felt it necessary to make certain she understood what she'd be facing the next day.

Laura nodded. "She will be. I know she will. You'll make it better, Nathaniel. You can sort anything out. I know you can. You'll sort this out too."

At her words, he felt an odd stirring in his chest that he ignored.

And he hoped his mother was right.

FIFTEEN

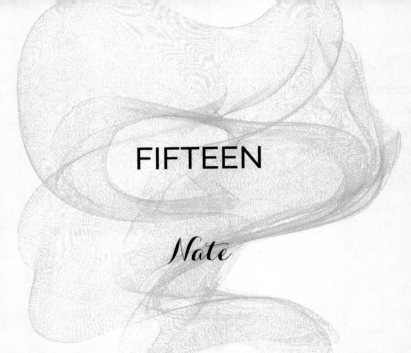

Nate

"WE'RE EARLY. WE'RE WAY too early. We're supposed to be there at ten, it isn't nine thirty yet."

Laura Roberts was fretting.

They were walking up the seafront beside the Victorian pier. Nate had driven his Aston Martin, leading with Laura and Victor in the Rolls following him.

Nate drove on his own. He had too much on his mind. He didn't want company on the trip to Somerset, especially not his parent's company, not that day.

Laura was in a state and Victor was actually visibly nervous.

Victor, Nate found upon arrival at his parents' home that morning, was coming along as well. This intention was stated in a tone not to be denied.

Nate would have denied his father but he had no desire to waste the precious time to do so.

Therefore Victor was along for the ride.

"We left too soon. We should walk on the seafront for half an hour, get a cup of tea. It's rude to be early," Laura worried, preferring to focus on her rudeness at being early than the fact that she was about to face the woman whose life her two children had all but destroyed.

Nate didn't care much that they were early nor did he care if it seemed rude. He wanted to meet his daughter and he wanted to see Lily. He'd lost eight years and if Lily's demeanor the day before was anything to go by, he was facing the battle of his life. He was set on starting straight away. He wasn't about to wait half an hour nor have a cup of fucking tea, which he never drank anyway.

They walked by the Royal Pier Hotel and the short street that led to Lily's terrace was a few paces away. Nate suppressed the urge to lengthen his strides and leave his lagging parents behind.

"What's that little girl going to think? How did Lily tell her about Nathaniel? How *could* she tell her? What kind of words can you use for something like that? How is she going to react?" Victor blustered. Not expecting a response to any of his rapid-fire questions, he finished with the dire prediction, "We'll have to find a psychologist."

Victor was beginning to sound like Laura, Nate thought with annoyance.

Then Nate couldn't think at all for when they were only two doors down from Lily's house, he heard, "Daddeeeeeeeeeeeeeee."

Flying toward him, her arms wind-milling wildly, her black hair streaming out behind her, was a beautiful little girl, her face alight with delight, wearing a pretty, sky-blue sundress.

A beautiful little girl that looked exactly like Nate.

Nate stopped dead because she didn't. She ran headlong into him, her head slamming painfully into his stomach, her arms flying around his hips to hold him in a fierce, tight hug.

At her touch, Nate felt something in his chest squeeze uncomfortably as one of his hands settled automatically on the soft, dark hair of her head, the other on her shoulder.

"Oh my God," Laura breathed.

"Tash! What are you . . . oh."

Everyone's eyes turned to Lily, who'd come running out of the house after her daughter. She stopped at the sight of them and her lips stayed parted in surprise.

"Oh my God," Victor breathed.

Lily wasn't wearing a pretty anything. She was barefoot, her face free of makeup and she had on a pair of faded, battered, what appeared to be army trousers and a skin-tight, lilac camisole that showed her thin shoulders and arms.

It also showed slight purple and yellow marks around her upper arms. Bruises that looked like they were made by a set of hands. Bruises that could only have been caused by Victor.

Regardless of this she somehow, to Nate, looked unconsciously, undeniably beautiful.

Before anyone could say another word, Natasha's head went back. Nate's hand dropped from it and she looked up at him, her dark eyes, *his* dark eyes, dancing merrily.

"I've been watching for you all morning. It seems like for . . . *eh* . . . ver! I thought you were *never* going to get here!"

Apparently, however Lily broke the news, she'd done it well.

Natasha's head jerked around so she could look at her mother but she kept her arms firmly around Nate's hips.

"Look, Mummy, Daddy's here," she told her mother unnecessarily.

At the sound of her calling him "Daddy," Nate felt that uncomfortable squeeze matched by a slice through his gut.

Lily's stunned gaze slid from the early-arrived crowd and then her face melted into a smile as she looked at her daughter.

"I can see that, baby doll."

Nate was staring at Lily's soft smile, feeling her endearment to her daughter, his daughter, *their* daughter, wash over him when Natasha's head came back around and she looked at Nate.

"Mummy told me last night you were coming," she informed him.

"Did she?" Nate murmured.

Natasha nodded gaily. "Yes, she told me she found out you were alive and you wanted to meet me straight away." Then she took her arms from around him, held them out at her sides and announced, "Here I am!"

Nate stared in fascination at the beautiful child he and Lily had created. She was, quite simply, not to be believed. Her eyes were sparkling, her heart was open and the sunny smile never left her gorgeous face. It was clear to anyone that she was happy to see him. Beyond happy. She was thrilled.

He had no idea what to say or do. Never, not once in his entire life had he been so uncertain of his next course of action.

Luckily, Natasha was not so uncertain.

She leaned into him. "Who are they?" she whispered loudly.

Nate looked around at Laura and Victor, who he had, while seeing and touching his daughter for the first time in her life, entirely forgotten.

He saw Laura had tears shimmering in her eyes. Victor was standing absolutely still, his chest puffed out with the effort he was making at holding back tears.

Nate settled his hand on the nape of his daughter's neck. He found it strange, how small it was, tiny and fragile, and felt a protective urge settle in him that was beyond his control, should he ever wish to control it, which he never would. He guided her closer to his body, moved to her side and out of the way so she could fully see her grandparents. He looked down at her as she leaned trustingly against his side. This he found strange, this unquestioning trust, strange and something else, something extraordinary.

"These are my parents," he answered her.

Natasha's expressive eyes rounded with surprise and her head again jerked back to her mother and again her body stayed in contact with Nate's.

Nate followed his daughter's gaze and saw that Lily hadn't moved, but she had been joined by a funny-looking man with a shock of black hair, black eyes, a pointed black goatee and a supremely rounded stomach. He stood with his hands on his hips, his feet planted so far apart he looked in danger of toppling over and he had an expression on his face so fierce, Nate was surprised the man hadn't turned Nate to stone.

This, Nate thought correctly, *must be Fazire.*

Nate's thoughts were interrupted by his daughter breathing the word, "Grandparents," in her mother's direction. Her voice sounded like someone had just bestowed a rich and untapped diamond mine on her as a gift.

At the sound of the catch of Laura's breath, a catch that heralded tears, Natasha's head swung back around. As if sensing innately that Laura needed it, Natasha disengaged from Nate and walked forward then ran the last few steps and threw herself, luckily less forcefully, at Laura.

Her arms closed around Laura's waist and she proclaimed, "Nanna!"

Immediately Laura burst into tears and Victor looked away, not willing to be unmanned in front of an audience, or at all for that matter.

Nate saw a movement to his side and turned to see Lily joining him, standing too far away for him to touch her. She was watching this meeting with a strange, benign expression on her face but held her body rigidly as if waiting for something to attack.

When Nate would have spoken, moved toward her, caught her attention in some way, Natasha tore from the embrace Laura was now giving her to hurtle herself at Victor and give him one of her fierce hugs with a cry of, "Granddad!"

Victor immediately dropped into a crouch and pulled the child between his legs, hugging her just as tightly as she was hugging him.

Lily allowed this for a moment and then she called to her daughter, "Tash, honey, come inside. I'm sure your, um . . . they would all like a cup of tea."

Natasha pulled away from Victor and looked him straight in the eyes.

"Do you want tea?" she asked him, her head tilting inquiringly to the side.

Victor didn't speak, likely couldn't speak, he just nodded.

She pulled free of Victor and half danced, half skipped back to Nate whose hand she grabbed.

"Great idea, Mummy." She quirked a smile at her mother and Nate's body stilled at the sight.

His daughter's smile, that familiar smile, was the only thing it appeared she'd inherited from her mother.

She had Lily's endearing, quirky smile.

Natasha continued, "While you make tea, I'll show them my bedroom!" She said this like it would delight and surprise them beyond their wildest imaginings.

Natasha pulled Nate forward with her hand tugging at his, and Nate walked toward the house. Lily fell in step behind them, *not*, he noticed, beside them.

As they drew nearer the house, Fazire still stood with hands on hips and with a ferocious expression firmly affixed to his face.

"That's Fazire, he's our special friend," Natasha made the introduction happily. "Stop scowling, Fazire," she warned him, her voice bossy, loving and teasing at the same time. She dragged Nate right past the other man who did not move an inch. Then Natasha whispered, "Don't mind him. He's been in a *really* bad mood for at least a *week*."

Of that, Nate had no doubt.

They entered the house, Lily's house, through the vestibule and an inner, lovely, stained-glass door. Natasha pulled Nate directly to the stairs as he glanced around to get a sense of Lily's home.

"I'll get the tea," Lily murmured, walking by them but not looking at them, then she said sternly, clearly making it an order, "Fazire, you can help."

Laura and Victor were standing in the entryway and Fazire walked, or rather *stomped* in behind them. He slammed the door and then carried on stomping down the hall, forcing Laura and Victor to jump out of his way, following Lily who had disappeared at the back of the house.

Natasha was tugging at Nate's hand, already two steps up the stairs and Nate looked at her. With one look at her excited, open, expressive face, he smiled at her.

Her face shifted somehow when she caught his smile and then she smiled back and said, "Mummy said you had a pretty smile. She said it was the most handsome smile she'd ever seen *in her life*. She said it made her belly do *somersaults*."

She bestowed this information on him without any idea of the enormity of its meaning or its effect, even though behind them Laura gasped.

"Come on!" Natasha urged excitedly.

She marched up the stairs, pulling him behind her but he barely took two steps when he abruptly stopped.

Hanging above the bottom stair he saw a picture.

The hall itself was painted soft beige with just enough peach to make it warm and inviting. The woodwork looked freshly painted in white but the wood of the banister and stairs had been refinished and was gleaming. The wood floors of the hall were also redone and those, and the stairs, had a muted-beige carpet runner.

This would have been cultured and classic, however, it warred with a set of fairy lights, each light surrounded by a delicate, muted-peach daisy, woven artistically through the rails of the banister giving it an offbeat feel. The only other adornment of the room was, every few steps, a picture in black and white in the same exact frame depicting the same subjects.

"My goodness," Laura breathed, looking at the first one.

In it Lily sat in a wicker chair that had been placed at the front of the house. She looked thin and wan and had a rug thrown around her legs but she was smiling tiredly, almost valiantly, at the camera. She held a bundled, tiny baby carefully, as if she was fragile and as if the baby was the most precious thing on earth to her.

The next photo was the same except the baby was older and Lily was standing instead of sitting, holding the baby on her slim hip. She was looking down at Natasha, her long hair tucked behind her ear, and she was again smiling. In the photo Natasha was gazing up at her mother, her chubby baby arm extended, her tiny fingers touching her mother's cheek.

The next photo was more of the same, this time Natasha, a toddler and standing, and Lily was crouched down and pointing to the camera, obviously calling the child's wayward attention to it. Again Lily and also Natasha were smiling.

Each few steps was another and another, eight in all, the same photo but different. They were all of Lily and Natasha in slightly different poses, none of them rehearsed, none of them formal, and in all of them Lily and Natasha were smiling.

Nate noted that Lily had cut her glorious red-gold hair from the length it used to be when he first met her, well past her shoulders, to the length it was now, just brushing them, sometime when Natasha was five.

"Those are my birthday pictures except the first one wasn't taken on my *actual* birthday because Mummy wasn't home from the hospital yet. Fazire takes them. My Gramma Becky taught him how. She was a photographer," Natasha informed them authoritatively as they hit the landing and she tugged him along through one of the middle of four doors.

Upon entry to his daughter's room, Nate was momentarily stunned speechless rather than regularly so.

The room was painted in the pinkest pink he'd ever seen. He didn't know such a pink existed. He thought that it might be a slightly better world if it that particular pink *didn't* exist.

"Well," Victor said, staring around him and struggling for something to say, "this is . . . er, pink."

Natasha giggled. "I know." She let go of Nate's hand and started dancing around the room. "Mummy said I couldn't have the pink I *wanted* because it was too *shocking*."

Nate found himself wondering what was more shocking than the pink Lily had agreed.

Natasha skipped to a set of shelves while Nate glanced around. There was a small desk with spindly legs that was painted white, a matching wardrobe and chest of drawers. The center of the room was taken up with a double bed with an intensely frilly, intensely girlie coverlet and it was festooned with ruffled toss pillows and stuffed animals. At the end, curled in a circle, was a fluffy ginger cat that completely ignored their arrival and continued existence.

Natasha gestured to the shelves.

"These are my books that Mummy used to read to me and now *I* read to *her*," she bragged happily then lifted her hand to point to a shelf higher up. "And these are my bears, which Miss Maxine gives me every year for Christmas. They're special bears she has made 'specially for me."

She danced over to the cat and picked it up with a hand in its middle. The cat, obviously used to this, let its entire enormous, fluffy body go limp so that it was doubled over in her small hand.

"This is Mrs. Gunderson, my cat," Natasha announced. "Fazire thinks it's a silly name and not nearly nice enough for an animal of such a dignified breed. Mummy calls her Gunny. Mrs. Gunderson doesn't sleep with me because I move around too much, she sleeps with Mummy."

Natasha cradled the cat as she took them on the rest of the tour of her room, which should have been short considering there wasn't much to it. However she seemed bent on introducing them to every item that had even the minutest meaning to her, which was most of it.

Suddenly she stopped, dropped the cat, which made a quick getaway, put her hands on her hips, much like her friend Fazire, and looked around.

"Well!" She threw her arm out dramatically. "That's my room. Now I'll show you Fazire's. I *love* Fazire's room."

Without being given an option and entirely unable to stop themselves in the face of her exuberance, they trooped out into the hall again. Laura and Victor glanced speculatively at each other and then at Nate as Natasha guided Nate by pulling at his hand. She walked to the front of the house and threw open Fazire's door with a flourish, dropped Nate's hand and skipped in.

Looking around he noted it was unlike any room he'd ever encountered, especially a man's bedroom. It was painted the deepest, darkest aubergine and was all but filled with an enormous bed covered in a satin coverlet, which instead of standard pillows, had a pile of turquoise-colored round ones with buttons in the middle. Strangely it had a framed, signed poster of a baseball player on one wall and a bookshelf entirely covered, indeed exploding with books on another.

Natasha jumped on the satin coverlet and stated a question to which she expected only one answer, "Isn't this a *great* room?"

Laura said quietly, "Are you supposed to be jumping on the bed, my darling?"

"Oh, Mummy doesn't mind," Natasha answered, still jumping. "Or at least she's given up telling Fazire and I to quit."

Laura's startled eyes turned to Nate at the very idea of the big, round man jumping on a bed. Nate found himself biting back laughter at his daughter's easily announced incongruity *and* his mother's startled gaze.

Unlike Lily, who seemed to have worn down over the years, losing her dazzling *joie de vivre*, Natasha was flourishing. She was bubbly and sparkling and obviously very, very happy.

Nate was, quite frankly, awed by all that Lily had created. His daughter, the welcoming house where all its occupants had their own space that was exactly like they wanted it, brimming with their personality (considering Fazire's room, however, Nate had his doubts about Fazire's personality). It was overwhelming that his thin, delicate Lily could have made something so wonderful against such odds.

Interrupting his thoughts, Natasha threw her legs out and expertly, clearly having much practice, landed on her bottom and bounced off the bed.

"Now! Mummy's room!" she announced, grabbing Nate's hand and forging out the door.

"I don't think—" Laura started, obviously uncomfortable with the idea of intruding on Lily's privacy, but Natasha wasn't listening.

"I don't like Mummy's room much. Mummy says she'll get to it though, ee . . . ven . . . chu . . . ah . . . lee," she sing-songed the word she obviously heard often as she walked to the back of the house.

Natasha threw open another door and dragged him inside and it was almost as if he'd entered another home altogether.

And not a very nice one.

The room was tidy and the bed was made. Other than that, there was nothing good about it.

The walls had been stripped of wallpaper but never re-plastered or painted, some of the old paper left in places. The bed was old, the mattress lumpy and all the furniture scarred, mismatched and in disrepair. The wardrobe door hung open drunkenly, exposing the clothes shoved inside the small space, shoes lined up underneath it that didn't fit in the closet. There were books piled on the bedside tables and on the floor that was old, unfinished planks without even a throw rug to cover them.

There were no pictures on the walls or any ornamentation or decoration in the room. The only thing Nate could see was a big picture frame on the battered dresser. In it the Lily he knew from eight years ago was hugging a dark-haired man while a woman with white-blonde hair hugged Lily from behind, her head on Lily's shoulder.

The cat strolled in, jumped agilely up on Lily's bed, sauntered to her pillow and curled up again for another nap.

The room was devoid of personality, not a room you'd want to spend any time in and, somehow, utterly sad.

"Now do you want tea?" Natasha asked, blissfully ignorant of all the room said about her mother's sacrifice, again tilting her head with her question and then, without waiting for an answer, she grabbed Nate's hand again and tugged him out of the room.

As he passed his parents, Nate could see his own stricken thoughts at the sight of Lily's room openly expressed on their faces.

"Nathaniel—" Victor said in a low voice as Natasha pulled him past.

He was saved from answering when Natasha turned her head to look over her shoulder at her father.

"Nathaniel," she said to him. "I'm named after you." She continued to tug him down the stairs. "Mummy said 'Nathaniel' is the name of a gentleman, a good name, a strong name. She *really* likes your name," she finished when they'd walked into the lounge.

"Tash, what are you filling their heads with?" Lily asked her daughter softly as they entered, a small smile tugging at the corners of her lips.

The lounge was again painted in a soft beige, this with bright-yellow tinge. The furniture was nice but obviously inexpensive and bought for comfort and with a view to lasting. Lily stood by the fireplace looking out of place even in her casual clothes. The likes of Lily didn't worry about her furniture's durability. The likes of Lily stood comfortably in opulent throne rooms.

Next to her was Fazire who had his feet planted apart but now his arms were crossed on his chest and resting on his protruding stomach. He still looked madder than a bull and had his head tilted back at an unseemly angle so he could stare down his nose at them even though he was barely an inch taller than the petite Laura.

Everyone stared at each other and no one said a word.

"Tea!" Lily said loudly, sounding desperate and jumping for a tray on a low table in front of a sofa.

Nate noted, distractedly, the teapot was chipped.

He also noted that she had not made him tea, which he did not drink, but automatically and without a word or a glance in his direction, handed him a mug of black coffee.

This he *did* drink.

The significance of this gesture, of his daughter telling him stories about her mother speaking of his smile and his name, hit Nate with the strength of a train.

Lily wasn't lost to him as he feared nor was she shattered like she looked.

She was simply broken.

And broken he could fix.

He watched her closely.

And then he smiled.

She'd put on a muted rose-colored cardigan, which had a thin, lilac ribbon embroidered with flowers running one side of the buttons. This was done obviously to cover the bruises on her arms.

She busily made tea as if her life depended on it, performing this task with the finest of hostessing skills. She distributed the refreshments, taking a coffee herself and stepping back to stand beside Fazire.

Once she settled into place, everyone stared at each other again.

Moments passed and no one said a word. The silence became uncomfortable. Then it became excruciating.

Laura gazed worriedly at Lily. Victor gazed assessingly at Fazire. Fazire glared at everyone in turn. Natasha looked expectantly from one adult to the other.

Finally Fazire opened his mouth, sucked in an enormous breath that should have evacuated the air from the room and was clearly about to speak when, sounding slightly hysterical, Lily shouted, "Photo albums!"

Fazire's mouth clamped together with an audible clacking of teeth and he glowered at Lily who had denied him whatever grand statement he was about to make.

"Photo albums," Lily repeated, slamming her cup awkwardly on the mantel, which also held a variety of framed family photos. "Fazire takes tons of pictures. You can catch up on Tash through Fazire's photos."

"What a lovely idea," Laura said softly but Lily didn't look at her. In fact Lily was studiously avoiding looking at anyone and had been since they entered the room.

"I'll go get them," Lily offered and practically ran to the door.

"I'll help," Nate said, putting down his mug, intent on having a moment alone with her. The first moment they'd had alone in eight years.

Lily stopped, whirled and stared at him wearing an expression of horror mixed quite liberally with fear. She opened her mouth to speak but before she could utter a word Fazire spoke.

"*I'll* help," Fazire declared, also moving to put down his tea.

Nate straightened and looked at the bizarre man.

"I said I'll help," he noted in a low tone.

"And *I* said *I'll* help," Fazire returned, clearly not reading nor wishing to read Nate's warning glance.

"Let Nathaniel help." Laura courageously entered the burgeoning fray.

Fazire's angry stare swung to Laura.

"Let Daddy help," Natasha said, bouncing up on the sofa and looking at them all with bright eyes, oblivious to the tension in the room. "Fazire doesn't like climbing all those stairs anyway. He usually floats up and he can't do that while you're all here."

Natasha settled on the couch equally oblivious to the horrified look her mother was throwing her way or the surprised ones her father and his family were aiming at her.

"Fine," Lily bit out, breaking everyone out of their shock at the little girl's strange words. She turned her eyes to Nate and, he noticed, she had carefully schooled her features. "Nate?"

Without waiting for his response, she spun again and stamped out of the room.

He followed her slowly up one set of stairs where, he noted, she paused to close the door to her bedroom, and then up another.

There were several more doors off the next landing, and she walked into a room that was obviously used for watching television. A large, plush corner sofa took up most of the comfortable space. The room also had several sets of inexpensive but stylish connecting shelves that were lined with books, ornaments, more framed photos and an enormous collection of photo albums. Nate noted vaguely that in all the money he'd paid his interior designer, his penthouse still seemed cold and uninviting. Yet Lily, who had no money, created a home that was warm and welcoming.

She immediately walked to the shelves and pulled out an album.

"You take this." She turned and handed him the album.

He took it reflexively saying, "Lily, we have to talk."

She grabbed another album and completely ignored him.

"And this." She extended the book to him and he accepted it.

"Lily."

She yanked another album free from the shelf.

"And this." She held it toward him but he didn't take it.

Her eyes still on the shelves, she jerked the album at him to indicate he should grab it but he ignored her.

"Lily, we need to talk," he repeated.

"Okay, I'll take this one," she decided magnanimously, tucked it under her arm and turned to grab another.

Nate walked to the sofa and threw the albums on it. Then he went to the door. This he closed. Firmly.

She froze, one hand ready to take out another album, and she stared at him.

"What are you doing?" she inquired.

"We're going to talk," he told her, striding back to her.

She turned smartly back to the shelf.

"Alistair says we can't talk. Alistair says that we should talk through our solicitors. Alistair told me to tell you whatever you have to say to me you should say it through him."

She had started obsessively piling her arms with albums.

Nate reached her, placed his hands on her shoulders, gently pulled her away from the shelves and then divested her of the albums and dropped them on the deep seat of the couch. This he did without her resistance mainly because she was stunned into immobility.

He faced her.

"We're done talking through solicitors," he informed her.

"Alistair says—" she started, her body going rigid as if girding for attack.

"I don't care what Alistair says," Nate cut her off.

"Well I do."

"We need to talk," Nate patiently repeated himself.

"We've nothing to say," Lily retorted, breaking out of her statue-like stance and starting for the couch to retrieve the albums.

As she passed him Nate caught her by the elbow and halted her. She tilted her head to look at him, her eyes beginning to fire.

"Nate, take your hand off me."

He ignored her and kept his hand where it was. He was not about to let this opportunity pass.

Suddenly he said quietly, "Thank you for naming Natasha after me."

She blinked at him. Then she blinked again.

He took advantage of her momentary confusion.

"Thank you for making her so lovely," he murmured softly.

Her mouth dropped open.

And in that moment he said what he'd been wanting to say for twenty hours.

"I thought you left me."

Her mouth snapped shut, her eyes closed down and she pulled her arm free.

"We're not talking about this," she stated flatly.

Nate went on, "I came home and you were gone, everything was gone. I thought you'd left me."

"Why on earth would I leave you?" she snapped, obviously not wanting an answer and her body noted she'd dismissed the subject. It did this by moving toward the sofa but he caught her again and gently pulled her back toward him.

Her eyes moved to his hand on her arm. "Nate, I asked you not to touch me."

She was trying to twist her arm free but he kept his hand there, just above her elbow, far away from the bruises.

"I thought you left me," he said again, needing her to hear it, needing her to *understand* it.

"You said that already," she clipped, tilting her head back and there was definitely fire there now. It was mingled with weariness, but it was there.

This pleased Nate. It pleased him very much.

"Jeff must have taken the note. If I'd known—"

She interrupted him, making a sharp, frustrated noise in her throat. Giving up on freeing her arm, she decided simply to move her body away from him and took a step back.

He didn't allow this either. His hand slid down her arm and before she knew what he was doing, his fingers laced in hers and he drew her closer.

She shook her head, her hand pulling at his, saying, "It doesn't matter now. It was a long time ago. It's over."

She was staring at the couch, staring at the albums, clearly wanting to carry on with her task.

Nate continued, determined, "My secretary was ill, I had a temp.

She lost messages."

Lily shook her head again, equally determined to ignore him.

"I moved. *We* were moving. I'd bought a new flat. I hadn't mentioned it because we were too busy with . . ." he paused and went on, "other things. I was going to tell you that night I came home. That night you left."

She tried to tug her hand free, her head no longer shaking from side to side but jerking. If she put her hands to her ears at that moment, he wouldn't have been surprised.

He tightened his hand in hers. "If I'd known I wouldn't have returned your calls."

At this announcement, her eyes flew to his, her head stopped swinging and his other hand went to her waist.

Nate finished, "I would have flown to Indiana to be with you. Lily, I'm sorry about your parents."

She looked into his eyes and he saw the sorrow flash in hers, whether it was at his desertion or her parents loss or both he did not know, but at the sight of it, the strength of it, he felt it settle somewhere deep within him.

Then her eyes cleared and the shutters came down.

"Thank you, Nate," she said carefully, with studied politeness. "Now, are you finished?"

"No," he said calmly, watching her closely.

The shutters flew open again.

"Well I am," she snapped. "No more talking!"

She again tried to jerk her hand free but he tugged it gently but forcefully and at this unexpected pull, she came forward on her toes, falling into him. Her hand went to his chest to break her fall. He felt it where it touched him, searing through his shirt like a brand, and his other arm immediately closed around her waist.

"No more talking?" he asked, his tone, as well, deceptively polite.

"That's right. No more talking," she agreed, struggling to pull free.

In a flash, he decided to play a dangerous game, to take a risk, to move ten steps forward before the door in front of him was even opened the barest crack.

He could, he knew, slam right into it.

Or it could open at the last minute and let him enter.

He weighed his options in mere seconds and took the risk.

"All right, Lily," he replied gently. "We were never very good at talking."

And then his head began to descend slowly toward hers.

As he came closer, she arched her back against his arm to get away from him, her eyes wide with disbelief.

"What are you doing?" she asked.

His hand released hers and stole around her, creeping up her back to press between her shoulder blades and bring her back to him.

"I'm going to kiss you," Nate answered.

"You are not!" she snapped, her voice filled with surprise and anger.

"Yes," he stated inflexibly, "I am."

His hand went up further, slid along her neck into her soft hair to hold the back of her head. Her body came into contact with his, her breasts brushing his chest, her hips a whisper away and he fought the urge to crush her against him.

"Take your hands off me!" she cried.

He dipped his head and brushed his lips against hers.

"No."

Still struggling, she demanded, "Let me go!"

Against her lips, he said, "This time, Lily, I'm not letting you go."

And then he kissed her.

The minute his lips pressed against hers she froze in his arms, not trying to struggle but keeping her body perfectly rigid.

His lips coaxed and teased but she didn't react. She stayed still and motionless and entirely unresponsive.

Nate wasn't buying it and he wasn't giving up.

He ran his tongue across her lower lip but her lips didn't budge.

"Open your mouth," he demanded boldly.

She shook her head, her hair sliding against his arm.

His other arm tightened at her waist bringing her into full contact with his frame.

"Lily, open your sweet mouth. Let me taste you again."

She made another noise in the back of her throat, this guttural with some emotion he could not decipher.

Nate decided to take this as a good sign.

"No?" he asked softly, his lips still on hers.

She didn't move.

Undeterred, he tried another tactic.

He slid his mouth across her cheek to her ear.

"Do you know," he murmured in her ear, kissed her there and he felt her still body turn rock solid, "that I remember everything. I have this . . . ability," he flicked his tongue against her earlobe, "and I never forget anything."

She kept her body completely controlled. One hand was flattened against his chest, pressed between them. Her other hand was at his waist putting pressure there to push him away.

He moved to rest his forehead against hers, his nose along hers, and his hand slid from the back of her head to cup her jaw, his thumb stroking her cheekbone.

"I remember everything about you," he told her, looking into her eyes. Those remarkable eyes hadn't changed, hadn't faded, with their pale-blue irises ringed in midnight. "All these years they would torment me, those memories. The sound of your voice, your laughter, the sight of your smile, the feel of you pressed against me while you slept."

She shook her head, her forehead rolling against his, both of her hands pushing against his chest now to get away. Her eyes were filled with fear.

Nate kept going. "I thought I lost you but I never forgot, *couldn't* forget. You were so sweet, incredibly sweet. The taste of your mouth, the taste of you between your legs, your hands on me, your mouth on me, the feel of you underneath me tightening around me when you came."

Her lips parted. In shock at his words, he knew.

And he didn't care.

"That's it," he whispered encouragingly and he kissed her again, his tongue sliding inside.

She fought for a second then she gave in with a soft moan.

Nate felt a searing of triumph as her hand at his chest slid up and around his neck, her other arm went around his waist and she held him fiercely there as if she'd never let him go. Her head tilted one way and Nate's slanted the other and her tongue touched his.

And she tasted exactly as sweet as he remembered.

Sweeter.

He deepened the kiss as she leaned forward and fit her body into his just as she used to, wriggling to get closer, press deeper, like she wanted to be absorbed. His arm tightened at her waist as his hand did the same at her jaw, holding her head tilted to his. He felt his body harden with need, eight years of need as eight years of yearning filled the kiss, surged through his frame, heating his blood to that familiar fever that he never felt for anyone else.

A fever that was only for Lily.

He groaned into her mouth and she shivered as she accepted it, her hand sliding into his hair to hold his head to hers.

The kiss was desperate and wild with eight years of longing and he was completely lost in her.

But she was not lost in him.

The kiss had proved to him that nothing had changed in Lily, except one thing.

She was a mother.

With mother's ears and a keen mother's sense.

She tore her lips from his and turned half stunned, half passion-filled eyes to the door.

Slowly, Nate followed her gaze.

And in the doorway stood Natasha staring at them with wide-eyed wonder.

Natasha's face split into an exquisite, gleeful smile and the little girl broke into a run.

Before Lily could disengage from his arms, Natasha slammed into them, throwing her arms around both their waists and burying her face in the spare space between them.

That moment for Nate, who had never had such a moment in his entire life, was so profound it nearly brought him to his knees.

But he had to remain standing to support Lily and Natasha who were both leaning into his body and his arms.

The hand Nate had at Lily's face dropped to the back of his daughter's neck.

Lily's head lifted from her sober contemplation of Natasha, the girl still pressed at their sides. He noted, when he looked in Lily's startling blue eyes, she'd had time to get herself under control.

She looked him right in the eyes and whispered fiercely, "This doesn't change anything."

He shook his head and smiled down at her, knowing she was wrong.

Softly, still shaking his head, Nate informed her of this important fact.

"You're wrong, darling. It changes everything."

SIXTEEN

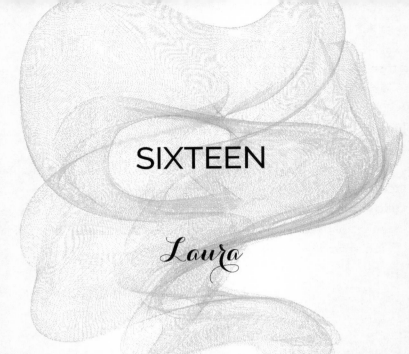

Laura

LAURA SAT SIPPING HER tea and watching both Lily's friend, Fazire, and her husband, Victor, silently squaring off.

And in doing so, she worried.

This strange Fazire, surprisingly, didn't seem frightened of Victor. He hadn't even seemed frightened of Nate, and nearly everyone was frightened of Nate. Her son was that kind of man, dynamic, magnetic, tall, powerfully built. You took one look at him and you knew, no matter what, you should *not* mess with him.

Victor was older, softer but still held a certain menace that only Laura and, eight years ago, Lily could see through.

Unfortunately, it appeared Fazire could see through it too.

Victor obviously didn't like that. He'd put a great deal of effort into honing his legendary menace.

"They're taking a long time. Tash-child, go see what they're doing," Fazire ordered, his arms still crossed on his chest, his head still tilted back ludicrously to stare at them down his sloped nose as if he was used to a greater height.

"Let them be. They've things to discuss," Victor contradicted as Natasha began to do what she was asked.

The child glanced at Victor and then settled back in the couch again and turned to Laura.

"There's lots of photo albums, *lots and lots*. Fazire likes to take pictures," Natasha explained her child's idea of what was taking her parents so long.

Laura silently hoped there were hundreds of albums.

Thousands.

"I can't wait to see the pictures, my darling," Laura smiled at her granddaughter then, as she had been wanting to do since she saw her, she touched the soft skin of her cheek. "Do you know how lovely you are?" she asked, mainly because she couldn't help it.

The child's response startled and delighted her.

Natasha nodded happily. "Oh yes. Mummy calls me the most beautiful girl in the *whole world*."

She giggled to herself at this idea, as if it was funny, as if it was not the absolute truth.

Laura thought that she was the most beautiful child she'd ever seen. Who would have thought Nathaniel's intensely masculine features in feminine, child-like form could be so striking.

"Tash," Fazire called warningly and dropped his chin to stare down at her in a practiced way that expected obedience.

"Oh, all right," Natasha gave in, sounding mock disgruntled, and she scooted to the end of the couch, found her feet and skipped out the door.

The minute she was out of sight on the stairwell, Victor pounced.

"They need time together," he snapped at Fazire.

Fazire turned to face Victor and shook his head slowly.

"They do not." Each word was said with absolute certainty.

"There are things Nathaniel needs to explain." Victor was leaning forward at the waist, trying to hold his temper.

One look at her husband and Laura said soothingly, "Victor."

Laura knew that this Fazire meant a great deal to Lily. Laura had heard Lily talking about him, she told Laura stories about him. He was far younger than Laura would have guessed, considering he was with Lily's family before she was born and he looked to be in his forties.

It simply would not do to have Victor go head to head with him in Lily's living room on this, their first, most delicate visit with her.

Fazire, still not seeing any of Victor's notorious menace, retorted, "Then he should explain them to *me*. *I* was the one who stood outside your door when your daughter told Lily he was dead. *I* was the one who stood looking into the devastated eyes of a twenty-two-year-old pregnant girl who was all alone in the world except for *me*. *I* was the one who called the ambulance when the blood was pouring out of her and she nearly lost Natasha. *I* have been at her side all these years, while *he* lived two hours away and didn't bother to travel the distance to knock on the front door."

Victor's face was turning an alarming shade of red and Laura stood to put a restraining hand on her husband's arm. Every word the man said pounded into them both like sledgehammers.

Fazire wasn't finished.

"And *I* was the one who she came to after she'd gone to *your* home days ago, intent on finally telling you about Natasha, which she'd been talking about doing since Tash was born. She'd even felt guilty about it, not going to you, even though she's had barely two pounds to rub together for eight years. *I* was the one who saw the state she was in when she returned and *I* was the first one to see the bruises *you* gave her."

The red in Victor's cheeks was now there for another purpose.

"We thought she'd—" Victor began.

"It doesn't matter what you thought," Fazire cut him off. "Anyone who spends an hour in Lily's company knows she's worth a trek up the side of a treacherous, threatening volcano to get her back, much less a two hour automobile ride."

Finally, having had his say, Fazire turned away and dismissed them, sipping daintily from his teacup. He idly watched as Mrs. Gunderson sauntered in the room, took one look at him, blinked as if communicating to him that his short, effective tirade was well-stated then sauntered out again.

Laura decided to play mediator. "We have to all get along, for Nathaniel and Lily's sake. For Natasha's sake."

Fazire's gaze slid to her. "There is no 'Nathaniel and Lily.' Lily won't have it. Lily is through with your son. And, unfortunately, I can assure you that the Lily you knew all those years ago is not the Lily of today. When the Lily of today won't have something, it simply isn't to be had."

Laura felt a sinking feeling in her stomach and her dismayed eyes flew to her husband, but he was looking at Fazire and Laura saw that Victor was smiling.

"What you don't know, Fazire," Victor proclaimed, "is when my son wants something, he finds a way to get it."

Fazire squared off again with Victor. "We shall see."

At that, there was a great clamor from the stairwell and Natasha came down, grinning from ear to ear and carrying a photo album. She ran into the room and slapped it down on the table in front of Laura.

"Here's the first one we should look at. It's the most recent but it has the *best* pictures, eh . . . *ver*," she announced.

Lily and Nathaniel followed more slowly, both carrying albums of their own. Lily walked into the room with her cheeks flushed becomingly, making her look more healthy and alive than they'd seen her in these recent days.

However, her eyes were wary.

Nathaniel, on the other hand, walked in looking very pleased about something.

Laura glanced at her husband and that sinking feeling lightened wonderfully.

Before anyone could say anything, another great racket came from the hall.

"I'm late, I'm late." They heard before they saw the body behind the voice. "I know I'm late. Tesco was a *crush*. The Witches Dozen was a madhouse. I barely . . ."

The door was filled with a large, very pretty, older lady who looked somewhat like Elizabeth Taylor. She was wearing a long, amethyst-colored caftan liberally threaded with silver. She accented this with lots of silver jewelry that jangled noisily and very high-heeled purple mules with pointed toes, festooned with sequins. She was carrying a baker's box and four, dangling carrier bags from Tesco.

She stopped dead at what she saw. First Natasha kneeling on the floor, opening an album. Then her eyes shifted to Laura. Onward to Victor standing beside Laura. Next to Fazire scowling ferociously. Then to the blushing Lily.

Finally, closest to her, she spied Nate.

At the sight of him, her eyes bugged out comically, her mouth dropped right open and she freely gaped at him.

Seconds into her astonished stare, she tore her stupefied gaze from Nate to look at Lily. Her eyes narrowed on Lily's face then shifted back to Nate.

After a moment, her mouth snapped shut again and she seemed to come to some conclusion. She walked into the room, right to Nathaniel and Laura held her breath.

"You," she stated, that one word crackling with meaning then immediately her face melted into an absolutely stunning smile, "must be Nate."

She leaned in and kissed his cheek.

Laura's breath went out in a rush and, if she wasn't mistaken, she also heard Victor's do the same thing.

Nate walked to the table, set the three photo albums on it and came back to the woman.

"I'll take that." And without waiting for a response, he divested her of the box and two of the bags.

"Gallant!" she declared in a near shout as if he'd thrown himself bodily over a puddle so she wouldn't have to get her elaborate mules wet.

Laura was intensely relieved that all her years at drilling gentlemanly behavior into her son were finally paying off.

"Since Lily seems unable to speak and Fazire isn't polite at the best of times, I'll introduce myself," she announced. "I'm Maxine Grant, family friend." She was looking at Nate when she said this but then her eyes moved to Laura. "You must be Laura," she stated warmly.

Laura nodded and walked to the other woman, her hand extended.

Maxine, Laura learned quickly, was not the type woman who shook hands. When their hands met, Maxine's closed over Laura's firmly and, with a hearty tug, she pulled Laura forward and kissed her on one cheek.

After this, her eyes looked over Laura's shoulder and she took in Victor. The warmth in her face and voice froze. "And presumably, you're Victor."

Victor, who was paying dearly (even Laura had to admit he deserved it, no matter how much she loved him and understood his actions) for his behavior of a few days before, nodded and correctly read that he would be receiving no kiss on the cheek.

"Maxine," Fazire proclaimed her name as if he was about to make a royal announcement, "you forget this is *not* a joyous family reunion."

Natasha's head jerked up in surprise, "Yes it is, I just saw—"

"Right!" Lily cried, interrupting her daughter, moving forward and setting her albums on the table with the others. "It's time for elevenses."

Laura saw Nate grin as he watched Lily, and at the sight Laura felt that lightening feeling in her belly as it flew to the stars.

Lily walked back to Nate, ignored the devastating grin—indeed, she didn't even look at his face—and pulled the box and bags out of his hands. She did this carefully, as if contact with his skin would burn her like acid. She moved industriously to the door and threw over her shoulder, "Maxine, would you mind helping?"

Without further ado, both women exited the room.

Everyone else stood and waited then Fazire made the peculiar proclamation, "*I* have some channeling to do." He stomped to the door, whirled and stood, spearing all the adults in the room each with a glare. "A *lot* of it." Then he stomped out.

Before anyone could react, Natasha called, "Daddy, come take a look at this."

Nate's gaze shifted to his daughter and his eyes warmed almost palpably.

Laura noted he was happy. She noted that, even though she had no idea what was happening, whatever was happening, Nathaniel thought it was going well.

Laura felt the tension completely ease out of her as Nate went to sit on the couch. He reached forward and gently pulled his daughter between his legs. Together, both of their identically dark heads bent, they looked at the album.

Victor moved to join them as Laura stood uncertain.

"I think," she said and all eyes turned to her, "I'll go and help Lily and Maxine."

"You do that, love." Victor gave her an encouraging wink but Laura waited for Nathaniel's approval.

The tips of his mouth moved up nearly imperceptibly and he nodded once.

She needed no more encouragement and she nearly ran into the hall.

Eight years ago, Lily Jacobs had come into their lives and everything had changed. Laura couldn't have explained how it happened if someone was forcing her to do so with a gun pointed at her head. It was simply a matter of fact that Lily was supposed to be with them, part of their family.

She *belonged*.

Then something terrible happened (and Laura was trying very hard not to think of what that was as it was too painful to bear).

Now, not just Nathaniel, but they *all* had work to do to win Lily back, win her trust and bring her back to her rightful place.

As she approached the back of the house where she saw the kitchen, her steps slowed when she heard the voices.

Laura was not the type of person to eavesdrop. Indeed she found the very idea appalling. But something about Lily and Maxine's hushed voices, their tone, made her stop.

She pressed herself against the wall unseen and she listened.

"Lily, talk to me," Maxine was urging, "tell me what's happened."

"Nothing," Lily answered and even Laura, who could not see her face, knew it was a lie. It was also said in a tone that clearly stated she was not discussing it.

"You didn't tell me he was that good-looking," Maxine said and Laura heard the noise of carrier bags rustling.

"Yes I did," Lily returned.

"You . . . did . . . *not*. He's *impossibly* handsome," Maxine noted.

"Maxine, I don't want to talk about this," Lily stated firmly.

"*Unbelievably* handsome," Maxine was undeterred. "You didn't do him justice when you described him."

"Maxine! I've waxed poetic about Nate's looks for years!"

At that, Laura smiled to herself and leaned a little closer to the door, careful not to get close enough to be seen.

"You still didn't do him justice," Maxine muttered.

"I'm not talking about this," Lily snapped, clearly losing her patience.

"Then we'll talk about why you're blushing." Maxine was like a dog with a bone. She was not, Laura thought delightedly, going to let it go.

"I'm not blushing," Lily denied and, Laura thought, lied.

"You are!"

"Maxine, drop it." Lily's tone was full of warning.

"No. What happened? Did he say something? Do something? I hope he did something," she said fervently.

"Maxine—"

"Lily, sweetling, you can tell old Maxie."

"He kissed me!" Lily uttered in a disbelieving whisper.

This was met with silence, and Laura, surprised herself at her son's forward behavior, leaned even closer to the door to hear Lily's reaction.

Finally, Maxine broke the silence. "Did you kiss him back?"

"No! Yes! Well, not the first time," Lily answered.

"He kissed you *twice*? How late was I?" Maxine asked in a muted shout.

Lily didn't bother responding to that.

"Was it nice?" Maxine pushed.

"Yes, it was nice. It was always nice with Nate." Lily said this in a voice that made it clear she was not happy that it was nice.

"I'll bet it was nice," Maxine muttered. Then she shot off a set of rapid-fire questions. "Did you talk? Did he explain? Did he say anything?"

Silence.

Maxine pressed on, "He must have said something, must have told you why he didn't come to you."

More silence.

Maxine kept at Lily. "He wants to marry you."

Utter silence.

"In two months!" Maxine, now, was losing patience.

"I'm not talking about this."

"Lily!"

There was a sharp noise as if something was slammed on a counter.

"He promised me he was never letting me go! He told me he'd take care of me!" Lily hissed.

"Sweetling—" This was said placatingly and Laura didn't have to be in the room to see Lily to know what she was feeling. It was blindingly apparent from the emotion trembling in her voice.

"No, Maxine. You of all people know what it's been like, what we've been through. No. He promised me—" She broke off, not able to go on with her thought then she continued, "For eight years, I thought he was *dead*."

There was a rustle of movement and then, "I do know, sweetling, but he's *not* dead and he's here and—"

Lily interrupted her friend, her voice now was bitter and the sound of it broke Laura's already wounded heart.

"I believed him. I trusted him. And he didn't come for me. He thought I left him, just like that." Laura heard a snap. "*Me* leaving *him*. It's ridiculous! And with no explanation, no reason, just packing up and moving away after what had happened between us. He didn't come after me. Even if he thought I'd left, he didn't come for me, to ask me to explain, to convince me to come home. He lied. He said he wouldn't let me go and then he did, without saying a word, without doing one single thing to stop it."

Maxine spoke, "Perhaps you should talk to him, perhaps he has an explanation."

The sounds of busy work resumed.

"Too little, too late," Lily returned. "We've struggled, no . . . *I've* struggled. I had to depend on you and Fazire and . . . and . . . he's a man who can transfer seven million pounds into someone's bank account in a day. You've seen him! He dragged me into a room with solicitors and threatened to take my daughter away from me. He thought the worst of me. He thought I was some flighty, besotted idiot who went and got herself pregnant and then hid the knowledge from him for years." Laura heard the determined noises of Lily staying busy. "He can't explain that. I don't want to hear anything he has to say. It's over. We'll agree a visitation schedule and I'll have to see him when he comes and gets Tash and when he brings her home. That's it. The end."

"Lily, I can't help but think you're making a mistake," Maxine warned and Laura felt a moment of hope.

Then, at Lily's next words, that hope was dashed.

"No, I *already* made the mistake, eight years ago. Now I'm protecting myself. I couldn't endure it if it happened again and, Maxie, I need you to stand by me."

More noises and then a muffled, "You know I will. I always have. I want what's best for you."

The conversation was over and Laura stood in the hallway, wondering what to do.

She should, of course, tell Nathaniel.

She should try to talk to Lily, to tell her about Nathaniel and why he would think she would leave him. Why, Laura knew in her heart even though he'd never told her, Nathaniel let her go. Laura wanted to explain all that was her son because she knew, she *knew*, Lily would understand.

But it was not her place.

Nathaniel would not thank her for sharing the information about his former life. He wore it like a badge of honor at the same time he hid it like a dirty secret.

Laura, like Victor, thought Nate could do anything. She thought this because he'd proved it time and time again. He didn't need anyone. He had taken care of himself since he was born. He'd never asked for a thing since she'd known him. If he wanted it, he got it for himself.

This time, even though he didn't know it, he needed his mother.

And she was going to be there for him.

Laura waited until there was enough time for the two women in the kitchen to be assured she hadn't overheard anything and then she walked in, smiling brightly.

Once in the room, Laura asked, "Can I help?"

SEVENTEEN

Lily

IT WAS NEARLY CLOSING time and Lily, caught in her own thoughts, most of them not very good, the rest of them supremely confusing, sat behind the counter of "Flash and Dazzle," Maxine and Lily's store in town.

Lily had bought in to the store several years ago using the funds left over from the sale of her childhood home. She'd held on to them just in case some other calamity happened and in those days, calamities were happening with alarming frequently. The refrigerator breaking down (twice). The clutch going out in the car. The washing machine overflowing and flooding the house.

At first, Fazire used to take care of these with a flick of the wrist but the Great Grand Genie Number One had channeled him and warned him if he did it any more, it would be considered Lily's last wish and he'd have to leave them. And there was no way Lily would allow Fazire to leave them. He was the only family they had.

Fazire had been furious, he couldn't actually get a job because he had no skills, save magic, and furthermore, he didn't exist in the human world and had no passport or driver's license. He'd started their air journey from Indiana eight years ago in the opened bottle in the luggage compartment, formed himself and magicked himself into the passenger area to sit with Lily.

He couldn't drive a car, they frightened him. "Machinery," he said with a shudder to hide his fear, "is common."

In those days, he couldn't do much to help, except magic away problems. However, he also couldn't go against the Great Grand Genie Number One. The consequences would be dire.

Therefore, for years Fazire had been magic-less except for floating, of course, and the occasional creation of three hot fudge sundaes.

Luckily, Flash and Dazzle had been doing a booming trade and still was. Every item in the store was handmade by talented designers and artists, each piece the only one of its kind. Two of their jewelry designers had become immensely popular, and Maxine had found this woman who made the finest, loveliest, handcrafted sweaters that Lily had ever seen. People came from far and wide to buy a one-of-a-kind sweater, dress or piece of jewelry.

Maxine had wanted to expand and open a store in Bath but didn't have enough capital to do it. As she had helped Lily incredibly over the years, Lily took the chance and invested in Maxine's expansion. It had been a good investment, increasing her income just enough to make their financial situation move from "critical" to simply "grave."

Maxine now spent her time flitting from one store to the other, bedazzling her customers with her extravagant personality, customers who came for the goods but came back for another dose of Maxine, and taking care of her clerks as if they were all favored daughters.

Lily managed what she now thought of as "her" store. She'd been working there (except for the brief time she lived in London and the time she had been unable to work because of her pregnancy with Tash) for nearly a decade.

She loved it there. She kept the flowers in the window box and tubs outside bright and cheerful all year long. She designed the displays of goods with a cautious eye for detail. She took care of her own clerks and all their various and sundry girl problems like they were her younger sisters. It was perfect as Lily could walk to work and thus not tax her stubborn car. She could make her own hours. And she could have Tash there whenever she wanted.

It wasn't exactly comparable to being an award-winning, jet-setting, bestselling novelist but it put food on the table.

That day, like every day, Lily wore clothes and jewelry she bought from the store wholesale or she wouldn't have been able to afford them. Flash and Dazzle was a *very* exclusive shop. Lily's dress was salmon colored with spaghetti straps and dainty hot-pink flowers embroidered in it. The bodice fit her like a glove down her torso to flair very slightly at the hips and it fell ending mid-thigh. She wore this with a pair of hot-pink flip-flops and a set of brightly colored, glitter-encrusted bangles in every shade of salmon, peach and pink jingled at her wrist.

Lily had no idea, whatsoever, that one look at her stylishly sporting Flash and Dazzle inventory, made the majority of sales in the shop (though Maxine knew this, for certain).

She also had no idea that even in her current state of slenderness, her glorious beauty had not faded over the years. In fact, it had deepened with maturity. Her heartbreak had only added a mysterious allure.

She'd never learned to come to terms with her beauty and still didn't fully know it existed. She had a feeling she was no longer the ugly duckling, though. She wasn't deaf or blind and she certainly wasn't stupid.

What Lily was, that day, was avoiding home.

It was Saturday. It had been Wednesday when Nate and the Roberts had come to meet Natasha. Nate was back today, having arranged horseback riding lessons for Natasha. This was her daughter's most desperate desire, but as these lessons cost nearly forty pounds an hour, Lily had been unable to afford them. She had been saving up to give them to her for Christmas. The fact that Nate could afford them without blinking an eye, Lily found highly annoying.

Now, Lily had seven million pounds in the bank, money that Alistair was arranging to put in trust for Natasha. Lily wasn't going to touch even a single penny of it.

She decided this stubbornly, even though Fazire tried to talk her into keeping at least some of it to finish the final rooms in the house. This included the entire garden level, which had yet to be touched, and the three rooms she hadn't started on the top floor. Not to mention her disaster of a bedroom. Fazire told her to put some in savings and to give some more to Maxine, who wanted to open another store in Cheltenham. He tried, with great determination, thus throughout the conversation floating precariously close to the ceiling, to convince her to invest in her own future.

Lily would not hear a word of it.

It was not her money. It was Nate's money and now Natasha's money.

And that was that.

And Lily had made another decision, this one strategic.

She had decided to avoid Nate altogether and she didn't hesitate to put that particular plan into action.

Lily had not been home when Nate arrived that morning. She left Fazire to watch over Natasha and hand her over to Nate when he arrived. Fazire, incidentally, wholeheartedly agreed with her Dodge Nate Plan.

She didn't even want to meet him in a conference room with solicitors, considering the last time he'd backed her up against a wall and held her face like it was the finest piece of crystal.

She certainly didn't want to be alone with him, considering the last time they were alone, he'd kissed her.

Kissed her!

It was insane and it was, quite simply, unacceptable.

She forgave herself for giving in to the kiss. She'd been wanting to kiss Nate for eight long years, wanting to touch him, hold him, have him back and never, ever let him go. She was allowed to give in to a moment of weakness, just that once.

But not again. Never again.

The rest of that day, when Natasha met Nate and the other members of her burgeoning family, had gone relatively well. Lily had been surprised at Victor and Laura's appearance but, if she could handle Nate, she could certainly put up with Victor and Laura for a few hours.

They'd served Maxine's treats and had more tea and coffee. Conversation was awkward and stilted and mostly made up of Natasha's excited gibberish, Maxine's hilarious quips and Laura's soft, careful comments.

Then Laura suggested a walk on the seafront, which Lily encouraged with great enthusiasm, running up the stairs to drag her genie out of his bottle (Fazire was furiously channeling his friends to tell them the latest episode in the Lily Saga) and plan her strategy with her ever-helpful friend.

At the last possible minute, Lily explained she had just remembered an urgent errand she had to run. Nate had glanced at her with a look that was both annoyingly patient and more annoyingly knowing, but she'd ignored him.

She said her brief good-byes and disregarded Laura's disappointed look. She rushed to her beat up Peugeot, coaxed it to start and took off as fast as the little car would take her, which admittedly wasn't very fast.

Fazire, as planned, called her mobile when the coast was clear.

She and Fazire had carefully arranged their next avoidance tactic.

Unless Fazire phoned her, Lily was to work at the shop all day and go to the grocery store after. This, she hoped, would give Nate plenty of time to have his visit with Tash and leave. Horseback riding lessons didn't last all day, only an hour. Even still, over a bottle of wine the night before, Lily and Fazire had made up a half a dozen excuses for her to leave again straight away in case Nate was still there when she arrived home (it wouldn't do for him actually to *know* she was evading him).

Alistair encouraged her avoidance of Nate, even demanded it. He was currently working with Nate's solicitors to set a visitation schedule and make it plain that Lily had no interest in what they were calling a "reconciliation."

Nate's solicitors were refusing even to broach the subject of visitation, demanding reconciliation and had gone so far as to present Alistair with a prenuptial agreement. This, Alistair returned after Jane had shredded it. Alistair didn't read it and certainly didn't give Lily the opportunity to do so, even if she had wanted to, which she did not.

She tried not to think of what Nate had said while they were retrieving the photo albums, though she was quite unsuccessful.

He'd thought she'd left him, which was absurd, and this confused her. He had not come after her and this angered her.

That he didn't know that Jeff and Danielle had plotted to keep them apart was obvious. That he accepted her leaving without even trying to discover why dumbfounded her. Especially since now, he clearly intended to have her back.

Then again, when he thought she'd left, there was no child involved. Now there was, and if there was anything Lily understood, it was the importance of family. Lily didn't for a second think that he wanted *her* but that he wanted *them*. More than likely Tash, with Lily as a companion and willing bed partner thrown in to sweeten the deal.

And Lily wanted no part in that.

It was closing time and usually Lily was happy to go home to Tash and Fazire on a Saturday when they'd get fish and chips and stroll the seafront or pop in a DVD.

Tash liked Pixar.

Fazire liked Westerns.

Lily didn't care what they watched.

Instead, she locked the doors, saw, very slowly, to the business of tidying the store, locking away the register drawer and seeing to the most minute task that would hold her back. Then she went to Tesco, and instead of whipping around the store in her normal, busy-mother-on-a-mission frenzy, she checked product labels, assessed quantities and spent vast periods of time contemplating the inventories of the larder at her home before she decided on a purchase.

She packed the car, carefully placing every bag safely in the boot as if she'd be graded on its arrangement. It was strange, having time on her hands. It was an alien feeling she hadn't had in so long, she couldn't remember the last time she had it.

Yes, she could, when she lived in London with Nate.

Then she wandered back to the cart store to return her trolley, humming to herself idly as if she had all the time in the world.

Finally, against her will for the first time in her life, she went home.

A gleaming, sleek, sporty car was parked at the front of her house, dashing all hope that Nate had already left and Fazire had just forgotten to phone.

She expertly, from years of practice, parallel parked the Peugeot into the spot behind the Aston Martin (Nate, she saw, had not changed his predilection for fast cars), mentally preparing for what was to come. She went over her excuses, deciding which was best—an emergency trip to the mall because her hair dryer was broken, which it was not but everyone knew a woman could not live a single day without her hair dryer.

Taking as many bags as possible from the boot, she struggled, arms laden, to the house.

She was barely halfway up the walk when the door was thrown open.

"Mummy!" Natasha flew out with her usual spiritedness, followed urgently by Fazire who had a look on his face that could only be described as stormy. "You would not be . . . *lieve!*" Natasha cried excitedly.

Nate followed Fazire and Lily fought back her reaction at seeing him casually strolling from her house. She couldn't count how many times she'd dreamed of that very vision coming real.

She found it immensely annoying that he was *more* charismatic, *more* attractive, *more* handsome than eight years ago. He wore jeans and a long-sleeved chambray shirt, the sleeves rolled up partially at his forearms, and he looked immensely masculine.

"Believe what?" Lily asked, trying to smile at her happy daughter at the same time ignoring Nate and finding both difficult.

She decided that, too, annoyed her.

Fazire walked by her, flashing her a glance filled with barely contained ire.

He muttered as he passed her, "Tash *confiscated* my mobile thingie-whatsit and would not *allow* me to use the house line."

Then, on that strange announcement, he stomped to the boot to get the rest of the groceries.

"Daddy has been busy today. Busy, busy, busy," Natasha told her with delight. "Fazire wanted to call you but I wouldn't let him because it was a surprise!"

Nate walked straight to her.

"Lily," he greeted.

She spared him the briefest glance and started to look back at Tash to ask about this "surprise" when Nate leaned into her. She had stopped to talk to Tash but now she reared back to avoid Nate.

He simply reached in and took all of her carrier bags, of which there were five, and *he* spared her a glance, his, again, annoyingly knowing. Then calmly, as if he had carried groceries into their house every day for the past eight years, he turned and walked into the house.

She glared at his back and decided she found that annoying as well.

"Come look, come on, come on, come on!" Natasha urged excitedly.

Tash grabbed her hand and tugged Lily forward. Lily threw a look over her shoulder at Fazire who was carrying the last three bags into the house. His lips were thin and his face was set.

Fazire, Lily knew, took Nate's defection personally. He had, he thought, been the one to bring Nate into Lily's life through her wish. Even though Lily tried to talk him out of it, Fazire felt personally responsible for all that happened to Lily. She knew it weighed on him heavily, and he was determined to chastise himself and had even gone so far as to vow early retirement from Genie-hood considering the enormity of his blunder.

"Mummy, come on!" Tash demanded and Lily allowed herself to be pulled into the house, up the stairs and to her bedroom.

Then she saw her "surprise."

In the doorway to her room, she came to a dead halt. Her eyes widened. Her mouth dropped open. And she stared.

"You can't go in because the floors are drying. They'll be back tomorrow to put in the new furniture. Isn't it great? It's just like *Changing Rooms*, except not done yet."

Tash's excitement was barely contained. She was practically dancing in glee.

Lily's room had been transformed. All of her furniture was gone, not even a trace of it in the hallway. The walls were smooth and had been painted in the palest blue. The woodwork was gleaming with a new coat of white gloss. An enormous ceiling rose had been affixed to the middle where also an intricate elegant light fixture dangled glamorously. The cornices had also been replaced, looking beautiful, classic and clean. The floors had been sanded and varnished.

Lily looked down at her watch.

She'd left that morning at eight. It was now six thirty.

She could not believe it had all been done in that time. It took her six months just to paint the hall.

"There were, like, seven men here. I couldn't believe they could get all of them in your room but they did. They even hoovered and dusted when they left so it would be tidy when you came home," Tash explained and then breathed in awe, "Isn't it lush?"

"It's lovely," Lily murmured, now way beyond annoyed.

So far beyond annoyed, it wasn't funny.

She was ready to do battle.

"Do me a favor, baby doll, and help Fazire with the groceries." Tash was so thrilled at what she thought was her father's grand gesture, she didn't notice her mother's glittering blue eyes. "And, ask *your father* to come up here. I'd like a word with him."

"Okay," Tash agreed readily.

Blind to Lily's mounting fury, her daughter raced headlong down the stairs, her natural ebullience ratcheted up twelve notches to immeasurable at all the good fortune that she thought had befallen them upon the arrival of her father.

While she waited, Lily paced the landing. Every time she turned back and caught a glimpse of her room, her temper flared even further out of control.

When she caught a glimpse of Nate's dark head sedately ascending the staircase, without a word, she broke out of her pacing and ascended the stairs that took them to the next floor. She wasn't going to confront Nate on the landing. She needed privacy for what she had to say.

She walked angrily to the living room and stood, hand on the door while Nate silently followed her and entered the room. When he did, she slammed the door loudly and whirled on him.

"How *dare* you!" she shouted, letting her rage loose.

"Lily."

This was all he said. He had crossed his arms on his chest and was watching her closely. She knew he didn't miss a thing. He *never* missed a thing.

Not that she was exactly trying to hide her fury.

His gorgeous face, she noted, her anger hitting the stratosphere, was carefully controlled. She decided his control annoyed her most of all.

"Where's my furniture?" she snapped.

"Gone," he said shortly.

"Bring it back," she demanded.

"It's gone," he stated unyieldingly as if he had every right to toss out her belongings without a word to her.

He walked toward her and she, unfortunately, was standing in front of the door she herself had closed. She had no retreat and realized her error immediately.

Instead of moving back and being pinned by his body and the door, which she knew in recent experience he'd do, she stood her ground and he came up to her and stopped.

He was close to her, *very* close. So close she could smell his tangy, earthy cologne. So close she could feel the heat from his body. Her belly threatened a gymnastics lesson and she resolutely ignored her reaction to his proximity. Letting herself go once was allowed, even expected. She had been, of course, pining for him for years.

To do it again would be a catastrophic mistake.

"I want it back," she clipped, barely controlling her careening emotions.

"It's not coming back. It's gone. New furniture will be delivered tomorrow."

"On a *Sunday?*" she hissed in disbelief. Hardly anyone did anything on a Sunday in England, except eat a Sunday roast and, perhaps, do a touch of gardening.

Nate shrugged.

Of course, the omnipotent Nate McAllister with his seven million pounds could get anyone to do anything he wanted.

She lost control of her careening emotions and what's more, she didn't care.

"I want you out of my house," she ordered, her eyes blazing, her body rigid with fury.

"We're going to dinner," Nate stated matter-of-factly as if she'd just stop, deflate, give in and say, "Oh, okay, whatever you wish."

At this she lost her mind.

"We are *not* going to dinner. *You* may take Tash to dinner but *we* are not doing *anything*," she yelled.

"I already told Natasha we're all going to dinner. She's looking forward to it."

If she wasn't mistaken, he'd moved in the barest inch.

Lily remained exactly where she was.

"Well, then, I guess you're going to learn the painful lesson of telling your daughter she can't have something she desperately wants because I'm not going to dinner with you."

His eyes flashed at her words, reading correctly that Lily had, over the years, been forced to learn the excruciating lesson of disappointing their daughter.

His hand reached up and she stared in shock at it until it moved out of her eyesight. It then traced her hair at her temple, pushed its heavy weight back and tucked it behind her ear.

His eyes watched the progress of his hand then they moved to hers. He spoke gently, reacting to what her words had meant but obviously he was still not to be denied.

"Yes, you are."

"No, I'm not."

He leaned in again, his hand dropping to her shoulder, this time his movement could not be missed or mistaken.

"Yes, Lily, you are."

It was then *she* moved in, going up on her toes to put her face so close to his it was barely an inch away.

"If you think you can stroll into our lives and turn them upside down with your money and power and . . . whatever, and . . . and . . ." She couldn't find the words. She was too angry to speak.

"And what?"

"I don't know!" she shouted in his face.

"I'll not have you sleeping in that room the way it was," he declared.

Again, her mouth dropped open at his nerve and sheer arrogance.

"It isn't *your* choice!" she raged.

His hand moved to cup her jaw.

"I've never seen you this angry." His voice was soft, contemplative. He was watching her with a warmth in his dark eyes that very nearly, but not quite, stole her breath.

"We barely knew one another," she snapped. "You've never seen me a lot of things."

Ignoring her, he remarked quietly, "You're incredibly beautiful when you're angry."

Again, she gawped at him, so stunned at his unexpected compliment, she was unable to react when he stepped forward, forcing her back the step it took to pin her against the door. His warm body came up against hers and his hand tightened at her jaw, his other hand settled on the door beside her head.

"You're incredibly beautiful always, but angry, you're magnificent," he murmured softly

His eyes had dropped to her mouth. The mood had shifted and she was most definitely not prepared for it.

"Get away from me," she breathed, half frightened at what *she* would do, half angry at what *he* was doing.

"Come to dinner with me," he coaxed, his deep voice like velvet.

"No," she denied stubbornly, refusing to give in to that voice and tried to jerk her head away, but in her current position, it was impossible.

"Come to dinner with me," he repeated, as if the exchange of words they'd just shared hadn't happened at all.

"I . . . said . . . no!" She didn't wait for him to ask again, she rushed on, "You need to step away right now. You may take Natasha to dinner and bring her home. Then your solicitors need to agree with Alistair a schedule for you to see Tash. I don't want to see you again. I don't want you in this house. I don't want—"

"We're getting married," he stated unequivocally, his voice again smooth and silky, and the gymnastics team in her belly started to do their warm-up stretches.

She put her hands on his abdomen and shoved with all her might.

He didn't move away, instead, his arm closed around her like a vise, crushing her against his body. His other hand dropped, also coming around her, higher on her back so her breasts were pressed against him. His head was bent so that his eyes looked into hers, his hard, beautiful mouth a breath away.

And then he spoke and his voice was no longer smooth and silky, nor was it gentle and nor was it coaxing. It was hard, low and full of steel and it surged through her like it was alive and breathing.

"I've lost eight years of you. Eight years. I don't know what you've suffered in those years but you've got the rest of our lives to tell me and I have that time to make it up to you," he stated firmly then went on.

"This, Lily, I assure you I'll do."

It took every bit of willpower she had not to let his words penetrate her armor. Her hands had been forced away from his stomach when he pulled her to him and now she clutched the fabric of his shirt at his waist, pushing it back as hard as she could.

"You've made me promises before, Nate," she reminded him heatedly.

"I know," he ground out, his eyes still drilling into hers.

"You broke those promises."

He didn't hesitate and he didn't deny it. "I know."

She glared, waiting for him to go on, to say something, anything that would make it better.

He didn't.

"We're over!" she yelled hysterically.

She couldn't take much more.

"We haven't even begun," he promised.

"I'm not going through it again!" she cried, lost in her panic, lost in her fears. Her anger had flashed and as usual was quickly gone and now she only wished for escape.

Her life may not have been the heaven it had seemed to be when she'd been with Nate so long ago, but it was a good life, a contented life, and she wanted it back.

"*You won't have to!*" Nate barked, shocking her by losing his own temper.

He was no longer cool and casual. He was in the throes of his own personal storm.

Lily should have acceded to the force of it for it filled the room, pressed into her like a slab of marble.

But she didn't. She couldn't.

There was too much to lose.

"I don't believe you," she accused.

"Fine. Don't believe me. But our daughter has two parents and for the rest of her life she's going to enjoy both of them. Together. She's going to enjoy the safety of a loving home, her parents living together, taking care of her. Not shuttled back and forth. Not being forced to adjust to two homes, two lives. You saw her when she found us together. You know she wants it."

"You can't have everything you want, believe me, Nate, I know." His eyes narrowed dangerously at her words but recklessly she went on, "It's a difficult lesson to learn but she might as well learn it early, rather than to grow up a hopeless dreamer like her mother and get crushed somewhere along the way."

She could have sworn his face registered the barest flinch but he continued.

"You can't tell me, given the power to offer her what she most desires, you wouldn't move heaven and earth to do it," he bit out.

"She'll adjust," Lily snapped even though he was, unfortunately, right.

Lily *would* move heaven and earth to give Tash what she wanted but just then she wasn't giving an inch.

"She'll be devastated," Nate correctly predicted.

"You don't know her enough to make that judgement," Lily aimed at her target and hit a bull's-eye. She knew this because his eyes started glittering angrily and she knew his control was stretched nearly to the breaking point.

"I've changed my mind," he clipped. "You're not magnificent when you're angry. You're incredibly annoying and unbelievably stubborn when you're angry."

"I'm not stubborn!" she denied stubbornly.

His face, if it could be credited, moved closer and he changed tactics so swiftly, her head began to swim.

"You want me, Lily, and you know it."

"I don't!"

Even she knew it was a lie.

"You want me," he stated baldly. "Shall I prove it to you?"

Frantic, because she knew what was coming, she threatened, "Kiss me again and I won't be responsible for what I do."

"I know *exactly* what you'll do."

And without giving her the opportunity to retort, his lips crushed down on hers.

This time she didn't hold herself stock still. This time she struggled, fought, pushed against him and tried to pull away. She clawed at his sides, tearing at the fabric of his shirt.

His tongue touched her lips and a lone gymnast executed a perfect round-off and her whole body stilled at the sudden glory of it.

As usual, he immediately sensed her capitulation. Surprisingly, he pulled away but not enough to allow her escape. Instead, he half carried, half dragged her to the sofa, and before she could make good a getaway, he pushed her backwards onto it and his heavy, warm body landed on top of her.

"Stop, Nate," she demanded, scrambling beneath him.

"No," he refused, and before she could say another word, his mouth came down on hers again.

His mouth was not gentle. It was hard, insistent, demanding. It was also familiar. It was also exactly what she'd wanted, wished for and dreamed of for eight years.

Not another man had touched her. She'd been on a handful of dates without even a goodnight kiss (well, perhaps a peck on the cheek). Lily had been too wrapped up in her life, her problems, her responsibilities. She didn't have time for men.

And no one compared to Nate. It was a simple statement of fact.

His mouth moved to trail down her cheek to her jaw.

"Please stop," she whispered on a plea. Her anger was gone, replaced by longing—eight terrible, lonely years of longing.

"No."

"Please, Nate," she begged.

In answer, his hand moved on her leg, smoothing a caress all the way up her thigh, pulling her skirt up with it, her skin quivering at his intimate touch.

His hard body pressed against her, so familiar, so warm, almost fe-vered. She wasn't going to be able to deny her body much longer the attention it craved.

"We can't," she pleaded.

"We can," he growled against her throat, the rumble of his voice moving through her until she shivered.

He felt it, she knew. He couldn't help but feel it and his mouth came back to hers and he kissed her again.

This time she didn't struggle. The minute his lips touched hers, they parted and his tongue slid inside.

And that was it. She lost her battle and she acquiesced as the gymnastics team in her belly—warmed up and ready to go—gave the performance of their life.

Eight years of grief and yearning poured out of her and she kissed him back, her tongue warring with his, her hands moving on his body, roaming over his back, down his hips, sliding over his behind. She'd forgotten how hard his body was, the tough sinew under his silken skin. She tore at his shirt, wanting the feel of him with nothing in the way. Once free of his jeans, her hands delved underneath the shirt to trail across his waist and up his back.

His skin was fiery to the touch.

It was too much, too soon. The tears came up the back of her throat, burning as her body burned under his touch.

His mouth never left hers, delivering its heady kiss, but one of his hands went to her breast, cupping it, finding her nipple with the pad of his thumb. She gasped against his mouth at the feel of him there, powerful shafts of pleasure shooting straight through her.

At her gasp, his kiss deepened and what was already wild became wilder. Years of grief changed to relief that he was alive, breathing, with her again, touching her again, kissing her again.

This time, *her* hands and mouth became insistent, demanding, her fingers rushing across his skin under his shirt, one of them moving to his belly, down, until she felt him hard against the palm of her hand.

The tears sprang from her eyes, falling silently along her temples as he tore his mouth from hers on a groan at her touch, his mouth gliding to her ear.

"Do you still want to stop?" His voice was rough with arousal but he sounded as if he wanted a response. As if he'd move away if that was what she desired.

She didn't answer, couldn't answer.

His hand tightened at her breast, his thumb swirling provocatively.

"Stop me now, Lily. It'll be your only chance."

Still unable to speak, she shook her head and Nate didn't hesitate. His mouth took hers in another searing kiss as both of his hands moved to her hips, pressing her against him, her hand, still between them, forced intimately flat against his arousal.

Just as quickly as he did it, he released her hips, his mouth and tongue everywhere, sliding down her throat, to her ear, along her collarbone, the edge of her bodice. He bent his head as one hand yanked her skirt up over her hips and without delay his hand went between her legs as his mouth closed over her sensitized nipple. He was doing both through her clothing, his teeth and tongue working sensuously at her nipple over her dress, his fingers pressing against her panties, using the silky fabric as tantalizing friction, and her body, already breathlessly alive at his touch, started vibrating.

"Nate," she breathed in wonder.

She'd forgotten how glorious it was. She thought she remembered but she'd forgotten.

He surged up again, his mouth against hers, his hand moved up to the edge of her underwear and then it plunged in.

"I've been waiting eight years to hear you say my name like that again."

Her breath caught at his words, the husky tone of wanting in his voice, as his finger found her and circled deliciously. She was clutching at him as the lusty spirals shot out from between her legs, his lips still touching hers but he didn't kiss her.

"Say it again," he demanded.

Her eyes had closed to concentrate on what her body was feeling and at his demand, they flew open and his black gaze was boring into her.

"Say it again, Lily," he commanded.

She bit her lip and his hand moved, his finger slowly, beautifully, slid inside her and at the feel of him filling her again, even just his finger, she couldn't help herself.

"Nate."

His mouth came down on hers hard as his hand worked at her and she pressed against it, kissing him back with desperate wanting.

Then, without warning, his head jerked up and his hand, his thumb at the core of her, one finger deep inside her, completely stilled.

"Jesus," he cursed, his hand moving swiftly but gently away from her, making her moan in pleasure mingled with disappointment.

He surged up lithely, pulling her along with him. She was dazed with passion, her legs trembling so badly she had to lean against him and hold on to his waist.

"Nate," she whispered uncertainly as one of his arms held her steady, the other hand yanked the skirt of her dress back in place.

His head came up at the sound of his name and he looked into her face, a satisfied grin playing about his mouth. His face, too, was still set with passion and at the sight of it, she sucked in her breath.

Briefly, he pressed his lips against hers.

Then he murmured, "Someone's coming."

And before this frightening thought could penetrate her desire-fogged brain, before she could get her buckling knees under control, before she could break away from him, the door flew open and Fazire was standing there.

Her old friend froze two steps into the room and took in the vision of Lily clinging to Nate and Nate holding on to Lily.

Fazire glared at them in horror.

Before he could utter a word, Natasha forged into the room.

"What's up?" she asked innocently, smiling happily at her mother and father standing together, seemingly the loving, embracing couple.

Lily was still recovering. Both fortunately and unfortunately, depending on how you looked at it, Nate was faster at his recovery and without hesitation he explained, his voice still slightly husky with desire.

"Your mother was just thanking me for the room."

With this, Nate's arm tightened around her waist before she could begin to pull away. Lily watched as Fazire's face turned as purple as the walls in his bedroom.

Natasha had no problem processing this explanation. It was, indeed, quite natural that Lily would wish to thank Nate soundly for his thoughtful gesture.

"Are we going out to dinner or what?" Natasha asked, her head tilting to the side. "I'm hungry," she went on in explanation before her mother could take her to task for her somewhat rude question.

Nate's head swung to look at Lily.

"Are we?" he asked softly and his lips turned up at the corners because, with one look at the soft gaze Lily was giving their daughter, he already knew the answer.

EIGHTEEN

Lily

LILY WALKED THROUGH THE heavy doors to enter the plush, elegant offices of Nate's company.

The last four days had been a tumble of activity and through all of it, Lily could think of only one thing.

Moving heaven and earth to make Tash happy.

Saturday night, they'd all gone out to dinner. Natasha and Nate, it was clear to see, were quickly forming a bond. Lily was somewhat surprised at how easily Nate showed affection to his daughter. It wasn't lavish or showy. It wasn't desperate to impress or please. It was genuine and beautiful and Tash responded to it immediately.

This visibly annoyed Fazire, but the genie loved Tash enough not to let it show (too much).

One day, they were barely scraping by, Natasha's entire family made up of a busy mother, a genie-father-esque figure who was more of a playmate, however, Fazire *had* learned over the years to do the laundry, was quite adept at ironing and could make a mean tuna casserole, and the outlandish Maxine.

The next day, literally, Tash had a dashing, handsome, rich, obviously caring father *and* doting grandparents.

Horseback riding lessons were hers for the asking. A seven million pound trust fund was waiting for her to turn twenty-one making it so she would never want again. Rooms could be transformed in a weekend as if by magic.

But this was Nate's magic rather than Fazire's, which perhaps was one of the reasons why Fazire disliked Nate so intensely, for Nate too could grant wishes. Even wishes that hadn't been expressed.

Tash's world had doubled, opening up before her with extraordinary beauty. It was, quite simply, a miracle. The wished for, hoped for, longed for, but never expected, miracle.

Natasha was delighted and Lily couldn't help but be delighted for her.

And Natasha wanted a family, it was clear. She'd heard the stories for years, not only of all the gloriousness that was Nate, but Fazire and Lily told her of Sarah, Rebecca, Will and their summers spent floating on inner-tubes on the pond, their big holiday extravaganzas and a million and one other things, both big and small, that made families so wonderful.

Tash, quite rightly, wanted that for herself.

Natasha had no idea what was happening with her parents and her confusion would be extraordinary, even devastating (as Nate predicted) if her mother, who had relayed so many glowing stories of her beloved Nate, didn't take him back gleefully and make them the family Tash craved.

And Lily, knowing how precious family was, couldn't help but want to give that to her.

After dinner, Tash and Lily had walked Nate to the car because Tash made her with a tug on her hand, the three of them walking together, Natasha between them holding both Lily's and Nate's hands.

Once there, he'd picked up Tash as if she weighed no more than a feather, and at seven, nearly eight and a tall child to boot considering her parents, she weighed a *lot* more than that.

She kissed him squarely on the mouth and threw her arms around his neck in one of her fierce hugs.

"When are you coming back?" she asked when she'd partially disengaged, her arms still resting on his broad shoulders.

"Very soon," he answered with a devastatingly handsome smile to which Tash, just like her mother, immediately reacted.

"Tomorrow?" she tried hopefully, making Lily's Avoid Nate at All

Costs Resolution fade to a memory.

Nate's eyes slid to Lily, who was trying very hard to control her expression.

"Maybe not tomorrow," he demurred. "But soon."

It was then that Tash rubbed her nose against Nate's.

Lily watched in fascination as Nate closed his eyes and something passed over his face. Something so intense Lily felt it go through her own body like an electric shock.

"Promise?" Tash demanded on a whisper, her face still close to her father's.

"I promise." Nate's deep voice was nearly a growl and Lily found herself swallowing at the emotion it betrayed.

Something about that growl, that emotion, all Nate's intensity made Lily's heart flutter, her chest squeeze and, lastly, it made her very, very curious to its cause.

She was standing with them on the sidewalk by Nate's driver's side door. When he put Natasha down, before she knew his intention, his arm shot out, hooked her waist and he pulled her to him.

She made a low noise of surprise, which was muffled when his mouth slanted down on hers in a hard but brief and unfortunately effective kiss.

"I want you here when I come back," he told her when he'd stopped kissing her, still holding her against his hard body, and she realized then he'd cottoned on to the Dodge Nate Plan.

She hesitated, trying not to look at Natasha who she knew was staring up at them gleefully.

Then she mumbled, "We'll see."

Apparently, that was good enough for him for he let her go, got in his expensive car and drove away.

"He's the bomb," Natasha said, using a term Maxine used frequently and watching her father go.

Lily stood looking at her daughter watching her father's car disappear and she saw the years stretching before her. Years of Nate bringing Natasha home, dropping her off and then disappearing from her life again for days or weeks, only to come back into her life for brief periods of time. Then again her daughter would be forced to watch him go.

And Lily asked herself, could she do that to Tash?

Lily crouched behind her beloved daughter, pulled her back to Lily's front and she rested her chin against Tash's shoulder.

"Happy, baby doll?"

Natasha was so happy she couldn't speak. She just nodded. It was the first time since Tash had uttered her first words that she'd been speechless.

Lily felt the emotion crawl up her throat, already knowing somewhere deep inside her what she should do but still incapable of allowing herself to do it.

Sunday, her new furniture was not only delivered and assembled but they went up to the top floor to where they'd stowed her belongings (the ones *not* tossed out by Nate) and returned them to her room so Lily didn't have to do it.

The bed was enormous. She'd never seen a bed so huge. It was a sleigh bed made of heavy, shining oak. A massive wardrobe twice the size of her old one and intricately carved like the scrolls on the bed stood against the wall. A thin, matching, six-drawer lingerie dresser, another wider dresser and two beautiful bed stands were added.

Gorgeous, delicate, lamps that matched the exquisite ceiling fixture stood on the bedside tables.

Gossamer curtains an even paler blue than the walls drifted at the window with heavy, slightly darker blue drapes hanging outside, all of this on stunning, scrolled wrought-iron curtain rods.

The floor was covered by an intricately patterned, deep-pile, fringed rug that Lily was fairly certain by its sheen was made of silk and likely imported from Turkey (she became certain of this because Fazire told her, Fazire knew a thing or two about rugs from Turkey).

And two pictures were affixed to the walls, ivory mattes in black frames with prints of fancifully drawn shoes that, on first sight, even Lily had to admit that she loved. They were so girlie and perfect she couldn't help herself.

The bed was covered in a fluffy, ivory coverlet trimmed in the blues of the walls and curtains, and there were two sets of three standard, downy pillows stacked side-by-side at the head of the bed encased in the varying blues and ivory in front of which stood gigantic European squares in soft cases that had a lovely swirl of all the colors as a pattern.

"It's bee . . . you . . . tee . . . full," Natasha breathed as she and her mother stood in the doorway staring at it.

It was more than beautiful. It was the kind of bedroom where dreams came true.

The room, however, was just the beginning.

Monday, she came home from the shop with Maxine who came over for dinner every Monday evening.

Maxine knew that Fazire was a genie. Maxine was also addicted to Fazire's tuna casserole and his equally adept hand at grilling a sausage and making the fluffiest mash potatoes in history. Maxine had further had an excited phone call from Tash and was eager to see Lily's new bedroom.

Natasha, as was becoming a habit, tore out of the house at their arrival, her black hair streaming behind her, her face awash with joy.

Fazire, as was becoming a habit, stomped out of the house, his black hair a mess as if his hands had torn through it repeatedly and his face awash with fury.

Tash halted two feet away from her mother, lifted her arm and pointed at the street. "Look Mummy."

Curious, both Maxine and Lily turned to look. Lily saw her Peugeot sitting there forlornly looking like it was begging to be put out of its misery and taken to the scrap yard.

"Isn't it lush?" Tash asked.

Confused, Lily stared. The Peugeot, even if Lily had enough money to have it valeted, could never be described as "lush."

"What are you talking about, sweetling?" Maxine asked.

"Can't you see it? Look! Behind Mummy's car. Daddy had it delivered today. It's a present for Mummy. The keys are in the house."

Lily's eyes shifted behind her car and she saw a sleek, handsome, shining, sporty, blue Mercedes convertible.

"Dearie me," Maxine exhaled in an unusual understatement.

Lily felt as if she'd been running for miles flat out then all of a sudden she slammed into a wall. Her breath, quite suddenly, had been knocked right out of her.

"Dearie me, dearie me, dearie me," Tash sing-songed and danced to the car, threw her arms wide and then she actually hugged it. Just as quickly, she turned back to them and asked, "Isn't Daddy *the greatest?*"

Lily was saved from answering when she heard the phone ring.

"I shall get that," Fazire grumbled from behind them.

Lily was still recovering from the car as she followed Tash, who was skipping delightedly into the house in front of them.

"What are you going to do?" Maxine asked, her voice both concerned and filled with awe.

"I don't know," Lily answered and indeed she didn't. She couldn't return the car and she had to use it. Natasha had hugged the damned thing, for God's sake.

"It's for you." Fazire was walking down the hall, holding the phone between his thumb and forefinger like it was a putrid piece of rubbish. He handed it to her and Lily, still stunned by the car, put it to her ear.

"Hello," she greeted.

"Lily." It was Nate and his velvet voice saying her name caused her to shudder.

She didn't need this right now. She could barely string two thoughts together. She certainly couldn't go head to head with Nate.

"Nate," she replied.

Conflicting emotions tore through her. She didn't know whether she should rail at him, for he was using her daughter against her, there was no denying that. Or whether she should thank him because the bedroom was fantastic, the mattress firm but comfortable and so much better than her old one it wasn't comparable. And Lord knew she needed a car. Though a Mercedes was definitely over the top. Or lastly, whether she should tell him to call Alistair if he wanted to speak to her and then hang up on him, which was what she *should* do. She knew this because Alistair told her more than once, in fact at least a dozen times.

She thought he was calling to ask if she got the furniture, the car, maybe to have a bit of a chat.

She was wrong.

He'd called her because he was angry. His voice was rumbling with it and she could practically feel it through the phone line.

"Your solicitor told mine that you've put the seven million in trust for Natasha."

She hesitated.

Why this would make him angry, she could not fathom.

"Of course," she muttered.

"*I'll* take care of Natasha. I've already set up a trust for her," he bit out.

Lily stood in her hall, her lovely fairy lights twinkling up the stairs. She didn't see this.

Already stunned, she became immobile with shock. Her daughter, just over a week ago, had some clothes in her wardrobe, a decent amount of toys, a selection of expensive bears Maxine had given her and the love of three people.

Now she had two trust funds.

Lily had no chance to voice a reaction even if she'd been able to come up with one, for Nate carried on.

"That money was for you," he clipped.

"I . . ." she began. She hadn't known it was for *her*. She couldn't even believe it was for her. She wouldn't begin to know what to do with seven million pounds.

"Release it from the fund," he commanded.

Too astonished to think straight, she replied honestly, "I can't. It's impossible to touch until Tash comes of age and then only she can get to it."

He didn't hesitate. "I'll have more transferred tomorrow."

"No!" she cried instantly, horrified.

He ignored her outburst. "If you give *that* away, I'll have more transferred."

"Nate—"

"Do I make myself clear?" he demanded.

"I don't want your money." She was beginning to surface out of her stupor.

Really, what next? Was she going to come home to a personal jet parked on a floating runway in the Bristol Channel behind her house?

"Apparently I don't, but I will," Nate declared.

This, Lily recognized immediately, was not a threat. It was a promise.

Without a word of good-bye, he hung up on her.

As promised, another seven million pounds (she called her bank, Maxine made her) was transferred into her bank account the next day.

"What are you going to do?" Maxine asked again that next evening as they were closing Flash and Dazzle.

"I don't know," Lily mumbled again, and still she didn't.

Even though she did.

"Sweetling—" Maxine said cautiously.

"I think I'm getting a headache."

This was true. Although it wasn't one of her migraines, she was definitely getting a headache. She felt badly using that ploy, but she knew in her heart of hearts that Maxine wanted her settled and happy and not to be so alone anymore. And it helped that the person Lily would be doing that with was *impossibly* handsome, a romance novel hero come alive.

And at that moment, she couldn't face the discussion.

At the mere thought of one of Lily's headaches, Maxine backed off. "Get home, have yourself a nice bath and don't think of any of this."

Maxine kissed her cheek, got in her tiny, old Mini that she'd had painted pink and which she refused to part with even though it was a worse clunker than the Peugeot, and drove off.

Lily walked home and she tried not to think of "any of this," but it was impossible.

As Maxine instructed, she had a bath. During her bath she allowed the thoughts and worries to crowd into her mind.

Then she made a decision. It took less time than she expected but then again, there wasn't much to it.

Marry Nate or don't marry Nate.

There were only two options and really only one, when you got down to it.

Fazire, who was living in a temporary fog of happiness that no further grand gesture had been made by Nate (he didn't know about the money and Lily wasn't about to tell him), made fish fingers and mushy peas for dinner, Tash's favorite, though Lily detested it.

After dinner, Lily climbed to the top of the stairs to the unkempt room where they kept their computer. She'd had dreams when she bought the house of making that room her office and writing her bestselling novels there. It was at the back of the house and had a gorgeous view of the channel, the pier, Flat Holm and Steep Holm islands and, of course, the coastline of Wales.

However, the room was still dingy with old stained carpet on the floor and wood chip on the walls. Not a place to inspire a brilliant novel, to tell stories of war widows and genies, glamorous female photographers and their intense, loyal lovers.

She turned on the computer, got on the Internet, found the train times to London and planned her trip. She spent some time paying bills and filing away paperwork, just to keep her mind busy and to avoid the call she had to make.

With nothing left to do to delay the call, she phoned Alistair at home (he'd told her she could).

"*Are you out of your mind?*" he'd yelled when she'd told him her decision.

"Alistair, I'm thinking of Tash."

"Marry me," he returned instantly.

For the second time in two days, the wind was knocked out of her without a physical blow to cause it.

As if his words weren't sheer lunacy (she barely knew him!), Alistair carried on, "If you want stability for Natasha, marry me. I don't have as much money as McAllister but I want kids and you'll both be well provided for. And fuck knows there is no way in hell I'd ever let you go."

She was silent. She didn't know what to say. He'd asked her on a date but this was ridiculous.

"Alistair, Nate's her father," Lily reminded him.

"Two visits and you're jumping at the chance to get back to him," Alistair returned sharply.

At these words, she took a swift intake of breath.

"I may be paying your bills but you don't have the right to speak to me that way," she said quietly.

"Lily, I sat there listening to your story, listening to what he did, what he gave up, what you went through and . . ." he stopped himself, unable to go on. Then he said, "Think about it, Lily, just think about it. I'm very serious."

He *sounded* very serious, that was not in doubt.

Then he hung up.

Resolutely putting *that* conversation out of her mind for she had far too much to deal with as it was, she then called Maxine and told *her* the plan, a little worried at what Maxine would say.

Alistair was a solicitor, he had a head on his shoulders and he'd blurted out a marriage proposal. Maxine was a character. She might shoot to the moon.

And what Maxine said *did* shock her.

"I think that's wise," Maxine said softly and without a hint of drama.

Lily sighed her relief then admitted, "I think I'm mad."

"No matter what happens, Lily, you'll always have Tash, you'll always have Fazire and you'll always have me," Maxine replied.

Lily nodded, her heart moving directly to her throat so words could not come even if she had them to say.

Maxine, obviously, couldn't see her nod but she knew it was there. "I'll cover for you at the store tomorrow."

"Thanks Maxie," she whispered.

"It'll be okay, sweetling," Maxine returned. "This time, I think it'll be okay."

The headache she'd staved off with the bath came back with a vengeance so Lily went to bed early. She also did this in an effort to avoid telling Fazire of the plan. He'd begin floating, talking pompously, making grand statements or perhaps even dire threats, and she wasn't up for that.

The next morning, she kept it business as usual. It was getting close to the end of school and Tash was getting antsy for her summer holiday. Fazire walked her to school the mornings when Lily had to get to the store early, which she told them she had to do that day, and Lily watched them go.

Then she tore back into the house, not enough time to take off the little dress she had put on to bamboozle Fazire and Tash into thinking she was going to work. She would have preferred to wear something business-like and formal, like a suit, but she only had one of those and she'd already worn it during a meeting with Nate. Therefore, the dress would have to do.

It was a dress she would normally wear to the shop, a deep raspberry color with a crossed bodice and empire waist. It fit her body snugly all the way down the hem brushing her knees. She wore this with a pair of funky, strappy, matte-gold high-heeled sandals that Maxine had given her the year before for her birthday. They were fine to wile away the hours sitting behind the counter at the shop but there was no way she would travel to London or anywhere in those high heels. However, if she didn't leave immediately, she wouldn't make her train.

And if she didn't leave immediately, she might change her mind. And if she changed her mind, what kind of mother would she be?

She took the Mercedes, the first time she'd touched it, mainly because she didn't have the time to waste if the Peugeot decided to be ornery. She needed to get to London, talk to Nate and get back before anyone was the wiser.

She needed time and privacy to break the news to Fazire and to know from Nate that Fazire's place in their family was solid or there was no deal.

She resolutely did not think about how different the Mercedes handled to her Peugeot. She would have plenty of time to think about luxuries, about how her life was about to change, about many things.

At that moment, she needed to deal with her situation. She needed to take measures to protect her daughter and different measures to protect herself. And she needed to do it soon before she lost her nerve.

During her two-hour journey she thought of all the reasons *not* to marry Nate.

She barely knew him.

She wasn't likely to know him because he rarely spoke.

He'd promised her important things and had reneged on those promises within weeks.

He'd made her wish from Fazire, something she'd waited for breathlessly for a decade, a nightmare and this hurt Fazire and Lily never wanted Fazire to hurt. Ever.

He had two siblings that where, clearly, Satan's spawn.

He'd made her hope for a bright future and then did nothing when that was put in jeopardy, which caused that hope to be snatched away.

She was still somewhat frightened at his father's temper.

And, lastly, it was clear he would expect the marriage to be a *marriage* and all that entailed, not an arrangement.

Then she thought of the reasons *to* marry Nate.

He was Natasha's father and he obviously, even after only two visits, adored her.

And every child needed a father.

Lily loved Will more than she could express and missed him every day of her life. If she had the chance to have Will back alive, breathing, walking, talking, she'd jump at it. She'd even sacrifice a little bit of herself (even a lot) to have him back.

And she would do no less for Tash.

Further, Nate would expect the marriage to be a *marriage* which would mean, at least for a while, Lily would have a mate, a partner, someone to share the burden.

And then there were the other, definitely more pleasurable bits of being *married,* married to Nate. Bits, she could not deny, especially after the last two times they'd been alone together, that she very much wanted.

So she made her choice.

And she knew it was costing her. The stress and strain was sneaking up on her and she felt it.

As the train pulled into Paddington, she felt the pain coming.

The headache, luckily, was muted not roaring. But it was there and she knew what it heralded. She didn't find herself a snack for fear of it coming back later to haunt her if she vomited, but she took two pain pills and prayed she was wrong about her prediction.

She used precious money that a day ago she'd never have used but she was, of course, in high heels and trying to fight an imminent migraine, and she took a taxi instead of the Tube to Nate's offices.

He'd left a card with Tash, telling her to call him whenever she wanted. Lily didn't know if Tash had taken him up on this invitation but she found herself hoping that her daughter did. It would have been the perfect conversation as Tash rarely kept her mouth shut and Nate rarely opened his.

She gave the driver the address and concentrated on keeping the headache in abeyance.

However, as she walked through the door to the plush offices, she felt the nausea building in her stomach and had to fight it back.

In her head, she tried to plan her strategy at dealing with the migraine. She tried to time the meeting with Nate. Would it take ten minutes? Fifteen? An hour? She hoped not an hour. And she tried to assess the possibility of the pounding intensifying to the point she was made invalid, wondering if she could make it back home on the train.

As the pain intensified, she decided she could not. She would need to get a hotel room for a couple of hours just to rest and let the migraine run its course. She'd be queasy and not herself when it was over but she thought she'd likely be able to get home hopefully in time.

Lily had not told Nate she was coming. She wanted the element of surprise. She was giving in but he had to give in too. She wasn't stupid and she wasn't going to make the same mistake twice.

She wasn't moving from Clevedon. If he wanted Tash, he'd have to come to them.

She walked to the reception desk, which seemed an impossible distance from the front doors. The walls were some sort of highly-shined wood paneling that Lily found way too bright for her sensitive eyes to take. The reception desk was a huge semicircle made of the same wood that could easily have sat five. But only one very pretty woman sat behind it.

"Hi," Lily greeted, fighting back the sick feeling in her stomach. "I'm Lily Jacobs, I'm here to see Mr. McAllister."

The girl's eyes traveled the length of Lily but Lily barely noticed. She had to put her hand to the desk to steady herself as she saw the flashes in her eyes.

No, no, no, she thought, *not this soon.*

It was coming on quickly, far more quickly than normal. Most likely the strain of the last few weeks, all the shocks, the emotions.

"Is he expecting you?" the woman broke into her thoughts.

"No, but it's important. If he's free, I'd like to speak with him."

The girl watched Lily for a moment and asked, "Are you all right?"

With effort, Lily focused on her, "Just a headache."

She carefully assessed Lily and said, "I'll ring his office, won't be a second." Her voice was kind and then moments later she went on, "Hiya,

Jennifer, there's a Ms. Lily Jacobs here to see Mr. McAllister. She says she doesn't have an appointment but it's important."

Lily leaned more of her weight on her hand on the woman's desk. Soon, she knew, she might not be able to hold herself upright.

The receptionist was on hold and she put her hand over the mouthpiece and said to Lily, "Why don't you sit down? Jennifer's ringing him now, I'll . . ."

She stopped talking and Lily concentrated closely on her face. If she didn't she just might throw up. The flashing lights in her eyes were now zooming and the pain in her head was magnifying alarmingly.

The woman's eyes widened and her lips parted at whatever she heard on the phone.

Lily didn't care. She wasn't going to make it. She needed to find somewhere to lie down immediately. Somewhere quiet, cool and very, very dark.

"Mr. McAllister is coming down himself," the receptionist breathed as if the Lord Almighty had rung to invite her to a picnic. She was staring at Lily with new interest but she didn't like what she saw. "You're *not* okay," she accused but it was soft, thoughtful accusation, and she surged from her chair and made her way around the desk.

Lily moved to face the desk fully and she put both her hands on it to hold herself up. She dropped her head and started to take deep breaths. She felt the woman's hand on her back and tried not to flinch at the touch. Touch was not good.

"Is there something I can do?" she queried. "Do you need a glass of water? Let's get you seated."

Lily nodded, a seat would be good. Standing was bad, very, very bad.

She was beyond speech, beyond much of anything. The pain was at her left temple, unexplainable, indescribable, twisting pain.

"Lily." She heard the deep rumble of Nate's voice saying her name but she didn't turn.

"Mr. McAllister, I think something's wrong with her," the receptionist murmured.

Nate was at her side in less than a second. She felt him rather than saw him, her eyes were squeezed shut.

"Jesus, Lily," he muttered, his heavy, warm hand replacing his receptionist's at her back and his other hand went to her waist where he gently turned her to face him.

In doing so, she had to give a great deal of her weight to him as she took her hands from the desk. His body tensed at the unexpected burden and her hands moved to the sides of his waist to hang on for dear life.

He pulled her to him with one hand, bracing her weight against his body while his other hand went below her chin and tilted her face to his.

Unseeing and unfocused, she looked in the vague direction of his face.

"Nate, I think I need to lie down," she whispered.

He moved suddenly then and she cried out. Sudden movement was not good. *Any* movement was not good.

But then she was freed of supporting herself at all because she was lifted in his arms. She rested an arm around his shoulders, a hand on his chest and her head in the bend of his neck.

This was a far better place to be than standing.

"Call Jennifer," he barked, walking away. The walking away part wasn't so good. It was movement and she made a noise of protest in the back of her throat. At the sound of it, his strides lengthened. "Tell her I want my physician at my flat immediately. And I want her to phone Mrs. Roberts. Tell my mother Lily's here and she's ill."

They were going somewhere, she didn't know where but she hoped they got there soon or she'd vomit all over Nate's lovely suit.

"Lily, do you know what's wrong?" he asked.

"Headache," was all she could manage to say and this she said very quietly in hopes he'd catch the hint and stop talking so loudly. Or, better yet, at all.

"This isn't just a fucking headache," he responded tersely, his voice rough with concern.

She didn't reply. He was right for one and for another, she was loathe to open her mouth.

They'd arrived somewhere and he set her on her feet but didn't make her take her own weight as he held her against his body then shifted her and she was finally, blissfully sitting.

In a car.

In terror, she surged up and out of the car, slamming straight into him.

"No!" she cried and the pain shot though her head like a bullet. She winced, not knowing her already pale face became ashen.

"Lily, for God's sake, what's wrong?" She looked up at him, tried to focus through the excruciating pain and Nate looked at her face. "*Christ!*"

The word was an explosion. She winced at the noise of his voice.

"Migraine, Nate, I can't ride in a car. The motion will make me sick. I can't bear it. Can't endure the movement. I need to lie down. Now," she explained and the effort of words completely exhausted her.

"You have to get in the car, darling. We're in a car park. We'll be home soon," he assured her, his voice now back to gentle.

"The car park is fine." And at that moment, lost in the pain, it was true. She would have lain anywhere, just as long as it was down, it was quiet and she no longer had to move. "I'll just lie down by the car."

He didn't listen. He pushed her in the car, carefully but forcefully, and before she could surge out again, he buckled her in. He wasted no time getting in the driver's seat and setting them in motion.

Nate, just as in memory, drove hard and fast, this time out of necessity. Lily leaned forward, put her elbows on her knees and her head in her hands to keep it as still as possible.

But in the end, Lily lost her control of the pain and she had no idea she was keening, emitting low, frightening, animal-like noises of sheer agony.

NINETEEN

Nate

NATE CARRIED LILY UP to his penthouse, the entire time she kept her head pressed into his neck with such force he felt his pulse beat against her.

And she hadn't stopped making that horrifying noise.

The elevator opened at the top floor, his floor as he owned the whole of it.

As if waiting for the sound of the elevator, the lone door in the small but opulent hall opened and Laura stood there. The minute she saw them, or more to the point heard Lily, the blood drained out of his mother's face.

"Oh my God," Laura breathed.

Without hesitation, Nate walked past her, through the living room, down the hall and directly to his bedroom. Beside the bed, he put Lily on her feet but kept her weight braced against him.

"What's wrong?" Laura asked but Nate didn't answer, he was looking at Lily and she was wincing.

"No light," Lily whispered.

Immediately Nate ordered his mother, "Shut the drapes."

"Pardon?" Laura asked.

"The drapes!" he clipped, his voice impatient and curt.

Laura ran to the windows as Nate's hand went to the zipper at the back of Lily's dress and tugged it down gently.

"What can we do?" he asked Lily softly.

"No light," she repeated as he finished with her zipper and carefully guided the skirt of her dress over her hips. She knew what he was doing and she lifted her arms in submission but he could tell the movement took great effort. "No noise. Noise, very bad. Cool, wet flannel," she finished.

The room went dark as Laura closed the drapes on the floor-to-ceiling windows that lined one side of the room. She then rushed to them while Nate pulled the dress free of Lily's arms, all the while bearing her weight against the length of his body.

"I'll get something for her to wear," Laura offered, taking the dress from his hand and throwing it across the bottom of the bed.

"No clothes. Can't bear it," Lily muttered and Nate's hand moved to the clasp of her bra and deftly undid it while Laura gave up on her offered errand and leaned forward and pulled back the covers to the bed.

Nate slipped the bra off her shoulders.

"Get a cool flannel," he ordered his mother and Laura ran to the bathroom.

He set Lily in bed and went to work on her shoes, which, he decided with annoyance, regardless of how sexy they were, could be used by banks to keep money safe, their straps were so complicated. Once he had both off and dropped them to the floor, he pulled the covers over her.

"Do you have any medication?" he asked.

She shook her head and flinched then pressed it to the pillows as she'd pressed it to his neck while he carried her up to the penthouse.

"Nothing works," she answered.

"The doctor's coming," Nate told her as he sat on the edge of the bed and pulled her hair gently away from her neck.

"Won't help," she mumbled.

He felt a frustrated fury surge through him. He realized vaguely that it had been under the surface since seeing her leaning helplessly against his receptionist's desk, but it had finally managed to get loose.

He controlled it, but barely.

"Lily, tell me what I can do," he urged.

"You're doing it," she whispered, pressing her head deeper into the pillows.

Laura came back to the room and handed Nate the flannel. He folded it and pressed it against Lily's forehead and she made a noise, this time not of pain.

"Yes," she breathed in such a rush of relief, it was as if he'd given her the elixir of life. She lifted her hand and pressed the flannel into her forehead with such force he could see the color of the flesh of her long, graceful fingers changing from pink to a harsh blush mingled with white.

The doorbell rang and Laura murmured, "I'll get it."

Lily whispered after Laura had scurried from the room, "Call Fazire, please."

"Of course," Nate assured her quietly.

"Tell him not to come."

Nate didn't respond.

"He'll want to come but tell him you'll take care of me." Her eyes fluttered open and slid to him but her head didn't move. "Tell him *I* said that."

Nate should have reacted to the importance her words, *wanted* to, but at that moment he couldn't. He heard his personal physician, Dr. Sims, coming into the room with Laura.

Lily closed her eyes and Nate rose from the bed to allow the doctor access.

"What's happened?" Dr. Sims asked.

"She says it's a migraine," Nate replied, his words clipped.

"Does she have them often?" the physician went on.

Nate couldn't respond because he didn't know. And this caused the control he had on his fury to slip a notch. If they'd had the last eight years together, he *would* have known.

"Yes." It was Lily who answered.

"How often?" Dr. Sims asked her gently, taking her pulse.

"Not often."

"Do you know your triggers?" he inquired, his voice soft and low.

"Stress," she answered and Nate's fury mingled immediately with a surge of guilt, which caused it to slip another notch. "Sometimes my period."

"Are you on your cycle now?" Dr. Sims asked.

"It's coming. The pain only comes just before," she replied.

"Let's get you sorted." The doctor glanced at Nate then to Laura. His meaning clear, they were to leave.

"I'm not going," Nate stated firmly.

Dr. Sims moved away and motioned Nate to follow. This he did but halted before they even came close to the door.

"Migraine sufferers need quiet, darkness, rest. I'll give her something to help her sleep. We'll talk outside but now she needs to be left alone and we need to get her to sleep. It's the best thing, sometimes the only thing for it."

Nate stared at Lily still pressing the flannel to her head and then glanced at the doctor.

Wishing only to speed the process of her recovery, he nodded and walked out of the room. Laura had already gone.

In the living room Laura was gathering her things. She heard rather than saw Nate come into the vast room.

"I'll go to the shops, get her a nightgown, a change of clothes . . ." Laura needed something to do and she had nothing therefore she was creating busy work.

Nate stopped her hasty exit. "I need you to call Fazire. Tell him she's here and she's not well. Tell him that I'm taking care of her. Please tell him Lily said that."

At the words "I need you," Laura's head jerked around. At the word "please" her face melted and her eyes began to shimmer with tears.

Nate had never said the former to her in his life. And the latter he rarely said to anyone.

She immediately dropped her bag and rushed toward the kitchen saying, "I'll do that now." Then she stopped and swung around. "What's the number?"

He smiled at his mother, feelings of immense gratitude at her being there when he needed her, when Lily needed her, warring with his anger. Nate told her the number he'd only used once but, as per usual, he'd memorized.

She muttered it over and over to herself as she ran to the kitchen.

Nate stopped himself from getting a drink, which he very much needed. He couldn't get Lily's appalling whimpering out of his head and he couldn't lose his fury at his feeling of powerlessness. That was not a feeling he was used to and he very much did not like it.

But he couldn't have a drink. It was before noon and furthermore, Lily might need him.

Laura came back in the room. "Fazire says he wants Lily to call him when she's better. He wants her to know he'll take care of Natasha. And he wanted to know why she was here," she reported.

Nate pulled his hand through his hair and then stopped it at his neck to squeeze away some of the tension that had settled there. "I've no idea why she's here. She showed up at my office and by the time I arrived at reception, she was barely able to stand."

When his secretary had told him a Lily Jacobs was waiting in reception, he'd immediately thought it was a good sign. She had been consistently adamant they talk through their solicitors. Her solicitor was a pit bull, constant demands, constant threats and Nate was told in no uncertain terms (through his own solicitors of course) to stay away from Lily.

This Nate ignored.

Lily's arrival in London was an unexpected surprise.

He knew he'd broken through on the first day with her. She responded to him and what's more, Tash had, spectacularly.

He also knew by the way Tash talked, a great deal, about what her mother had said about him, that Lily had been pining for a "dead" Nate for years.

And finally, Nate definitely knew that she'd gotten lost in him the last time they were together. One didn't get as angry as she was without feeling *something*.

Nate knew a fair few things about anger. There was the mean kind and there was the emotional kind.

Lily didn't have a mean bone in her body. Lily's anger was emotional, something deep inside her driving it. And whatever that something was drove her to react to his kiss, his touch, in her familiar, uninhibited way.

That something, whatever it was, at this point was everything to Nate.

Nate could work with something.

Furthermore, with one look at their daughter's hopeful, happy face, she had given in to a family dinner. He'd known eight years ago she'd never break up a family and he was betting on the fact that hadn't changed.

When his secretary had told Nate she was there, he'd wasted no time in going to her. But, regardless of this, the reason for her visit was a still mystery.

It could be a yes or it could be a no.

Nate was counting on a yes.

He dropped his arm and shook off his thoughts. He'd know soon enough and Nate was a patient man.

He watched as Laura glanced at the hall that led to his bedroom then back at Nate.

"Do you think Natasha sees her like that?" she asked quietly.

Nate thought of his daughter and the coat of Teflon that Lily had obviously painstakingly crafted around Natasha to ward off anything that would affect their daughter's high spirits and good humor. They had little, but Natasha needed for nothing and had no idea what she was missing or, indeed, from her personality, any of her mother's struggles or sacrifices.

He doubted seriously Lily would expose her to what he'd just witnessed.

He shook his head in answer to his mother's question.

It was then the doctor entered the room and walked toward them.

"How is she?" Laura asked, her voice coated with concern.

"I gave her a mild sedative. Unfortunately, there's not much we can do but wait it out. She says they go away after she's had a sleep. It's just finding sleep through the pain."

"I'll check on her." Laura moved toward the hall but stopped at the doctor's next words and turned back.

"No, don't. She needs peace and most of all, she needs quiet. She has to fight this on her own. She told me they only last a few hours, she just needs sleep."

"What causes it?" Laura asked.

"A variety of things." He was efficiently packing his bag. He'd been called away from a hefty patient schedule. However, when Nate McAllister called, anyone who got the call instantly did his bidding, even general practitioners.

Laura's tone was coated with concern when she queried, "Is it . . . could it be something serious? Something—"

"Mrs. Roberts, it's likely nothing," Dr. Sims assured. "She says she's been suffering them since she was a child. If you're worried, get her to see a neurologist, get an MRI."

Nate spoke for the first time since the doctor came into the room. "Set it up."

Dr. Sims shifted his surprised eyes to Nate. "I'm sorry?"

"Refer her to a neurologist," he ordered.

"She might have already seen one. Sometimes the pain is stubborn and they might not be able to tell you much. She obviously knows her triggers, how to cope."

"Do it," Nate clipped out.

At his tone and the hard, set look on Nate's face, Dr. Sims nodded.

"Tomorrow," Nate demanded.

"Of course," the physician finished, settling his bag, "She should be fine in a few hours. If anything happens, call me."

Then he was gone.

Laura was back at her handbag, gathering her things.

"I'll do a little shopping. She should stay with you tonight," Laura stated decisively. "I'll make sure she's comfortable."

His mother walked to Nate and gave him a kiss on the cheek and then she too was gone.

At these sudden departures, Nate found he had time to think.

However, Nate didn't want to think. He didn't want to think of Lily alone and battling pain in his bed. He didn't want to think of Lily suffering that way again, much less that she'd done it since she was a child. He didn't want to think how little he knew her even though he remembered even the most infinitesimal detail of every moment he'd shared with her.

Therefore, he didn't think.

He phoned his office and had them courier work to him but told them under no circumstances to ring the doorbell. He took off his suit jacket and his tie, loosening the buttons of his shirt at his throat. He quietly checked on Lily twice, both times, thankfully, she was sleeping. His mother arrived several hours later with enough glossy shopping bags so that Lily could stay a month, much less a night.

Through this time, Nate kept his mind on his work and he waited. And he kept absolute silence. And he kept careful, deliberate control on his fury.

Hours later, he walked away from the dining room table where he'd set up his temporary office rather than working in his study, which was on the other side of the apartment and too far away from Lily. He went into the bedroom to find a change of clothes, hoping Lily would now sleep through any noise.

When he arrived, the bed was empty. Lily was gone.

He stood stock still in the door, a strange sense of unease filling him even though he knew she couldn't have really gone.

Then he heard a noise and his head jerked around.

She was wearing his dressing gown and standing in the doorway of the bathroom. She was leaning against the doorjamb, the balls of one foot pressing against the top of the other.

He remembered her standing exactly like that eight years ago. Nate had remembered that vision of her, their first night together, time and again over the years.

That once painful memory sliced through him. If Lily was in London to tell him "no" then he'd have this memory to add to his tortuous inventory.

With determination, he set that thought aside.

"Are you feeling better?" he asked in a quiet voice.

She nodded, pushed away from the doorjamb and walked to the bed.

He walked toward her and while he did so, he spoke. "Is the pain gone?"

"Yes. I just feel weird afterwards. Exhausted but able to function. I don't know. It feels like I've been in some kind of battle."

She stopped by the bed, leaned over and grabbed her dress. He stopped by her, reached out and gently pulled her dress from her fingers.

"You have," he stated matter-of-factly.

She was staring at her dress in his hand and, at his words, her eyes lifted to his.

"I haven't. It's no big thing. It's just a headache." She was trying to pass it off as if it was nothing.

Nate never forgot anything but even if he had that luxury, he'd never forget the sound of her keening.

"Trust me, you have. I saw you do it."

Clearly not wishing to argue, she changed the subject and asked quietly, "Can I have my dress please?"

He tossed it on the bed deliberately out of her immediate reach. She watched it land and made no comment. It was then Nate noted that she looked slightly dazed.

"Laura bought you a nightgown, or, if the bags in the other room are any indication, twenty of them," he told her.

A ghost of her quirky smile played about her lips and Nate registered it in his mind as his body instantly reacted to the sweet, familiar sight of it.

"Laura does like to shop, doesn't she?" Lily whispered as if to herself and her words sounded almost fond.

She didn't expect an answer to her question and Nate, unable to control himself any longer, pulled her cautiously toward him and slid his arms around her.

Her head tilted back but, surprisingly, she didn't resist his embrace. Instead, she lifted her hands to rest on his biceps.

"Are you all right?" she asked, her eyes peering closely at him through the darkness of the room.

"No, I'm not all right." He surprised himself by answering honestly.

She sucked in her breath sharply then inquired, "What's the matter? Is it Tash? Fazire?"

He interrupted her. "It's you."

"Me?" Her eyes widened.

At her response, he let out a low, humorless laugh that caused her to come closer to him, her face changed as worry filled it.

"Nate?"

"Why are you here?" he asked suddenly.

She wasn't following and her worry turned to confusion. "Here?"

"In London. Why did you come to see me?"

Again, her face changed, this time to a sort of sadness.

"Nate, I think you're changing the subject." Her voice was so soft, if she was any further away than in his arms, he wouldn't have heard her.

He didn't answer.

"You said you aren't all right," she reminded him. "Why aren't you all right?"

He still didn't answer. Something stopped him. He didn't know what it was but whatever it was always stopped him. It stopped him from speaking, stopped him from letting anyone close, stopped him from trusting anyone with his thoughts, his feelings, anything about him.

Even Lily.

She waited. Her patience thinned and he watched it in silence.

Then she exploded, "Damn it, Nate, talk to me! What's the matter?"

At her outburst, the sudden loudness of her voice after he'd placed such a high price on silence because of her pain, not to mention the fact that he felt, after the episode of hours before, as if she could shatter into a million pieces and be lost to him again but this time forever, he admitted tersely, "You scared the hell out of me."

Her face changed again, this time to understanding. And she didn't pull away from him. He thought she would at his admission but she didn't. Her fingers tightened on his arms reassuringly.

"Oh, Nate, it's just a headache," Lily whispered.

"Stop saying that, Lily. It isn't just a headache. I've never seen anything like that in my life."

She, to his complete astonishment, tried to tease. "Then you must have lived a very sheltered life."

"No, Lily, I haven't," Nate returned instantly, each word clipped and she immediately realized her mistake, but he didn't allow her to dwell on it or remonstrate herself for it. Instead he informed her, "You have an appointment with a neurologist tomorrow."

"I do?" This time, her expressive face filled with surprise.

And it was then, unusually belatedly, that it dawned on him that her face was expressive again. Her guard was down. She was standing in his arms lightly pressed against his body and not trying to pull away.

She was talking to him and hadn't once mentioned the name Alistair. His arms tightened, bringing her deeper into his body.

"Yes, you do," he said softly, feeling it rather than knowing it. The reason why she was there.

"Why? There's nothing they can do. I've been to doctors," she told him.

"Humor me," he returned.

"Nate—"

"Do it for Tash," he muttered, bringing his hand up to tuck a heavy sheaf of her extraordinary hair behind her ear.

"I don't have to, Nate. I've had the headaches since I was a little girl, just a few then. They came more often when I started my period. Every other month before my cycle and any time I got overstressed."

"Lily?"

"Yes?"

"This discussion is over," he stated flatly.

She stared at him, her expressive face turning rebellious and he realized then how much he missed her.

He knew he missed her. He knew it. He'd lived with it for years, most especially the last couple of weeks.

But now that she was back, now that she was truly Lily, her smile quirked, her face telling him exactly what she was thinking before she opened her mouth to speak, he felt her loss like a blow.

And her return like a blessing.

He bent his head to brush his lips against hers and she only stiffened slightly in his arms.

Progress.

"Let's talk about why you're in London," he suggested in a tone that said it was anything but a suggestion.

"Can I get dressed?"

"No."

She gasped.

Then, a moment later, she sighed.

"Can we do it in another room?" she asked huffily.

"No."

"Nate—"

"Now *you're* avoiding the subject."

Her lips puckered and her eyes slid away from him.

Any residual fury at his ineffectiveness in the face of her pain ebbed out of him as he sensed victory.

"Before I say what I'm going to say." Her eyes came forward and her hands came between them to fidget together against their chests, "I'm going to warn you that I have certain conditions."

His arms moved from around her, he took hold of her hands in his and he pulled them gently behind her back, pressing her soft body fully against his.

"Nate!" she exclaimed.

"Just say what you have to say Lily."

"Let go of my hands."

She was avoiding the subject.

"You were fidgeting," he informed her.

"So?"

"It was distracting."

"Trust me, you'll listen to what I have to say."

"It wasn't distracting *me*. It was distracting *you*."

Her head jerked sharply, she stared at him a moment and then the quirky smile played about her lips but didn't come out in full force.

"You're too perceptive for your own good," she grumbled but didn't mean it. There was a hint of admiration to her words, and at any other moment in his life he would have allowed himself to feel pleasure at it.

Not at this moment, however. This moment was too precious to allow his mind to wander to anything but her.

"Lily." His voice held a warning.

"What now?" she asked.

"You've something to say?" he prompted.

"All right, fine," she mumbled but then didn't say anything.

He waited. She kept her quiet.

He waited. She puckered her lips and slid her eyes away again.

He waited. She slid her eyes back and looked at him, opened her mouth then closed it again.

"Lily," Nate repeated then he couldn't help himself. He felt his body begin to shake with laughter.

"Are you laughing?" she groused, locking on to another subject to dodge the one she was avoiding.

He released her wrists but held her where she was with his arms still about her. He bent his head and buried his face in the fragrant hair at her neck.

"Just tell me you'll marry me," he demanded against her neck, his voice filled with amusement, his body shaking with it and something very close to the feeling he'd had when his daughter first threw her arms around him stole into his heart.

"I'll marry you," she whispered and his arms tightened like steel bands.

Something powerful and innate surged through him, something enormous and profound and unbelievably pleasurable. Better than the most intense orgasm he'd had (a climax he'd had with Lily, he remembered it clearly, the fifth time they'd made love).

"But I have conditions," she informed him.

He lifted his head and stared down at her already deciding he'd be willing to give anything.

Almost.

"We're not moving to London," she stated. "You'll have to move to the house in Clevedon."

Without hesitation Nate replied, "Done."

Lily seemed surprised at his quick agreement and it threw her off for a moment but then she recovered. "You have to accept Fazire, no matter what."

This time he hesitated and she opened her mouth to speak but before she could say a word, he bit out, "Fine."

"And he lives with us."

Nate nodded. He'd accept her strange friend Fazire. He'd live with the entire British Army camped in his living room if it meant being with her, having her in his bed and having his daughter just down the hall.

"Say it," she demanded.

"Fine," he allowed.

"And if anything ever happens to me, he stays with Tash as long as Tash wants him."

Nate watched her closely. He found this demand more than a little strange, as if Fazire was a possession to pass along.

Correctly reading from her face this meant a great deal to her, he agreed with another nod.

At that she relaxed against him.

"That's it?" he inquired, finding himself relieved. She could have asked for more, much more, diamonds and pearls, jet-set holidays, mountain chalets in the Alps.

But she didn't ask for any of that and this time she nodded.

"Now we'll discuss my condition," he told her.

Lily tensed again immediately. "What conditions?"

"Not conditions, condition," Nate replied. "I only have one."

She stared at him, her widened eyes had narrowed.

Nate carried on, "No more children. If you want another baby, we'll adopt."

Her eyes instantly grew wide again. "Nate, it was just a bad pregnancy. There's no reason I can't—"

He cut her off, "Just a bad pregnancy like your migraines are just headaches?"

Her mouth snapped shut and she pursed her lips.

Then he asked suddenly, "Are you on birth control?"

"No."

This announcement shocked him. "Do you use another form of birth control?"

She was beginning to squirm and looking more than a little uncomfortable.

He couldn't care less about her discomfort.

"Answer me, Lily," Nate demanded, giving her a mild shake.

"No."

"Why the hell not?" he snapped.

She glared at him but didn't answer.

"Answer me." Nate was beginning to get angry.

She'd graduated from Oxford, for Christ's sake, she wasn't stupid.

She'd nearly died during her last pregnancy, hell, she *did* die. She should be protecting herself.

He hated the idea of another man touching her, especially since, in the beginning, she had only been his. But as much as he detested it, he understood he had to let go of that now. She was back, Natasha was theirs, his entire focus was on their future.

"Did they use it?" he asked, not exactly thrilled about talking about her lovers but he had to know.

Consideration to contraceptives wasn't something he'd taught her in the brief time they'd had together. Indeed, he'd avoided it with calculated purpose, but he could imagine she'd learned a great deal in eight years.

"Who?" she queried, looking mystified.

"The men you've been with."

Even in the dark room, he saw her face pale.

She kept her silence for a moment and then said, "Nate, I really don't think it's any of your—"

He shook her again this was slightly more than mild.

"Nate!"

"Lily, you're going to be my wife. Considering my condition on our impending nuptials, this subject would eventually come up."

"I didn't agree to your condition," she told him.

"You aren't getting pregnant again," he retorted.

"Really, I—"

He interrupted her. "We'll get you to a GP tomorrow as well and get something arranged."

He had decided to give up. She was definitely more stubborn than he remembered and there were other ways he wished to spend these moments, vastly more enjoyable ways, *not* arguing about birth control and *definitely not* thinking about her other lovers.

Even so, he couldn't stop himself from muttering, "It's stunning, someone as obviously intelligent as you would be so immensely dense about protecting herself with contraceptives."

She stiffened in his arms. "I am not dense."

"Considering the fact you nearly died in childbirth, yes, I'd say you were dense," Nate bit out curtly because the subject was so important, considering what happened with Natasha, and Lily's nonchalance about something that important intensely annoyed him. Therefore he instantly decided he liked the idea of arguing about birth control.

"I hardly need to fill my body with pills or be fitted with ... with ... some sort of apparatus if I wasn't taking anyone to my bed!" she snapped, her eyes firing and a blush so fierce he could see it in the dark crawling up her cheeks.

His body stilled and his arms tightened. "What did you say?"

"You heard me."

"All right, I'll ask another question. What did you mean?"

She seemed at a loss for a moment. Clearly her agitation and her recovery from the migraine were slowing her processes. Then she caught up.

"You're too smart for your own good, do you know that?" she inquired irritably.

"Don't change the subject and answer the question."

She looked skyward and for the first time she pressed against his arms to get away.

"This is mortifying," she told the ceiling.

At that, he knew.

He couldn't believe it but he knew. It was nearly as unbelievable as the fact that she hadn't been touched when he first had her. This was impossible to believe.

"There haven't been any others," he stated and her eyes flew to him. "Have there?" he asked softly.

She hesitated for a moment and then she said, "I know you think I'm the most, well, that I . . ." She made a strange, frustrated noise then burst out, "There just wasn't time!"

He realized she was making excuses like this news was a bad thing. Like this wasn't a gift from the gods, like her return, like Natasha, like the fact she'd just agreed to marry him.

"Lily." His voice was low with meaning but she was beginning a roll.

"There was always something. When Tash was young, I was recovering then after that I was just too tired. Then there was work, laundry, Tash, Fazire, the damned *car*. I mean, there wasn't *time*."

Nate tried and failed to cut in patiently by murmuring, "Lily."

She talked over him. "And then there's finding someone. I mean, Nate, there are a lot of losers out there. *A lot.* You would just not *believe.*"

She was underlining her words again like he remembered she'd do when she was agitated. It was so very *Lily*, not meek, mild, world-weary Lily, but *his* Lily, spirited and hilarious.

Nate's body started to shake with laughter and relief and what he'd felt before, something he didn't recognize but now he knew was triumph mingled liberally with joy.

"Lily." His voice was suffused with mirth.

She ignored him and her eyes rolled to the ceiling. "And some of the things they *said*. One guy even told me I had nice breath! He complimented *my breath* as a pick up line. *Please* tell me you've never done that." Her gaze came back to him at her query, she finally felt his body shaking and her eyes narrowed. "What's funny?"

He decided he didn't want to read her thoughts in the darkened room and with effort he let her go but laced his fingers in hers. He walked to the window, dragging her with him and threw open the drapes. Then he immediately pulled her back into his arms.

"I asked, what's funny?" she demanded.

He smiled down on her and her face changed when she saw it. He noted some of the old expression she used to wear when she looked at him shone through and the joy he was feeling intensified exponentially.

"Darling, as much as I hate the thought of you going it alone with Natasha for eight years, I hate the thought of you with anyone else more. So, I hope you'll forgive me when I tell you I'm glad you haven't shared your beautiful body with anyone but me."

"Well!" she huffed, clearly at a loss for what to say and she turned her face away from him so he couldn't see her expression.

He tilted it right back with a hand at her jaw and he saw confusion in her eyes, confusion and relief. "Now that *that's* out in the open, do you agree to my condition?"

Again she looked adorably confused when he switched to an earlier subject and he noted for future reference that she was foggy after a migraine.

Then her expression cleared.

She sighed. Hugely.

"I suppose," she gave in.

His arms tightened and his head descended.

"If we can adopt," she interrupted his descent.

"We'll adopt," he said against her lips.

"Okay," she whispered, her body melted into his, and finally, gratefully, he kissed her.

TWENTY

Lily

LILY WOKE UP ALONE in Nate's colossal bed.

She'd never seen a bed so huge in her entire life. It was even bigger than the bed he'd bought *her* and she thought that was the biggest bed she'd ever seen.

She listened for a moment to the silence in the enormous room and wondered where Nate was. She rolled languorously to her side to see if there was an alarm clock and she saw it was nearly nine thirty.

She blinked at it in surprise. She hadn't slept that late in years. Lily didn't even think she had the capacity to sleep later than seven o'clock.

She rolled onto her back and contemplated the ceiling and the softness of Nate's sheets, which were otherworldly soft.

Nate, she realized, if he was anything like he used to be, must be at work.

She threw the covers back and headed to the bathroom while thinking rather contentedly about the night before and, especially, more than contentedly, that morning.

Surprisingly, Nate hadn't made love to her after they'd agreed to get married. He'd finally kissed her (after their mortifying exchange about contraception that she did not want to remember, ever).

But that was it.

Well, not *it* exactly as he kissed her a great deal throughout the evening, held her from behind and nuzzled her neck as she was talking to Fazire (luckily Fazire knew she was usually disoriented after a migraine and thus didn't press her as to why she was, all of a sudden, at Nate's place in London) and linked his fingers in hers while they ate the food he'd had delivered.

Later, they'd finally gone to bed, Lily wearing one of the nightgowns Laura had bought her.

Laura didn't purchase twenty nightgowns. She'd purchased three, four sets of underwear, two outfits, three pairs of shoes and two huge bags full to the brim with toiletries and cosmetics of every size, shape and color. Laura could shop for England in the Olympics and win the gold medal, hands down.

Once in bed, Nate had pulled her back to his front and wrapped his arm around her waist. Then he'd pressed his face in her hair just like he used to do, and in that moment Lily had given herself the momentary luxury to allow the eight years simply to melt away.

She laid in bed waiting.

Nothing.

"Um . . . Nate?" she'd whispered into the dark room.

"Mm?" The murmur sounded behind her and his arm tightened about her waist.

She didn't know what to say. So she said, "Never mind."

She realized she was slightly disappointed. Then she realized she was more than slightly disappointed. She hadn't exactly gone there to throw herself at him, just piece her family back together. But they *had* just agreed to pledge their troth. Certainly some sort of celebratory consummation effort was in order.

"You're not yourself," Nate said softly.

"What?" Lily asked.

"I'll make love to you when you're recovered. Right now, you're still not yourself."

"Oh," she whispered.

Something about that made her heart flutter. She didn't understand completely why but she felt it was important.

"Go to sleep, darling," he murmured into her hair.

She decided she liked it when he called her darling. She knew she shouldn't but that didn't change the fact that she did.

Exhausted from the day's events, in fact the events of the past two weeks, and in his comfortable bed with his warmth behind her, she fell into a deep sleep the like of which she had not had for years.

She woke what seemed a year later, rested, relaxed, contented . . . and aroused.

"Nate?" she mumbled sleepily.

Apparently Nate had decided she was herself again, for at the sound of her voice he took his hand away, which had been up the hem of her nightgown, cupped at her breast with two fingers not so idly fondling her nipple. He flipped her on her back and in an instant he became her entire world. His hands, his mouth, his tongue, they were everywhere and the vague sense of relaxed, contented arousal boiled away in seconds as hot desire flooded through her.

She gloried in it, had been waiting years for it and now she knew it was finally to be hers.

Within minutes he had her meager clothing off her body and the heat surging through her like a burn. She was moaning his name, her hands in his hair as his mouth was at first tormenting one breast then the other then down, down . . .

He stopped and his head jerked up, dislodging her hands. Abruptly his body fell to the side, its weight coming off her and his immense heat leaving her made Lily feel suddenly cold.

Disoriented, she tilted her chin down to see what had stopped him and her body stilled at what she saw.

Nate was lying on his side, up on his elbow and his eyes were riveted to her belly.

It had been eight years since anyone had seen her naked and in the heat of the moment, the thrill of the sensations, she'd forgotten all about it. She wasn't the biggest fan of her body, in fact, she mostly disregarded it. It did what it was told most of the time and that's all she required of it.

Now, she felt vulnerable and embarrassed, especially that he was looking at her stomach. It wasn't precisely her favored area of her body (not that she had a favored part of her body).

Lily's flushed face started to burn and she looked down to see what caught his attention and saw the scar from Tash's C-section.

It wasn't hideous but it *was* a scar and scars were never very attractive. She saw his hand reach out toward it and she grabbed it in embarrassment before he could touch her. She wanted to throw the covers over her but his eyes moved to hers.

The instant they locked on hers, she became mesmerized by them. They were glowing with something she couldn't read but whatever it was made her forget her embarrassment entirely.

"Tash?" he asked, his voice husky.

She nodded, wondering what he was thinking.

Then to her astonishment, his head bent and his lips touched the scar at one end and slowly ran along the length of it.

"Nate," she whispered.

Witnessing his tender gesture, the tears suddenly came, clogging her throat, making her voice croaky.

And then she couldn't think of crying, couldn't think of his tenderness because he'd shifted his body and his head was going down even more, his mouth finding her between her legs and all she could think about was what he was doing to her, what he was making her feel and the absolute beauty of it.

He made her climax with his mouth, and while she was in the throes of it, the waves of pleasure sliding through her body, he surged up and filled her.

She cried out his name as he drove into her, not being gentle in the slightest, his thrusts were sheer, controlled violence. It was a possession, a claiming, and his hand came between them, went straight to the highly sensitized core of her even before she'd completed her orgasm, bringing another one instantly.

She was panting, clawing at his back, mindlessly whispering his name between breaths, wrapping her legs around his hips as the glorious sensations tore through her at having him again. She loved the feeling of him slamming into her just like she'd dreamed so many nights and even daydreamed during the light hours.

And finally, when she was certain she'd live for eternity in the heady spasm of a climax, his hand came from between them, both his hands lifted her hips and he drove into her one last time, moaning his release into her mouth.

After, Lily lay there, the weight of Nate pressed against her, his face buried in her neck, her limbs wrapped lovingly around him, and she allowed herself the tiniest moment of joy that they finally, after years and years, had the beauty of what they used to share back.

He lifted his head and his mouth came to hers.

"Sweeter than I remembered," he murmured against her lips and she was so intoxicatingly spent she could do nothing but nod.

Lily didn't remember that he'd told her that he *did* remember everything. Therefore, she had no idea what his words meant.

It wouldn't have mattered anyway. She'd just had a multiple orgasm during a coupling with a lover, not just a lover, her dream man who she thought had been dead for eight years.

She was beyond processing the importance of murmured statements after climax.

Instead, she immediately began to drift to sleep. Her eyes were closed and Nate was stroking the hair away from her temple. She thought that felt nice.

"Lily?" She heard his soft, deep voice still rough with desire.

"Just going to rest my eyes a bit," she mumbled something her grandmother Sarah used to say before napping. She wrapped her arms and legs tighter around him, he was still on top of her, still inside of her and she nuzzled her face in his neck.

On her trip to dreamland, she felt Nate's body shake with amusement and normally she would have found this irritating but she was, at that moment, way, *way* beyond irritation.

It had, Lily thought as she took a shower in his shower cubicle that could have easily fit three (or even more) people, been a little slice of heaven. As she scrubbed the peony scented bath gel that Laura bought her into her skin with the fluffy sponge Laura also bought her, she looked around Nate's state-of-the-art bathroom (it took her five minutes to figure out how to work the taps in the shower) and distractedly realized it was bigger than Natasha's bedroom.

This luxuriousness brought other things to mind.

Marriage to Nate, Lily thought, might not be that bad.

Firstly, Natasha would have her father.

Secondly, Natasha would learn how to ride a horse, indeed, at the rate Nate was going, she would likely own one by the end of the week.

Thirdly, perhaps, just perhaps he *would* take care of them.

He certainly dropped everything to take care of Lily yesterday. She'd seen his work spread across his massive, twelve-seat dining room table last night. She could imagine what a penthouse apartment cost not to mention being able to throw around fourteen million pounds in a week, buy her a Mercedes *and* whatever Nate had arranged for Tash's trust fund.

Eight years ago, he'd worked relentless twelve-hour days and even, sometimes, made business calls to different time zones in the evenings. It likely wasn't so easy for Nate McAllister to drop everything because the wayward mother of his child happened by for a surprise visit and then had a medical semi-emergency.

She stepped out of the shower and toweled off, wrapping the thick towel around her hair and sorting through Laura's various tubs and bottles. It was at least a two year supply for Lily, even if she could have afforded those brands, which she couldn't.

While Lily lotioned her body and went about putting on her face, she also resolutely set aside *how* Nate took care of her yesterday. She didn't think of his soft voice or the intense feeling flowing through it when he spoke. She didn't think of him carrying her urgently to the car or pressing a flannel to her head or urging her to tell him how he could help. And lastly, she tried not to think of his admission that she scared the hell out of him and what that might mean.

They would be husband and wife so they could be mother and father to Tash, a family whole at last, just as Lily had while growing up. Lily was happy to accept all that came with it, the companionship (if it lasted), the lovemaking (which was *very* nice and always had been), the security (clearly Nate could take care of them financially, they most likely would never have to worry again about the fridge breaking down and what that might mean to their grocery budget).

She would let him, indeed welcome him into her home, her life, her family and her bed.

But she was going to have to guard her heart.

Nate wasn't going to let her into his that was clear. She'd practically had to beg him to tell her she'd scared him with her migraine.

Therefore, she wouldn't, *couldn't* let him into hers.

Not again.

They were, she thought as she put on one of Laura's outfits, strangers that somehow seemed to be closer, have more of a history than they actually did, merely because everything had been so intense, so much compacted into such a short period of time.

But they *were* strangers and Lily had to remember that.

She combed out her wet hair one last time as Nate had no hair dryer (alas), mussed it with her fingertips and she looked at herself and her new outfit in the mirror.

The skirt was so long it was to her ankles, white, flowy and tiered with a pretty, minty-green, gauzy top that was nearly so sheer you could see through it. Its wide neckline fell off her shoulder, exposing the strap of the pastel-green camisole and matching bra she wore under it. The top was belted at the waist with a piece of wide fabric that matched the blouse.

Laura had exquisite taste. Lily tried not to think of the expense of the clothes. She knew the designer names in the labels and shuddered at what they likely cost. She resolved to find a way to pay Laura back and soon. She really didn't want to be indebted to the Roberts.

Lily strapped on the gold sandals she'd worn the day before and walked out of the bedroom and down the hall in search of food to quell the growling in her stomach. She wondered if Nate still had his groceries delivered but figured he likely did. The idea of Nate wandering the aisles of a grocery store was so preposterous it made her smile.

Lost in her thoughts, the smile still on her lips, she walked into Nate's gigantic living room and stopped dead as she saw both Nate and Victor standing around the work that was still spread out all over Nate's dining room table.

Nate's head jerked around when he saw her enter the room. He was holding a file open, the papers arched for him to read and his face had been blank. The minute he saw her though, his lips curved into one of his breathtaking smiles that a lone gymnast in her belly liked especially and therefore executed a perfect back handspring at the sight.

Lily ignored the gymnast and her antics and her eyes flicked to Victor.

He was smiling at her too, his far more tentative. She didn't know what to make of that so she nodded to him silently.

Nate was approaching her, his long legs eating the distance swiftly, and she tilted her head back because, within seconds, he was at her side.

"Good morning," she said as she gazed up at him.

"Morning." His low voice rumbled and his head came down to give her a brief but hard kiss.

His strong hand settled at her waist and flexed there and her hand went up to flatten on his shoulder to push back, not wishing to engage in a Nate-style public display of affection in front of his father.

His head came up and he completely ignored the pressure of her hand.

"How are you feeling this morning?" he asked.

"Better." She watched his black eyes flare and instantly took his meaning. "Good," she whispered for his ears only and felt the blush creep up her cheeks just like she was a twenty-two-year-old virgin and not the mother of a seven-year-old girl.

"Good?" His voice had a faint teasing tone that the lone gymnast also liked, very much, and the corners of his lips tipped up in a lazy grin.

She leaned into him conspiratorially, her eyes shifting around his shoulder to Victor then back to him.

"Your father," she said, *sotto voce*, reminding him they had company.

For some reason this made him snatch her into his arms and he buried his face in her hair as he chuckled against her neck.

And somehow, making him chuckle, Lily felt that she'd just reached the top of Mount Everest, even to the point of having trouble breathing as she'd reach such altitude.

He let her go, though she felt it was somehow with reluctance, when the mobile phone on the dining room table started ringing. Nate strode back to the table and she watched him go, thinking he had such a powerful gait that it was beautiful, like the trained power of an athlete.

Then her eyes fell on Victor.

She felt funny around Victor. He'd hurt her in more ways than putting his hands on her in violence to the point of bruising her. He'd broken her trust by doing it.

She thought of him, when she first met him, as a kind of father figure in absence of Will. Now Will was gone and both Tash and Lily were left with Victor, and Lily didn't know what to think of that.

He'd done what he'd done out of love and loyalty for Nate but it still didn't change the fact that he'd lost his temper to the point of manhandling her.

"Lily," Victor greeted softly as she walked toward him cautiously.

Her eyes moved to Nate who had answered his phone. He was talking on the mobile but also watching her, watching *them*, and not missing a thing. He was not, this time, inspecting a bug under a microscope. Nate's dark eyes were active, engaged and *aware*.

"Do you want some coffee?" Victor pointed to a silver service and Lily nodded.

"I'd kill for some coffee," she answered and Victor moved to get her a cup. "Two sugars and milk," she told him.

"I'm not surprised you like it sweet," Victor mumbled to himself as he poured her a cup. "Laura made it so you don't have to worry. It tastes good. You just missed her. She left not five minutes ago."

He offered her the cup and Lily took it.

"Please thank her for me, for what she did yesterday, for the clothes." She put her arm out to show him her outfit. "If she gets me the receipts, I'll pay—"

"Rubbish," he snapped and she tensed immediately, her eyes flying to Nate, who she noted, regardless that he was on the phone, was watching her so closely she couldn't imagine he heard a word that was said by the person on the line.

She moved her gaze back to Victor and she just stopped herself from taking a step back at the intensity she saw in his eyes.

"We owe you more than a pretty skirt," he was saying.

"I'm sorry?"

"Jeff, Danielle . . . me. We owe you more than some bits of fabric."
Lily held her breath at his words and he lifted his hands in a gesture of
agitated frustration then he spoke with surprising bluntness. "How do
you go about paying a girl back for eight years of her life, marking her
with bruises?" He was still intense but seemed, underneath it, lost and
uncertain.

She was shocked at his honesty, shocked and touched.

"Victor . . ." She moved toward him, responding to the lost and uncertain bit and without taking a sip she set her coffee back on the table.

She was only feet away from him when Victor announced, "I disowned them."

At these words, Lily froze.

Then she breathed, "What?"

"Jeff and Danielle. Cut them off without a penny. The wills are already changed. Nate, you and Natasha inherit everything."

Lily blinked.

"But they're your children," she protested, forgetting for that moment how truly hideous they both had acted, taking her note, not telling
Nate her parents had died, telling Lily Nate was dead. This was not the
behavior of kind, good people.

But disowning them?

Sarah had always threatened to disown Lily or Becky or Will, depending on who angered her, but it was always an empty threat and she
didn't have much to give anyway, not like the Roberts did.

But to go so far as do it?

"Yes," Victor replied firmly. "They are my children and for that reason
they have whatever's left in their trust funds and I've left them to their lives
each with a good education to make something of themselves, finally."

Lily took another step forward.

"I hope you left the door open, just a crack, in case they're sorry and
they come back," she said softly, and hesitantly she put her hand lightly
on his arm.

He looked at his arm where her hand rested and then at her. The
intensity drained from his eyes and the Victor she knew replaced it.

"You have a kind heart, Lily," he told her quietly. "I'll take them back only if they convince you and Nathaniel to forgive them. Not before and if you don't, not ever."

She squeezed his arm and moved into him another several inches. "Laura?"

Victor put his hand over hers on his arm. "She agrees."

Lily closed her eyes as the pain of another mother ran through her. She opened them again and said, "It had to cost her."

At that he said something strange, something that made Lily immensely curious, scared her out of her wits and, most importantly, it rocked her to her core. He said it in a low, quiet voice that was meant not to be heard outside their *tête-à-tête*.

"Nathaniel had suffered enough in his life. He didn't need to suffer the last eight years. Laura knew that and I know it too. He's our son, they hurt him. What were we meant to do?"

For the briefest second she thought it was a statement in the guise of a question but then she realized he expected her to answer. To tell him she approved, to give him other guidance or show him another way.

She shook her head, and because her answer was unworthy, she turned into him and closed her arms around his shoulders, enfolding him in a hug.

She closed her eyes tightly and whispered in his ear, "I don't know what to say."

His arms came around to embrace her and there was violence in it, an affection so strong it took her breath away.

An affection and intensity that was just like her father's.

"Just be happy," he mumbled into her ear, his voice shaking with emotion, and at the sound of it, the feel of his embrace, she burst out crying. She wished she hadn't but it was all too much, she couldn't help herself.

So lost was she in her emotion, she barely registered it when Victor turned her into Nate's arms and she cried into the hard wall of his chest. Cried for her gullibility, cried that she'd believed Jeff and Danielle, cried for what they all lost, including Laura and Victor, cried for what it cost them and cried for, well, everything.

Finally, when she'd spent her tears, she arched back against Nate's arm and she saw him take something from Victor and then he handed her a handkerchief. She wiped her eyes but he still lifted a hand to slide his thumb along her cheekbone.

"All right now?" he asked in a gentle voice and she nodded.

After nodding, she contradictorily shook her head and his dark eyes flickered with worry.

"I'm hungry," she admitted on a trembling smile.

She watched as he grinned, the concern in his eyes fled and he bent his head and brushed his beautiful, smiling lips against hers.

"I'll take you to get something to eat and then to the neurologist," he told her and broke away.

"Let me fix my face." She began to turn from them but stopped, hesitated and then leaned into kiss Victor on the cheek.

This startled a smile from the older man and it was not in any way tentative.

Lily felt, inexplicably, like an important piece of her life, thought lost and left gaping, had been put back, snug and comforting, into place.

She hurried from the room as she heard Nate ask, "Are you okay here?"

Victor replied, "Yes."

"You know what to do?"

And then Lily was out of earshot, but she wasn't listening anyway. The words, *Nathaniel had suffered enough*, were ringing in her ears.

"DO YOU STILL HAVE A motorcycle?" Lily asked.

"Yes," Nate answered.

"Then I have another condition."

Lily watched Nate smile.

They were in his Aston Martin headed back to Somerset. It was after their delicious brunch at a posh patisserie in Kensington, her neurologist's appointment (complete with an unnecessary and costly MRI) and the GP appointment (she was now in possession of birth control pills, but as it took a month for them to be fully effective she was also fitted with a diaphragm).

After all of this, she hoped she didn't have to see another doctor for at least twenty years.

Although she had to admit to one highlight of her medical experience.

Upon leaving the GP's examination room, she saw Nate sitting and waiting for her. The ankle of one of his long legs resting atop the knee of the other, his dark, handsome head bent to study a pile of papers in his lap. He was completely oblivious to every single woman in the room staring at him with longing, surreptitious glances.

And then, as if sensing she was there, his head came up and he watched her coming toward him, his eyes moving lazily from the top of her hair to the tips of her toes. His face registered a sort of triumphant satisfaction, communicated such a smug possession that she could swear that *he*, rich, powerful, tall, lean, urbane, gorgeous Nathaniel McAllister was proud to be with *her*, sheltered, plain, naïve, Indiana-girl Lily Jacobs.

The very thought of it made her nearly trip on her fancy high-heeled sandals and fall flat on her face.

Luckily she did not for that would have ruined the moment and he rose when she came closer. Again, as was becoming his custom, his hand moved to rest on her waist, his fingers pressing into her there as if he wished to brand her.

"All set?" he murmured, his eyes and voice warm.

She nodded and, she couldn't help herself, she did it happily.

She could also swear, as they left, Nate's hand at the small of her back guiding her through the waiting room, that she saw one mother of a sick, snot-nosed child lean to another sitting beside her, jerk her head frustratedly in their direction and mutter, "Figures."

They'd gone to the car and started straight away to Clevedon.

Lily had been surprised at this and wanted to go back to the penthouse to get her things but Nate assured her it was "being seen to."

"What's your condition?" Nate asked pulling her out of her reverie and her reaction to his smile.

"If you take Tash on the cycle, you can't drive it the way you drove it when we were together. You have to be more careful," she told him.

"Agreed," he replied instantly then went on, "But what about when

I take *you* on the bike?"

"Oh, I'm too old for bikes," Lily responded airily, her body thrilling a little bit at the thought of being on a motorcycle again, especially with Nate.

This thrill she tamped down with firm resolution.

At her words, he let out a sharp bark of laughter that filled the car and she smiled to herself at the sound of it.

"You already broke your own condition anyway."

She was letting their easy banter relax her even further. She hadn't felt this carefree in, well, since she last was with Nate.

"I beg your pardon?"

"This morning when we, when you . . ." She broke off and thought how to put it delicately. "We didn't use any protection," she informed him.

"Yes we did."

She was watching the scenery but at his words her head snapped around to stare at him.

"We did?"

"*I* did," he amended.

"You did?" she queried in wonder.

"Obviously, I did it right," he muttered to himself.

"How . . . ?" she mumbled then went on, "Forget it, I don't want to know."

His answer was to take her hand from her lap and lift it to his mouth, brushing her knuckles with his lips all the while his eyes never left the road.

The lone gymnast in her belly liked it when he did that too.

Later, Nate expertly parallel parked in front of Lily's house, and before he'd fully helped her alight, Natasha had flung the front door open to the house and was rushing to them.

"Mummeeeeeee," she cried and Lily had just stepped on the sidewalk when Tash's body slammed into her and her thin arms closed around Lily's hips.

"Hey, baby doll." Lily bent to kiss the top of her shining, black hair, the blue gleaming in it from the still-strong sun.

"Daddy!" She disengaged and threw herself at Nate to give him one of her fabulous hugs.

He bent as well but to pick her up. He swung her in front of him and her legs closed around his waist and linked at the ankles behind his back as her arms rested around his shoulders.

"Natasha," Nate murmured.

"Your things arrived," Tash informed him cheerfully and Lily's once contented, now startled gaze moved from her daughter to Nate.

"Good." He was smiling at Tash.

"What things?" Lily asked, vaguely realizing Fazire had also come out of the house and was emanating genie rage all the way down their front walk.

Nate didn't answer but his eyes moved to Lily's.

"What things?" she repeated.

She'd asked Nate but Tash answered, "About a million suitcases and some boxes. There's a few things for you in some glossy bags but not *nearly* as much stuff as for Daddy."

At her daughter's words, Lily crossed her arms in front of her, started to tap her toe and she glared at Nate.

He put Natasha down and Lily's eyes cut to her daughter. "Go inside a sec, Tash, I need to speak to your father."

Tash presented her with a child scowl. "You're always needing to speak to *my father*."

Lily raised her eyebrows and Tash read the meaning swiftly after years of seeing her mother give her that look. She had lots of practice reading the meaning. Unfortunately, Lily hadn't learned about the eyebrow raise tactic until it was almost too late.

Tash ran inside and Fazire, with a jerk, followed and slammed the door behind them.

Lily whirled to Nate.

"Do you want to tell me what's going on?" she snapped.

"Are we going to have this conversation on the pavement?" he inquired blandly, even in asking the question, he sounded like it was all the same to him.

Her hackles rose. There was simply nothing that penetrated his armor.

"Yes, we are."

"You told me to move to Somerset," he reminded her.

"I didn't mean today!"

"When did you mean?"

She closed her mouth and glowered at him because she thought that was her safest bet considering she didn't have an answer to his question.

His eyes changed, they became hard and glittering and she felt a thrill of fear at the sight.

"I've lost eight years. Eight years of you and seven years of my daughter. If it's within my power not to lose another day, I'll not lose it," he told her, the force behind his deep voice almost like a physical thing. "And it's within my power."

She had to admit, he had a point. Although she wasn't going to admit that to *him*.

"It seems everything is within your power," she grumbled perhaps a little unconvincingly.

Nate didn't respond.

"So that's it then. One day you live in London, the next you live in Somerset. Easy as that?" Lily asked.

"You did it for me," he stated matter-of-factly.

"I didn't have a penthouse and a multi-gazillion pound company to run!" she retorted.

He took a step toward her and one of his steps brought him within an inch of her. His hand went to her jaw and she tilted her head back to look at him. His eyes had lost their steel and were glittering with something altogether different.

"Are you worried about me?" he asked softly.

"Well, what are you going to do?" she flared. "You can't exactly commute two and a half hours one way. You'll be on the road five hours a day. You'll be home in time to kiss Tash's forehead while she sleeps."

"I'll figure it out."

His hand was at her waist again, his fingers biting into her there.

She turned her head and looked at her house.

Perhaps she hadn't thought this through.

He was right. They might as well start this family thing right away.

No use delaying it if they didn't have to. Except *Nate* was the one who'd be paying the price. She'd had Tash all this time. Fazire and Maxine were always an enormous help, she hadn't been alone.

He hadn't been nearly as lucky as her. *He'd* had Jeff and Danielle (and Victor and Laura but that was beside the point).

And she couldn't get Victor's words out of her head. They'd been bedeviling her all day.

Nathaniel had suffered enough.

What, exactly, had he suffered?

"Maybe we should move to London," Lily mumbled, staring at his chest.

"Natasha is settled here," Nate replied instantly. "Eventually I'll move some of my staff to Bristol offices. It'll work, Lily."

She wasn't convinced. "We should talk about this."

Her eyes lifted to his face as his arm slid around her waist. "You're not giving up anything else for me and certainly Natasha isn't," he declared then promised, "It'll work."

Lily sighed and warned, "I'm not sure how Fazire is going to cope with you being here."

Nate's lips twitched. "He'll adjust."

She sighed again. "I suppose."

He drew her into his body and looked at her with an intensity that caused *all* the gymnasts to wake from a wee nap and start to tumble.

"This is going to work," Nate vowed, that vein of steel going through his words.

Lily lifted her hands, rested them on his chest, leaned into him and relented, "Okay."

Because there was really nothing else to say.

TWENTY-ONE

Lily

LILY HAD TO ADMIT, Nate was right per usual, it *did* work.

In a way, if you didn't count Fazire and a variety of other things.

Okay, perhaps a great many other things.

Okay, perhaps it seemed *only* to be working for Nate and Tash. And Tash was the most important so Lily tried not to worry about it too much.

Although she did worry, just not too much. Instead of worrying about it twenty-four hours a day, she only worried about it during waking hours, which she thought consisted of "not too much."

After Fazire heard the news that Lily and Nate were getting married *and* Nate was moving in, there had been a genie explosion that had to rock the Genie Richter Scale at about two hundred and eleven.

"Have you forgotten these last eight years, Lily-child?" Fazire stormed after fifteen minutes of bluster and shouting. He was floating so close to the ceiling he had to tilt his head to the side to accommodate his altitude. All of this was done while Nate was taking Tash out for a treat from The Witches Dozen in order to give Lily time to break the news privately.

"Why does everyone keep going on about the last eight years? I wasn't alone. I had you and Maxine. We didn't starve or live out of a cardboard box, for goodness sake!" she exclaimed.

"*That* is easy for *you* to say. *You* didn't watch *you* slowly fade away, day in, day out, year after year," Fazire returned, his dark eyes narrowing angrily.

"What's that supposed to mean? I took care of Tash and *you* well enough!" Lily's own temper was coming to the surface.

Fazire didn't respond, just floated towards his bottle. "Just mark my words, if it happens to you again, Fazire will *not* be here to pick up the pieces."

Shocked and angry, Lily breathed, "Fazire, I can't believe you just said that."

Lily was stunned and she truly disliked it when he referred to himself in the third person. Not that he could go anywhere until she had her final wish but the fact that he threatened to go somewhere was shocking, to say the least.

He turned his head away from her in a magnificent genie pout and his body began to vaporize but the words hung in the air.

"I've some channeling to do. The other genies are just *not* going to believe *this!*"

For the next week Fazire held resolutely to his pout even though it was like Nate wasn't even there. Nate got up at an ungodly hour every morning, woke Lily (only partially) with a kiss, and went to London. He came home at an ungodly hour every evening, kissed the sleeping Tash (who didn't wake for anything) and turned the sleeping Lily into his arms.

Lily didn't know how he could do it, he was running himself ragged.

But he did it, day after day (after day).

Although Nate *wasn't* there, all that was Nate definitely was.

Workmen arrived the day after he moved in with the edict to finish the house to Nate's plans and Lily's decorating specifications. There wasn't just one of them or even two but a dozen workmen milling around the house, which according to Fazire was another black mark against Nate's name in Fazire's Book, as Fazire rarely left the house and he didn't like company very much.

And then there were the interior designers, three of them, showing her paint chips, fabric swatches, handing her catalogs of a dizzying array of bathroom fittings, furniture, wall coverings and the like. Amongst these she was to choose, to coordinate, to give them her "vision."

Nate also ordered every item in the house that had a plug and was more than a year old, which was all of them, to be replaced by state-of-the-art, top-of-the-line items. He further decreed that any piece of worn-out or cheap-appearing (and thus likely to wear out) item in the house, which was most of it, be replaced.

The designers drifted through the house pointing at this sofa. *"That has to go."*

And at that bookshelf. *"That has to go."*

And the other chair. *"That should never have been created in the first place."*

It was part hilarious, part humiliating and part annoying, mostly the last part.

Lily called Nate's office in London.

"It's too much too soon," she told him while watching her living room furniture being carted out the door.

"It's too little too late," Nate retorted firmly.

Quite clearly they were in a stalemate. And even more clearly, they were *not* going to discuss it because they didn't have time to discuss anything and probably wouldn't discuss anything even if they had time.

Lily had also transferred her financial burdens firmly onto his very strong shoulders mainly because he'd demanded she do it. Seven million pounds in the bank or no, all the bills were immediately switched to be debited from his accounts.

This, for some bizarre reason, he'd commanded she do the very first morning he awoke beside Lily in their new bed. As it was an ungodly hour and she'd been half asleep at the time, she didn't put up much of a fight and simply told him sleepily where she kept her household files.

"I do not like this," Fazire said, standing outside the door of a room on the top floor.

It used to be a room that held junk.

Now three workmen were diligently making it into the bathroom part of a master suite for Lily and Nate that was to make up most of the top floor.

Lily tried cajoling. "When this is done, you'll only have to share the bathroom with Tash."

Fazire turned cold eyes to her, unimpressed.

Lily kept trying. "You can have my bedroom when we move out. It's lovely in there now."

Fazire's eyes turned to stone at this reminder of Nate's grandiosity.

"Fazire, I'm doing this for Tash," she finally whispered.

His eyes flickered for a moment and then he whispered right back, "I know you, Lily-child. You'll lose your heart."

"No I won't. I promise, Fazire. I know *exactly* what there is to lose and I'm not going through it again," she replied fervently.

So fervently she half believed it herself but the other half wasn't so sure anymore.

In just days Nate was demonstrating, in every way, he was intent on taking care of them *and* exhausting himself *and* (likely) bankrupting himself in order to do it.

Fazire watched her closely for a moment, nodded, although it was clear to see he was not convinced, likely seeing the stronger other half, and then he floated down the stairs even though she'd asked him not to do any of his genie antics in front of the workmen. Fazire really didn't like stairs, going up *or* going down. Luckily the workmen were too busy to notice.

The next week, Nate's temporary office in Bristol was ready for him and life changed again in the seafront terraced house.

Nate was a force of nature *not* living in the house. He filled it with his quiet dynamic when he actually spent time there.

It was then Fazire's genie pout switched immediately to open hostility. If he'd been allowed to do magic, there would have been hell to pay. Instead, he burnt Nate's toast all week even though Tash's and Lily's was perfection, accidentally misplaced Nate's car keys twice and kept moving Nate's mobile phone to various deep regions in the house.

This last backfired as Nate would ring his phone with Lily's mobile and Tash would run around the house trying to find it just like it was a game. Fazire would watch this with an expression that clearly said, "Foiled."

Tash, on the other hand, moved directly from blossoming under the loving care of the possibility of a complete family unit straight to full, glorious bloom when that family became a reality.

Nate still worked ungodly hours but he was always there for break-fast, even getting up first to wake Tash for school. This not only allowed Lily to sleep in but also had the unprecedented bonus of the usually morning-grumpy Tash flying out of bed full of energy and good cheer.

And he was always home at the very latest to put Tash to bed.

This he did by laying in it with her, his big body stretched out on her girlie comforter, holding one side of her book while she rested her head on his chest and held the other. In this position he listened to her read.

He could and did do this for hours, to Tash's delight. She was a su-perior reader for her age and liked to show off her skill. They did it even sometimes until after her bedtime which Lily allowed, telling herself they were both making up time.

Lily would watch them surreptitiously. She couldn't help it. Her daughter was so full of joyful happiness it was a pleasure to see.

And secretly Lily loved watching Nate with Tash. She'd dreamed of it for years, thinking it would never be a reality. And the reality, for Tash, was better than any dream Lily could create.

As for Lily, Nate's being home more often meant making up time in an entirely different way.

Just as eight years before, they didn't share their deepest secrets, hopes, wishes and dreams over romantic dinners or during pillow talk. Just as eight years before, they barely talked at all.

But just like eight years before, they made love.

A lot.

Nate couldn't seem to get enough of her. This Lily understood be-cause she seemed equally to want him more after every time they'd been together.

However, this time it was different. This time she held herself back.

Or she tried.

It was difficult. It was *Nate*, her wish, her romantic hero come alive (again).

This time, though, she enjoyed the beauty of their lovemaking, par-ticipated in it, allowed him to teach her new things and take her to new heights, but she never let herself go.

Or mostly she didn't.

Well, perhaps sometimes she managed to think about *trying* not to let herself go before she let herself go.

And sometimes, something would happen. Something profound and extraordinary. Something Lily didn't understand but she desperately wanted to even though she told herself over and over again that she didn't.

Some door would open to Nate's heavily-guarded soul, allowing her to catch a glimpse and then it would shut before she got a good look inside. Just like when he'd run his lips across the scar on her belly.

Once, in the heat of the moment, his hand was between her legs making her ache with longing and he was kissing her in a way that caused her to stop breathing and then he'd shifted over her. In a smooth, swift movement, he'd entered her and she so loved to have him inside.

She'd put her hands to either side of his face, lost in the moment of being joined with him. She looked him in the eyes and said exactly what was in her heart.

"You're so beautiful."

His whole body stopped, went statue still and he'd stared at her before saying something strange and heartbreaking.

"Only you see that, Lily."

It was Lily's turn to go statue still but Nate didn't allow her to stay that way for long. His mouth took hers in a fierce kiss and his hands coaxed her back to squirming underneath him.

After, when he'd tucked her back to his front and buried his face in her hair, she thought about what he'd said.

Lily couldn't imagine Nate, so confident, so powerful, would think that only *she*, Lily, saw his beauty. It was plain for everyone to see and everyone looked, mainly women.

At the very least he had to know how Victor and Laura felt about him. And now Tash.

She wanted to talk to him about it, tried to find the words but three things stopped her.

Firstly, Nate himself. Even if she had found the words, he wouldn't have answered. He wouldn't open up to her, hadn't done it before and wouldn't do it now. Not that Lily had tried but she couldn't bear the thought of the door being slammed in her face.

She had no idea why he had let her go all those years before. Even though he thought she left him, why he had not come after her looking for answers (for they were his due). No one just ups and leaves for no reason. It was simply not good form.

Lily still found the idea of her ever leaving him utterly ridiculous. But he thought she had and Lily had a strong feeling it had something to do with why he was so closed off, shut down, locked away.

Secondly, she wasn't sure she wanted to know what was in his soul. After Victor's dire words, Lily feared it, whatever it was. Even though she desperately wanted to know, she also just as desperately *did not*.

This brought her to the third reason, how she would react if she knew what was behind that guarded door to his heart. Worrying about it meant she cared about him and getting him to open it may mean her needing to open hers. And that she wasn't sure she could do again even though, if she was honest with herself, she knew that it was happening already. It was, quite simply, *Nate*.

All of this made her want to shout at him, beg him to speak to her, trust her with whatever it was that was behind that closed door to his soul.

Because if he just told her, if he made the first step then she would know he trusted her. It would be like a gift. Almost like the gift of Tash.

It also made her want to kick him in the shin for being so bloody minded.

Lily did not shout at him or kick him in the shin as much as she wanted to do both.

Instead, she did the next best thing.

She talked to his mother. She didn't mean to, but it happened all the same.

And it didn't go very well at all.

THE ROBERTS HAD DECIDED TO come on the weekends.

This they decided without much input from Nate or Lily, it was simply just going to happen.

This, Lily knew, was in order to see and get to know Tash. But also it was to see Nate. Since they'd adopted him, he'd been a regular fixture in their lives. Without their other two children, they were alone together.

Coming to the second weekend that Nate was in Somerset, he was strangely tense.

He always seemed aware, on edge, attuned to everything around him. However that weekend it was magnified and all this seemed entirely centered on Lily.

Nate was now in the occasional habit of holding one of his hands at her hip, his fingers biting into the flesh there as if they wanted to fuse with her skin. But that weekend, anytime she was within touching distance, his hand went to her, his fingers pressing into her. Further, he seemed unable to let her out of his sight, leveling his dark gaze on her as if he wanted to pin her to the spot, as if he expected she'd go up in a puff of smoke at any minute.

"I tell you, Victor is driving me up the wall," Laura complained, breaking Lily out of her reverie as they walked along the seafront to have coffees and cakes at The Witches Dozen.

Nate and Tash were strolling ahead of the pack, hand in hand. This sight gave Lily a sense of contentment that she told herself she felt for Tash.

Victor and Fazire were striding behind Nate and Tash.

There had been serious animosity between Victor and Fazire, even more than Fazire held against Nate, but Fazire was beginning to lose his battle against Nate. It was difficult to continue to be hostile against someone who did not react, at all, whatsoever.

However that day, Fazire and Victor seemed to have reached a détente. A détente that was quickly eroding as Victor was trying to convince Fazire to turn his obsessive love of baseball to soccer.

Laura, Maxine and Lily were lagging behind, way behind, and Lily was keeping a close eye on Fazire who, she could tell, was about to blow.

Laura and Lily hadn't needed words to put their relationship back on track. The Saturday before, when the Roberts came to visit, without a word Lily had put her arms around Laura and Laura immediately burst into sloppy tears. Lily joined her, they'd cried themselves spent in each other's arms then they'd leaned back, took one look at the other's face and burst out laughing.

That had been that.

Laura went on with her rant.

"He's supposed to be semi-retired but he'd go into the office every day. Now, with Nate not being there, he doesn't go. Instead he stays home and asks questions. 'Laura, where's such-and-such?' or 'Laura, where's so-and-so?' And then, 'Why in bloody hell do you keep it there?' Even though it's been there for twenty-five years and he's never questioned it before."

Maxine was laughing quietly and Lily was watching closely as Victor was comparing George Best to Ryne Sandberg and Fazire's face was turning alarmingly purple.

"Then he *moves* it to where he thinks it's better suited to be and then *I* can't find it and have to ask *him*. I kid you not, I plotted his murder yesterday while eating a full bag of Malteasers. It's the perfect murder and I'm pretty sure I could get away with it."

Maxine stopped chuckling quietly to let out a burst of raucous laughter and Lily smiled as she caught Laura's hand to give it a reassuring squeeze.

Nate and Tash both looked around at the sound of Maxine's laughter and Lily transferred her smile to her daughter. When she swung it to Nate, it faltered.

He didn't return her smile. He didn't seem to be enjoying their jaunt during a sunny summer day. Nor did he seem happy that his whole family was together. He seemed wary, guarded, or more guarded than usual, and even poised for action.

What action that would be, Lily could not fathom.

"I think there's something wrong with Nate," Lily blurted out and Maxine and Laura turned startled eyes to her at the sound of the concern in her voice on what seemed such a happy day.

She watched as Nate turned away and guided Tash into the coffee shop just as Fazire cried, "Sandberg was an All-Star, Golden Glove, MVP. He could do much more than *kick a ball with his foot!*"

At Fazire's words, Victor's face started to turn alarmingly purple.

"What do you mean, Lily?" Laura asked, cutting Lily's attention away from Fazire's heated outburst and Victor's not surprising response.

Lily stopped dead on the pavement and watched Nate and Tash disappear into The Dozen. Laura and Maxine stopped too and Lily turned to them, looking from one woman to the other.

"I don't know. I can't describe it. He's not the most happy-go-lucky person in the world. He's always on edge in a way. But lately, he seems somehow . . ." she paused, fighting for words and not finding them. "*More* on edge," she finished lamely.

Both Laura and Maxine shifted their gazes to the door of the coffee shop, which Victor and Fazire were walking through, both men's arms gesticulating wildly. The women's gazes swung to look at each other. Then they moved to look at Lily.

"Lily," Laura said, "my son is a rather . . ." she seemed at a loss for words too and continued, "*intense* man."

"You can say that again," Maxie mumbled.

"I know *that*." Lily lifted her hand to pull her hair back from her face and held it at the crown at the back of her head, tugging at it gently in frustration. "I can't explain it so I'll demonstrate it."

Both women nodded encouragingly in perfect synch.

Lily carried on, "Whenever he's near enough to touch me, he puts his hand at my waist like this . . ."

Lily dropped her hand and put one on both women's hips, just like Nate did, her fingers pressing into their skin.

As Lily's hands dropped away, Maxine said helpfully, "I think, sweetling, Nate is somewhat, er," her gaze slid to Laura and then back to Lily, "possessive."

"I know *that* too!" Lily cried and then continued. "But it's not that. I swear it's like he wants to fuse with me. I can't explain it but it isn't only that. He's started to look at me like, I don't know, like he thinks I'm going to . . . to . . . disappear. Go up in smoke. *Poof!*" She exclaimed, lifting both of her hands to the sides of her face and splaying them dramatically with a whoosh.

Laura's face slowly lit with understanding and Lily pounced on it immediately.

"What?"

Laura looked toward the coffee house and then back at Lily. Her understanding now tinged with something bittersweet and alarmingly sad, making Lily's heart beat a little faster in hopes of learning something *and* in fear of what she might learn.

"It's your anniversary," she whispered.

"My what?" Lily asked, not expecting to hear *that*.

However, whatever Laura was talking about also dawned on Maxine.

"Dearie me, that it is," Maxine breathed and she, too, looked in the direction of The Dozen, her face contemplative.

"*What?*" Lily exclaimed.

Laura put her hand out to touch Lily's arm. "My darling, the last time . . . before . . ." She broke off and shook her head as if to clear it. Then she closed her eyes for a long moment clearly struggling with herself about something. When she opened them, they were bright and direct. "You disappeared after two weeks."

Lily stared at her still confused. "And?"

Laura's hand squeezed Lily's arm.

"And it's been two weeks," Laura finished as if that explained everything.

Lily shook her head, still not comprehending and Laura moved closer to her.

"The last time you were together, you disappeared into thin air after two weeks. Nathaniel left home in the morning and you were there. He came back in the evening and you were gone, not a trace of you left. Just like you disappeared in a puff of smoke." She paused as Lily's eyes widened in understanding. "Now you've been back together for two weeks and Nathaniel, well, Nathaniel would know the significance of that. He'd remember it. He remembers everything."

"But Laura, I didn't disappear. We . . ." Lily stopped and bit her lip, then forged ahead. "We don't have to go into that. But Nate knows that I didn't go anywhere then, and I'm not going anywhere now."

Maxine chimed in, "The mind plays tricks on us, sweetling. We can know something rationally but not believe it. Trust me, I'm the most irrationally rational person there is, or is that the most rationally irrational?" she asked Laura and Laura gave her a weak smile.

"This is ridiculous, Nate can't think . . ." She didn't finish, couldn't fathom it. He was there, she was there, Tash was there, the Roberts, even Fazire seemed to be behaving himself, or as close as Fazire could get. She started again. "I'm not going to go anywhere."

Laura cut in, "There are things about Nate you don't know."

It was at these words that Lily's frustration at not knowing about Nate, not understanding why his shields were up, why the impenetrable armor shrouded his heart, broke through like a rocket.

"Yes, you're right. There's *a lot* that I don't know about Nate," she clipped out in a low, angry voice. "A lot he doesn't say, a lot he doesn't share. He didn't let me in eight years ago and he isn't letting me in now. And not letting me in before meant that he let me go. Do you know what that means for now? How that makes me feel? Especially now, with Tash? I'm living with a complete stranger!"

"Lily—" Laura interrupted but Lily continued on a roll, and it was difficult stopping one of Lily's rolls.

"He didn't trust me then and he doesn't trust me now and I'm telling you, I'm sick of it. I can't ask, because he won't tell me. I can't—"

"Lily—" It was Maxine this time but Lily was not to be stopped.

"It's like . . . like, he's encased in ice *and* a suit of steel. I can't reach him. Even if I were to try to pick away at it, take a blow torch to it, somehow he's just . . . simply . . . *removed*."

Laura moved in closer, grabbed both of Lily's arms and gave her a bit of a shake.

"Lily, quiet!" she whispered urgently. "You're making a scene and they may come out."

"I don't care!"

In fact, Lily quite liked the idea of a scene. Maybe if she made a scene she might get somewhere.

Laura shook her head again and started to look panicked.

Lily grabbed hold of Laura the same way Laura was holding her. "You have to tell me, Laura. If you know what it is, what's behind that door that Nate has so firmly closed, you have to tell me."

Laura shook her head, her panic turning strangely to fear.

"Please, you must," Lily begged.

"I can't. It's not my place. He'd never forgive me. He hides it. He puts so much effort into hiding it, like it was wrong, like it was dirty. Yet he seems somehow . . . *proud* of it. But he'd never forgive me if I told you, never. And, Lily, I couldn't bear to lose him, he's the only child I have left."

There it was again, "wrong" Laura said, "dirty." And Victor had said "Nathaniel suffered." All these ominous words that described him, and Lily, who he was supposed to be marrying, spending the rest of his life with, who was the mother of his child, didn't seem to have the right to know.

She'd had enough of the secrets, hints, hedging and silence. She was sick to death of it. Whatever it was caused her to lose him eight years ago and it was pulling her firmly away from him now. Or, more to the point, keeping her distant.

Nate, she instantly decided, wasn't the only one who could close down.

Two could play *that* game.

Lily abruptly let go of Laura and turned back the way they came. "I'm going back to the house."

"No!" Laura and Maxine exclaimed at the same time.

"You can't go back. You have to stay with him. If you go back he'll be worried," Laura went on.

"Let him be worried," Lily flared. "At least that will mean he feels *something*."

Laura's face changed again, this time to motherly disappointment. "Lily, you know that's not fair. You know that Nathaniel feels *everything*, especially for you."

"No, Laura, I don't know that. If he did, he'd trust me with whatever this horrible secret is." Laura closed her eyes in despair and Lily didn't wait for her to open them again. "Just tell them I have a headache and that I went back."

Without waiting for a response, she turned and practically ran back to the house (as much as she could run in flip-flops).

Once Lily arrived home, she halted in the entryway and looked around.

She didn't know what to do. She had nothing *to* do anymore. No chores, no errands, nothing. And that made her frayed temper completely disintegrate.

The master bed chamber, as Fazire sarcastically anointed it, that Nate had commanded wasn't due to be finished until the next week.

Her office (the only other room upstairs now due to the enormity of the master suite, the living room had been moved to the garden level) that Nate had ordered her to decorate wasn't finished yet either.

Nate had hired a housekeeper who came in once a week and cleaned and did the laundry and the ironing too, which made Fazire none too happy.

"What next?" he'd demanded to know. "A chef so I won't be able to cook either?"

Nate paid the bills. Nate had groceries delivered. His secretary set up an account on the Internet—with Waitrose, no less—and all Lily had to do was click on her choices and *voilà!* they arrived the next day.

She was, quite simply, overwhelmed by him. He was everywhere, taking control of everything. Or taking *care* of every*one*.

Except he wasn't there at all.

"Lily?"

It was Nate's voice and she swung around and glared at him, automatically determined to make some headway, penetrate his shields, get *some* reaction from him, *any* reaction.

He was standing in the inner doorway. The hall was shadowy, the sunlight was coming in behind him and she couldn't see his face.

"You!" she yelled nonsensically.

He started to move forward, the powerful masculine grace of his movement, and Lily's admiration of it, somehow grating on her nerves and he ignored her bizarre outburst.

"Laura said you had a headache. Is it a migraine?" His voice was soft and normally she would have thought his concern was sweet.

But she was beyond that now.

"No, it's not a bloody migraine!" she cried, stamping her foot in frustration.

Nate stopped less than a breath away, his hand reached out to her waist and his fingers bit into her there. Lily could see his face and his concern was plain as day. And still, it didn't stop her.

"What is it?" he asked, his voice low, his tone guarded.

She should have read it, been more considerate with her words but she wasn't in the mood.

She grasped his hand at her waist and pulled it up between them.

"It's this!" she exclaimed. "It's the housekeeper, the workmen, the decorators. It's everything." She finished with, "It's *you!*"

At that, she abruptly released his hand and watched the shutters instantly go down in his eyes, shielding her from his thoughts, cutting her off.

"That's it, Nate, close down. I expected no less." Lily's voice was edging toward bitter.

He moved into her and Lily stood her ground.

"What's this about?" His voice was even lower. A different kind of a low, a rumble that was so lethal it skidded across her skin like the flat of a blade.

"You tell me!" she shouted, tilting her head back and moving into him in an unsuccessful attempt to be menacing.

He said nothing.

She waited.

He still said nothing.

Then she stopped waiting, pulled away and ran up the stairs to their bedroom, threw open the wardrobes a shade hysterically and started to throw her clothes on the bed. She had no reason to do this but it seemed a good attempt at a grand gesture.

If he was worried she'd leave, she'd make him think that she would, she'd force him into the confrontation they should have had eight years ago.

Lily decided a grand gesture was the only thing that would get a reaction from Nate. And, for some reason, she needed a reaction from Nate. She needed it desperately.

She'd thought she could do this, live together and keep her heart apart. But, apparently, she couldn't. It just wasn't in her.

Because this was *Nate*. She'd known the instant she laid eyes on him that he was hers.

And he *was* hers.

Except, he wasn't.

On her second pass to the wardrobe, Nate's hand seized her wrist and he swung her around, clothes flying everywhere.

"Talk to me, damn it," he snarled, his dark eyes glittering with menace and something else she could not read.

"You're a fine one to tell *me* to talk to *you*. If you were a superhero, they'd call you Silent Man," Lily yelled.

He used her wrist to pull her closer and he leaned into her, his face barely an inch from hers.

"You were talking to Laura. What did she say?" he bit out and Lily realized he was angry.

No, furious.

And it was barely contained and it scared the hell out of her.

He seemed no longer sophisticated and urbane. He *was* dangerous and predatory.

But still, Lily didn't heed the warning look in his black eyes.

"Nothing!" she shouted into his face. "Not one damned thing. I asked her about you but she wouldn't say a word!"

She saw a flash of relief cross his face before he hid it and she actually growled.

"What is it?" she cried, twisting her wrist free and grabbing fistfuls of his shirt at his chest. "What's the damned secret about you that everyone is so intent on keeping?"

Nate's hands hit her waist and he brought her closer but she resisted. He won, not surprisingly.

"It's nothing," he stated, his voice edging back to calm.

"It's not nothing!" she exclaimed, yanking at his shirt.

"It's *nothing!*" Nate barked, all calmness gone in a wink.

Lily jumped at the ferocity in his voice but she still didn't stop, and she pulled him even closer to her, her face a breath away from his.

"Well, Nate, it's something to me. Whatever it is kept you from me for eight years. Whatever it is made you think I'd leave. Whatever it is made you let me go. Whatever it is, is holding you back from me *now!*"

When she finished her last dramatic statement, Nate jerked away from her and turned on his heel. Lily opened her mouth to call out to him, that they weren't nearly finished but he stopped at the door and threw it shut with such a vicious slam the pictures on the walls shuddered in their frames.

At this, she jumped again and could do nothing but stare at him, slack-jawed.

Definitely predatory. And definitely *dangerous*.

He strode directly to the bed, bent and with a swipe of his arm, sent her clothes flying.

At this, her eyes widened in alarm.

Then he strode, with determination, to Lily who stood rooted to the spot. He grasped her hips and lifted her upwards.

She cried out in surprise, threw her legs around his hips and grabbed his shoulders to steady herself as he turned her to the bed. Then she was falling, holding on to him as she went backwards, her back hitting the bed and Nate landed square on top of her.

"You think I'm holding back?" he growled, his eyes back to glittering dangerously, his face barely an inch away.

Regardless of all she had just witnessed, she threw caution to the wind. It *was* a grand gesture after all and she started it. She had to have the courage to follow it through and see where it ended or she might lose everything.

So she flung at him, "Yes!"

And then she felt his hand yank the skirt of her dress up around her waist.

"Nate!" she cried as she realized his intent and he buried his face in her neck, conveniently hiding his from view.

"You have more of me than I've given anyone," he snarled against the sensitive skin at the base of her ear and then she felt his tongue there.

She tried to push him away as the gymnasts, who didn't seem to care about the dramatic events that had brought them to this pass, started to warm up with cartwheels.

At the gymnasts' antics, Lily stopped pushing him away and slid one arm around him and the other hand into his hair, trying gently to move his head so she could see his face.

"I don't mean this. I don't mean here, in the bedroom," she whispered.

It was as if she didn't speak, one of his hands skimmed with delicious intent across her belly up to her breast, his thumb expertly finding her nipple through the fabric and rubbed tantalizingly against it. Even though she tried to control it, Lily felt her insides melt.

"I've given you more than I gave my adoptive family," he murmured, his voice turned silky and was still at her ear, the deep timbre shooting tremors through her.

"Nate, don't do this. We've always been good at this. *Talk* to me," Lily begged.

He ignored her and his lips edged along her jaw to her chin as his hand went between their bodies, teasing at the edge of her lacy panties.

With his lips against hers, he said, "More than I gave my mother."

She gasped as she realized he didn't mean Laura. It was the first time he'd spoken of his birth mother since, well, the only other time he'd ever spoken of her on their first date in the park.

Her gasp was cut off by his lips taking possession of hers in a brutal, demanding kiss. A kiss that was meant to tell her something. A kiss that coincided exactly with his fingers stopping their tantalizing play. They shoved the delicate fabric of her underwear aside and two of them entered her in a beautiful invasion.

She immediately moaned against his mouth, instantly responding to his touch. Her arms went around him, her hands pulling his shirt out of his jeans so she could run her fingers along the hard muscles of his back, so she could feel the immense heat of his skin.

"So wet," he muttered against her lips, "only for me."

And touching her, he seemed somehow taken away from the current tense conversation. His voice almost reverent, disbelieving. The sound of it broke Lily's heart.

His fingers started moving, she could think of nothing else, not their argument, not his secrets, just what his hand was doing to her.

"Only you, Nate," she agreed softly.

At her words, he dropped his forehead to hers and closed his eyes, that look coming over him that was so raw and intense it shook Lily to her core.

He kept his lips against hers as his hand worked its magic but he didn't kiss her. He'd opened his eyes and they bored into hers as his hand sent electrifying shockwaves of pleasure shooting through her body.

Finally, he said against her mouth as his thumb swirled and she cried out sharply as he brought her closer, ever so closer. "You're not leaving me, Lily."

She shook her head.

"Say it," he growled.

She pressed against his hand, so close, she was nearly there.

"Please, Nate."

"Say it," he demanded.

"Nate," she breathed against his mouth, one hand coming up to delve into his hair, hold his face to hers.

"Lily." His voice was a low, velvet rumble.

She opened her half-shut eyes and looked directly into his black ones.

"I'm not leaving you, Nate. I'll never leave you," Lily declared, her voice trembling with a feeling that had nothing at all to do with what his fingers were doing.

A feeling that had everything to do with what was in her heart. What had been in her heart since she was fourteen years old, and what she knew was her wish come true when Nate had saved her from the purse snatcher.

And then his mouth crushed down on hers and he let her soar, his hand taking her to glorious heights, where he always took her. His mouth absorbed her cry of pleasure as her hands clutched at him, her hips pressing into his fingers.

As the shudders receded, he fell to his side, gently pulling her with him and righting her skirt at the same time. Then he cradled her in his arms protectively, slowly stroking her back.

Her face was pressed into his throat and she felt vulnerable and exposed. He had taken her to a beautiful place but he did not join her there.

Still removed. Always removed one way or another.

"Nate?" she mumbled against his throat.

"Mm?" He was in his own place again, his own thoughts, far, far away from her. She was beginning to recognize when he was with her and when he was gone.

Quietly, in a voice so small she was surprised he heard it, she whispered scant words that held deep meaning, "I need you here, with me."

His hand stopped stroking and his arms tightened around her, taking her breath.

"You have me."

She shook her head against his neck, mutely denying his words.

"You have me, Lily. I promise."

She knew she didn't.

But Lily experienced a colossal change of mind. A life-changing one.

Even an earth-shattering one.

Instead of putting all her energies into guarding her heart against him (which clearly wasn't working, it *was* Nate), she was going to try to open his heart to her. She was going to use everything that was in her power, such as it was, maybe even go so far as to use her last wish to open *his* heart.

She had no idea if she would succeed, but, Lily determined in that instant, she was damn well going to try.

TWENTY-TWO

Nate

NATE LEFT THE OFFICE early wishing to get home.

Home.

Where Lily and Natasha were.

And, of course, Fazire.

Tash had called, telling him there was a surprise waiting for him there.

He couldn't imagine what kind of surprise it could be, in the month since Lily's dramatic tirade, complete with tossing clothes out of the wardrobe, his life had been full of surprises.

Pleasant surprises. Extraordinary surprises.

The kind of surprises and the possible intent behind them being something he'd very much like to believe, but found, through years of experience with disappointment, he could not.

IT HAD STARTED THE NEXT morning after Lily's scene.

She had woken early, very early. She slid quietly out of bed obviously making an effort not to disturb Nate. This effort was for naught as she knocked into the bed twice, cursed under her breath and nearly fell over as she dressed. Knowing she was being careful for his sake, Nate kept his eyes closed when what he wanted to do was drag her warm body back into bed.

When time passed and she didn't return, Nate got up, pulled on a pair of jeans and went in search of her.

He found her in the kitchen wearing a pair of very short, thin, cotton drawstring shorts patterned in stripes of soft pink and purple that showed off her long, shapely legs. With this, she wore a pink camisole and an old gray cardigan that had seen better days which he immediately decided to replace with something else, something new, something made of cashmere.

She was standing in the middle of the kitchen with her hands on her hips staring at the countertop with what appeared to be confusion.

Wondering at her mood after their row the day before, Nate approached her from behind silently on bare feet and cautiously slid his arms around her waist.

The afternoon before she'd promised not to leave him, said she would *never* leave, but Nate didn't trust that. He'd learned early not to trust and nothing had happened in his life to alter that lesson.

He knew she wanted more from him, she wanted it all and he couldn't give it to her. He felt, as he did eight years before, like he was living on borrowed time. Like once she found out who he really was she'd not only want to stay far away but now keep Tash from him as well.

Nate wouldn't allow that.

And to stop it from happening he'd do whatever he had to do. Including keeping his past from the both of them.

Not that Lily was giving her all to him. The open-hearted Lily who let her excitement at life bubble out of her at the slightest provocation was gone. The laughing Lily who told stories about her beloved family had faded. No matter what he did to rectify his past mistakes, to erase the last eight years of her making do and scraping by, she was still different.

Wary, watchful and closed.

She jumped when he touched her and whirled, nearly knocking his chin with her head, and her soft, fragrant hair whipped across his face.

"Nate!" she cried, her expression clearly showing disappointment at seeing him and he felt something lurch painfully in his gut. She looked over her shoulder at the countertop then back at him and announced on an exaggerated pout, "You've spoiled my surprise."

Then she stunned him by sliding her hands around his waist and tilting her head to the side, the disappointment fading as she gave him one of her quirky smiles. At the sight of it, he sucked in his breath and he felt every muscle in his body tense.

Her smile was exactly as he remembered. Not wary, not watchful, not closed in any way. Open, happy and one of the sweetest sights he'd seen in his life.

She leaned slightly into him, her breasts brushing his bare chest, her chin forced to tilt back further so she could look into his eyes.

"I was making you breakfast in bed," she informed him cheerfully.

He glanced over her shoulder at the evidence that, indeed, he had interrupted her in the middle of preparing food.

With the knowledge of her intentions and understanding that her earlier disappointment was not directed at him, Nate didn't know what to do. Nate was not the kind of man who didn't know what to do and he didn't like it.

No woman had made him breakfast in bed. No woman had even made him breakfast. Not a single one of his lovers had done anything for him, given him a present, brought over a bottle of wine or prepared dinner for him. They were happy for him to buy dinner, presents, even holidays, but the women in his life were used to being taken care of, being spoiled. Nate had played the game mainly because if he didn't, they'd turn whiny and demanding. He'd learned it made life far more peaceful and furthermore, he could afford it.

This was an entirely new experience.

Lily seemed not to notice his surprise.

"Once I got started, though, I didn't know what to do. You never remark on your food, say what you like. You just . . . *eat*." Her smile hadn't faltered, in fact, her voice sounded almost teasing. She gently pulled away from him and threw her arm out towards the food on the counter. "I decided bacon, eggs and toast was my best bet. Everyone likes bacon, eggs and toast. Then I realized I don't even know how you like your eggs!"

She laughed softly, finding this amusing and came back to him, casually putting her arms around his waist again and resting her entire torso heavily against his tightened chest.

"You know, I feel like I've known you for years but I've really only known you a few weeks. Isn't that funny?" She drooped her shoulders and tipped her head back to stare up at him with her extraordinary eyes, the blue so clear, so deep, so open, Nate felt lost in them.

Lost in her eyes, lost in her mood, lost in Lily.

So lost, he didn't answer.

"So," she whispered, "how do you like your eggs?"

Her question took him away from his silent contemplation of her. She sounded as if his answer meant everything in the world to her.

He looked warily down on her, his body tight, not knowing whether to give in to the relief he felt at her new attitude or worry at what she was hiding behind it.

"I'll like them any way you cook them," he answered, noncommittal.

Something he could not read flashed in her eyes, something that looked strangely like determination and her arms tightened about his waist.

"Scrambled?" she asked.

"That'll be fine," Nate replied.

Her smile came back. "How about fried? Do you like that better than scrambled?"

"Either," he answered.

"Poached?"

"Fine."

At this, her eyes lit and she shook her head and laughed, her entire body vibrating with it. For a second she dropped her forehead against his chest, giving in to her bizarre moment of amusement then she flipped her head back again, nearly clipping his chin. She lifted her hands to either side of his face, pulling it to hers and she stunned him further by kissing him briefly, the laughter still on her lips.

She hadn't touched him of her own accord outside of bed since they'd been reunited.

"What am I going to do with you?" she mumbled, clearly not wanting an answer as she carried on, her voice very soft. "How do you like eggs best, Nate? Please tell me."

This trivial piece of information *did* mean something to her so he sighed then responded, "Poached."

Both of her hands went straight up in the air as if she was calling a goal in an American football match. With this gesture, her back arched, pressing her front closer against him.

"Success!" she cried happily and loudly, her face alight with triumph and Nate felt the brittle edge go off his morning at the sight. An instant later her face fell dramatically and she exclaimed, "Oh no!"

"What is it?" he asked.

"I don't know how to poach an egg."

It was then that Nate started laughing, all tenseness gone, the edge smoothing out and his arms tightened around her as her hands dropped to hold him at either side of his neck. She leaned up and kissed him again.

"Never fear," she declared, pulling away from him and turning, all business, toward the counter. "I saw someone do it on a cookery program once. I think you have to get the water going in some kind of centrifugal thingie-ma-bobbie and crack the egg in it. I'll figure it out."

On this, she got busy and opened the bag of bread.

Nate allowed himself a moment to let his relief show. He allowed it because, with her back to him, Lily couldn't see it. She seemed so happy, so much the old Lily he wanted time to revel in it. He reached out and pulled her back into his arms, burying his face in the hair at the side of her neck.

It wasn't often that Nate felt hope, so when he did he knew it was a precious thing.

And at that moment, he felt hope.

Not a forever kind of hope. That hope, he knew, didn't exist. But a hope for now.

"Nate?" She was pulling slightly away in an effort to see his face but not get out of his arms. "Is something the matter?"

He lifted his head and kissed her nose. "Nothing."

Again, something flashed in her eyes but instead of her face closing off as it normally did when he didn't give her the answer she wanted, she leaned back into him. The midnight blue in her outer irises had moved in towards the pupil.

"Now that we have breakfast semi-sorted, perhaps you'll give me a good morning kiss?" she prompted softly, her voice timid but her eyes were inviting.

This wasn't the old Lily. This wasn't even the new Lily.

This was an altogether unknown Lily.

She'd never asked for a kiss before and Nate didn't need to be asked twice.

Both Fazire and Victor arrived in the kitchen at the same time interrupting a good morning kiss that had become pleasantly heated.

"Sorry, sorry . . . we'll come back." Victor edged back out when Nate reluctantly lifted his mouth from Lily's and turned his gaze to the two men.

"I'll not come back!" Fazire grouched, flagrantly ignoring the scene he'd just interrupted and stomping in. "I need coffee immediately."

Lily pulled away from Nate and approached her friend.

"Fazire!" She grabbed Fazire by the cheeks and pulled his head to her, tipping it down and kissing it on the top. "Nate likes his eggs *poached*," she imparted this on her friend as if she'd just been the first to decode the enigma machine.

After he was released, Fazire looked from Lily to Nate and back to Lily. He shrugged his disinterest in the news and went to the coffeepot.

Nate leaned his hip on the counter and nodded to his father who straggled in wearing his pajamas and a dressing gown.

"Who made this?" Fazire demanded to know, his lip curled in disgust. He was holding the coffeepot aloft and staring at Nate angrily deciding Nate *had* to be the culprit.

"I did," Lily answered, busily lining bacon on the grill pan.

At Lily's admission, Fazire wasn't deterred in his ire.

"It looks like water," Fazire accused, transferring his angry eyes to her.

"It does *not* look like water. Just because you can't chew it, Fazire, doesn't mean it isn't any good." She tossed her head and looked over her shoulder at Victor who had decided to seat himself at the kitchen table to watch the show. "Fazire likes his coffee strong."

"I gathered that," Victor commented.

Lily threw a startlingly bright smile at Victor and went back to work. Even though she'd turned her back to him, Victor stared at her in frozen wonder for a moment then his eyes slid to Nate.

Then Nate's father smiled and slowly he winked at his son.

THAT EVENING, AFTER VICTOR AND Laura had gone, Fazire had disappeared to his room and Nate had listened to Tash reading before he tucked her in to sleep, Nate had gone to find Lily.

She was sitting in the sun room in a new wicker lounge with a bright-blue cushion edged in a soft beige, her legs curled beneath her, her head bent, reading a book. Mrs. Gunderson was sleeping in a tight cat body curl next to her.

With Nate's money and Lily's choices, everything in the room was of far better quality and vastly improved style. The furniture was wicker, woven plump with thick, dark reeds. The windows had been replaced with timber-framed, double-glazed, sparkling panes. The walls had been repainted in clean linen and large potted palms were placed attractively around the room. The day outside was gray, but the room had a soft glow from lamps with bulbous beige bases with crisp shades sitting on wicker tables by the lounge and in between the two chairs opposite it. A square, glass-topped, wicker table sat in the center of the arrangement holding a huge crystal globe vase filled high with irises.

Nate felt a sense of satisfaction seeing Lily sitting there peacefully reading with her cat. It was the kind of room Lily should be in, expensive and elegant, and it was the kind of thing Lily should be doing, reading and relaxing, not running around taking care of everyone.

He'd been studying her for some moments when she sensed him, her head coming up and her face, which had been concentrating on her book, relaxed into a small smile.

"Is Tash sleeping?" she asked.

Nate felt something uncurl inside him at her simple question. It wasn't important. It wasn't profound. Just a mother asking a father if their child was sleeping.

Yet, to Nate, it was the most intimate question anyone had ever asked him.

"Yes," he answered.

Lily put her bookmark in her book and set it aside but she didn't rise.

"She loves to read to you. I think it's the highlight of her day."

Nate made no verbal response but that thing unfurling in his chest loosened further upon hearing her remark.

Finally he spoke. "I don't want to interrupt your reading." She shook her head to indicate she didn't mind and he continued, "I've been meaning to tell you that tomorrow morning we have an appointment at the Registry Office to begin the process—"

He didn't finish as suddenly Lily hurled herself out of the lounge and across the short space and threw herself bodily at him, rocking him back on his heels. Mrs. Gunderson went flying on an angry cat meow at her rapid movement.

Lily's arms went around his shoulders and with a little hop, her legs went around his hips and he reflexively put his hands under her bottom to hold her steady against him.

She was pressing her cheek against his and holding him tightly.

"What's this?" he whispered into her ear.

Her head jerked back and she looked at him, her eyes bright and tears were glimmering at their bottom edges.

"You said in Alistair's conference room you were going to marry me but then you didn't say anything about it again. You said two months. It's been nearly a month already!" He had no chance to respond to her overwhelming reaction as she went on excitedly. "We'll fix a date tomorrow, yes?" she asked and he nodded, finding himself pleased by her extremely positive response.

She leaned into him and again put her cheek against his.

"I have so much to do! I have to find a dress and Tash needs a dress. And we have to get invitations." Her head jerked back and she looked at him again, all sign of tears were gone, her eyes were alight and dancing. "A small wedding? In the Registry Office?"

At her question, he nodded again and with a soft pull, she released her legs from his hips and he let her go. He watched as she kept talking excitedly and walked around the room, turning off the lamps.

"Fazire will need something to wear and then there are flowers. I think peonies. Mom loved peonies. It's the Indiana state flower, did you know that?" She didn't look at him as she asked the question, nor did she wait for a response.

"We'll need a photographer. I don't want one of those Nazi photographers that take seventeen hours to pose all the photos. It should be a fun day. We should be drinking and eating, not spending all our time having our pictures taken. What do you think?"

Before he could answer, she stopped and jerked erect after turning off the second lamp.

"I know! Fazire can take the photos!" She clapped her hands in front of her excitedly and Nate remembered her doing precisely the same thing when he'd given in to her motorcycle ride on their first and only date. The sight of it made his chest expand in a way he'd never felt before. It was warm. It was pleasant. And he had no idea what it meant. He had no idea that it heralded contentment and security, two things he'd never felt in his life.

He had not even come into the room and was still standing in the doorway. He leaned against its jamb and continued to watch her.

He didn't stay very long in his position. Lily walked toward him, grabbed his hand and led him out of the room through the living room and up the stairway to their bedroom. The entire time she talked and she planned.

She asked him if he wanted dancing then didn't wait for his answer and decided there should be dancing.

She asked him if he wanted to wear a morning suit then didn't wait for his answer and decided that was too stuffy for a Registry Office.

She asked him if he wanted speeches then decided there *must* be speeches.

In the bedroom, after he'd closed their door, she turned into his arms.

"Just leave it to me. I'll take care of everything. I'll call in Laura and Maxie and we'll have it sorted in no time." She pressed her index finger in his chest. "*You* just need to be responsible for the honeymoon. Can you do that?"

His arms tightened and he smiled into her shining face.

"I think I can manage that."

She tipped her face up to him and smiled.

THREE DAYS LATER, NATE WAS in his new Bristol office in a meeting, two of his transplanted staff seated in the chairs in front of him awaiting instructions, when the buzzer went on the phone.

When he was in a meeting, the buzzer never went on his phone.

Ever.

Nate wasn't a cruel boss but he was a demanding one. He expected his staff to work hard and smart, to be ambitious but not greedy nor backstabbing and to be forthcoming with good ideas and constructive criticism. He rewarded them for these things. The more of them they demonstrated, the better they demonstrated them, the larger the reward.

If they failed to demonstrate them, they were gone.

However, Nate was not friendly with his staff. He didn't take them out for drinks. He didn't buy them Christmas presents, although he did give them generous Christmas bonuses. He didn't share his personal life with a single soul in the office or out of it, for that matter. He did not encourage this behavior amongst his managers and their employees either. He expected work to be work, he expected success, he expected absolute professionalism and he led by example.

He was not a doting father to a corporate family.

He was the respected, removed commander of a very tightly run corporate army that, day after day, achieved remarkable results.

It was his edict that he was never to be disturbed during a meeting unless it was urgent. An edict like all of his edicts that was always strictly obeyed.

Therefore, when the phone sounded, both of his staff jumped in surprise.

Nate hit a button on the phone. "Yes?"

"Ms. Jacobs for you," his secretary, Jennifer, said over the intercom, adhering to his command that any time Lily called, *any* time, she was to be put straight through.

Nate didn't spare his two employees a glance (if he had, he would have seen their eyes widen in surprise). He just picked up the phone.

Lily had called him once to complain about her living room furniture being carted away.

Tash, on the other hand, called him every day when she got home from school to tell him every minuscule piece of news that she felt might be of import, which was practically every second of her day. Nate looked forward to his daughter's calls. Natasha was talkative but clever, incredibly clever. She had at her command a great number of words, and she used them well and often, far better than people three times her age. It was clear Tash was advanced and Nate was already looking into special schools for her, something, he thought vaguely, he really should discuss with Lily.

Nate had learned quickly that Tash's calls were to come on a regular schedule and he had Jennifer clear his diary for that hour, without exception.

But Lily had only called once. There was no more furniture to be hauled away and most of the work was being completed that week. He had no idea why Lily would call and he was concerned it was not good news.

"Lily," he greeted her.

"Hi! You busy?" she responded brightly, her light-hearted tone taking him by surprise.

Nate was busy. Nate was always busy.

"No," he replied.

There was a pause. Then she asked, "What're you doing?" And she spoke as if she was calling just to chat, as if she did this every day.

He sat back in his chair, taken aback by this latest development that was the New Lily and finding himself wondering at her intentions.

His glance slid past his two employees who were pretending (poorly) not to listen into their normally cold and indifferent boss's unprecedented conversation with the unknown "Ms. Jacobs," a woman for whom he would interrupt a meeting without even the briefest hesitation.

He ignored them.

"Working," Nate answered.

She let out a carefree laugh then remarked, "Of course."

"Lily, is there something—?"

She interrupted him. "Tash is going to be on school holidays soon and I think we should plan a family trip."

Nate froze at her unexpected words.

He'd had family holidays with Victor and Laura but as Victor worked constantly, they'd been few and far between. During those holidays Jeff had taken every opportunity to torment Nate in his own special way while Danielle had taken her own opportunities to torment Nate in entirely different ways.

Nate did not have fond memories of family holidays.

Then again, Nate had very few fond memories and most of them centered around two weeks eight years ago and his most recent three.

Not knowing any of this, Lily continued, "I'm thinking Disneyland Paris. Tash has been wanting to go there forever and I've never—" She stopped abruptly and then quickly went on, trying to cover her reference to what she and Natasha had done without him over the years. A reference she knew would put Nate on edge. "Anyway, we'll all go for a few days and then Fazire can take Tash to the park and perhaps you and I can go into Paris for a day, or a couple of days, just the two of us. I've never been to Paris."

Nate was silent at this suggestion of a stereotypical family holiday with the inclusion of an intimate couple's getaway.

Lily was also silent.

Lily's silence was expectant.

Nate's was stunned.

And pleased.

She finally broke it. "Well, what do you think?"

"I'll have Jennifer set it up," Nate replied.

"Yippee!" she shouted so loudly that he had to take the phone away from his ear and he couldn't stop a small grin from forming on his lips as he heard her unconcealed glee.

Nate was also relatively certain his two employees heard her cheer. Especially since they glanced at each other with knowing looks and they *definitely* saw his heretofore unseen grin.

"I have to go," Nate told her, his grin gone and he was sending a cold look to both his staff, which immediately wiped any speculation off their faces.

"Oh, okay." Her voice sounded disappointed, and at that Nate felt that strange, relaxed feeling in his chest again. "When will you be home tonight?"

"The usual time."

"Oh, okay," she repeated then hesitated then she sighed deeply, and if he wasn't mistaken, meaningfully, then she said, "'Bye."

"I'll see you later."

He waited for her to hang up. She didn't.

"Lily?"

"Nate."

"Hang up," he commanded.

"*You* hang up," she retorted.

His eyes lifted to his employees again and one of them had dropped her head to stare at her lap, the other one was looking to the side and his lips were twitching.

"Lily, I have two of my staff in my office with me."

"Oh!" she exclaimed. "If you were busy, why did you take my call?"

"I've missed enough of your calls in the past. I won't miss another one," he responded and the steel in his voice, a far more familiar sound to them, caused both of his employee's faces to go instantly blank.

Lily's tone was warm and soft. "Nate."

Lily saying his name in that tone went straight through him.

"I have to go," he repeated, this time with a reluctance that he allowed to be read in his voice.

"'Bye," she said, that one word sweet and intimate, and Nate felt it almost as if it was a physical touch and that thing in his chest loosened just a bit more.

TWO WEEKENDS LATER ON A Saturday afternoon came the most profound of a month full of surprises.

Nate and Victor had finished going over some business in Nate's new study on the garden level. Father and son went in search of everyone else and found them in Lily's office on the top floor.

The house was complete, the workmen and decorators gone, the furniture and appliances replaced and it was now what Nate considered a home appropriate for Lily and Natasha. A home of consequence and quality for his family. A home *he* provided for them. The kind of home they deserved. The kind of home he would work until he died to be certain they always had.

The mortgage was now settled and Lily owned the house free and clear.

The furniture and fittings were all top of the line and even if something happened to him, she'd not have to replace them for decades.

Lily had stamped it with her quirky style that was both refined and offbeat. Muted colors mixed with bold, classical, elegant furniture twinned with distressed cottage-style antiques, the walls and most surfaces adorned with Fazire and her mother's framed photographs of family and her home in Indiana.

Lily had decorated her office in eggshell white with furniture upholstered in grass-green with lilac and sunshine-yellow toss pillows and accents.

The usually tidy room was covered in opened magazines and catalogs with pages torn out and strewn all over the place. There were also torn and frayed swatches of fabric dotting the floor and several surfaces.

Fazire was reclining in his usual armchair, and he was, for some reason, partially covered in an enormous swathe of taffeta the color of an eggplant. Maxine, wearing a turban nearly the same shade as Fazire's swathe but not a part of the afternoon's planning session, instead a part of her own bizarre ensemble, was seated at Lily's white, spindly-legged desk, clicking through photo after photo on Lily's laptop. Laura was reclining on Lily's chaise, an enormous book open on her lap displaying invitation selections.

"No purple," Lily decreed as Victor cleared the door and Nate stopped in it, taking in the scene.

"It has to be purple!" Maxine cried in a tone that said she'd absolutely *expire* if whatever it was they were discussing was not purple.

"I agree," Fazire announced pompously.

"No purple," Lily repeated.

"Pink!" Tash shouted over the conversation.

Lily was on her knees on the floor, her bottom resting on her calves that were folded underneath her. Four magazines were opened in front of her and swatches of fabric in every color of the rainbow were arrayed around and amongst the magazines.

Tash was standing behind Lily, her body pressed against her mother's back and her arms around Lily's neck. Lily was lightly holding on to Tash's elbows, keeping her daughter close.

"No pink, baby doll," Lily said softly then bent her head to kiss a spot just above Natasha's wrist, and at this sight Nate felt a warmth seep through him, starting in his gut and emanating upward.

"Gray. A nice, soft, dove gray," Laura suggested. "No one ever uses gray."

"What are you talking about?" Victor sat next to Laura on Lily's green chaise longue.

"Wedding colors," Maxine answered. "Fazire and I are agreed on purple. It's the only color that has more than one vote."

"Purple isn't very Lily, Maxine," Laura put in.

"Dove gray is *definitely* not Lily," Fazire stated firmly.

Nate leaned against the doorjamb and crossed his arms on his chest, surveying the scene with a vague sense of satisfaction.

Lily's eyes lifted to him, they dropped to where he was lounging against the jamb and then back to his face. Then he was arrested when he saw a secret, intimate smile play at the corners of her mouth before she looked away.

"It's *Lily's* wedding. She should pick the color," Victor noted logically.

"Lily, can I speak to you privately?" Nate cut in to the discussion, deciding to assuage his curiosity about her smile, the answer behind which he very much wanted to know, rather than wait for a determination of what their wedding colors would be, the answer to which he didn't care about in the slightest.

Everyone turned to stare at him, but without hesitation Lily kissed Natasha's arm again, gently disengaged from their daughter, stood and followed him out of the room, down the hall and into their newly completed bedroom.

Their room she had decorated in rich indigo, sharp vermillion and deep violet, somehow managing to make it both comfortably masculine and softly feminine, a place in their home that Lily was able to make for them both together and separately.

Once he closed the door behind him, she slid her arms around his waist and leaned her weight into his torso, a habit she had formed the last several weeks. It was something she did often, in fact, most every time she was near him.

"What's *your* favorite color?" she asked, her head tilted back and that strange, knowing smile still visible on her face.

One of his arms went about her, the other hand cupped her jaw, his thumb running along her cheekbone.

New Lily, he saw, was firmly in place. She was a mixture of his sweet Lily, the Lily he had saved from the purse snatcher, the mature but not lost nor broken Lily, and something else altogether. She was cheerful, playful, teasing, loving and relaxed. She was also something different, something alluring and mysterious, as if she had a secret but not a bad one.

A delicious one.

She'd begun spending the evenings in her office writing, using the laptop Nate had bought her or writing longhand in notebooks.

Natasha would sit with her and watch the new flat screen television using her headphones or Tash would sit in Nate's study when he was there, watching his flat screen television and wearing her headphones. Fazire would often join them when they were in Lily's office, Fazire sitting in Lily's grass-green armchair, his feet up on the ottoman, reading one of his books (Fazire didn't join Tash in Nate's study, however).

Lily had also started the habit of calling Nate regularly at his office, not every day but several times a week.

She had nothing to say and didn't want to know much of anything. She'd ask what he wanted for dinner (he never had a preference, food was food). When he'd be home (he was home the same time every night, except five minutes earlier each time). What he was doing at that particular moment (always working). Did he want Chinese takeaway that night (again, food was food). How he felt about beef Wellington served at their wedding reception (he only cared about Lily being legally tied to him, he didn't care what they ate after that came about).

It was clear she didn't really care about his answers, in fact, didn't demand them as he often didn't give them. It seemed, instead, as if she simply wanted to talk. As if she wanted a brief connection with him during the day and this connection had no strings. There was nothing loaded in their conversation. No wrong answer he could give. It was just her way of establishing a connection, any connection.

Each time she called, he dismissed anyone who was in his office with a sharp nod of his head, turned his chair to face the window, sat back and rested his ankle on his knee. Then he let her blather on, just like he let their daughter do when she called.

When Lily phoned, it too became known around the office as uninterruptible.

Without exception.

And during the last two weeks after Tash was in bed, there were three occasions when Lily asked Nate to go to the pub with her.

They quietly walked together down the sea path to her local. There, they sat outside by the sea, Nate drinking vodka and ice, Lily having a glass of white wine. Eventually, she'd lean into him and rest her head on his shoulder, his arm would slide around her and together they would watch the water.

She didn't ask probing questions. She didn't demand details of his past. Often, something in her thoughts would make her sigh but he never asked her about it and she never offered any explanation. Other times she'd break the silence and tell him about her family, her father, her mother, her grandmother, her old limestone house. These stories could be sweet, they could be funny but always they were tinged with her grief.

After a few drinks, they'd walk slowly home, taking their time and holding hands, and he'd take Lily to bed and make even slower love to her.

After those three nights, Nate noticed he'd had the most restful nights of sleep he could remember and he could remember every night of his life.

Once, when he had work to go over, needing to make detailed notes before a meeting the next day, he'd stayed late in his study asking Lily, for the first time that he had been in Somerset, to let Tash read to her so he could finish.

In the wee hours of the morning, Lily came down and knocked on his door. When he called her in, she jumped up and sat on the side of his desk and began a sweet and strange interrogation, asking him questions about what he was doing and what his work involved.

He calmly, but not very informatively, answered. He had work to do, it was late, he wanted to finish and join her in bed and he knew she had to be in the shop in only a few hours. He was trying to ignore the soft skin of her thigh that rested next to his forearm. He was trying to ignore when she'd lean forward and point at a graph on a document and ask a question, her cleavage bared to his view. He tried to ignore it when she regarded him levelly, her eyes warm, her thumb between her bared teeth, her mind obviously somewhere else, somewhere better as she watched his lips form brief words to answer her questions.

Eventually, she giggled, threw her hands in the air and stared for a moment at the ceiling. She then jumped off the side of his desk, grabbed his wrist and held it out so she could slide into his lap.

And seated there, she asked one final set of questions that swiftly ended the late night interrogation.

"What's a girl have to do around here to seduce her fiancé? I mean, how obvious could I be? Should I do a striptease? Roll around on your desk naked?"

She didn't finish, couldn't, as his mouth cut off her words.

And she did end up on his desk naked but she didn't have to roll around.

In their bedroom with the entirety of both of their family next door talking wedding colors, Nate's hand drifted from her jaw to tuck her hair behind her ear.

"My favorite color?" he repeated.

"Yes, *you* pick our wedding colors," she demanded, her tone teasing.

"Lily, my favorite color is red," he told her, her eyes widened and she burst into laughter, her body pressing closer to his.

"Dracula's wedding!" she shouted and Nate hoped Laura didn't overhear, her heart would explode. "I love that! I'll wear black with blood-red petticoats and carry red roses and you can wear a tuxedo with one of those crosses at your neck. We'll be the talk of the town."

Nate smiled at her outrageous suggestion as she snuggled closer.

"I'd rather not," he replied dryly.

"Me neither." Her sexy, knowing smile was gone and her quirky grin was back. "What did you want to talk to me about?"

"Nothing," he replied.

For some reason, her hilarity and the loss of that smile caused his curiosity to recede.

Her arms tightened around him and she kissed the underside of his chin.

Then she said, "Come on, Nate. You had something to ask?"

"It isn't important." He dropped his other arm to her waist, but to his surprise she let out an exasperated noise, pulled away and then, sharply, she pushed him towards the bed with both her hands at his chest.

He didn't move.

"What are you doing?" he asked as she planted one foot behind her and began to shove his chest with her full, leveraged weight behind her shove.

He still didn't move.

She ignored his question and muttered to herself, "Forget it, you aren't going to budge." And then she stopped shoving and started to unbutton his shirt.

At her bizarre and unexplained behavior, his voice was edgy and he grabbed both of her wrists.

"Lily, what in bloody hell are you doing?"

Her head came up and she leaned into him, ignoring his tone and allowing him to hold her wrists but now pressing her chest tantalizingly against his.

"I'm making you talk," she explained with a jaunty grin.

"I'm sorry?"

Without warning, her head bent to the middle of his chest where she'd managed to get his shirt unbuttoned. He felt her tongue on his skin and fire swept through him.

He jerked her back by her wrists.

"Lily, Natasha is in the next room."

Her grin turned devilish.

"Then you better talk quick before I ravish you." She leaned in again and ran her lips along the underside of his jaw and he felt his body's immediate reaction even as he bit back a smile.

"Ravish me?" he said, amusement in his voice.

His hands loosened on her wrists and she put them to good use, pulling his shirt free of his jeans.

"You think I can't do it?" Her head came up with her challenge and the midnight had nearly taken over the pale blue of her eyes.

He slid his hand into her hair at the left side of her head and gently fisted it at the back to hold her face tilted to his.

His head descended and softly, against her lips, he said, "Oh yes, darling, I think you can do it."

He felt, rather than saw, her smile and that feeling stole through him.

"Tell me why you wanted to talk to me," she coaxed, her hands edging lightly up the skin of his back.

He wasn't proof against her playful mood and he gave in. "Tell me why you were smiling."

His eyes were less than an inch from hers and he saw hers turn confused as her brows knitted.

"I'm smiling because you just admitted I could ravish you—" she began.

He shook his head and kissed her lightly then let his lips slide down her cheek to her ear, "Before, in your office, when you saw me in the door."

She moved back and looked at him, and there it was, that knowing look in her eye, the smile twitching her lips.

"That?" she asked.

He nodded. "That."

The smile deepened and, if it was possible, her eyes warmed further and she explained, "Remember when we first met, after Victor brought me back to his house and I was coming down the stairs when the police were there?"

Of course he remembered. He remembered like it happened only an hour earlier.

"Yes."

"Well, you were leaning against the wall like the hero in a romance novel then and you were doing it again just now. And I remembered when you did it then and how much . . . how you . . ." She stopped for some reason and started again, "How I so very much wanted you to notice me when I saw you leaning against the wall like a romantic hero. And, well, and then you did, er . . . notice me that is."

Her comment took him outside the playful mood, her words shaking him and he stilled.

"I'm sorry?" he queried.

She smiled at him, her eyes both alluring and dancing. "You're just like the hero in a romance novel. I should know, I've read *hundreds* of them. So has Maxie, you can ask her. I *promise*, she'll agree with me."

Before he could reply, she pulled away, brought her hands up between them and started counting things.

Things about him.

Things that made his stomach clench, his chest ache and his throat close.

At the same time he felt all this, conversely, he also felt like bursting into laughter.

"First, you are inconceivably, *impossibly* handsome," she began. "And you *lean* very well."

"I *lean* well?" he asked incredulously.

She nodded vigorously. "*Very* well," she assured him as if leaning well was a trait akin to honesty, integrity, diplomacy and generosity all rolled into one. "And you're tall and dark and narrow-hipped—"

"Narrow-what?" Nate interrupted her but Lily ignored his interruption.

"And you're very clever. Beyond clever. You're brilliant. And you're hard-working. You're virile and fierce—"

"Lily—"

"And rugged—"

He couldn't help himself, he started laughing.

Rugged?

"Lily—" he tried interrupting her again but she stopped ticking off her hilarious list and put her hands on either side of his face and what she said next made all amusement flee.

"You're everything I ever wanted. You're exactly what I wished for when I was fourteen years old. Exactly. You can ask Fazire. I told him what I wanted and then, years later, there you were. And you were perfect. I knew it the minute I laid eyes on you. I knew who you were and I knew I wanted you and I knew you were *mine*."

Nate stiffened, his body going stock still, and he shook his head, pulling away from her, putting distance between them and he felt his shields go up. He didn't put them up. They went up automatically.

Softly, as a warning, he told her, "You have no idea who I am."

She didn't allow him to retreat. She closed the distance and wrapped her arms around his waist, holding on tightly.

"I know *exactly* who you are."

He shook his head again, once, a definite negative but she kept talking, this time her voice was fierce and there was an iron edging her words.

"You're Nathaniel McAllister. You're my lover. You're the father of my child. You take care of your family. You'll never let us go without again and you'll never let me go again." She flattened herself against him and lifted her lips against his. "Nate, you're *mine*. *You* belong to me and I belong to *you*."

He felt her words tear through him.

If she knew about him, her words wouldn't be so fervent, so determined.

He lifted his hands to either side of her face.

"You're right, Lily, I'll never let you go but you've no idea who I am."

She kissed him silent and then said softly, "You can have your secrets. I don't care about them. You can tell them or you can keep them. But Nate, I know who you are. I may just have learned your favorite color but I *know* you'll never let me hurt again. And you wouldn't have done it before if you'd thought it was within your power." Her gaze, which had been intent, lightened and she finished, "By the way, Jeff doesn't lean. He slouches."

At her quick change in topic, her tone moving from impassioned to playfully informative, unusually, Nate lost track of the conversation.

"I beg your pardon?"

On a wicked grin she said, "Jeff, your brother, he doesn't lean like a sexy romantic hero, like *you* do. He *slouches*, like a snotty schoolboy."

At that, Nate finally allowed himself to give in to laughter. Letting the rest of it go. Burying it deep so after she knew, after she went away, he could take it out and savor it.

Snatching her to him, he threw his head back and roared with laughter, holding her close.

Nate nor Lily had any idea that the inhabitants of the room next door went silent and listened to him laugh. Two of them smiled. One of them giggled. The last scowled.

In their bedroom, Lily's mouth against Nate's neck, when he stopped laughing, she said quietly against his skin, "Something else you should know, *I'll* never let *you* go either."

And Nate felt her words were less words and more a vow and his arms tightened around her.

NOW HE WAS ON HIS way home, to his most recent surprise, another day bringing him closer to the end, another day he had to relish as he waited for his good fortune to run out.

TWENTY-THREE

Lily & Fazire & Nate

"DADDEEEE!" TASH YELLED, AND they heard her crashing through the house to get to the front door.

Lily was in the kitchen helping Fazire prepare dinner. At her daughter's cry, she knew Nate was home. She knew this because Tash's exuberant shout had become the nightly ritual upon Nate's arrival home.

However tonight there was a bit more excitement behind the mad dash.

Lily's eyes flew to Victor who was sitting at the kitchen table going through some papers.

It was Thursday. Victor and Laura weren't due to visit until Saturday but Lily had recruited Victor in her latest strategy to get Nate to trust in her, in their family, in happiness.

She wasn't lying to him when she told him she didn't want to know his secrets. She didn't want to know, she didn't care what they were. Whatever they were wouldn't matter in the slightest.

She just wanted him to believe, believe in her, believe in their family and believe in himself. She knew he didn't. She was shocked by that knowledge but she knew it was there all the same. It held him back, kept him away from her, kept him removed and she wanted—no, it had now become a need, she *needed* him. She needed him for Tash *and* she needed him for herself.

She wasn't making a lot of headway, no matter how hard she tried (and she'd been trying *very* hard). So she'd decided to pull out the big guns and enlist Laura and Victor. It was a desperate measure but she didn't care about that either. She wasn't too proud to admit she was desperate.

This was her family she was worried about.

Lily would do anything.

Catching her look, Victor grinned at her.

Lily grabbed a tea towel and dried her hands quickly, throwing a nervous smile at Victor, then one to Fazire.

Fazire was watching her closely. Fazire, Lily noticed the last couple of weeks, was watching *everything* closely. Even closer than normal. Especially Nate.

Lily didn't have time to worry about Fazire. She rushed out of the kitchen and down the hall, feeling nervous. Why, she didn't know. She wanted this to be perfect, to be meaningful, to put at least one dent in that armor around Nate's heart, to watch just one drop melt off the ice that encased it.

Laura rushed into the hall from the living room, her eyes wide and excited. When she spied Lily, she gave a little giggle. At the same time, both women's hands searched for the others', they clasped them tightly and walked out the front door.

Tash was dancing around Nate and the brand-new, bright-red Ducati motorcycle that was sitting on the front walk, an even brighter red, huge bow adorning it.

Victor had chosen the bike because Lily didn't know anything about Ducatis. Nate had one of course, in London, but he didn't have one in Somerset. Victor had assured her this bike was the best, the most expensive, the top of the line and it certainly looked it (*and* cost it). Victor had arranged for it to be delivered and Lily had paid for it out of her seven million pounds. It was the first time she touched the money. Victor had also decided that he and Laura had to come to watch the presentation, certain it would be a doozy.

It was a doozy all right.

Nate was staring at the motorcycle.

Tash was shouting.

"Mummy bought it for you! Isn't it pretty? She says you'll take me for a ride. She got helmets and everything! One for you, one for her, one for Fazire and even a small one, *for me!*"

Nate's eyes went from the bike to Lily, who had stopped just outside the front door, and Laura had stopped beside her. Lily felt Fazire and Victor move in behind them.

She smiled at Nate.

Nate frowned at her.

"Do you like it? Do you like it? Do you like it?" Tash sing-songed, still dancing around the bike.

Nate was still glaring at Lily seemingly frozen to the spot.

Lily was confused at his glare and her smile faltered.

"I wish to speak to you privately," Nate announced, his voice sounded controlled, formal. He came unstuck and stalked toward her.

"Nate—" Lily started but he was already there, grabbing her hand and pulling her into the house, right through Victor and Fazire, going so far as shoving his father out of the way.

"He likes it! Daddy always speaks to Mummy *privately* when he's happy," Tash yelled.

Lily felt relief because what Natasha said was true. Nate carefully shielded Tash from any of his more amorous displays of affection. He was openly affectionate with Lily in front of anyone, holding her hand, touching her, brushing his lips against hers. But if he wanted something deeper and more meaningful, he did it behind closed doors.

Nate dragged Lily up the stairs, all the way up to their bedroom. He pulled her inside and then he slammed the door. Slammed it so hard it felt like it shook the house.

Lily stopped several steps away from him, tilted her head to look at him and smiled, woefully misinterpreting the intensity behind his actions.

"I take it you like the bike," she said through her smile.

Nate stared at her, his eyes didn't look happy. In fact, he looked angry. Very angry.

Her smile faltered.

"Who paid for that bike?" Nate asked, his voice dangerously calm.

She blinked at him, again beginning to be confused and the smile melted from her face.

"I did. It's a present from me," she replied.

"I already have a bike."

Lily felt her heart sink. "I know. But it's not here and I thought—"

He interrupted her. "What money did you use to pay for that bike?"

Her body jerked and she realized, too late, where she went wrong. All of a sudden the gesture seemed silly. Indeed, it *was* silly. He'd paid for his own present.

"I used the money you gave me," she answered in a small voice.

She felt tears start to prick her eyes. This was not going well at all.

"Lily, I told you, that money is for you." Again, his tone was calm, even, low and still dangerous and she could tell he was angry.

"Yes, I know," she went on. "It's mine, that's why I bought a present with it, er, for you."

He kept his body still and the distance between them. She could tell this took an effort. She could tell he wanted to approach her and, for some reason, shake some sense into her and all of a sudden she felt afraid.

"You don't use that fucking money for me. I don't need a goddamned bike. I thought I explained this but I'll explain it again," he continued, using patience, what appeared to be *extreme* patience. "That money is yours. You use it for you."

"Nate—" she began only to be interrupted again and it was clear his patience had quickly run out.

"I've got everything I need right here in this goddamned, *fucking* house!"

Even though Nate's words were beautiful (in a way), Lily winced for two reasons.

Firstly, he'd lost his temper and his voice was raised. In fact, he was shouting and she'd never seen him that angry. He was, quite simply, enraged.

Secondly, he was cursing flagrantly. He didn't shy away from a curse word but he also didn't use them very often. And certainly not in a raised voice that could be overheard by his daughter who he went to great pains to protect from anything he felt might be inappropriate.

Surprisingly, considering Nate didn't talk much, he wasn't finished and he was getting louder.

"And you don't use it on Natasha. *I'll* take care of our daughter."

"Nate—" she tried again, using what she hoped was a soothing voice, but he interrupted her again and he was even louder.

"And you don't use it on Fazire. It's clear you took care of Fazire, and anything you used to take care of, now, *I* take care of. Is that understood?"

Lily was losing her fear and beginning to get angry. Therefore she didn't reply because she was attempting to control her own temper.

He took a giant stride forward, which meant when he stopped he was an inch away, and he dipped his face to hers.

Stubbornly and angrily, she held her ground.

"*Is that fucking understood?*" Nate roared and she'd had enough.

She was just trying to do something nice. She was just trying to melt his heart. She was just trying to *make him happy*.

"Don't yell at me!" she yelled.

"Tell me I'm understood!" he yelled back.

"I can't use seven million pounds on me!" Lily returned just as loudly, head tilted back, hands clenched into fists at her sides and shouting in his face. "You pay for everything! The groceries! My new car! You bought me a new cashmere cardigan that I didn't even *need* just a week ago! You even paid off the mortgage! What am I going to do with seven million pounds?"

"Go shopping. Go to a spa. Fly to fucking Paris and watch the collections and buy every stitch of clothing at Chanel. Get a manicure every day. It doesn't matter. Just use it . . . *on you!*" Nate shouted back.

Her eyes narrowed on him. "Go . . . go . . . you want me to go *shopping* with seven million pounds?" she spluttered (still loudly). "Get a seven million pound manicure?" she yelled nonsensically.

He took a step back, his eyes still glittering with anger but she could tell he was trying to control himself.

"I don't give a fuck. Just don't spend it on anyone but you," he demanded (also still loudly) and then started to turn away toward the door like they were done talking or, more to the point, yelling, which they *were not*. Then he turned back. "I'll have the money for the bike transferred into your account."

"Don't you dare!" she shouted but she shouted it at his back. He'd opened the door and disappeared.

She stared at the space where his back used to be and she realized she was breathing heavily, her heart was pounding and she'd never been so angry in her entire life.

Lily took a deep breath then a second one and through that one she heard another door slamming somewhere far away but it still shook the house.

Nate's study.

At the sound, she stopped trying to calm herself and stomped out of her room. She then stomped down the stairs. Then she stomped down the second flight of stairs right past Victor, Laura, Fazire and Tash and even Mrs. Gunderson, who sat beside Tash, tail twitching. They were all standing in the hallway, their eyes, in unison, watching her progress as she rounded the ground floor landing and stomped down to the garden level.

She walked right up to Nate's closed study door and without knocking she threw it open, stomped inside and then *she* slammed it shut.

He was standing behind his desk, papers in his hands, for some reason the brightly colored plastic box that held her household files was opened and on top of his desk.

She ignored the box and ignored the searing glance he aimed at her.

"We're not done," she announced.

"We're done," Nate retorted.

"We are not!" Lily yelled.

Calmly, he looked back down at the papers in his hands, dismissing her.

At this, Lily threw her head back and screamed blue, bloody murder. When she was done, she tipped her chin down again and glared at him. He was most certainly looking at her now, with narrowed eyes and knitted brows.

"Good!" she snapped. "I have your attention."

With that she advanced on him, rounding his desk. He turned to face her and she halted a foot away from him and lifted her finger.

"It's *my* seven million pounds. You gave it to *me*!" she shouted and with every verbally-underlined word, she poked him in the chest. "If I want to buy you a motorcycle with it, I'll *bloody well* buy you a motorcycle. If I want to buy you a prized pedigree *King Charles spaniel* that costs the moon, *I'll* buy it for you. If I want to commission *blind nuns* in a convent in the *depths* of the Pyrenees to craft you the finest *tailored shirts* fashioned from silk spun from a *near extinct* species of silk worm, *I'll* do it! Now, is *that* understood?"

After she stopped shouting, Lily saw emotions warring on his face and she couldn't latch on to any one of them but she thought she glimpsed amusement as well as anger there. And something else. Something she definitely couldn't read.

"If something happens to me, I want you to be taken care of. I don't want you wasting that money on me," he told her, his voice much softer but his dark eyes were intense.

"Nothing's going to happen to you," she snapped, not feeling any less intense and her voice was not one iota softer.

Finally, he touched her. He dropped the papers he was holding on his desk and his hands settled on either side of her neck, one of his thumbs moving to stroke her cheek.

When he spoke again, his voice was gentle. "If there comes a time in your life when I'm not in it, I want to know you'll want for nothing."

"That's *not* going to happen!" she yelled, now her raging feelings even *more* intense knowing she hadn't made the tiniest nick in his armor, not even a scratch.

Furthermore, she was beginning to get scared.

Why would there be a time when he wasn't in her life?

"Nate, I'm not letting you go," Lily declared, scowling at him to hide her fear. "Whatever is going on in that head of yours, forget it. I'm not letting you go. You're not letting me go. No matter what."

"Lily—"

"No! No matter what!" she snapped. "*Now* we're done talking."

She pulled her neck away from his hands and stomped back to the door, feeling relatively pleased with herself, feeling she'd made her point.

"Lily," he called and she halted, hand on the door, and whirled around to glare at him again, not wishing to lose ground. Even if she hadn't put a scratch in his armor, he'd have to be an idiot not to understand what she just said and Nate was no idiot.

"What?" she clipped.

He watched her a second and she realized whatever emotion that had hold of him was gone. She knew this because his lips were twitching.

"After . . . that," he started, his voice was no longer angry, there was no intensity and there was no gentleness either, he was definitely amused, "I hesitate to mention money again, but you've a separate bank account with a goodly amount in it." He pointed to the paper on his desk that he'd been studying when she'd arrived.

She stomped back around the desk to stand beside him, snatched up the bank statement and stared at it.

It was Tash's school fund.

"It's clear you could have used that money. I'm wondering why—" he began.

"I never touch that. That's Tash's school money," Lily answered his unasked question, tossing the bank statement down on his desk.

He stared at her, eyes blank. "I'm sorry?"

She turned to him and put a hand on her hip. "Tash's school money. Tash is a gifted child. It's not just me who thinks so as a doting mother, so do her teachers. They told me she'd benefit from a special school. Those schools cost money, *lots* of money. I've been saving—"

Something shifted in the room and that something emanated from Nate and the power of it made Lily stop speaking. It was something she didn't understand but Nate didn't look amused anymore. He also didn't look blank. His eyes were burning into her so intensely she felt they'd scorch her skin.

"You did without to save money so Natasha could go to a school for gifted children?" he asked.

Lily felt a shiver slide across her skin at the tone of his voice. Again, she couldn't put her finger on it, didn't know what it was but it meant something to him. Something profound.

"Of course," Lily said quietly, knowing, in her experience of families, in her experience of people, an experience she *didn't* know was vastly different from his, that any mother would do the same. Those two words were said with the kind of certainty that someone would declare the sky blue and the earth round. "Can I spend my seven million on that?" she ventured carefully.

Tash could go to the best school in the world with seven million pounds.

Nate didn't answer her. In another abrupt change of mood, he swept her in his arms and held her so tightly she couldn't breathe. He buried his face in the hair at her neck and for long moments he didn't speak and he didn't let her go.

"Nate," Lily whispered, "I can't breathe."

At her words, his arms loosened but he still didn't let her go.

Finally, after whole minutes slid by, he lifted his head and looked into her eyes and what she saw made her not able to breathe again. It was raw and aching and the weight of it fell on her like an avalanche.

"No," he said softly. "I'll pay for Tash's school."

She nodded immediately, not wanting to do anything to deepen that ache in his eyes.

"I've already noticed she's advanced for her age," he went on.

"*Significantly* advanced," Lily told him.

He smiled, that awful look thankfully melting from his face. It warmed and he bent his head to kiss her lightly.

"Significantly advanced," he agreed against her mouth.

"Like her father," Lily continued, staring close up into his eyes.

"Like her mother," Nate parried.

She shook her head and put her hand to his cheek.

"What am I going to do with you?" she whispered.

"Help me select a school for our daughter," he responded without hesitation. "I've already made a shortlist."

Her eyes rounded at his announcement then she grinned and leaned into him, dropped her hand from his cheek and wrapped both her arms around his waist.

"Okay," she answered.

Lily pressed her cheek to his chest and she felt him rest his on the top of her head.

And, Lily realized, joy beginning to bud in her heart, that she'd done something ages ago, something that was for Tash, something that no hugs, no afternoon phone calls to his office, no expensive motorcycles could do.

What she'd done for their daughter, *his* daughter, rent a huge, gaping hole in his armor.

She closed her eyes tightly and felt hope.

"Lily?" he called against her hair.

"Yes?" she whispered, her eyes opening.

"Please don't buy me a King Charles spaniel. I'm not fond of small dogs."

She closed her eyes again, this time with laughter.

THE MOTORBIKE ROARED UP TO the front of the house, Nathaniel's tall, lean body on the front, Tash's small, lean body holding tight to him on the back.

Fazire did *not* like motorbikes. He had not liked Will's and he did not like Nathaniel's. What was in Lily's head when she bought that bike, Fazire did *not* know. To Fazire, motorbikes were certain death on two wheels.

After her father stopped the bike, turned it off and shoved down the stand, Tash jumped off the back and pulled off her helmet like she'd been doing the exact same thing every day since the day she was born.

Fazire, Laura, Victor and Lily were standing at the front of the house watching the father and daughter pair. Lily went forward as Tash ran to her.

"Did you like it, baby doll?" Lily asked as she arrived at her daughter.

"I loved it. Loved it, loved it, loved it!" Tash cried, throwing her arms around Lily and jumping up and down, shaking Lily with her excitement. Then she stopped jumping and she leaned back, her arms still around Lily's waist. "I tried to make him go faster but Daddy wouldn't, no matter how much I begged and *pleaded*," she finished dramatically.

"Thank goodness for that," Laura muttered, with feeling, under her breath.

Fazire's eyes turned to Laura and they shared their first look of complete accord.

"Your turn," Fazire heard Nathaniel's deep voice say and his eyes moved back to the tall man and he saw that Nathaniel was looking at Lily.

"Oh no," Lily said, backing up a step then two. "I'm too old for bikes."

"Oh Mummy, you must go! You must!" Tash cried, rounding her mother and putting both hands on Lily's behind and pushing forward while Lily still retreated, Nathaniel advancing on her.

"Nate—" Lily said warningly and Fazire understood why. Nathaniel's face had a set look and he was grinning.

Fazire sighed.

Lily was going to be next on the bike.

Fazire heard a squeal, quickly followed by another one as Nathaniel made it to Lily and lifted her up, swinging her around, and with quick, long strides he carried her toward the bike. The first squeal was Lily's, the second squeal was Tash's and the little girl was jumping up and down again, clapping.

"Go, Daddy, go!" she encouraged.

"Don't forget her helmet!" Laura called, turning to rush into the house.

"On their first date, he took her on his bike," Victor said beside him and Fazire's eyes moved to the man at his side. Victor sounded like he was talking to himself and Fazire realized this was true when he saw the faraway look on Victor's face. "He never brought her back and I knew he wouldn't. That night, after he called to tell me she wasn't coming home, I never would have thought it would have ended so soon." Abruptly, Victor stopped speaking.

Whether this was because the pain of the memory or something else, Fazire didn't know but something flashed on the other man's face as he watched the pair and Fazire's eyes swung back to Nathaniel and Lily.

"Oh my—" Laura breathed, now back and holding Lily's helmet.

Nathaniel was zipping his leather jacket on Lily and for some reason Fazire saw this brought tears to Lily's eyes. After Nathaniel was done with the zipper, Lily threw her arms around his neck and kissed him. Not a soft, demure kiss but a kiss the like little Tash shouldn't see. Surprisingly, because Fazire knew Nathaniel was very careful with these sensitive, private matters, Nathaniel's arms closed around Lily, pulling her deep into his body, his head slanted and it became a kiss that little Tash *really* shouldn't see.

"Fucking hell," Victor murmured words Tash shouldn't hear but she'd heard a lot of them that day, also from her father.

Fazire's arm shot out and he pulled Tash to him and covered her eyes with his hand.

"Fazire!" Tash shouted, trying to yank his hand away and Lily and Nathaniel realized what they were about. Their lips disengaged, though their arms didn't, and the pair looked at their audience.

Fazire could see Lily blush.

"There are children in attendance," Fazire snapped across the expanse, dropping his hand from Tash's eyes.

Nathaniel's gaze sliced to Fazire but other than that he made no response.

"Fazire!" Tash shouted again, planted her hands on her hips and gave him a pouty look. He glared right back at her. They were locked in a staring contest, which Fazire would win because he had lots of practice with Becky, Lily and seven years with Tash, not to mention he was immortal so he had all the time in the world.

Laura moved forward with the helmet and Tash lost the contest as she turned, crossed her arms on her chest and looked toward her parents.

"Can you let Tash read to you tonight? We might be a while," Nathaniel said to his mother.

"Of course," Laura replied, clearly pleased with the offer to spend more time with her granddaughter.

Nathaniel turned to Natasha and he didn't have to say a word. She ran forward and gave goodnight hugs and kisses. The one to Lily was a hug about the waist and a kiss from her mother who bent down to do it. Nathaniel lifted her up, Tash wrapped her arms and legs around him and kissed him soundly on the mouth before she pressed her cheek to his shoulder and, after a few moments locked together with Lily looking on, a smile on her face, Nathaniel set her down.

Tash stepped back to hold Laura's hand. Nathaniel got on the bike, Lily got on behind him, wrapped her arms around him tightly, put her chin on his shoulder and they shot from the curb far faster and far, *far* more dangerously than he'd gone when Tash was on the bike with him.

"He's the bomb," Tash whispered, watching them go.

Fazire had had enough.

He turned to Victor.

"We must speak," he announced.

Without waiting for Victor to reply, Fazire stomped into the house, down the stairs and into their new family room.

It was just like the old family room except it had a bigger, fluffier, more attractive corner couch with a big ottoman in the front that could sleep three small, active children. Fazire liked this couch. The old one was comfortable but he could retire on *this* couch. This couch was more comfortable than the hundreds of cushions that made his bottle a home.

There also was an enormous flat screen television set affixed to the wall. Fazire liked this television too. His westerns came alive on that television. Clint Eastwood looked like he was actually in the room.

There were also nicer, sturdier, more attractive bookshelves and more of them so he could have much more space to fill photo albums and put framed pictures.

In fact, Fazire liked the whole house. He liked the KitchenAid mixer and blender. He liked the new refrigerator, which was like the ones in America that actually had room enough to fit food in it for more than a day. He liked Lily's office and the fact she had time to write.

He liked a lot of facts about Lily. The fact that Lily was smiling again. The fact that Lily was laughing again. The fact that Lily's face rarely looked pinched and worried about money or Tash or anything.

Anything, that was, except when she looked at Nathaniel.

Fazire had decided he'd done his job well. It just took a long time for it to realize. Like a gestation period for babies. Lily *had* asked, with her wish, that she and her lover go through trials and tribulations. Unfortunately, Fazire was a wee bit *too* good at granting his wishes (he always had been, he thought with little humility). When he tied Lily's life to Nathaniel's with her wish, he'd chosen the exact right man and she'd been given everything she wanted.

However, at fourteen years old, she didn't understand that all those terrible troubles the heroines in her books went through in real life hurt. That the words were just words on a page, but in real life, the pain was immense. Trials and tribulations to prove your love were exactly that, *trials* and *tribulations*.

And Lily wasn't through with hers. Neither was Nathaniel. Not just yet.

Victor followed Fazire into the room and closed the door behind him.

"What now?" Victor asked, wary eyes on Fazire.

Fazire wanted to float. He really, *really* wanted to float but he kept his feet on the ground for now.

"Tell me," he commanded in his best genie voice.

"Tell you what?" Victor asked, not, unfortunately to Fazire's way of thinking, a human who liked to be commanded.

"Tell me about your boy."

Victor's body grew tense and he did not respond.

"I can fix him," Fazire announced.

"What did you say?" Victor asked.

"I can fix him. You tell me about him, what's stopping him from giving himself to Lily, I can tell Lily and she can wish for it and I can fix him," Fazire explained.

Fazire didn't want to do this, not in a million years. He didn't want to go back into his bottle and be passed along to the next greedy, grasping, vengeful human. He wanted to watch Tash grow up. He wanted to watch Tash's daughter grow up. And her daughter and . . .

"You're mad," Victor cut into Fazire's dismal thoughts.

"I'm not mad. I'm here for a reason. I know you humans think I'm strange and I don't care. I think you humans are strange because you humans *are* strange. However, I've got a purpose in Lily's life and I'm quite prepared to—"

"We *humans*?" Victor asked, watching Fazire closely.

Fazire nodded, crossed his arms on his chest above his belly and tilted his head back to stare down, or more to the point, *up* his nose at Victor. "Yes, you humans."

"And what are you?" Victor queried.

"I'm a genie," Fazire announced.

Victor's brows snapped together, he stared and then his face got a little scary even for Fazire who wasn't scared of anything.

"You think you're a genie," Victor said slowly and incredulously.

"I *am* a genie."

"You think you're a genie and you're living with my granddaughter, Lily, my son—"

"I *am* a genie," Fazire repeated.

Victor stared at him for long moments then he crossed *his* arms on *his* chest and said quietly, "Maybe we need to find you a home. Someplace comfortable—"

"I have a home. *This* is my home and then there's my bottle and—"

"Dear God," Victor breathed, his brows coming unknitted and he looked no longer frightening but concerned.

Fazire sighed. There was nothing for it.

Therefore he floated. He crossed his legs under him and he snapped his fingers so his human clothes immediately changed to his genie clothes including the fez, gold armbands and earrings.

Victor's concerned look was gone. His head was tilted back to stare at Fazire drifting five feet up in the air and Victor's mouth was open.

"Sarah, Lily's grandmother, was my first mistress. She gave her wishes to her daughter Becky, Lily's mother," Fazire explained, staring down at the stunned and speechless Victor. "Becky couldn't have babies so she made a wish and I made Lily. I made her perfect and sweet, just what you see. But I wanted her to have humility—"

Fazire explained how Lily used to be, even magically floated a photo album out, an act that startled Victor and made him take two steps back, and flipped it to the right pages so Victor could see the chubby, plain, adolescent Lily, something else that made Victor look like he could not believe his eyes. Then Fazire told Victor about Lily's wish and where Nathaniel came into this mess.

"It was the most complicated wish *ever*," Fazire informed Victor. "Now he's back and it seems her wish came true. I was channeled last night and told I was nominated for Best Wish of the Century Award. So far this century, I'm the only one nominated. I figure I could win. No one has ever had a wish like *that*."

Victor stayed mute, didn't utter a sound throughout Fazire's explanation.

Fazire floated closer to him and closer to the floor.

"Now," he said softly instead of commanding it because it meant a great deal, a great deal to Lily. And even though it also could mean that Lily would use her last wish and he would go away, he wanted to give this to her. He wanted to fix Nathaniel. He wanted it for Lily and, these last few weeks, watching the tall, proud, intelligent man and how he looked at and treated Lily and his daughter, he wanted it for Nathaniel too. "Tell me about your boy so I can fix him."

Victor closed his eyes slowly.

He opened them again, sat down on the couch and put his head in his hands.

Fazire snapped his fingers and he was in his human clothes. He floated low until his feet touched the floor. He walked over, sat on the opposite side of the couch to Victor and he waited.

Victor's head came up and he looked at Fazire. He seemed startled for a second as he hadn't realized Fazire had changed back but he recovered quickly.

"I can't believe you're a genie," Victor whispered.

"If you tell anyone, I'll have to kill you," Fazire lied. This was entirely untrue but he'd always wanted to use that line.

Victor shook his head.

"Does Tash know you're a genie?" Victor asked.

Fazire nodded.

"Does Nathaniel know you're a genie?" Victor went on.

Fazire shook his head.

"Fucking hell," Victor breathed.

"You really shouldn't use that kind of language, *especially* with a youngster in the house," Fazire admonished.

Victor just kept staring at him.

"Tell me about Nathaniel," Fazire prompted.

Finally Victor relented. "I'll tell you about Nathaniel but you have to give him time. And Lily time. If they don't seem to be working it out on their own—"

"I'll give them time," Fazire interrupted.

"You can't tell Lily right away," Victor pressed.

"I won't tell her right away." Finally in exasperation Fazire snapped, "I'm a genie! I know what I'm doing."

Really, what could be so bad about Nathaniel? It was obvious to anyone he was a good man. Fazire even *wanted* to dislike him and he couldn't hold out for more than a few weeks and Fazire was really good at holding a grudge. He once went three hundred years holding a grudge against another genie. He was famous for it.

Victor interrupted his thoughts and started talking. While listening to the terrible tale, Fazire stopped thinking.

When Victor stopped talking, Fazire said immediately, "I *must* tell Lily."

"You tell her, I'll have to kill you," Victor threatened and even though Fazire was immortal, he still felt a thrill of fear.

"Why would he—?" Fazire started.

"I've no idea," Victor cut in.

"But it's nothing to be ashamed—" Fazire continued.

"I know," Victor interrupted again.

"I can't fix that," Fazire admitted and it was true. He couldn't. *No one* could fix that.

Except but one person.

"Lily can," both Fazire and Victor said in unison.

NATE WAS LYING IN BED, covers to his waist, some papers in his hands he should have gone through that evening rather than taking his daughter and Lily on motorcycle rides.

Instead of reading them, he was thinking about the rides, Tash's excited babble in is ear, Lily's body pressed against his.

He was also thinking about the only present he'd ever received from anyone outside his adopted family. A present from Lily. She hadn't bought him a tie or a watch. She'd bought him a motorcycle. No half measures for Lily, he was discovering.

Lastly, he was wondering if there were blind nuns in the Pyrenees who made tailored shirts out of rare silk and he was hoping Lily didn't have their phone number.

Lily walked out of the bathroom wearing another pair of short drawstring pajama shorts, these were light blue with green polka dots and they were topped by a fitted green camisole. She was rubbing lotion into her hands and arms that made the room smell of almonds. He noticed and was pleased to see that she'd gained some weight in the past weeks, her too-thin body filling out into the lush curves he was more familiar with and he vastly preferred.

He watched her walk toward the bed, graceful and unaffected, having no idea that even in her pajamas she was more elegant than any woman he'd ever met.

She jumped up and landed on her knees at the end of the bed, sitting on her calves. Her eyes found his and she smiled at him, but Nate noticed her smile was warm but guarded.

He gave up all pretense of reading and tossed the papers on the bedside table.

"What's on your mind?" he asked, correctly reading her face.

Her eyes lit with a knowing look, not surprised he surmised her troubled thoughts and asked about them. To Nate's way of thinking, time was too precious not to cut to the chase immediately, most especially any time with Lily.

She tilted her head to the side and bit her lip.

Releasing it, she said, "Promise you won't get mad?"

Nate wanted to laugh but he didn't. Lily on the end of their bed smiling at him, however guarded, Tash downstairs asleep and exhausted from an exciting day that centered around Lily's generosity, his parents in Lily's old room, now the guest bedroom—with all that, there was practically no way he *could* get mad.

Of course, after what he expected she considered his irrational response to her giving him a present, a response he knew wasn't at all irrational, he could understand her concern.

"I won't get mad," he assured her softly then, deciding she was too far away, he commanded in an even softer voice, "Come here."

She shook her head, her smile fading and he felt something constrict in his chest as he witnessed its loss.

"I need to tell you something and I think I better do it from here."

He kept silent and felt his shields go up as he watched her warily.

She took a deep breath.

"It's all my fault," she declared.

He stayed silent at her strange declaration.

She hesitated and then spoke again. "Everything that's happened to us. It's all my fault."

He still didn't speak, this time because he could not imagine how Lily had turned things around in her head to think that *anything* she'd done could make what had happened to them her fault.

"You see," she went on, "these past eight years, I knew I should, I wanted to, but something always got in the way, but I always knew I should go to Victor and Laura and I didn't."

Finally he understood her worry. His shields went down and he broke his silence. "Lily, darling, come here."

She shook her head again, her red-gold hair brushing her shoulders.

"I need you to know. I need to say this. Nate, I couldn't afford it. I could have called them but what do you say? I was ill, at first, but that's no excuse. I mean, I got better then it was *years*—"

"Lily—" he interrupted but she was on a roll and getting agitated. He knew this because she jumped off the bed and began pacing.

"I wrote them letters, dozens of them, trying to explain. I thought I could do it better by writing it. I'm a good writer, a long time ago, I even won awards. I never told you that." She stopped and looked at him as if shy of this admission then she brought up her hands and her fingers started to fidget, clenching and unclenching. "If I'd gone to them, if I'd called, just sent one letter, I can't even understand myself why I didn't send—"

Nate decided this was enough.

He threw off the covers, knifed off the bed and advanced on her. He was not about to allow her to berate herself for Danielle and Jeffrey's deception, not after what she'd been through.

She didn't retreat but when his arms went around her, she kept her hands between them and pressed them against his chest. She tilted her head back, looked at him and he saw her eyes were tormented. At the sight, he felt fury blaze through him but, as he'd promised her, he kept it firmly under control.

She went on quietly, "I thought they knew about my parents dying. I thought they knew and they didn't care about me enough to—"

His arms tightened but her hands pushed against him to keep some distance.

"Lily, I don't want to hear—" he started.

She shook her head again. "You have to know that's what I thought, even though it sounds awful. I thought they might be like Jeff and Danielle. I know it wasn't right but part of me—"

He saw the tears spring to her eyes and he decided it was a good thing he'd likely never see his sister and brother again for he would not be responsible for what he did.

"I need to explain to them. I need to apologize," Lily went on.

His arms went from around her and he wrapped his fingers around her wrists. Pulling her hands from between their bodies, he gently maneuvered her against the length of him. When he released her, she slid her arms around his waist and leaned into him and he framed her face with his hands.

"Let it be," he said softly.

"I can't," she replied. "They have to be wondering. Nate, it was seven years I had their granddaughter and I haven't even told you about my wish yet. When I do, you'll understand, it's all my fault—"

At the torment in her eyes, Nate wanted to throw something across the room. He wanted to do someone (and he knew *exactly* who) bodily harm. Instead, he kept careful control of these reactions and he hushed Lily by touching his lips to hers.

When he'd moved an inch away, he looked deep into her eyes and repeated, "Let it be, Lily."

She was, he noted, not ready to let it be.

"I can show them the letters. I still have them, every single one. And I have to tell you about Fazire, what I wished, how this all comes down to me."

One lone tear slid down her cheek. Nate brushed it away with his thumb and decided their conversation was finished. He wasn't going to allow Lily to blame herself for their loss, and he was definitely not going to stand there and watch her cry.

"It's over, everyone is moving on," Nate explained quietly. "There's no reason to go back. Just let it be."

Her eyes changed in a way that he could swear barely masked fear. She leaned into him further, her arms tightening around him.

"Will you?" she asked.

"Will I what?" he returned.

"Will *you* let it be? Will *you* stop working yourself to death to prove to everyone you're sorry for something you didn't do? Will *you* stop taking care of everyone and realize we're all in this together? That we're all supposed to take care of each other? That we're a family, you and me and Tash. And your parents. And Fazire. Do *you* know it's over and we're moving on? Will *you* let it be?"

Unusually for Nate, he hadn't seen it coming. He hadn't realized she was negotiating him to this pass. He hadn't noticed her bringing his guard down, battering his shields and going in for her soft, tender kill.

"Lily—" His voice sounded rough to his own ears and he felt his chest begin to expand and relax.

He'd never had a family, a functional unit where people took care of each other. He had Laura and Victor, but he owed both of them his life and everything he was. Jeff and Danielle had never been family.

But, of course, he couldn't tell Lily any of this.

"Please don't transfer the money for your cycle into my account, Nate," she whispered, cutting into his thoughts. "Please let me do something nice for you."

Instead of speaking his answer, he tightened his hands on her face and she showed she understood his non-verbal assent by tightening her arms around his waist.

She came up on tiptoe and, her mouth against his, in a voice so soft he could barely hear her, she murmured, "For a lot of reasons, because there *are* a lot of reasons, I love you, Nate."

He felt and did everything at once.

A surge of joy flew through him so strong he thought it had to have burned a path through his gut straight to his heart.

Before it could bring him to his knees, he bent and slid an arm under hers. Lifting her, he carried her to the bed, his mouth taking hers in a hot, demanding kiss.

At the same time, of their own accord, his battered shields slammed up and locked into place.

Her arms went around his neck and she kissed him back as he planted her in their bed, coming down on top of her.

When his mouth moved to her jaw, ear, neck, she repeated, "I love you, Nate."

The words tore through him and he silenced her with his mouth, yanking at her clothes, pushing them down, pulling them up, throwing them aside.

When he was done, she pressed her gloriously naked body into him, running her hands over his fevered skin, wrapping a leg around his hip, sliding her lips across his jaw, nipping his shoulder with her teeth.

"I love you," she said against his neck.

"Quiet, Lily," he growled, taking her mouth in another hard kiss, working her with his hands and fingers, bruising her lips with his own, forcing her silence.

When she was squirming underneath him, her fingernails on one hand scraping the skin of his back, her other hand moving between them to wrap around him, it was then he thought it was safe to take his mouth from hers and he used his lips, teeth and tongue in ways he knew would send her soaring.

"Nate, I love—"

His mouth came back to hers to stop her words. To assure her silence, he spread her legs, positioned himself and slammed into her wet softness. She gasped against his tongue at the sudden, savage invasion but her body instantly began to move with his. She dug her heels into the bed to lift her hips, inviting and absorbing his violent thrusts.

He knew it was happening, felt it building in him as it built in her, he felt her tighten around him, her breath coming in short, quick pants, her arms holding him close. He experienced another kind of joy as he heard her cry out his name when she climaxed. Only then did he let go the control he had on his body, grinding into her sweet softness until he found his own release.

He allowed her to take his weight for brief moments, staying connected to her intimately, carefully filing away the feel of her under him, wrapped around him, before he rolled away.

Nate heard her soft mew of protest as he pulled out, something she did every time as if the loss of him tore an important part of her away. He cataloged the sound amongst his many memories as he gently arranged them in the bed, yanking the covers over them and holding her close to his side.

She didn't speak, so he did.

"I won't transfer the money," he allowed, giving her that one thing as he'd be taking away everything else.

He felt her smile against his shoulder and she snuggled closer. He knew she thought she was closing in on sweet victory of the war she'd been waging for the last month.

"Thank you," she whispered and by the tone of her voice Nate understood it meant the world to her.

He also realized that he'd made a colossal mistake.

Nate had been selfish. He'd wanted it all even when he knew he couldn't have it, shouldn't have it, but he took it anyway. He knew it the minute he'd watched her walk down Laura's stairs to talk to the police after the man had tried to snatch her purse.

He knew she was not for the likes of him.

He knew it then and he knew it now.

She thought their eight year drama had all been her fault but he knew she'd been a trusting innocent, a virgin, an Indiana girl who'd never even had a boyfriend.

It was Nate who'd taken all she was willing to give and all she was willing to give was *everything*. He'd forced her to sleep with him on their first date, forced her to move in with him after one night, purposefully made her pregnant to bind her to him then left her to face the consequences of his actions on her own. Then, when he found her again, he forced himself into her life, her home, her bed, her family and took even more.

Now he had it all and he wasn't worthy of it.

He should have set up visitation with Natasha. He should have taken only what Lily was willing to give and allowed her to keep him at arm's length. He should have worked at shielding *her* heart instead of letting her fall in love with a man who didn't exist. A romantic hero, in her mind, who was, Nate knew, no romantic hero at all.

Now she thought she was in love with him but she didn't know who he was, what he was, where he came from.

When she found out, and eventually, Nate knew with certainty, she would, it would be all the more devastating to her.

Therefore, he had to commit one final act to take care of her, protect her and their daughter.

He felt Lily's weight settle into him but Nate didn't sleep that night.

Instead he lay awake, feeling her soft, warm body pressed into his side, listening to her breathing, stroking her skin and hair and purposefully creating one last, precious memory.

TWENTY-FOUR

Lily

LILY WAS TERRIFIED.

It was the day before her wedding and everything this past week between her and Nate had gone wrong, terribly wrong, completely wrong, cataclysmically, heart-wrenchingly *wrong*.

"Has Nate arranged somewhere else to sleep tonight? It's bad luck to see the bride on the wedding day," Maxine said, wearing another flowing, amethyst caftan, this one threaded across the front with matching beads. She was smiling, but cautiously, unaware of the content of Lily's rampaging thoughts but knowing they were there.

"Yes," Lily answered quietly, averting her eyes but feeling both Maxine's and Laura's on her.

"Lily?" Laura asked carefully.

Lily jumped up from the couch in the front sitting room and started pacing, having no idea her habitual practice of pacing when she was anxious was speaking more than a million words, and *not* that she was having the usual pre-marital jitters, but something far more dire.

"Nate's made arrangements," Lily announced. "I've insisted he take Tash with him. They'll meet us tomorrow at the Registry Office in Bath."

"Tash is going with Nate?" Maxine asked slowly.

"Yes, I think it'll be good for them to have this time alone together.

Though Fazire is also going with them," she contradicted herself and then remembered Victor's announcement upon news that Nate was staying elsewhere that he'd accompany him as well. "And, as you know, Victor is going to be with them too so, really, Tash won't be alone with Nate, as such." Now she was both rambling and making little sense.

Maxine and Laura looked at each other.

"Fazire. Why?" Laura asked.

Lily didn't respond. She wasn't going to tell Laura that she didn't need Fazire right now. She could barely cope with Maxine and Laura's gentle concern. Fazire was chomping at the bit to speak to her. He'd been waiting for his moment for a week, finding Lily closing him down at every turn. Lily knew his patience, what little there was of it, was running out.

But Lily had made up her mind. She was going through with this and she didn't want Fazire to talk her out of it.

IT HAD BEEN OVER A week since she gave Nate the motorcycle. Lily had been so certain she'd made headway that day with the way he'd reacted to her saving money for Tash's school and the violent, stormy, uncontrolled way he'd made love to her after she'd told him she loved him. Then he had given in and let her buy him the bike without paying her back.

She'd been so certain she was melting his heart.

She'd been so certain she'd torn holes in his armor.

However, the next morning everything changed.

Drastically.

He'd kept his normal routine, waking Tash, having breakfast with them but he was removed. More removed than his usual, he was *entirely* removed. Lily felt it, she saw it and it sliced through her.

Before leaving, he'd picked up Tash for their daily, Tash-wrapped-around-Nate-smack-on-the-lips good-bye, giving their daughter a warm smile. Then, unusually, he'd given Lily only a peck on the cheek. Even that, Lily had the uncomfortable feeling, was done for Tash's benefit.

Nate had come home later than was his norm (Lily had been noticing he'd been coming home earlier and earlier each night). He'd read to Tash but then went directly to his study without a word to Lily.

Lily had decided to give him space. She'd gained ground and didn't want to push it. She went so far as to go to bed without saying goodnight. She had made it her practice to visit him in his study for a goodnight kiss if he was working late, something she knew, or thought, they both enjoyed.

Nate had come up much later than usual but she had been awake, lying in the dark waiting for him. He didn't turn to her. He didn't make love to her. He didn't pull her back into his front and burrow his face in her hair. Instead, he turned his back to her and went to sleep, just . . . like . . . that.

Throughout the weekend, Nate worked in his study all day each day and well into the night. He even avoided Victor and Laura, although he welcomed Tash sitting and watching television in his study. He didn't make love to Lily or pull her to him when he eventually sought their bed.

Victor, Laura and Fazire were casting strange, knowing glances amongst themselves, but Lily knew better than to ask. Though she had to admit she found it peculiar that Fazire was participating in this behavior, especially with Victor. Fazire had warmed a bit to Nate but never to Victor.

When the quiet and now openly concerned Victor and Laura left Sunday afternoon, Lily gave Nate his head until he left Tash's room after she'd read herself to sleep and he headed straight to his study.

Lily followed him, knocked on the closed door and entered at his word. He barely glanced at her when she walked in and she felt her blood run cold.

"Nate?"

"What is it, Lily?" he asked, not lifting his eyes to hers after his first brief glance, his question sounding as if he didn't much care about her answer and her cold blood slowed as ice crystals formed.

"Is something the matter?"

Her voice was timid and unsure and his head came up at the sound of it. She felt a flicker of hope at the warm look she thought she caught in his eyes but then he shuttered them.

"I'm busy, Lily. We're getting married next Saturday and then away for two weeks on honeymoon. I've a tremendous amount to do."

This seemed plausible and Lily gave him a relieved but weak smile and walked to the side of his desk and stopped, wanting to touch him but for the first time in a long time, afraid.

"Can I do something to help?" she asked softly.

At this, for some reason, he laughed without humor. The sharp bark of it was harsh and it grated against her already frayed nerves.

"You could leave me to it," he suggested when he was done with his anti-amusement, his eyes on her and they were hard and blank, telling her clearly she was an unwelcome distraction.

Lily remembered that look. She had seen that look. He'd leveled it on Danielle on numerous occasions.

Her heart stuttered in her chest but she nodded and slowly moved away. Very slowly. Snail's pace slowly. Moving slowly while hoping he'd call her back for a kiss, a touch, something, *anything*.

He did not.

He also did not turn to her when he finally came to their bed.

He was gone before she awoke, he didn't wake Tash but he did leave a short, unaffectionate note for Lily (and a longer, very affectionate note for Tash) saying he left early for the office.

That afternoon, sitting behind the register in a quiet moment at Flash and Dazzle, she'd phoned him at the office.

He'd said he'd never miss another one of her calls and he hadn't. She expected her calls came at times when he was busy but he always took them as, she now knew, he always took Tash's calls when she phoned him when she got home from school.

"Mr. McAllister's office," Nate's secretary Jennifer answered.

"Hi Jennifer, it's Lily. Can I speak to Nate?"

Jennifer was quiet for a moment and Lily felt the now familiar stutter in her heart. These past weeks, Lily had chatted to Jennifer, and although they'd never met, they'd built a rapport.

This time, however, Jennifer didn't invite even a short chat.

Instead, she said softly, "I'm sorry, Lily. Mr. McAllister said he was not to be disturbed under any circumstances."

Lily swallowed and nodded even though Jennifer couldn't see her.

"That's okay," Lily replied, trying to do it brightly and fearing she failed. "Can you tell him I phoned?"

"Definitely," Jennifer assured her.

When Lily got home from Flash and Dazzle, she found that Nate's edict of not being disturbed didn't apply to Tash who was, as ever, awash with news of her telephone conversation with her father. Although this wasn't news from Nate, as Lily suspected Nate couldn't get a word in edgewise and wouldn't try anyway. It was more Tash's news said in the form of, "I told Daddy . . ." and, "Then, when I described it, Daddy laughed."

Instead of Nate taking Tash's calls and laughing with her making Lily feel content, it made her fear and alarm turn to anger, which she nursed quietly under Fazire's watchful glare all night.

Nate didn't make it home for Tash to read to him, nor did he call to say he'd be detained.

Lily monitored her daughter closely to see if her very astute senses were noticing anything different between her mother and father. However, Nate was shielding Tash from this and treating her exactly the same even while his behavior to Lily was significantly different.

As Lily shut down the house for the night, Nate still not home, Fazire approached her in the hall.

"Lily-child—" he started gently, his eyes soft on her.

"No, Fazire," she held up her hand as if to ward him off, "not now."

Then before he could press as Fazire was wont to do, she'd run up the stairs. She got ready for bed but didn't get in it, instead she paced. And she waited. And her mind tumbled over its thoughts, none of them good.

Very late, she heard Nate enter the house but he didn't come up, and as minutes ticked by, she went in search of him.

She found him in their back garden, now lushly appointed with planters, pots and beds brimming with flowers and greenery, all of this well-tended by a weekly gardener. She was stunned to see him standing at the balustrade by the cliff looking toward the Victorian pier smoking a cigarette. Not since their night on Laura and Victor's stoop had she seen him smoke a cigarette or even smelled it on him.

She stood just outside the new French doors to the garden and called, "Nate?"

His body jerked and his head snapped around to look at her through the darkness. She was just as stunned that she'd surprised him. He was always alert to anything but most specifically her. Sometimes she felt he knew she was approaching a room even before she'd cleared the door.

She couldn't imagine what had him so lost in thought but she wanted to know, needed to know and damned well was *going* to know.

She walked across the garden and stopped in front of him.

"You're smoking." Her voice was a soft accusation.

"Yes, Lily, I'm smoking. And you're standing in the garden wearing your pajamas," he replied as if her transgression was as bad as his.

"When did you start smoking?" she ignored his comment.

"When I was nine," he responded immediately, nonchalantly sharing a piece of his history with her like he did it every day and this information hit her like a blow.

Dear God, who started smoking when they were nine? She thought but he didn't allow her to respond.

He went on, "Get back into the house."

She blinked, momentarily thrown by his harshly-voiced command coming so quickly after he'd shared something personal about himself, something she hadn't had to wheedle out of him. Determined to get to the bottom of what was bothering him, she decided to ignore it.

"We need to talk. Something's—"

"Lily, get back into the fucking house. No woman should stand outside barely clothed, especially not you. You're the mother of my child, for God's sake. This is a terraced house. The neighbors can see you."

She had to shake her head trying to clear away his words, his tone, his meaning.

"Nate, it's nearly midnight, no one—"

"Get back into the *fucking* house," he snarled savagely, losing patience and leaning into her so menacingly, she couldn't help but take a step back.

She hesitated, her heart stuttering again.

Then she squared her shoulders, determined to have it out even if it was midnight and she was in her pajamas. Yes, they were pajamas and yes, there wasn't much to them but *she* wouldn't describe herself as "barely clothed" for goodness sake.

"Don't speak to me that way," she snapped. "We have to talk. Something's wrong with you and I want to know what it is."

Without answering, he turned away from her and resumed his

contemplation of the pier.

At this action, she tried a different tactic.

She stepped into his line of sight and put her hand on his arm.

"Nate," she said in a gentler tone, "please talk to me."

He looked down at her like he had when he was standing in his parents' foyer and Victor was shaking her. Like when they were in the conference room that awful day talking about Natasha's custody. As if she was a not very interesting bug he was watching crawl across the pavement.

Pulling all her courage to her like a shield, she threw pride into the wind and leaned into him, putting her arms around him even though nothing about him was inviting her actions.

"Talk to me," she urged, all her love for him in her words.

He didn't touch her. Instead, he calmly flicked his cigarette over the cliff as if she was a mile away instead of holding him in her arms.

"Nate!" she cried, beginning to panic. "Talk to me."

That was when he touched her. His fingers went into the hair on either side of her head and held her there while his mouth slammed down on hers in the first kiss he'd given her in days.

It was not a loving kiss. It was hard, insistent, greedy, taking everything while giving nothing in return.

She was too happy he was touching her, kissing her, to let it register. She simply opened her mouth under his and gave him everything as she'd always done.

Lily heard his groan and was thrilled by it, but inexplicably he tore his mouth from hers. Then she was being lifted, carried, not to their room but downstairs to the family room. All the while he kissed her in that awful way, his mouth then moving to her neck, shoulders, behind her ear, his teeth sinking into her flesh in a dangerous, erotic way.

He kicked the door to the family room shut behind them and threw her on the couch, following her down. He pulled off her clothes, tore off his own, his actions not gentle, nor were his mouth and his hands on her naked body, and it finally slid into her consciousness that he was not the same.

This wasn't violent, stormy passion.

This was selfish and devouring.

"Nate—" she whispered, trying to slow him, trying to reach him.

"Shut up, Lily," he growled against her mouth and on those ugly words, he changed.

Instead of taking, he was giving but not in his usual way. It was like he was driven to force a response from her, to bend her body to his will and, damn it all, she loved him too much to deny him. She gave then she gave more then even more.

And he took it, all of it, everything.

Until she was there, waiting, needing him to come inside, her heart pounding, her breath coming in gasps, her body on fire for him.

"Nate—" she whispered again urgently, using her hands at his hips to try to bring him to her but he pulled away.

Her eyes opened and looked into his and she felt her heart rip apart at what she saw.

His were blank but his hand between her legs moved enticingly, and her hips, of their own volition, pressed against him.

"Beg," he demanded, his voice rough and sharp.

Lily stared then blinked, thinking for a moment she hadn't heard him correctly.

"Wh-what?"

"You want me, Lily?" he asked, then his head descended and his mouth moved along her cheek to her ear.

As he did this, she nodded.

"You want me then beg," he said into her ear.

She felt her chest seize as emotion filled it even as he manipulated her with his hand and her body betrayed her.

"Nate—"

"I want to hear you say it. Say, 'Please, Nate, fuck me.'"

At his shocking demand, a demand so *not* Nate it was frightening, the tears crawled up her throat and his mouth moved from her ear to her breast, sucking in her nipple sharply, sending waves of pleasure through her. He rolled his tongue around it as his thumb simultaneously rolled at the core of her, knowing from what was now months of experience she loved this, responded to it, it made her soar.

This time, she fought it.

"Please don't do this," she pleaded and he came back over her.

"You want to know my secrets?" he asked and her head jerked.

She wasn't keeping up with his lightning-quick changes of mood, his shifting of topics, his shocking behavior.

His hand was still working at her and she was close to climax, could feel it coming. She closed her eyes, arched her neck, wanting it to come so this would all be over and, hopefully, they could talk.

His hand went away.

Her eyes snapped open and her chin jerked down to look at him.

"Do you want to know my secrets?" he repeated.

"No!" she cried, louder than she should in a house harboring sleeping people, one of them their daughter.

His mouth silenced her and she struggled but his hand came back, tormenting her and her body swiftly descended into need even as she continued to fight it.

With supreme effort, she tore her mouth free. "Stop, Nate."

His thumb swirled and she couldn't help herself. It felt so good, she moaned low in her throat.

"You don't want me to stop," he taunted cruelly at her moan. "As ever, you're gagging for it."

She bit her lip and knew he was right and she hated herself for it. She couldn't stop her hips from pressing against his hand, her hands from roaming his back even as her eyes caught his in the darkness. She could see them burning into her, not with love or with passion but with ruthless determination to have exactly what he wanted.

"These are my secrets, Lily. This is who I am."

She shook her head fiercely.

She wouldn't believe it, *couldn't*.

"I know who you are. I wished for—"

"Beg," Nate interrupted her words with his demand.

She shook her head again.

Nate smiled. A terrible smile that captivated her even as it repulsed her. Then he *made* her beg. With brute strength and merciless skill, he brought her to the edge of climax and took her away, time and again, until she could bear it no more, and she felt if she didn't have release her body would shatter.

Holding him tight, wrapping her arms around his back, her legs around his hips and bringing her lips to his, she whispered, humiliation warring with desire and losing, "Please, Nate, please fuck me."

And he did.

It was hard. It was fast. It was rough and there was no love in it and she climaxed so magnificently, she felt for a moment she *had* shattered, gloriously. And after she didn't hate herself for it, she *detested* herself, her weakness and part of that was because she felt disloyally like she detested *him*.

Nate.

Her wish.

Her dream man.

Her everything.

Immediately after he was done, he knifed away from her without regard for her sensitive body, put on his clothes and, looking down at her, he said, "I'm going to London. I'll be back Friday."

Then he was gone.

And Lily lay naked and exposed, staring into the darkness, into the space where he'd been, trying to still her mind then trying to catch a thought and failing at both. Finally, she wrapped a blanket around her body, curled up into a little ball and she cried.

After she slept. Then she waited.

And she tried to hope.

ON WEDNESDAY, SHE CALLED HIS mobile. She knew he was talking to Tash, still shielding their daughter from whatever it was that was falling apart between them. But he didn't contact Lily. She phoned his mobile in the morning not wishing to go through another humiliating episode with Jennifer. He did not answer. Then she rang him mid-morning then the afternoon.

Still no answer and she felt hope quickly dying as he missed call after call that he promised he'd never miss.

She left the shop early and made certain she was home when Tash got home from school so she could latch on to the phone when Tash was done speaking to her father.

"Mummy wants to talk to you," Tash said on a giggle as she watched Lily pacing in the kitchen, Fazire's assessing eyes on her, regarding her from his seat at the table.

Lily nearly snatched the phone out of her daughter's hand when Tash offered it to her.

Lily had been thinking about it, trying to find a reason for his abrupt change to such hostile behavior and she'd convinced herself that she'd pushed too hard, got too close, made a mess of things by trying to break through and she was ready for retreat. Even having Nate removed was better than this.

"Nate, I—"

"Lily, I don't have time for this now," he interrupted her before she got started. "Call me later."

And, without another word or waiting for her to respond, he hung up.

She stared at the phone finding it difficult to breathe, her heart stuttering so much she felt like it would come to a halt. She looked at Tash who had been grinning at her but her grin faded as Lily put the phone on the receiver.

"Didn't Daddy—?" Tash started.

"Daddy's really busy, baby doll. Getting ready for our honeymoon," Lily explained quietly, not believing a word she said but hoping that Tash would.

Luckily, her daughter bought her lie, her grin came back with a vengeance and she skipped out of the room.

"Lily-child," Fazire spoke and started to float and Lily knew what that meant and she was having none of it.

She shook her head and when she heard Tash cooing to Mrs. Gunderson somewhere in the house, she said one word to Fazire, knowing he'd know what she meant, "Tash."

With that she ran, ran out the front door, ran down the street, ran past the pier, along the seafront path, straight to the bandstand and stopped. She stopped her feet, her heart and her thoughts and she started walking fast, breathing heavily, making her body work hard so her mind wouldn't. She walked until she felt she would drop and only then did she turn toward home.

Later that night, when Fazire and Tash were both asleep, she tried Nate again.

He answered his mobile and in the background she heard what sounded like a busy club or restaurant.

"What is it, Lily?" he asked instead of greeting her, obviously seeing her name displayed before answering his phone.

"I just wanted to say—" she began tentatively, not sure what she wanted to say but needing to say it all the same.

But as she spoke she heard, in a purring, female voice that was *very* close to the phone, "Nate, our table's ready."

Nate didn't even try to cover the mouthpiece when he responded, "In a minute, Georgia."

Lily's legs buckled from under her, and powerless to stop herself, she dropped and sat on the bed. It felt like it took a year for her to turn her head and look at the clock on the bedside table.

It was past ten at night and Nate was out with Georgia, his old girl-friend, a woman Jeffrey had thought he was ready to marry. He was away from Lily the week before their wedding, in London, out on the town with another woman.

"Lily." She heard her name sound in her ear as if from far away but she had herself together enough to note that Nate's voice sounded impatient.

"It—" She cleared her throat, her body numb, her mind blank and she had no idea her voice betrayed exactly how broken she felt. "It's nothing, Nate. Enjoy yourself."

Then she'd hung up even as she heard him start to say her name again.

Her mobile rang in her hand almost immediately but she engaged and disengaged, disconnecting Nate without a word, and she then turned it off. The house phone rang and she picked it up out of its bed, hit the button for on then hit the button for off and then on again, listening to the insistent ring tone until it grew urgent and even longer and at long last, it silenced.

She rolled on her side in the bed, pulled the pillow over her head and again, keeping her thoughts at bay with an extreme effort of will, she cried herself to sleep, which was, she was realizing, the only way she *could* get to sleep.

The following morning at the store, Maxine cornered her.

"What on *earth* is going on?"

It took effort but Lily lifted her eyes to Maxine's. "Nothing," she lied through her teeth. "Why do you ask?"

"Why do I . . . why . . . ?" Maxine spluttered. "You're marrying your dream man in two days and you look like hell. I'm sorry to say it but you do. You look pale. Your eyes are all puffy. You should know, Fazire called me—"

"Don't listen to Fazire. He doesn't know what's going on," Lily broke in.

"Do *you* know what's going on?" Maxine flashed back.

Lily responded automatically, "Nate's an important man. A lot of people depend on him. He hasn't had a holiday . . ." Lily stopped.

She had no idea when he'd last had a holiday.

She had no idea about a lot of things about Nate.

What she *did* know was that he was guarded. What she *did* know was that he had secrets. What she *did* know was that eight years ago he demanded that she move in and then promised her the world. Two weeks later, when she needed him the most, he broke all his promises and let her go. Now, eight years later, the same thing happened with slight differences.

And, two months later . . .

What?

He'd warned her, she knew. He'd kept himself removed. He'd kept his distance. He'd planned for a time when she wouldn't be in his life, nearly told her there *would* be a time—but besotted fool that she was, believing in genies and dreams and wishes—she hadn't listened.

For the first time in years, she felt her confidence lying about her in tatters. She felt that she hadn't lived up to whatever promise Nate had seen in her when he got her back. That this brilliant, rich, sophisticated, *impossibly* handsome man could never find what he needed in her.

Never.

"Just, please, Maxie. Let's not talk about this. I'm getting a headache," Lily finished on another lie, something she was doing with alarming frequency these days.

Maxine bustled up close and looked Lily in the eyes. "Don't give me that headache business. I know something's not right and—"

Before she could finish, Lily's mobile rang. It was sitting face up on the counter and both Maxine and Lily's eyes swung to it.

The display said Nate Calling.

Both Lily and Maxine reached for it. Luckily Lily got to it first for she knew Maxine, in her current mood, would probably make hideous matters far, far worse.

Lily hopped off her stool and swiftly rounded the counter, taking the call and putting the phone to her ear.

"Nate?" she answered.

"Don't you *ever* fucking hang up on me again and turn off the phones."

Lily halted dead in her getaway from Maxine as Nate's furious words hit her ear, his rage vibrating through her body like a lethal current.

He was the one who was out with an ex-girlfriend. *He* was the one who humiliated her on her own family room couch, or more to the point *his*, he'd bought it, but still, it was in *her* house and *she* hadn't had the old one carted away. *He* was the one who was sneaking cigarettes in the garden at midnight. *He* was the one who wasn't speaking to her. *He* was the one who was tearing her heart to shreds.

Lily could take it no more, she snapped.

"How dare you!" she shouted into the phone.

"You have my daughter in that house and if something happened, I couldn't get through. You kept her from me for seven years, Lily. Don't you ever play that fucking game again."

Lily's body went rock solid and she fired back, "I cannot believe you just said that to me."

He ignored her. "I'll be home tonight."

"Don't bother," Lily retorted acidly.

"I'll be home tonight," he repeated then *he* hung up on *her*.

Lily stood with the phone to her ear, anger, humiliation and pain coursing through her so strongly, it took long moments before she realized Maxine was standing right in front of her.

When Lily's eyes focused on her, Maxine looked no longer angry and determined to get to the heart of the matter. Maxine looked scared.

"What just happened, sweetling?" she asked, her voice soft, gentle, coaxing.

At her friend's tone, the fight slid out of Lily and her vision dissolved as tears flooded her eyes. Maxine's arms went around her, holding her tight.

"I don't know," she whispered. "I don't know." And she repeated those words again, then again.

"Hush, sweetling. Hush," Maxine murmured and stroked her hair.

When Lily pulled herself together, Maxine gave her a lilac, lace-edged handkerchief to dry her eyes and let the matter drop but the frightened look never left her face.

By the time Lily got home, terrified that Nate would already be there, her lie about the headache had come true. It wasn't a migraine but it was close.

Fazire, she noticed immediately, was blustering and ready to blow but he took one look at her, and as he'd done countless times before, he ushered her to her room. He got her a cool drink, some tablets, ran her bath and then kept Natasha occupied so she wouldn't miss her mother while Lily battled the pain.

Lily took the pain killers, took her bath, closed the curtains and went to bed with a cool flannel at her brow, fighting against the headache until the medicine worked and she finally found sleep.

"Lily?"

It was Nate's voice, gentle, questioning, and she thought for a moment she was dreaming.

She opened her eyes and saw his muscular thigh on the bed. Of course Nate noticed immediately she was awake, even though she'd closed her eyes nearly as quickly as she'd opened them.

"Fazire says you have a headache." Nate's voice was so soft, he was talking in a way that it seemed he thought his words were alive and could cause her harm.

"I'm fine." Lily kept her eyes closed and her voice neutral.

"Is it a migraine?" Nate asked and she felt his fingers tucking her hair behind her ear.

Lily squeezed her eyes tight at his soft, sweet, *familiar* touch and the pain shot back into her temple so she was forced to train her body to relax.

She couldn't keep up with him and she didn't have the strength to try. She suspected that even though he'd lost interest in her, he didn't want the mother of his child's brain to explode.

"I'm fine, Nate. It's not a migraine." She lifted her hand to the flannel, threw it aside and turned so her back was to him, all this she did without looking at him. "Go to Tash. She misses you."

"Can I get you anything?" He'd not been deterred by her turning her back to him, now he was stroking her from neck to waist, pushing the covers out of the way to do so.

She wanted to move into his hand, wanted it so much she could taste it in her mouth, feel it in every pore of her skin.

Instead, she steeled herself against it.

"No. Like I said, I'm fine."

"Lily—"

"Go away, Nate." She wanted to sound exasperated but instead she sounded something else and even to her own ears she was pretty certain she sounded defeated.

He didn't go and he also didn't say anything more. What he did was shift on the bed so he could sit and stroke her back.

She held her body tense. Feeling the tears in her throat, she swallowed them down. She was no match for his attention (this *was* Nate) and slowly her body relaxed, and finally she fell back to sleep.

When she woke again, it was the dead of night. Nate's front was pressed to her back, his arm was wrapped tight around her and he'd buried his face in her hair.

Lily laid there a second, allowing herself, for one last time, to pretend.

Then she pulled away, got up and quietly exited the room. After missing dinner, she found she was hungry and she made herself a sandwich. Taking her sandwich with her, she went to the family room, turned on the TV and ate. She didn't watch the TV, however. Her mind was on other things. It was on her beautiful house, her beautiful appliances and furniture, her beautiful new car, her bank account filled with more money than she could ever spend.

Nate had done an excellent job. She could live without him and in doing so give their daughter a beautiful home, drive her around in an expensive car and make certain she had everything her little heart desired.

He hadn't been angry that in her turning off the phones he couldn't get through to *her* if something had happened.

It had all been for Tash, she realized, pain and bitterness searing through her.

All of it.

In fact, she wouldn't be surprised if he *had* told Danielle to tell her he was dead all those years ago, tired of the naïve, clinging farm girl and ready to cut her loose. She'd probably been an interesting diversion, an inexperienced virgin. Men liked that. But once he'd got what he wanted, the interesting part obviously became not so interesting.

But finding that he had a child and also finding that Lily was going to put up a fight, a fight that it would be difficult for him to win (considering what she now convinced herself was his behavior, his lies, his deceit, just like his brother and sister), he went about winning it another way.

And he enjoyed the spoils of victory in the meantime.

But when she'd told him she loved him, that was something he didn't need, didn't want and immediately and remorselessly, he threw it away.

Now that she knew her place, now that he'd made it blatantly clear with that debacle in the very room she was lounging in at that moment, he knew he had her where he wanted her. He'd hold her in the night, take from her when he wanted and leave her when he didn't.

She was still nothing but a naïve, Indiana farm girl and not for the likes of him except for the tedious fact that she was the mother of his child.

Understanding this made it easier, she told herself (but she didn't really believe herself). She knew where she stood. She knew why he wouldn't give her what she needed, why he wouldn't give her anything of himself.

Because it wasn't hers to have.

Maybe, she hoped, one day he'd give it to Tash.

On this thought, she fell asleep on the couch only to be woken what seemed like minutes later because she was being lifted in the air.

Automatically, her hands moved around Nate's shoulders.

"What . . . ?" she began, vaguely noticing he'd turned off the television and the light.

"You sleep with me." Nate's voice was back to harsh, gone was the softness he'd shown her when she had the headache.

"I don't think—" she started again as he cleared the room and headed for the stairs. She tried to push out of his arms but they went tight as steel bands.

"You sleep with me," he repeated, again roughly and in a tone that would accept no denial.

"Let me down," Lily demanded and he did, on the ground level landing but he took her hand and dragged her up the next two flights of stairs. As they were close to Fazire and Tash's rooms, Lily didn't make a peep and didn't pull away.

Once they were in their room, he closed the door and dragged her straight to bed where he brought them both to a halt.

"I don't understand why you—" Lily turned to him but he interrupted her again.

"What will Tash think if she sees you sleeping on the couch?" Nate snapped.

It felt like he'd punched her in the stomach and at the same time her heart shattered.

"Of course," she murmured, "Tash."

It was all for Tash. Looking back at the last two months, she knew that everything he did was for Tash. A mother and father, living together, for Tash.

She made her decision. Surprisingly this time it wasn't difficult.

She yanked her hand from his and crawled into bed on his side where he'd stopped them, making her way to her own and settling, her back to him.

He joined her in bed, flicked the covers over them and hooked her about the waist, dragging her across the bed and into the warmth of his body.

She tried to pull away but in her ear, he hissed, "Lie still."

"Tash doesn't care *how* we sleep, Nate," Lily snapped back, her tone bitter.

She gave an almighty pull and slid away. Then she waited, tense, for him to pull her back.

He didn't.

She didn't fall asleep but she heard (she thought, but she was wrong) when he did.

Hours later, when it was time, she got up, took her clothes, her makeup and everything she needed and locked herself in the bathroom and didn't come out until she was ready to face the day.

And to face Nate.

When she opened the bathroom door, it was Nate who was pacing. He was wearing dark-blue pajama bottoms, what he'd been wearing last night when he'd dragged her to bed, and he was pulling a hand through his hair.

Upon the door opening, he stopped and swung to her. His hand didn't fall but stayed at the back of his neck and he stared at her. Not like she was a bug under his scrutiny, not blank, not detached, but she couldn't tell what she read on his face and she no longer cared.

She tried not to care about how beautiful he was, standing there with his muscular chest, tight stomach, black hair, dark, intense eyes and powerful frame but she couldn't.

Perhaps, she thought distractedly, with practice she'd be able to do that.

One day.

His eyes looked her up and down and then settled on hers and they stared at each other what seemed hours but was probably minutes.

Finally, he dropped his arm.

"We have to talk," he told her.

She shook her head and walked into the room. Dumping her cosmetics on her dressing table, she turned to him.

"The time for talking is over," she replied, feeling strangely that even though it had been only a few days since the time she would have begged him to talk to her, *did* beg him to talk to her, it felt like forever ago. She walked to the door but he stopped her with a hand on her arm, his fingers closing around it painfully as he swung her to face him.

"You're going to listen to me," he demanded.

She yanked her arm away and when he moved to regain hold, she clipped in a horrible voice, a voice she'd never heard pass her lips in her life, "Don't you *touch* me."

At her tone, Nate went completely still.

Lily went on speaking in that voice. "I'm going to marry you tomorrow like you want, for Tash. I'll sleep in the same bed with you and we'll pretend we're a cozy family. You can go to London and do whatever you need to do with whatever women there you need to do it with and I'll . . ." she faltered, not knowing what to say, then rallied and told him honestly, "Do without."

"Lily—" he broke in but she kept going.

"I've done it before, I'll do it again. This will be fine. It'll all be fine and Tash will never know."

"Listen to me—"

"She'll never know!" Lily spoke fervently but kept her voice low so neither Tash nor Fazire would overhear. "No one will ever know," she said like she was trying to convince herself.

Feeling she'd made her point, she turned and had her hand on the door handle, sensing escape, but she was thwarted as he swung her back around, his arms closing around her tightly, bringing her up against his body and to her shock, his face went into the hair at the side of her neck.

"Lily, I want to tell you about—"

Her body became stiff as a board.

"Take your hands off me."

He took his arms from around her, but her hope that he was doing as she asked was dashed when he immediately framed her face with his hands.

"You need to listen to me. You need to know who I am before you marry me tomorrow. You need to know so you can make the right decision and whatever that is, I'll—"

"I know who you are, Nate. You showed me Monday night, remember?"

He closed his eyes but not before (she could *swear*) she saw that familiar aching pain slice through them.

He dropped his forehead to hers then opened his eyes again and he admitted, his voice harsh but not with anger, with emotion, "I was trying to push you away. I thought it was the right thing to do, but when you heard Georgia, your voice, Christ, Lily, your voice. I can't get it out of my head. I was out with her parents. They've been family friends for years. She wasn't supposed to be there."

Lily shook her head and tried to pull free of his hands. This didn't work so she stood her ground and glared at him.

Now it was *her* shields that were impenetrable, or at least she told herself that. She'd clean *these* particular wounds later.

"Lily, my mother was—" he started.

"Stop it!" she shouted and with superhuman effort yanked her face from his hands and took a step back.

She was beyond caring who was in the house. She had to get out of there. She had to get out of there and away from Nate as soon as she could. She never thought she would feel she needed to be away from Nate but at that moment she needed it more than breath.

"I don't care anymore, Nate," she lied, caring more than anything but getting very good at lying with all the practice she'd had recently.

His eyes narrowed. Of course, he saw through her and she knew he didn't believe her but he kept his distance, though the distance between them wasn't much, she was thankful for it.

"The time to tell me was eight years ago," she informed him. "I don't care anymore. I get it, Nate. I understand. I'm just the plain, silly, hillbilly girl who got infatuated with who she thought was her romantic hero."

At that, Lily laughed, the acid resentment in the sound causing Nate's controlled features to wince and he moved toward her again, but she quickly retreated, lifting her hand to keep him at bay. His eyes dropped to her hand and he halted.

He opened his mouth to speak but Lily got there first.

"I was so *stupid* to think *you'd* want *me*." She pointed at the both of them in turn. "Stupid, stupid, *stupid*. You, the dashing, brilliant, wealthy, impossibly handsome, *unbearably* handsome hero wanting silly old *me*. The nobody, Lily Jacobs. Fat, stupid, *ugly* Lily Jacobs."

She swallowed her laughter this time on a tear-clogged gulp, not even knowing what she was saying anymore.

Her eyes shimmering with tears she refused to shed, she therefore missed Nate's stunned look of disbelief as she continued.

"Who you are now is the father of my daughter. That's it. The end. You need to keep up the pretense and find somewhere to stay tonight and you're taking Tash and Fazire with you. This is so you don't see me before the wedding. Bad luck."

She *did* chuckle at that, again completely without humor.

She finished with, "I'll see you tomorrow." And she said this with finality, this time *her* tone brooked no response.

She turned her back on him, opened the door and fled as fast as her feet would carry her (which wasn't very fast seeing as, for confidence building purposes, she'd put on a pair of fancy, strappy, hot-pink, high-heeled sandals with a big flower at the toe to go with her fancy, body-skimming, hot-pink sundress).

Nate did not follow.

It was her turn to leave a note to Tash, saying she had to get to work early.

Then she got in her fancy new Mercedes and drove.

She didn't go to work, not until it was time.

She simply drove and drove. Blanking her mind and installing armor around her already frozen heart.

NOW SHE WAS BACK AT home, waiting for Nate to come and pick up Tash and Fazire. Steeling herself to spend a jolly night with Laura and Maxine, celebrating her last night of freedom before the big day. They'd planned champagne and an orgy of food, and Maxine had brought CDs to which later they would dance drunkenly as Lily and Maxine and often Fazire had done in the past.

Lily was so far beyond celebrations with champagne and dancing, it wasn't funny.

In fact, she wasn't certain she'd ever laugh again.

The door flew open and Fazire crashed their not yet-started party.

"Lily-child, I must speak to you *now*," he commanded grandly.

Lily's eyes went to the window. She saw Nate angling out of his Aston Martin and she immediately understood Fazire's imperious and slightly panicked demand.

She felt the familiar thrill race through her at the sight of Nate as she watched him move gracefully toward the house, but she tamped it down and looked back to Fazire.

"Not now, Fazire, we're in the middle of a bachelorette party." This, too, was a lie.

Fazire looked from Lily, to Laura, to Maxine, to the champagne that lay in its ice bucket unopened, the glasses unfilled sitting around it. Then his eyes went back to Lily.

"I will *not* be denied. My room. Now." With that he stomped out and she knew he very much wanted to float and a little bit of her deep down inside felt badly for him.

Lily got up and followed him, but at the door, she closed it and turned back to Maxine and Laura.

Maxine knew the consequences of disobeying Fazire and her mouth dropped open in horror. Laura, who didn't know, still looked a little frightened.

"Sweetling, you should go with him," Maxine urged.

"No," Lily answered.

Maxine and Laura looked at each other again.

"Daddeeeee." They heard Tash's joyful shout in the hall.

Lily went straight to the champagne and started preparations to open it, deciding that getting drunk, very drunk and soon, was the best possible course of action at this juncture.

Again, Maxine and Laura looked horrified as Lily ignored her imminent and supposedly beloved-beyond-reason husband's arrival to the beautiful abode that he'd provided for her, doing five years of work at Lily's pace in two months and far better than Lily could have managed or afforded.

"Aren't you, erm . . ." Laura started hesitantly, "going to greet Na-thaniel?"

"He knows where to find me," Lily stated with deep and false uncon-cern and then popped the cork just as the door flew open again.

"Yipeeeeeeeee!" Natasha shouted and ran across the room. "Can I have some champagne, Mummy? Please, please, please!"

Nate entered the room behind his daughter and Lily ignored him too.

Mrs. Gunderson sauntered in, jumped up next to Maxine and settled in for the show.

"Ask your father, baby doll, he might have something special planned for you tonight." Finally, Lily's eyes met Nate's. "And he wouldn't want to be *delayed*," she finished with ill-concealed meaning that Nate was expected to come and quickly go.

Maxine and Laura's heads swung to look at Nate as did Mrs. Gun-derson's, tail twitching expectantly. He was standing in his expensive, superbly cut, dark-gray suit looking impossibly, *unbearably* handsome.

Tash ran to him and threw her arms around his hips, tilting half her body back and she cried, "Can I Daddy? Please, please, please!"

Lily watched as Nate's hand settled on the crown of his daughter's head and then slid down to stroke her cheek gently, all the while he looked down at her with a soft expression on his face. She steeled herself, too, against the warm rush that the sight made her feel.

She hadn't seen him since she ran out on her tirade this morning. She also hadn't heard from him and she didn't care. This also was a lie. Now she was lying to herself and she didn't mind one whit (that too was a lie).

His head lifted and his eyes locked on Lily's, or more to the point, skewered her to the spot.

"Of course you can have some champagne," he said to Tash and Lily noted the intensity of his eyes but also that they were impossible to read. All she saw was that they weren't blank or detached but burning.

Laura and Maxine (and Mrs. Gunderson) swung their gazes back to Lily.

"Of course!" Lily exclaimed, too loudly. "We'll *all* have champagne. What a splendid, idea, Nate. You of all people know we have *so much* to celebrate," she finished cattily and the ugliness felt foreign on her tongue.

Laura, Maxine and Gunny swung their eyes back to Nate, but before he could respond Fazire stormed in. He glanced at Nate, gave him a nod then he looked back to Lily.

"I thought I told you we were speaking in my room," he snapped.

"Fazire, just in time," Lily said, clapping with mock-delight. "We're all having champagne before you and Nate and Tash go to Bath. It's Nate's idea. Isn't he *the bomb?*"

Fazire blinked at her and Tash giggled, her daughter failing to read her mother's sarcasm although everyone else certainly didn't. Fazire's gaze, too, went back to Nate.

Lily ignored everyone and extended her hand to her daughter. "Come on, Tash. Let's get extra glasses."

Tash skipped to her, her small hand closed around Lily's and for the first time that day, Lily felt a modicum of comfort.

No matter what her life would bring, no matter what new horrors, she'd always have Tash and now Tash would have everything—a family, grandparents, a stable home (in a way) that was plush and posh, trust funds, horseback riding lessons.

Everything.

Yes, Lily decided, she would live for that.

And on that thought, her face softened and she gave her daughter one of her genuine, quirky smiles. She was so wrapped up in her misery she had absolutely no idea the effect her smile had on the room, particularly one of its inhabitants, the *impossibly* handsome one.

"Just a sip, my baby girl," she warned as she and her daughter made to leave the room.

"Okay." Tash was thrilled to have the decadent treat and was smart enough not to push it.

They met Victor on their way to the kitchen, he was on the ascent from the study. His eyes on Lily were kind and very, *very* worried.

"We're having champagne in the sitting room before you all go to Bath," Lily announced breezily as she walked right by him.

"Lily, can we have a quiet moment?"

"Nope. Champagne then you're off. Not much time for chats," Lily answered with a dazzling, false smile thrown over her shoulder.

Delivering that, she nearly ran to the kitchen and tried to pretend she didn't see Victor's face fall.

They had champagne and Lily felt the tension in the room acutely, even though, thankfully, it appeared Tash did not. Everyone toasted Nate and Lily's future. They all tried to be cheerful. Finally, champagne drunk, Nate and Victor loaded the cars, Tash going to the Aston Martin and Fazire to Victor's Jaguar.

Lily trailed behind Tash and Nate. She gave her daughter a hug and kiss and settled her into the car. Slamming the door with a wave and a blown kiss, she turned and nearly collided with Nate.

Before she knew what he was about, his arm was around her, he stepped back, dragging her with him, one step, two, three until they were away from the car but still in eyesight of everyone and everyone was watching. His other arm coming around her, he positioned them so his back was to their audience and Lily was shielded, shielded from everyone but Tash.

Then he kissed her.

It was a real kiss, not false, not fake, not demanding and greedy. A real Nate Kiss that took her breath away.

When he lifted his head, his eyes bore into hers, their intensity rooting her to the spot.

"You'll be there tomorrow?" It was a question.

"Of course," she answered automatically.

"No matter what, you'll be there tomorrow?"

She was still trying to recover from the kiss but she thought she could hear fear in his tone.

This, she told herself, had to be the champagne even though she'd only had one glass. She had no idea where he was going with this. His mood swings were enough to make her dizzy, if his kiss hadn't already done that.

"Yes, Nate," she replied, digging deep and finding her shields. She threw them up and she did it on purpose with grave determination. "I would never, ever, disappoint my daughter."

His eyes flashed but instead of letting her go, getting angry or speaking, he kissed her again. This was a real, *real* Nate kiss, open-mouthed and branding. A kiss the like he'd barely ever given her in front of Tash, much less when their daughter was only three feet away and likely watching, avidly.

When his head came up this time, Lily was leaning into him for support.

"Lily—" he started, but he stopped.

She blinked at him, her recovery from the last kiss taking a wee, bit longer.

"What?" she breathed when he didn't go on.

"Tomorrow we begin . . ." he said and Lily stared, not knowing what he was on about, then he finished, "again."

With that, he let her go.

She almost staggered at the loss of his strong support but caught herself. She turned and watched him get in the car and she waved dazedly as he drove her daughter away, Victor and the scowling Fazire following them.

Maxine and Laura came up on either side of her.

"Lily, I think it's time that I—" Laura said.

"Party! It's time to party!" Lily cried and, without caring what they thought, she ran into the house.

TWENTY-FIVE

Nate

THEY HAD ROOMS AT the Royal Crescent Hotel in Bath.

Nate had taken them out to dinner and then walked his exuberant, excited daughter through the opulent Georgian city with a quiet Fazire and Victor following them. Back in their rooms, Nate let Tash read to him before she went to sleep in one of the two bedrooms in their suite. This was not an easy task, considering her anticipation for the festivities of the next day.

Through this all, he'd kept tight control on his thoughts and put up with Fazire, who he knew was barely containing his desire to make some grand statement, and his father, who was also barely containing his desire to have a heartfelt talk with his son.

Nate was coasting on pure, adrenalin-fueled fear.

He hadn't felt fear since he was a young boy. But he remembered what it felt like, though fear of a pummeling from one of his mother's drug-addled lovers was nothing to the gut-twisting fear he had of losing Lily.

Again.

His insane, misguided, absurd decision to show her who he was in his unique, obscene way, to hold her guarded against her own loving heart, had been the most extraordinary mistake he'd made in his life.

And he remembered each one he'd ever made.

Vividly.

He'd thought the last one, not following Lily to Indiana when her neighbor had told him she'd gone home, was bad enough.

This one had been worse.

This time he didn't have Danielle and Jeffrey to blame.

This time he'd broken her all on his own.

The glass of vodka he was holding snapped in his hand, he felt the shards tear through his flesh and watched, removed, as the blood formed, dripping mingled with vodka, to the carpet.

As he was watching, detached as he bled, there came a knock at the door. This was a strong knock but it was quickly followed by an overbearing one, or more aptly described, an overbearing *succession* of knocks.

His father and Fazire.

Nate took out his handkerchief and wrapped it around his hand. Ignoring the glass, vodka and blood on the floor, he went to answer the door.

Both men stood outside. Victor's face was grave. Fazire's, Nate registered in a distracted way, was the same. Fazire was also holding a photo album.

"We need to talk," Victor announced.

Without hesitation, Nate nodded and stepped aside. Fazire and Victor shared a surprised glance, clearly thinking they'd meet resistance.

Nate was beyond resistance. He didn't have the energy for it. He left them at the door, walked into the sitting room and lowered himself to a settee.

"What have you done to your hand?" Victor asked in alarm and Nate watched as his father checked himself from rushing forward.

"Broken glass." Nate calmly motioned to the glass on the floor and didn't explain further.

He didn't need to.

Both Fazire and Victor stared at the glass then stared at each other again. Victor closed the door, they walked forward in unison and sat opposite him.

"Is everything all right between you and Lily?" Victor asked, and at his question Nate threw back his head and laughed.

It was much like Lily's laugh that morning, stronger but just as mirthless and bitter.

When he was done, he leveled his dark gaze on his father and saw Victor had gone pale.

"No," he replied honestly.

"I didn't think so," Victor murmured, showing to Nate's surprise that he didn't know what to do next.

Fazire wasn't so uncertain. Lily's bizarre friend slammed the album on the table between them.

"It's time," he announced.

"Fazire—" Victor put in.

Fazire's gaze swung haughtily to his compatriot.

"It's *time*," Fazire insisted.

Victor leaned back and looked at Nate.

"Son, steel yourself," he warned in a dire tone.

Nothing, Nate thought, could penetrate the fear of what tomorrow would bring, not even Fazire.

Again, Nate was wrong.

Fazire started talking and Nate turned his eyes to the outlandish man.

"Many years ago, a man bought my bottle—"

"Your bottle?" Nate interrupted.

Fazire's hand came up. "Do not interrupt me, Nathaniel."

Nate looked at Victor then shrugged. Best to get this over with so he could make himself another drink, then another, and another until he was drunk enough to sleep and so that he could be hungover enough for tomorrow, when Lily came to her senses, he would have something else to think about when she left him at the proverbial altar.

"As I was saying," Fazire continued, "a man bought my bottle and sent it to a woman, his wife. She lived in Indiana and she became my friend. Her name was Sarah . . ."

Then, for half an hour, Fazire talked. He told Nate he was a genie. He told Nate about Lily's parents, Becky and Will. He told Nate about baseball games and lying in inner-tubes, floating hot summer days away on a pond. He told Nate he'd actually *created* Lily. Then he'd opened the photo album and showed Nate what Fazire called his "greatest mistake."

Nate's somewhat alarmed gaze swung to pictures of Lily, pictures he'd never, at a glance, recognize *were* Lily if he hadn't looked closely enough to see her remarkable blue eyes, or, in some of the photos, her quirky smile.

Stunned by the pictures of the chubby, plain (but not entirely unattractive, not with those eyes or that smile) girl that was his Lily, Nate listened further without interruption to Fazire telling him about Lily's obsession for romance novels. About the children being cruel to her at school (this, Nate had no trouble believing, even though everything else Fazire was saying had to be the ravings of a functioning madman). About the boy she had a crush on insulting her and breaking her fourteen-year-old heart.

Then Fazire told Nate of her wish, her wish for *him*, her wish for a romantic hero who would love her more than anything on earth and think she was beautiful.

When he was done speaking, Nate was staring at him.

"You're mad," Nate whispered, wondering if perhaps he should call a doctor, *now*.

Fazire looked at Victor and Victor nodded.

Then Fazire snapped his fingers and Nate heard a tinkling of glass. His gaze swung to the broken shards on the floor and he saw them jump around and, in the blink of an eye, disappear along with the blood and vodka stains.

Slowly, Nate stood.

"What the hell?" he muttered.

"I'm a genie," Fazire announced.

Nate's gaze swung to and narrowed on Fazire.

"You've been caring for my daughter," Nate stated in a voice so controlled it had a lethal edge.

"I wouldn't hurt Tash. I created her mother for goodness sake," Fazire blustered but Nate was having none of it.

He'd had enough of this strange man and he wasn't going to have some bizarre magician claiming himself to be a genie living with Lily and Tash. He knew from Lily mentioning on several occasions her "wish" that

Fazire had convinced her too that he was a genie.

Nate glared at him.

"Get out," he demanded knowing in that moment if Fazire didn't get out, Nate would bodily eject him from his life *and* his family's. "Right now."

Fazire snapped again and the room was filled with a voice, a voice that was achingly familiar.

Lily's voice but young, her voice that of a girl turning into a woman.

"Fazire, I wish one day to find a man like in my books. He has to be just like in one of my books. And he has to love me, love me more than anything in the world. Most important of all, he has to think I'm beautiful."

Nate froze at the disembodied words that seemed to dance through the air. There was no tape recorder and no speakers, the words just hung in the air, coming from nothing, nowhere, but they were all around them.

"He has to be tall, very tall and dark, and broad-shouldered, and narrow-hipped."

Nate's fingers curled into fists and he ignored the pain in his injured hand as he heard the words Lily spoke to him just weeks ago, smiling, teasing, telling him he was her "narrow-hipped" romantic hero who could "lean well."

"And he has to be handsome, unbelievably handsome, impossibly handsome with a strong, square jaw and powerful cheekbones and tanned skin and beautiful eyes with lush, thick lashes. He has to be clever and very wealthy but hard-working. He has to be virile, fierce, ruthless and rugged."

"Stop it," Nate demanded on the word "rugged" and Lily's sweet voice saying the same word she called him weeks ago but saying it years ago, in a wish.

The voice relentlessly went on.

"And he has to be hard and cold and maybe a little bit forbidding, a little bit bad with a broken heart I have to mend or one encased in ice I have to melt or better yet, both!"

Nate closed his eyes at the hope in her voice but wished instead he could stop his ears from hearing.

"We have to go through some trials and tribulations. Something to test our love, make it strong and worthy. And . . . and . . . he has to be daring and very

masculine. Powerful. People must respect him, maybe even fear him. Graceful too and lithe, like a . . . like a cat! Or a lion. Or something like that. And he has to be a good lover. The best, so good he could almost make love to me just by using his eyes."

At that, Nate opened his eyes and laughed, this time without bitterness.

He threw himself back on the settee and listened to a young Lily describing her deepest desire, her most heartfelt wish.

Him.

"Is that it?" Nate heard Fazire's voice ask. *"Are you sure you want this to be your wish?"* There was hesitation then Fazire went on, *"Very well."*

Lily's voice cut in. *"Don't forget that part about him loving me more than anything on earth."*

Her words and their fervent tone tore through Nate's gut.

"And!" Nate heard her burst out in desperation. *"The part about him thinking I'm beautiful."*

"Lily, you will be beautiful, you already are." Nate heard Fazire's disembodied voice assure her.

His eyes cut to the strange man and for the first time he looked at him with unguarded respect.

"Just, don't forget those parts. They're the most important," Lily reminded her genie, her voice shaky and, Nate thought, terribly, *unforgettably* sad.

"I won't forget any of it." Nate heard Fazire promise his beloved fourteen-year-old girl. A girl he'd followed through her trials and tribulations. A girl whose side he never left. *"Lily, my lovely, your wish is my command."*

The room was filled with the sound of a snap and it went quiet.

Everyone sat in stunned silence.

Victor, even though still pale, was grinning at Nate.

Nate's eyes moved to Fazire who, he should not at that point have been surprised but he was, Nate saw was floating and wearing a ridiculous outfit the colors of turquoise and grape, including a fez and curly-toed shoes.

Fazire was looking down his nose at Nate. "Nathaniel, I am *very* good at my wishes and if you don't *do* something and *soon*, I'll lose the Wish of the Century award," he declared.

"It's nowhere near the end of the century, Fazire," Victor explained.

"Time flies when you're immortal," Fazire shot back. "Competition is heating up. Just yesterday—"

Nate didn't let him finish.

He didn't have time to process the fact that Lily had her own personal genie. He just looked up at the man floating cross-legged in mid-air (something, Nate noted, his father didn't seem at all surprised about).

"Fazire," Nate cut in, and when he had Fazire's attention, he said simply, "Tash."

Fazire nodded. "Of course."

Then Nate grabbed his car keys and with long strides and without a look back, he walked out the door.

NATE OPENED THE FRONT DOOR to Lily's house, his house, their *home*.

It was late, but not late enough for the hen night festivities to be over, but he heard standing in the entry vestibule, no laughing voices, no tinkling glasses, no music and no merriment.

This did not surprise him.

A week ago he'd set himself the task of forcing Lily to fall out of love with him so when she found out about who he was she would not be destroyed.

At the silence of the house and Lily's recent behavior he worried that he had, as usual, succeeded swiftly and soundly in his aim.

He opened the stained glass inner door and stopped dead.

Laura, wearing a dove-gray satin dressing gown, her face free of makeup, her hair pulled back, was sitting on the stairs waiting for him.

Mother and son held each other's eyes for long moments then Laura got to her feet and came forward.

She lifted her hand to Nate's cheek and said softly, "I knew you'd come."

At her quiet assurance that she knew innately he would do the right thing, that she believed in him and Nate realized always had, Nate's arms went around her. Laura rested her cheek against his chest.

Finally she tilted her head back to look at him. "Lily's upstairs. We decided to have an early night."

Nate nodded and they disengaged. Then he took his mother's elbow and escorted her to the door of the guest room where he kissed her cheek and watched her enter. When she closed the door he turned with purpose to his and Lily's bedroom.

The door was closed and when he opened it the room was dark, the curtains drawn and he could see Lily's sleeping form in the bed. He walked to the side and stared down, noticing in the dim light she was curled around his pillow, hugging it close to her.

Quietly, he took off his clothes, dropping them to the floor. He then pulled back the bedsheets. He slid into bed carefully and pulled away the pillow, righting it behind his head and positioning his body in its place. Unfortunately, before he had completed this task, she woke.

"Nate?" she murmured, her voice husky with sleep.

His arm went around her quickly holding her tight against his body and he reached out and turned on the light.

She lifted up with her hand on his chest and blinked at him as his other arm closed around her, bringing her body over him so she was lying mostly on top of him.

"What is it?" she asked, still blinking but her face was clearing. "Is it Tash?"

"Tash is fine," Nate assured her quietly.

Lily stared at him then her eyes dropped to the clock at the bedside table. They came back to him and he saw, in that short time, she'd put her shields up. She looked wary and she tried to push away.

His arms got tighter.

"What's going on?" Lily asked.

"Do you know," Nate began conversationally, having mentally rehearsed his words in the car, doing this in order to shove away the thoughts and memories that had been pelting his brain viciously for the past week, "until Laura and Victor adopted me, I didn't know my birthdate?"

Lily's body stilled and she stopped trying to pull away.

"I'm sorry?" she queried, her face melting from annoyed and watchful to confused.

Confused, Nate thought, was good. Nate could work with confused.

So he went on, "I didn't know my birthdate until Laura and Victor adopted me and told me. It's the fourteenth of September."

Her head jerked at this news but she recovered swiftly and bit her lip then released it.

"How could you . . ." Her eyes shifted away and he could tell she was trying to decide how to respond.

Curiosity, he was pleased and hopeful to see, won.

Confused was good, curious was much, much better.

She continued, "Not know your birthday?"

"My mother never told me," Nate answered matter-of-factly.

Lily's eyes grew wide with shock, wary and guarded gone. She was staring at him with undisguised disbelief.

"Why on earth wouldn't your mother tell you?" Lily was holding her body still, tense and he sensed she was unsure how to react to his unprecedented sharing.

He wasn't surprised. He'd been behaving erratically, pushing her away and pulling her close, holding her at arm's length and then demanding her attention, yelling at her when she bought him presents, keeping himself from her and then, finally, brutally showing her who he was.

Or who he thought he was.

And he hadn't just been doing this for the last two months. He'd been doing it since they met.

"I never asked," Nate replied, quelling his thoughts to focus on the very important matter at hand. "She probably didn't remember considering most of the time she was drunk and when she wasn't drunk, she was high or, more often than not, both."

He watched as she closed and opened her eyes slowly as if this was beyond her comprehension.

"High?" Lily whispered.

"She was a drug addict, Lily," Nate responded softly then before she could react or put her shields back in place, he continued. "Her name was Deirdre."

At more news of his life, his history coming forth, Lily's eyes grew soft, and before she could control it, she said with a horrified reverence, as if he'd just shown her the fountain of youth and it was flowing with blood, "Deirdre."

Nate saw his opening and without delay he relentlessly pressed through.

"Until I went to school, I didn't know you washed your clothes."

He heard Lily's swift intake of breath and was heartened by the fact she wasn't hiding her reactions.

He talked over her gasp.

"The teachers reported me to Social Services and they came to visit my mother. She put on a show for them and from then on she made me take our clothes to the Laundromat so they wouldn't come back. Until I moved in with Victor and Laura though, I never knew you were supposed to clean your sheets."

He felt as her still body grew rock solid in horror.

Then she whispered, her voice shaky, "Your mother made *you* wash your clothes?"

He kept pressing through, sensing he was gaining an edge, knowing Lily had a kind heart and, after all, she'd wished for him.

He took advantage but ignored her question. "I stole food. I had to or I wouldn't eat. I had milk and cereal for breakfast, lunch and dinner. I didn't know any better," he told her then smiled. "And lots of candy. Candy was easy to steal. It fit in your pockets."

Lily did *not* smile and clearly found nothing Nate was saying amusing. She swallowed, not pushing away, not holding herself from him. He felt her melting into his body but she did not speak. She simply stared at him, her eyes unguarded, lips slightly parted, face soft.

That's when Nate decided it was time to let her know all of it.

"When I was eleven, I went to work for one of Deirdre's lovers. She had a lot of them and I learned early, because she didn't hide it, what having a lover meant in the physical sense." Nate watched Lily again bite her lip at this news but didn't hesitate and carried on, "I stole from her lovers too. Sometimes they'd catch me, which wasn't good, so I learned to avoid them, to be invisible or fast enough to escape them. If I didn't, they'd beat me. Sometimes, they'd beat Deirdre and I'd try to stop them so they'd turn their attention to me. Deirdre never tried to stop them."

"Didn't try to stop—" Lily repeated but Nate talked over her.

"Scott, one of Deirdre's lovers, put me to work making deliveries and doing pickups. I don't know what I moved but I didn't care. He gave me money and we never had any money. In the end Scott went away and I took a job direct with his boss. His boss wasn't a good man. He was a dangerous man but he paid me more money than I'd ever seen before. I was good at it—"

"Stop," Lily whispered and her voice and eyes were tortured.

"You have to know," Nate returned quietly.

He hated to see the look in her eyes but he believed with everything he was that he was correct, she *had* to know.

"I don't have to know," she repeated, contradicting his belief, her voice growing stronger.

"I was a criminal," Nate told her bluntly. "Since I could remember, I stole, I—"

Suddenly and forcefully she pulled free of him but not to escape. She sat up and glared at him.

"You were *not* a criminal!" she snapped.

Nate followed her up. "I was, Lily. I worked for a gangster. Whatever was in those packages—"

"You were eleven years old, for crying out loud!" she yelled and he knew she was agitated. He knew this because she was being loud even though Laura was in the house and Maxine was also spending the night. She was also shifting in the bed with intent, and before she could jump up and start pacing, he captured her in his arm. He pushed her to her back and rolled over her with his body.

Then he went on. He needed to say it all, get it out so she could make her decision.

"It doesn't change what I did, who I was and that person is the father of your child and tomorrow, if you don't back out, he'll be your husband."

Lily glared at him. "Are you a gangster now?"

Nate shook his head but responded, "Lily, there's more you need to know."

"Have you had a birthday party?" she asked, suddenly switching the subject what Nate thought was nonsensically and he stared at her, thrown for a moment, before replying.

"Lily, we're talking about me being—"

"Have you ever had a birthday party?" she interrupted him, squirming underneath him to get away.

"What does it matter?" he asked, pressing into her to keep her where she was.

"It matters!" she shouted and stopped wriggling in order to scowl at him.

"Why?"

"I . . ." she snapped, "I don't know why. It just does. Have you ever had one?"

"I never wanted one," he replied.

"Well, you're getting one this year," she declared on a huff. "I *cannot* believe you've never had a birthday party. What's your favorite kind of cake?" she fired off her question, eyes narrowed.

"Lily, I need to tell you the rest."

"Nate, I don't *care* about the rest. What kind of cake is your favorite?"

Nate stopped talking and stared at his bride-to-be.

He was telling her things of grave importance, things she needed to know before she legally bound herself to him. He was telling her things he'd never told anyone, not even Laura, though he knew that Victor knew and guessed he'd told Laura. It was likely that Victor told Laura everything.

But Nate was telling Lily things he'd hidden from everyone, all his hideous secrets, and Lily was talking about cake.

"I don't have a favorite cake," Nate responded.

"Everyone has a favorite cake, Nate," Lily informed him.

"Cake is cake," Nate shot back, impatient to get back to the subject.

"Cake is *not* cake. There's angel food cake and Victoria sponge. There's coffee cake. There's streusel cake. There's cheesecake. Don't *even* get me started on chocolate cake. There has to be hundreds of different kinds of chocolate cake." She hesitated and Nate, thinking she was finished with her bizarre litany of cakes, opened his mouth to speak but then she went on, "German chocolate, devil's food, chocolate sheet cake, chocolate mocha cake—"

Finally, he lost his patience and he interrupted her on a quiet explosion, "Lily, for Christ's sake!"

That was when her hands came up to either side of his face and she stared him in the eyes. He realized she wasn't looking at him with a wary, guarded expression nor were her shields up. She also wasn't staring at him horrified and repulsed that he'd slept in dirty sheets, had a mother who was a drunken drug addict and committed crimes before he was in his teens.

Instead, she was planning his birthday party.

And she was looking at him the way she used to look at him, with a look of awe, wonder, as if he was conqueror of nations, creator of worlds.

This hit him with the weight of a dozen anvils.

He felt that weight and a clutch in his chest even as he felt warmth spread through his gut and his voice was rough when he murmured, "Lily."

"I'm going to make you a cake," she promised softly, "every week until your birthday so you can pick which one you like best."

At her soft words, he felt the clutch in his chest release, completely and finally, leaving him free for the first time in his life to just *breathe*.

He pulled her tight into his arms, burying his face in the side of her neck and rolled to his back, taking her with him so she was on top.

"And we're going to have a big party," she continued speaking softly in his ear. "And we're going to have a big Christmas. But, before that, we're going to have a Fourth of July party and Thanksgiving—"

"I love you, Lily," he whispered into her neck.

"And we're going . . . what?"

He tilted his head back into the pillows and looked in her beautiful blue eyes. "I love you, Lily, more than anything on this earth."

For a moment she just stared at him, her eyes wide and filling with wonder. Then he watched, fascinated, as they brightened with tears.

"Really?" she breathed.

Keeping their eyes locked, Nate lifted his head and brushed his lips against hers. "Really," he said there.

"You love . . . *me*?" she asked, as if that was impossible to believe.

Because of Fazire's story, he now understood her disbelief that he could love her even if it still stunned him, and Nate knew he had to *make* her believe. His hand came up and tucked a sheaf of her heavy hair behind her ear.

"Yes, I love you," he said, his voice hoarse with feeling.

"But—" she began and he kept going, resting his palm against her jaw and running his thumb along her tear-stained cheek.

"I loved you the minute I saw you, elegant, untouchable, beautiful and not for the likes of me," he told her with complete honesty.

"Beautiful?" she whispered.

"When I first saw you, you were the most beautiful woman I'd ever seen and I remember everything, Lily, every woman I've ever laid eyes on. You were extraordinary, magnificent, so much so I couldn't even move." Nate watched as her tears came faster and his other hand came up to frame her face and wipe away the wetness with his thumb. Then he whispered, "You still are, darling."

Her face clouded and she pulled slightly away. "I have to tell you . . ." she whispered hesitantly and went on cautiously, "it's all a wish. You don't really see *me*. You see what Fazire—"

"I know about Fazire," Nate cut her off. "I know what he is. I know about your wish and it wouldn't matter." He watched her eyes grow round and he continued, "If there was no wish, no magic and no genies, I'd think the same thing. I see *you*, Lily, your natural elegance, your beautiful eyes, your fantastic smile, your lush body—"

"Stop," she cut in and rubbed her fingers across her cheeks, trying to brush away the tears even as she pushed his hands away but he held fast.

"You *are* beautiful, but I don't love you because you're beautiful."

She became still again in order to stare at him.

"Why do you love me?" she whispered and he answered immediately.

"Because you have the courage to jump on a purse snatcher's back. Because you have an unnatural abhorrence to litter. Because you act like a ride on a motorcycle is like being given the keys to a kingdom of dreams. Because you have the ability to make all the people around you love you even when they barely know you. Because you inspire loyalty. Because you made our daughter happy even when you were not. Because you created a comfortable, loving home for her even though you had no money."

"Nate, don't—" she interrupted, squeezing her eyes shut as if it would blot out his words but he didn't listen.

"Because you taste good and feel even better. Because you look at me like no one else has ever done."

"Stop," she broke in forcefully, her eyes flying open, "I want to tell you why I love you."

He felt his body get tense.

"Do you?" he asked quietly.

"Do I what?" she asked in return.

"Do you still love me?"

He watched her brows snap together. "Why wouldn't I?"

He smiled at her and he knew it was a smile filled with regret.

"I don't know, darling," he answered softly. "Maybe because I let you go, broke my promises, didn't take care of you, made you beg for—"

She lifted her hand between them and waved at the air while saying, "Oh that. I'm over *that*."

At this breezy announcement and her acting as if his constant betrayals of trust were akin to forgetting to take out the rubbish, Nate couldn't have stopped it if he'd tried, which he didn't, and his body started shaking with laughter.

He decided instantly that he loved that about her too, her ability to forgive though, in the same instant, he vowed he'd never do anything that she'd have to forgive, not ever again.

His laughter was short-lived when he heard Lily gasp.

"What's happened to your hand?" she cried.

Rearing back, she grabbed his wrist and stared at the bloody handkerchief tied around his hand.

"It's nothing."

She lifted her eyes from his hand to his face and glared at him and even with her angry glower, he could have kissed her.

"Right, nothing. Like my migraines are just headaches," she snapped.

"Lily."

She crawled over him, her hand latched to his wrist and pulled him out of bed.

"I want to see," she said, tugging him toward the bathroom.

"I said, it's nothing."

She halted and turned back to him.

"I *want* to *see*."

She underlined her words verbally and there she was.

He knew in that instant that he finally, irrevocably, had her back.

His Lily.

His.

She'd wished for him.

Him.

Nathaniel McAllister.

He was meant for her and she was meant for him. They belonged to each other. They belonged together.

Relief sweeping through him, he gave his wrist a swift yank. Pulling her off balance and into his arms, his head descended and his mouth took hers for a quick, hard kiss.

When he was done and he saw the smoky dark blue at the edge of her irises was creeping toward the pupil, he muttered in a voice that said, clearly, she really had no choice in the matter, "You can see when I'm done making love to you."

Without hesitation she agreed, "Okay."

It was then that he started laughing again but this, too, was short-lived because Lily leaned up on tiptoe, threw her arms around his neck and she gave him a hard kiss.

But Lily's wasn't quick.

MUCH LATER, LILY'S NAKED BACK pressed to his front, Nate buried his face into her fragrant hair.

He hadn't made love to her. She had pushed him to his back and she'd made love to him, her mouth and hands on him as she spoke softly, lips against his skin, telling him all the reasons she loved him.

Not because he was rugged, lean-hipped and wealthy with a broken heart she needed to (and did) mend.

But because he was, she said, brilliant. He was strong and people respected him. He kissed well and she mentioned something about gymnasts doing cartwheels and back handsprings in her belly, but he wasn't paying much attention because at the time she was saying it her tongue was tracing the ridges of his stomach, and he found he couldn't concentrate on her words. She told him he had a beautiful smile. She informed him, to his surprise, her parents would have liked him. She explained he was a good son to Laura and Victor. She said he was good at taking care of her when she was ill. And finally, she finished with the fact that he made her feel safe and he was an excellent father.

With her finishing words, he rolled her on her back and took over the lovemaking with such rigorous intent, she couldn't speak at all.

When they were done she'd again yanked him out of bed to see to his hand. She cleansed it, bandaged it and he'd allowed it, not letting on that she was the first and only person he'd ever let take care of him. He'd never even allowed Laura to tend to him but he didn't share this either. He would, just not right then. There were other things he needed to share.

Nate guided her back to bed. There he pulled her back to his front and quietly, he shared with her the rest of his life, speaking more words at one time than he ever had. He told her of growing up with Deirdre, of his mother not sending him to a special school when the teachers told her she should, of her murder, of Victor's part in saving him then Laura's, of Danielle's unwanted attention and Jeffrey's malice.

Through this all, she said nothing, simply rested her arm on his at her waist and laced her fingers in his. Often her body would tense but she didn't interrupt him.

Finally, when he was finished and silent, she whispered, "Why didn't you tell me?"

It was his turn for his body to tense. "I thought if you knew, you'd leave."

"Why?" she asked.

"You'd probably never seen a syringe filled with heroin or held your mother's hair when she was so drunk she was getting sick in the toilet," he explained.

"You thought I'd leave because you had a terrible, awful, horrible, useless, unspeakably bad mother?" she queried and at any other time Nate might have smiled at her dramatic description of his mother but it wasn't the time for smiles.

"I thought you'd leave because I did bad things."

"You didn't know," she defended him.

"I *did* know. I was young but I wasn't stupid," Nate replied.

"You had no choice," she returned immediately.

Nate didn't answer for this was true.

Finally he said, "It isn't a pretty story of genies and magical wishes or even lazing away summer days floating on ponds."

"No," she admitted. "But it made you . . . you."

"Yes," Nate allowed for this was true too.

"And I love you," she went on.

This time his arm tensed, pulling her deeper into his body.

"Yes," he murmured.

"And I wouldn't change a thing about you, except to erase what you've been through," she told him, snuggling even closer.

"I didn't want it to touch you," Nate shared. "It was ugly, dirty and I didn't want it to be a part of your life."

"*It* was ugly and dirty but *you* weren't," Lily replied in a voice vibrating with feeling and registering so low, he had to tilt his head closer to hear.

And what she said next shook him so deeply, any remaining armor he had around his heart fell away (although, there wasn't much left) and the quickly melting ice around it shattered.

"I'm proud. I'm proud of who you were, how you survived and what you've become. And I'm proud that you were an inspiration to make Victor see he should change his life so you and he and Laura could have a better one. And I'm proud that you love me and we made Tash together."

Nate closed his eyes and drew in his breath. Of all of it, he'd been dreading this moment the most.

He had one last admission to make that night.

"Lily, there's something else you need to know."

"All right," she said trustingly and, now vulnerable, knowing he'd come so far, she'd given so much and he had her back, he steeled himself against her reaction to his next words.

"I meant to get you pregnant," he announced.

She went completely still and Nate felt his chest constrict. Then she turned in his arms and looked into his eyes, hers were bemused.

"I did it with intent," Nate went on, feeling she had to know and hating himself for doing it as well as the fact he had to tell her. "I wanted to bind you to me. I knew how you felt about family and I thought making you pregnant would mean you'd never leave. I didn't know you were pregnant when you *did* leave but I did everything I could when we—"

"Thank God," she breathed, shocking him into silence with her words.

She smiled her quirky smile and Nate stared at her, dumbfounded by her reaction.

She moved in, brushed her lips against his and turned again, nestling contentedly into his body.

"If you hadn't," she carried on sleepily, clearly not upset in any way that he'd callously impregnated her in a selfish effort to tie her to him then left her to bear the child alone through a difficult pregnancy and a birth that caused her to die for two minutes and thirty-eight seconds, and then for seven years she'd reared Tash under supremely trying circumstances all without Nate's assistance, "we wouldn't have Tash and, well, anyway . . . thank God."

And that, Nate realized with a profound sense of relief, was that.

Nate again buried his face in her hair, laid silent and listened as Lily fell asleep.

He held her.

Then, for the first time in his life, at peace with himself, at peace with his past, Nate slept.

He woke before dawn and carefully pulled away so as not to wake her but she rolled into him and wrapped her arms around him.

She lifted sleep filled eyes to his, "Where are you going?"

He kissed her softly and murmured, "I have to go to Tash. Go back to sleep, darling."

She nodded, gave him a sleepy smile and let him go. The minute he exited the bed, she clutched his pillow to her.

Nate dressed, sat on the edge of the bed and tucked her hair behind her ear.

"You've seen me on our wedding day," she muttered into the pillow, not opening her eyes.

Nate bent down and touched his mouth to the skin at the back of her ear.

"I think we've had all the bad luck there is to have," he assured her.

Her lips came up in a half grin before she fell back to sleep.

Nate allowed himself a moment to watch her, a moment to feel the joy that had replaced the tightness in his chest, to come to terms with his newfound sense of contentment, security, belonging.

Then he left his soon-to-be wife and went to their daughter.

TWENTY-SIX

Everyone
Lily

"LILY, THE LIMOUSINE IS here!" Maxine called up the steps.

Lily stood looking at herself in the mirror thinking maybe, just maybe, Nate hadn't been bewitched by Fazire's magic.

Maybe she *was* beautiful.

Her dress was simple ivory silk, strapless, form-fitting, cut at just above the knee. At her waist there was a thin belt of the same ivory material with a small, silk-wrapped, square buckle. She had on a pair of pointed-toed, stiletto-heeled, ivory, sling-backed pumps. The only jewelry she wore was a one strand pearl necklace and matching bracelet with pearl studs in her ears, a set that Laura had given her that morning stating it was her engagement present from Laura and Victor. Her hair was swept back softly in a satin ivory ribbon tied in a bow at the nape of her neck.

"You look fab," Susan said from behind her.

Lily's eyes moved to the three girls in her bedroom with her. Susan, Emily and Lorna were her shop girls from Flash and Dazzle. The shop was closed for the day so the girls could attend the wedding and be involved in the preparations.

Susan was great with hair and thus she did Lily's for her wedding day. Emily was great with makeup, so ditto Emily's reason for being there. Lorna had no special skill but Lily was not about to leave one of her girls out and Lorna was the type of girl who wouldn't have allowed that anyway.

Lily could, considering the fact that she had a little less than seven million pounds in her bank account, have had the best stylists and makeup artists in the United Kingdom tending to her wedding preparations, but what would be special about *that*?

Maxine hustled into the room, all business.

"Come on girls, you better get going or you'll never make it to Bath on time and—" she stopped dead when her eyes fell on Lily. Then her mouth dropped open. Seconds later, she burst into loud tears.

Lily, Susan, Emily and Lorna all rushed toward Maxine, and Lily wrapped an arm around her friend.

"Maxine, what on earth's the matter?"

Maxine's tear-brightened eyes never left Lily. "You . . ." she started then sighed, "Oh, Lily." And Maxine threw her arms around Lily and gave her a tight hug. When she pulled back, she looked in Lily's eyes and whispered, "You're the most beautiful bride in the world."

Lily smiled thinking that, of course, Maxine would say that.

"Hear, hear!" Lorna shouted so loud and with such conviction that Lily jumped and Lorna downed the last sip out of her champagne glass.

"I'll say!" Emily followed suit with her champagne.

"Me too!" Susan chimed in, not drinking as Susan was driving all the girls to Bath.

"What's going on?" Laura bustled in, looking around the room, which bore the evidence of not only wedding preparations but of a hen morning that had started the minute Lily staggered, tired from a sleep-disturbed night, but still elated at the events of that night, into the kitchen to see a concerned Maxine and Laura sitting at the kitchen table.

Once their eyes hit Lily's happy, shining face, their concern melted, hugs were exchanged, tears of joy fell and the first of several bottles of champagne was popped open.

Lily felt on top of the world, on top of the universe, gliding along in heaven.

She had Nate. Finally, *completely*, he was hers. She wanted to climb to the roof and shout it to the entire town (this, she did not do, as her dress would be ruined).

Laura's eyes alighted on Lily and she, too, stopped dead and stared. "Oh, dear Lord," she breathed.

Lily moved to Laura and stood in front of her.

Putting her arms out to her sides, her heart thundering in her chest, she asked her soon-to-be mother-in-law quietly, "Will I do for your son?"

It was Laura's turn to burst into tears and she reached out and clutched Lily to her.

"You'll do. You'll more than do." Laura leaned away from Lily but didn't let her go. "I couldn't have made a better bride for my son if I had it in my power. Lily, you're *perfect*."

Lily felt tears fill her eyes at Laura's sweet words and Emily shouted, "No! Don't cry! Oh no!" She snapped at Lorna, "Get me my makeup bag, quick!"

Susan, Lorna and Emily swiftly repaired makeup damage on Lily, Maxine and Laura and then Emily shoved lipstick, mascara, blusher and a powder-blue, lacy handkerchief, the one her mother held on her own wedding day that was also the one her grandmother held on hers, in Lily's small, exquisite, ivory handbag (another gift that morning, this from Maxine) and they all ran down the stairs.

Lily stood on the pavement and waved off her girls as they shouted encouraging and somewhat raunchy words out their open windows as they drove away. Lily was giggling and smiling and thinking nothing, *nothing* could ever make her sad again.

However, she did not see the three people alighting from the car down the street as she had her back to it.

But Laura did and her face paled at the sight.

Tash

NATASHA ROBERTS MCALLISTER JACOBS WAS thankful that

Mummy had sent Fazire with them to Bath.

Daddy, Tash found, was *not* very good at doing a seven-year-old girl's hair and making it ultra, super beautiful for a *very* special day.

This, Tash thought, was okay considering her daddy was good at everything else. No one, she allowed, could be good at absolutely *everything*.

And anyway, Fazire had magic. He just snapped his fingers and Tash's hair had all sorts of fun, bouncy curls and was pulled back at the sides with pretty, sparkly clips. When he did this Daddy stared at Fazire in a funny way that looked both exasperated (Tash liked this word and knew what it meant) and amused.

It was a look that made Natasha giggle.

Daddy, Tash found out, now knew that Fazire was their special genie and he didn't mind. Tash knew he wouldn't and thought they should have told him *ages* ago. He was the best daddy *ever* and since Fazire was one of the family, even though he was a little strange, Tash *always* knew her daddy wouldn't mind.

Mummy was making her wear pale blue, like the color Daddy had used in Mummy's new, now old bedroom. Tash had not been happy about the blue, she'd wanted pink. Until she'd seen her pretty, frilly blue dress. Once she'd seen the dress, she didn't mind at all.

"Now that I've seen to Natasha's hair, *I* need to prepare," Fazire said in his I-am-a-genie-all-bow-to-me voice, and he disappeared in a poof of grape-colored smoke that drifted towards his bottle until it was gone.

Tash looked at her father.

He looked more handsome than anyone she'd ever seen in her *whole life*. And she remembered everyone she'd ever seen in her whole life, she remembered everything, though she'd never told anyone that. He was wearing a dark suit with an ivory shirt and a pretty tie the *exact* color of Tash's dress.

She moved to her daddy and, even though she was no longer a baby but now a big girl, her daddy was strong and he picked her up, just like always. She wrapped her arms and legs around him and nuzzled her nose against his. And, again, just like always, he nuzzled hers right back.

She pulled back, just a bit, and she took a deep breath because she had to ask what she'd been thinking about for *days*, for *weeks* but had always been too scared.

"Daddy?" she said, her voice timid.

"Yes, sweetheart?" her daddy replied and Tash felt something funny in her heart because he'd never called her sweetheart before and she liked it a whole lot.

"You're not, um," she stopped then rushed on, "ever going to leave again, are you?"

She watched her daddy's handsome face turn stunned then hard then soft and he said, "*Never*," in a way that she really, *really* believed him.

She took one of her arms from around his neck and put her hand on his cheek and said something else she'd been too scared to say.

"Today's a happy day and once it's over, do you think you'll hurt anymore?"

He blinked slowly and then asked, "Hurt? Tash, what makes you think—"

"I see it in your eyes," Natasha interrupted.

Mummy wouldn't like that Tash interrupted but she suspected Daddy wouldn't tell.

Her daddy's arms became tighter than ever and his hand went to the back of her head, his fingers sifting into her fun, bouncy curls and he pressed her cheek against his strong neck.

What he didn't do was answer.

"You're too sharp for your own good," he muttered and Tash had heard *that* before.

She had the suspicion that she wasn't too sharp for *her own* good. She was too sharp *for everyone else's* good.

"I don't want you to hurt anymore," Tash told him quietly, thinking they should get back to the subject because it *was* an important one.

Her daddy pulled back and looked her directly in the eyes, and looking at him she saw *her* eyes for she and her father had the same *exact* eyes.

"The hurt's gone, Tash," he told her.

She stared at him closely, trying to see any of the hurt there, in his eyes, his face, anywhere.

She couldn't find any so she smiled her quirky-sweet smile.

Then she cried, "*Yipeeeee!*"

And then she got her *bestest*, best gift of the day.

Her father smiled back at her.

Maxine

"I DO *NOT* BELIEVE THIS is happening.," Lily stood seething in her sitting room.

Maxine couldn't believe it was happening either. Time was ticking away. They should have left ten minutes ago. Instead these *odious* creatures were standing in the sitting room saying things to Lily, things . . . things . . . things . . . such *things* that Maxine was worried her ears were bleeding just hearing them.

It had been a fun, happy morning full of giggles, tears and champagne and they'd tackled the food they'd barely touched the night before (to Maxine's delight, she liked her food). Lily was Lily again. Fully Lily. The girl Maxine had met nearly a decade before, happy, giddy, full of life, smiling and open-hearted for all to see.

All was finally well in the world.

Then, watching Lorna, Emily and Susan drive away, Maxine had felt Laura stiffen by her side. She'd turned to see what Laura was looking at and she spied Alistair walking toward them, a man and woman with him.

"Alistair what are you doing here?" Maxine smiled at him.

Alistair didn't smile back.

That was when Maxine felt it. A wave of something horrid pounding at her back and she turned to see Lily, who was even paler than Laura and who seemed rooted to the spot, her mouth open in shock—supremely unhappy shock, Maxine felt it important to note—and Lily looked ready to commit murder.

"How *dare* you!" Lily cried, advancing on them. "Go away! Go! Get out of my sight! *How dare you!*"

The hard, angry look on Alistair's face softened as he gazed at Lily but he remained resolute.

"Lily, you must listen. Jeffrey and Danielle told me about McAllister," he implored. "Please, you *must* listen."

"I don't have to listen to a thing you say," Lily snapped and turned to Maxine. "Let's go."

Maxine was looking between everyone. She knew who Jeffrey and Danielle were and her eyes narrowed on them then they swung to Alistair and you'd have to be blind not to see her face screamed "traitor."

"We're going," Maxine declared, moving to Laura.

"I want to hear what they have to say," Laura said quietly, staring at her children and everyone stopped.

"Laura, the booking for the ceremony is firm. If we miss it or we're late . . ." Maxine put her hand lightly on Laura's arm. "We can't be late or they'll have to move to the next wedding. Saturdays at the Registry Office are booked solid. Lily and Nate were lucky to get the one they have and even still, Nate had to pull strings."

"You two go, I want to hear what they have to say," Laura replied then turned to Lily. "I'll drive your car. After I'm done here, I promise, I'll follow."

Lily was shaking her head but Alistair started speaking and all attention turned to him.

"Lily has to hear it."

"Lily's going to go marry my son." Laura's voice, which had been soft, now had a fierce tremor running through it. "*I'll* deal with Danielle and Jeffrey."

"I'm not leaving you alone with *them*." Lily's voice also had a vein of iron coursing through it.

Laura turned to Lily and took her hand. "You must go. Go to Nathaniel. I'll handle this."

"No," Lily shook her head again and said with finality, "We're family and family sticks together."

Before Laura could reply, Lily turned to Alistair. "You have ten minutes."

They'd all walked into the house. Lily didn't sit or offer refreshments and neither did Laura. Maxine was standing sentry. Alistair took his cue and stayed standing as did Danielle who, Maxine noted with ire, was staring about her looking at the newly furnished, sumptuous sitting room like she'd walked into a squalid hovel and Jeffrey who was staring intently, even hungrily (but not in a good way, in a way that made Maxine's skin crawl), at Lily.

"You now have nine minutes," Lily stated after they'd stood there for a while and no one but Lily said anything.

"Your fiancé is a criminal," Alistair stated bluntly.

Laura gasped.

Lily's eyes narrowed and her hands clenched to fists.

Maxine tensed.

Alistair went on, "Jeffrey and Danielle have had private investigators investigating him. I've read the reports. Not only was McAllister a petty thief and runner for a gangster, your soon-to-be father-in-law was a gun dealer."

Jeffrey moved forward and Lily took a step back so he stopped but, unfortunately, he spoke.

"Lily, they've both gone legit but you should know his mother was murdered. There's even the possibility he did it. That Nate murdered his own mother," Jeffrey said, his voice dripping sincerity, false sincerity. Even the biggest fool on earth could tell he was an out-and-out liar.

Then it started, the vile words spewing forth, not only from Jeffrey but also from Danielle. And not just about Nate, though the words about Nate were more shocking and sad than vile, but also about Victor.

Maxine found it took every bit of willpower in her not very full (at the best of times) reserve to stop herself from moving forward and scratching their eyes out.

"Quiet!" Laura suddenly shouted, finally stopping the words and all eyes moved to her. "Quiet," she repeated in a lower tone, her voice again trembling but this time with anger. "I thought," she began and then stopped, blinking and swallowing, visibly trying to get control. She eventually started again, "I thought I was ashamed of you before, of who you are, what you've become, all you've done, but now, now . . . now, I don't even know what to say. You aren't just no longer my children. From this point on *you no longer exist.*"

That was when it happened, Maxine was sorry to say. That was when her willpower gave out (but, it might also have been all the champagne she'd consumed that morning, she did, very much, like her champagne). She would, of course, look back and deeply lament her actions but it was beyond her control. She *liked* Laura and she *loved* Lily and she couldn't have stopped herself even if she tried.

Which she didn't.

For, after Laura made her statement, Danielle walked right up to her mother and slapped her across the face.

And *that* Maxine could not abide.

Luckily for Maxine, she had a partner in crime because Lily apparently was just as finished with the conversation and she didn't abide the physical abuse from daughter to mother either.

So both Maxine and Lily acted to put a stop to it.

Which was, it would turn out, *deeply* unfortunate.

Victor

"I CAN'T IMAGINE WHERE THEY are." Victor heard the girl say.

They were standing in the Registry Office anteroom. The guest list was few, some close friends of Victor and Laura's, Lily's shop girls and various and sundry other people neither Victor nor Nathaniel had ever met who were a part of Lily's life.

They were supposed to have gone into the ceremony room five minutes ago. If they missed their appointment, they'd have to reschedule.

Victor felt a sense of doom. All day Nathaniel had seemed, well, it was hard to believe but Nathaniel had seemed light-hearted, relaxed in a way that Victor had never seen before in his son. *Never.* Victor felt *certain* that Nathaniel had fixed things with Lily.

Now, he was not so sure.

Victor looked out the window and saw Fazire in a strange dark-purple suit, a turquoise tie and a camera hanging from his neck, pacing the pavement, glaring down the street as if he could force with his magical powers Lily's limousine to glide toward the entry, and he appeared to be talking to himself.

"Sir, we're going to have to ask—" one of the Registry Office personnel had approached Nathaniel who, Victor noted with mounting alarm, looked grim. Beyond grim. Grim tinged with what Victor was devastated to see was *resigned*.

Then Victor heard Nathaniel's mobile ring.

"We really must ask you to turn off your mobile," the Registry Office person said but snapped her mouth shut when Nathaniel's steely gaze sliced to her.

Nathaniel pulled out his phone, looked at the display and took the call just as Victor's mobile rang in his pocket.

"Lily." Victor heard Nathaniel say, his voice terse.

Victor pulled his phone out and saw on its display Laura Calling.

He engaged his own mobile as he heard Nathaniel say in terse clip, "You're *where?*"

Everyone's eyes swung to Nathaniel as Victor put his phone to his ear.

"Laura," Victor said into the phone but heard nothing but sobs. Victor felt the doom settle in his heart as his body went tense and he watched as rage replaced resignation on his son's face.

"What's happened, Laura?" Victor asked quietly, thinking he knew the answer.

He didn't.

"We're in . . . we're *all* in . . ." Laura stuttered. "*Jail!*" she wailed and Victor's brows snapped together.

Then what his wife said penetrated.

So Victor shouted, "*Jail?*" and Nathaniel's and everyone else's eyes swung to him as Laura babbled into his ear something about Lily's attorney then Jeffrey and Danielle, and just as Victor prepared to have a stroke, considering his blood pressure had to be skyrocketing and his anger had reached new bounds, Nathaniel strode purposefully to him, mobile still to his ear.

"I'll be there in less than an hour," Nathaniel was saying into his phone, his voice vibrating with fury. Victor watched as Nathaniel listened for a few moments, and when he spoke again he carefully controlled his voice and said softly, "Darling, I'll take care of it. I'll be there in less than an hour."

He flipped his phone shut and looked at his father.

"Laura, I have to go," Victor interrupted his wife.

"But Victor!" Laura cried.

Victor looked at his son.

"Nathaniel needs me," he said.

There was silence for a moment and then, with what he knew was hope in his wife's tremulous voice, she said, "Of course." Then, with definite hope, "I'll see you soon, my love."

He heard the disconnect in his ear and disengaged his phone.

"What do you need me to do?" Victor asked his son.

"Lily and I are getting married today," was all Nathaniel said.

Victor nodded that the message was understood and Nathaniel glanced at his daughter who was giggling with Lily's shop girls.

"Look after Tash," Nathaniel ordered.

Victor nodded again.

Fazire charged in and shouted to the room at large, "What in the name of the Great Grand Genie Number One is keeping them?"

Nathaniel didn't respond. With swift, long strides, he walked right past Fazire and out of the building.

"Now where is *he* going?" Fazire cried as Natasha, looking frightened, ran after her father but Victor caught her and swung her back.

"I have to go with Daddy!" his granddaughter yelled, straining against Victor's arms and reaching toward the door where her father disappeared.

"It's going to be okay," Victor soothed Natasha. "Something's happened and your daddy needs to go fetch your mummy."

Natasha moved shrewd eyes to her grandfather, looked at him closely and deciding either he was telling the truth or her father could sort out anything (likely the latter), her fear melted, a quirky smile tugged her lips and she said, "Okay."

She then skipped back to Lily's girls.

"Would you like to tell *me* what's happening?" Fazire, head tipped back, stared down his nose at Victor and Victor moved toward his odd friend and did as requested.

Fazire's face got as purple as his suit but Victor ignored him and turned toward the fidgeting Registry Office employee.

Then he commanded, "Take me to the person in charge."

Laura

AT FIRST THEY WERE TREATED abominably by the police.

What seemed like hours ago (but wasn't), back at Lily and Nate's house, Laura, trying to find her opening to intervene (but failing) in the highly escalated situation, had vaguely heard Lily's attorney call the police. The police, upon arrival, didn't seem to care one bit that the girl wrestling around on the floor with Danielle was supposed to be getting married in an hour. They'd carted the lot of them off to the police station and didn't allow them to use the phone.

Lily, to Laura's dismay, had seemed completely at ease with this.

Her dress remarkably had survived the wrestling match, although, to Laura's despair, her bracelet had been ripped off and her hair was in complete disarray.

Danielle had come out the worse for wear, however.

Alistair and Jeffrey had managed to pull Maxine out of the fray but it took both of them to control her as she tried to dive back in, all the while shouting encouragement to Lily who was in what appeared to be a struggle to the death with Danielle on the floor.

In the final moments of the battle, Mrs. Gunderson decided she'd had enough of sitting on the back of the couch and watching with feigned cat disinterest. She threw herself—hissing and claws bared—into action and scratched Danielle's arms and legs viciously, but surprisingly, or perhaps not surprisingly, the cat didn't touch Lily.

As they were sitting in the police station waiting for their chance to use the phones, Lily had smiled at Laura and said, "Don't worry. As soon as I can I'll call Nate and he'll get this all sorted out."

This, Laura had to admit, *did* make her feel a *little* bit better.

However it didn't change the fact that Laura's two rotten, horrible children had again spoiled things for Nathaniel and Lily and it was Laura's fault because *she* had wanted to hear what they had to say hoping, stupidly, that it was going to be an apology.

Lily wasn't wrong about Nate.

Ten minutes after Lily phoned Nate, an official looking person came to them looking embarrassed and casting accusing glances at the officers who had arrived at Lily's home and taken them away without regard to the celebratory circumstances, then didn't offer them a bathroom or the use of the phone for what seemed like ages.

Upon arrival, the officer smiled consolingly at Lily.

"Ms. Jacobs, I've had a call," he explained. "Please accept my *deepest* apologies. Your fiancé is on his way. In the meantime, let's get you some tea and a place to tidy up."

"Well!" Maxine stated grandly, standing and shaking out her flowing lavender caftan that was liberally sprinkled with sequins around the collar and hem. Maxine's outfit hadn't fared so well in the struggle. There was a big rip rent from knee to hem. "He offers *tea*. I *never*," she snapped.

"Could I *please* have some first aid?" Danielle asked snottily from her place down the hall, luckily *far* down the hall from where Lily, Laura and Maxine were sitting.

"And you would be?" the policeman asked.

"I'm Danielle Roberts," Danielle stated as if she was saying, "I am Queen of the Universe."

Laura closed her eyes in despair then opened them to see the man's back straightening.

"We'll get to *you* in a minute," he said dismissively and somewhat threateningly.

Laura noted Danielle's face registering deep affront but she tore her gaze away from her birth daughter and watched as the officer turned back to Lily and offered her his arm.

In a tone that was nearly reverential, he said, "Ms. Jacobs."

He also nodded to Maxine and Laura and they knew they were to follow.

Lily took his arm and they walked away, past an outwardly fuming Danielle, a surprisingly silent and guilt-stricken-looking Jeffrey and the glaring, pacing, unrepentant Alistair.

Laura tried very hard to ignore her children but Danielle was scratched and bleeding. Though she knew it wasn't *that* bad, Laura was still a mother and she couldn't help herself. Even though she vowed never to care, never even to *think* about her two children again, she opened her mouth to speak but Lily beat her to it.

In a whisper, Lily leaned into the policeman and suggested, "Maybe, before our tea, you could see to her scratches?"

At Lily's kind words, Laura reached out and caught Maxine's hand and felt Maxine's close around her own and squeeze with assurance.

Laura bit her lip.

Yes, she thought, *yes, my dearest Lily, you are* perfect *for my Nathaniel.*

Now they were sitting in an untidy but not unsavory office. They had tea and package biscuits, although someone had run out and bought Lily a skinny latte, such was Nathaniel's power, Laura was proud to note. Laura and Maxine had done their best to get Lily's hair back to its former loveliness. It looked fine but not nearly as fine as Susan's handiwork. And they waited for Nathaniel to arrive.

Laura felt her heart ache as she struggled to find the words yet again to apologize to Lily that her children had ruined *everything*. She closed her eyes tight, feeling the tears clogging her throat as she sat in a police station, of all places, with Lily on her wedding day, of all days, when Laura heard a giggle.

Her eyes flew open and locked on Lily who was giggling harder, louder, her body beginning to shake with it.

"I can't," Lily breathed and then let out an unladylike snort of laughter. She tried for control and started again, "I can't believe I wrestled on the floor of my sitting room in *my wedding dress*."

She threw herself bodily against the back of the chair and rocked with her laughter.

Maxine was laughing too, softly, as she got up and divested Lily of her latte. Lily's dress had made it this far, even if they had to wait another month, or, Laura hoped not, two, for an alternate date at the Registry Office, Lily could wear the dress again and she didn't need coffee stains on it.

"I had my money on you," Maxine said through her strengthening laughter. "You had her hair so tightly fisted, I thought you were going to yank it . . ." She stopped and gulped down laughter, her horrified eyes swinging to Laura, "Laura, I'm so sorry. She's your daugh—"

"She's nothing to me," Laura declared firmly and both Lily and Maxine's laughter died abruptly.

"Laura," Lily said softly and she prepared to stand.

Laura brought her hand up.

"No." Lily's movement arrested at Laura's word.

"But she's—" Lily started.

Laura pinned Lily to the spot with her gaze and Lily's mouth snapped shut. "No, she isn't. I have a daughter, yes, I still have a daughter. And she's sitting with me in this very room."

"Laura," Lily breathed and surged out of her chair.

Laura rose as well and they found themselves in each other's arms and both hugged tight.

"Mr. McAllister," they heard in respectful voice coming from behind the closed door, "I can assure you . . ."

The door flew open and Nathaniel stood there, his tall body tense, his eyes sweeping the room then they stopped on Laura and Lily.

"That'll do." Nathaniel's deep voice rang with authority, his gaze still on Lily and Laura but he was speaking to the police officer at his side.

"What I was saying is, I can assure—" the police officer began but stopped when Nate's angry eyes cut to him. "Of course," the officer went on, "I'll, erm, leave you to it." Then the officer backed out of the room.

Everyone stayed still and silent, the women staring at Nathaniel, Nathaniel staring at Lily.

Finally Lily broke free, ran to him and threw her arms around him. His arms closed around Lily and, as she pressed her cheek against his chest, he rested his on top of her head.

"It's okay," Lily whispered her assurance. "It's okay. We'll wait. We've waited this long. We'll just go have a party and then we'll have another one when we—"

Nathaniel lifted his head and looked down at his bride.

"We're getting married today," he declared, his voice implacable.

"But I thought—" Lily started, her head tilted back to look at her fiancé.

"Victor's dealing with it," Nathaniel cut her off and his eyes moved to Laura. "Mother, the limousine is waiting to take you and Maxine to the Registry Office."

The room stilled yet again and Laura felt a tightening around her heart and a tremble move through her body.

"Wha-what did you just say?" she whispered as she felt her heart travel to her throat.

Nate's carefully controlled face grew soft as he looked at Laura. "Please take our friend to the Registry Office," he said quietly, then finished, "Mother."

Laura stood rock solid at hearing her son call her "mother" for the second time in his life.

Then, shakily, her heart finally righting itself and feeling strangely, beautifully, buoyant, she nodded.

"I'll take Lily," he went on.

"Of course," Laura replied quietly.

Maxine was standing and watching, fanning her face with her hand and swallowing convulsively to stop the tears.

Lily didn't even try. She pressed her cheek against Nathaniel's chest and stared at Laura, tears sliding down her cheeks.

"Lily, careful," Maxine said. "You'll ruin your makeup."

"I'll fix it in the car," Lily assured her then she smiled. "Go," she ordered gently.

On trembling legs Laura walked towards the door, but as she would pass her son and his fiancée, Nathaniel's hand came out to stop her. She looked up to him and he bent to kiss her cheek. When he straightened, she bit her lip, nodding as she touched his shoulder. Then Maxine's hand slid through her arm and Maxine guided her through the door.

Lily and Nathaniel followed.

Jeffrey and Danielle were still sitting in the hall. Alistair had disappeared. Laura was pleased to note (she was *still* a mother), Danielle's arms were covered in plasters.

"Nate!" Danielle jumped up out of her chair and Jeffrey followed her, grabbing his sister to hold her back. "Listen to me, you must—"

First Laura and Maxine then Nathaniel and Lily walked right by the two without a word.

As usual, Nathaniel showed no reaction to seeing his ne'er-do-well siblings. It took a mammoth effort of will for Laura to glide by, she hoped serenely. She was helped by Maxine squeezing her arm and moving closer to her body in a show of support.

Finally they were out the door and Laura realized she was holding her breath. She let it go in a whoosh.

Nathaniel saw them both safely into the waiting limousine and closed the door firmly behind them.

As the limousine smoothly slid away, Laura and Maxine watched out the window as Nathaniel walked Lily to his Aston Martin.

"Can I just say?" Maxine started, still looking out the window, "He's *the bomb*."

For the first time in hours Laura felt mirth burble up inside her chest and then she burst out laughing.

<hr />

Nate

NATE WAS TRYING VERY HARD not to lose his temper while he drove fast, but not too fast, to what he hoped would still be his wedding. He didn't want them to crash in a ball of fiery flame in one last trial and tribulation to test their love before Lily's wish was finally, solidly, irreversibly granted.

Lily was sitting beside him in the Aston Martin leaning towards the opened mirror on the sun visor, calmly applying mascara and babbling.

"*Then*, Mrs. Gunderson jumped in, hissing and very, *very* angry and—"

"Lily," Nate cut into her rambling story, a story that for some reason Lily found hilarious but Nate most definitely did not.

"What?" Lily asked, screwing the top back on her mascara.

"I don't find this amusing," Nate told her.

"Well, of course not, you weren't there. You had to *see* it to *believe* it," she explained on a giggle, underlining her words with verve as she had been doing for the last half an hour. "I was *wrestling* on the *floor* in my *wedding dress*," she reiterated a snippet of her infuriating story that she'd already told him, one of the many snippets Nate found he detested most of all.

"Even if I'd seen it, I wouldn't find it amusing," Nate replied.

"Well, I do," she stated firmly and then she went on, saying words that shocked Nate even though he couldn't imagine ever feeling shock again, "Nate, I don't care what it says about me and I hope you don't think less of me but here it is, I'm *glad*. I would have *paid* for that opportunity. I told you what she said, what *they* said, her and Jeffrey, about *you* and also about *Victor*. And then she slapped Laura. I was itching to get at her. Slapping her *mother*! I just could *not* believe. What a *bitch*!"

That snippet of the story, Danielle slapping Laura, was the one he detested most of all. He was pleased he'd not known that part when he'd been at the police station or, he had little doubt, he'd be the one in jail likely locked in a cell after committing double homicide.

"Do you think less of me?" Lily asked quietly, interrupting his thoughts.

"No," Nate answered honestly.

"You're sure?" she pressed.

"Absolutely."

Silence, then in a bare whisper, she said, "I think I may have torn out some of her hair and I have to admit, I kind of feel badly about that."

Finally, Nate laughed and after a few seconds, Lily joined him.

It took a moment but it registered on Nate that this was the first time they'd shared laughter. They'd shared many moments of amusement, smiles, grins, he'd made her laugh, she'd (far more often) made him laugh but never had they shared a moment like this.

And now he had a life before him that would be filled with these moments.

His laughter naturally died and once it did, he found her hand and brought it to his lips. He brushed them against her knuckles and dropped their joined hands to his thigh but he didn't let hers go.

"Do you think Victor arranged for a new time?" Lily asked, Nate glanced her way and saw that surprisingly she was relaxed, happy and not at all affected by her tumultuous day.

"Yes," he replied, returning his eyes to the road.

"Well, if he hasn't, please don't be disappointed. We'll reschedule and—"

"He's done it," Nate said firmly.

"If he hasn't, then—"

"He has."

"If he hasn't—"

"Darling, he *has*," Nate said in a tone that was unmistakably final.

"Okay," she muttered, but rebelliously, under her breath, she said, "But, if he hasn't, I don't care. I have you now, married or not. It doesn't matter to me. Just as long as I have you."

He felt that becoming familiar feeling of happiness surge through his chest, his hand squeezed hers but reluctantly he let it go so he could downshift and stop at a traffic light in Bath.

"So," Lily changed the subject, "where are we going on our honeymoon?"

"It's a surprise," Nate replied, the traffic light changed and he moved forward, closing in on the Registry Office hopefully to find that Victor had succeeded in his task.

"Does it have a beach?" she asked.

"No," he answered, deftly executing a turn in the heavy traffic.

"Does it have mountains?" Lily tried again.

"No," he responded, feeling his lips twitch at her sweet interrogation.

"Is it in a foreign country?"

"Yes," he told her.

"Italy?" she queried, hope in her voice.

"No."

"France?" Lily went on doggedly.

"No."

She seemed stymied as Nate pulled up outside the Registry Office. He parked on the double yellow lines and the Aston would stay there. They could ticket him, he didn't care. He had millions of pounds. He'd happily pay a parking ticket or a hundred of them to shave off ten minutes of waiting to be married to Lily.

He got out and was rounding the car when she alighted from the other side.

"Please wait for me to open your door, Lily," he requested softly when he made it to her.

"Switzerland?" She ignored his request and kept at her former topic and Nate threw back his head and laughed.

He brushed his lips against hers and escorted her to the pavement, saying a firm, "No."

"Where are we going then?" She lost her patience and her eyes flashed but with happy frustration rather than true anger.

"I'm not telling you."

She dug in her heels at the bottom of the steps to the entry. Victor and Fazire filled it as Lily looked up at Nate.

"I never said I wanted it to be a surprise Nate," Lily stated then threatened, "I'm not going in there until you tell me."

Without hesitation, for Nate no longer cared if it was a surprise or not if it meant he'd have to wait any longer to get married, he finally relented and told her, "Indiana."

Lily's head moved involuntarily and she blinked.

"You're taking me to *Indiana* for our honeymoon?"

Nate slid his arm around her waist and pulled her toward his body.

When he felt her softness hit him, he bent his head to hers and, their faces a breath away, he said, "I want you to see this property I purchased. It cost a fortune. The people living there didn't feel like moving. In the end, I persuaded them. It's a limestone farmhouse with marble window sills and a big pond in the front yard."

Lily sucked in her breath and her eyes grew wide. Then he watched as they filled with tears and she leaned into him. Her hand went to his cheek, she whispered his name and he felt all the love in the world wash over him in that quiet whisper.

At his name on her lips said in that tone, Nate's head descended the rest of the way and he kissed her through her tears.

"Lily!" Maxine yelled from somewhere near but Nate didn't care where. "You'll ruin your makeup!"

Fazire

"NATE, IT DOESN'T MATTER," LILY said comfortingly to Nathaniel.

"It matters," Nathaniel said curtly to Lily.

Fazire looked on.

"There's nothing we can do. We have a full schedule," the Registry Office person said, wringing her hands.

"Son, I tried," Victor cut in and Fazire saw he looked completely dejected.

Fazire knew the proud man *had* tried, he'd watched him. Victor had tried *everything*. He tried coaxing, he tried threatening, he tried bribing. And nothing worked.

"She was accosted in her living room and mistakenly carted away by the police!" Maxine shouted dramatically. "Surely you can make an exception for *that*."

The Registry Office employee shook her head.

"But they've been waiting eight years." Fazire heard Laura say, her voice so sad it made Fazire sad too, or more sad than he already was. He was sad for Lily, for Nathaniel, for Tash, his glorious Tash who was looking on crestfallen, even for Laura and Victor who so wanted this for their family.

"Lily-child," Fazire said softly, knowing what he had to do.

Lily didn't look at him. She was staring up at Nate with love and concern shining in her eyes.

Fazire knew at a glance she had changed. Fazire knew that Nathaniel had healed her last night. That Lily had healed Nathaniel. That her wish had finally come true. That they would finally find happiness. For the rest of his genie days, and there would be *many*, he would live happily with the knowledge that he'd created that for his Lily.

But Fazire was still sad, sad for himself, sad that he was to be leaving them, his adored Lily, his beautiful Natasha and this fine man he'd grown to respect.

"Lily-child," Fazire repeated, his voice stronger and Lily turned to him, took one look and disengaged from her furious lover and moved to Fazire.

"Are you okay?" she asked softly, her hand light on Fazire's arm.

She was watching him closely, losing track of her own dire circumstances to worry about him.

"Use it," Fazire said and he found, to his utter astonishment, his voice was croaky.

Oh how the other genies would laugh if they ever heard *that*.

He cleared his throat and repeated, "Use it."

"Use what?" she asked, her eyes confused.

Fazire nodded his head toward Nathaniel and Lily looked over her shoulder at her fiancé.

"I want a word with the Registrar," Nate demanded.

"I've already spoken to the Registrar. *He's* already spoken to the Registrar," the employee pointed at Victor, and Tash leaned heavily, despondently, against her father's legs. Nathaniel's hand came to his daughter's shoulder reassuringly as the employee went on, "I'm *so* sorry. We'll schedule a new date for you as soon as we can."

Lily turned back to Fazire, her face pale and Fazire knew she understood.

"I can't . . . we can wait," she whispered, her eyes panicked.

"Look at them, Lily. Look at Tash. She thinks your Nathaniel can do anything. She thinks Nathaniel has a *different* kind of magic. To learn any different, Lily-child, you *know* it would break her heart."

Lily shook her head. This she did fervently, fear now filling her face and her fingers on his arm tightened as if she'd never let him go.

"Look at them," Fazire urged softly.

She shook her head again and she didn't look but she knew, she *knew* and so did Fazire. He knew she'd do anything for Tash and he knew she'd do anything for Nathaniel.

Her other hand came up to take hold of his other arm.

"Fazire," she whispered and she moved close, then closer, her arms locking around him.

"Use it, Lily-child," Fazire murmured softly in her ear as his darling Lily shoved her face in his neck.

"I don't want to. You'll go away and you're family. Family doesn't go away until they *have* to go away and you don't have to go away. You never have to go away." Fazire felt his Lily's body jolt then she whispered, "I love you Fazire."

Her voice broke on his name and her arms went so tight, Fazire didn't think he could breathe but luckily he didn't have to breathe so he just let her hold fast.

"I love you too," he replied, shocking himself because he meant it.

He meant it to the depths of his cynical genie soul.

The genie council for Best Wish of the Century had been wrong. *Lily* was the best wish ever granted.

Ever.

Since eternity.

"Use it," Fazire repeated.

"No," Lily denied.

"Lily-child, *use it*," he begged and felt her body jolt again.

She was silent for long moments then he heard her request in a whisper, "If I do this, you must let Tash say good-bye."

Fazire closed his eyes.

"No, I can't bear . . . no." It was Fazire's turn for his voice to break and he heard Lily's quiet hiccough of grief.

"If you go, I'll miss you," she was still whispering, her voice an ache.

"Use it, Lily," Fazire pressed, not sure he could take much more.

"We'll never forget you," she went on and he knew she was delaying. He knew she was trying to think of another way.

"Please, Lily, now . . . use it."

Her arms grew even tighter. "I'll write a story and forever it will pass down in our family so everyone will know about you," she promised. "How wonderful you are. How funny. How loyal—"

"Lily-child . . ." He felt moisture in his eyes and didn't know what it was for a moment before he blinked it away.

It dawned on him it was tears. Fazire, the great genie, was *crying*. He hoped that didn't get out. He'd never, in eternity (literally), live *that* down.

"*Use it*," he implored and at the tone of his voice, Lily's body stilled.

Then her face burrowed deeper into his neck and she spoke the words against his skin.

"Fazire, I wish to be married to Nathaniel McAllister, today, right here, right now, in the Registry Office in Bath."

Fazire pulled gently out of her arms and she stood before him, eyes shimmering with tears locked with his, she lifted her hands up in front of her and held them clenched together in despair as her lips pressed tight against each other to fight the tears.

Grandly, using his best genie voice, Fazire said, "Lily-child, your wish is my command."

He smiled at her sadly, lifted his hand and snapped.

Then the Great Genie Fazire disappeared.

TWENTY-SEVEN

Lily

LILY SAT ON AN elegant settee waiting, Tash resting heavily against her side, Maxine on her other side holding her hand.

Nate had demanded to talk to the Registrar and had disappeared behind a closed door.

Tash had noticed instantly, after her father left, that Fazire was gone and she'd asked after him.

Lily had lied, trying for a brave face, telling her that Fazire had forgotten something and would be back in no time. Lily would break the news to Tash later. Soon, she knew, Tash's mind would be on other, happier things, and Lily didn't have the heart to ruin her day any more than it already was.

Lorna came forward and handed Lily her bouquet made of full, white, fat, fragrant peonies, Becky's favorite flower.

"Just in case," Lorna whispered hopefully and moved quietly away.

"I wish your grandparents were here," Lily said to Tash, holding the bouquet to her nose.

"They are," Tash glanced at Laura and Victor.

Lily smiled. It was small and sad but genuine.

"Your *other* grandparents, baby doll."

Tash snuggled into Lily's side, wrapped her thin arm around Lily's waist and gave her a firm squeeze. "Me too."

And I wish Fazire was here, Lily thought fervently, throwing her thought out to the void.

She did it desperately hoping that the Great Grand Genie Number One monitored wayward wishes and granted them on a whim, even as she knew he did not (Fazire would have told her, the Great Grand Genie Number One wasn't much on humans, even though those he oversaw served them).

Vehemently in her head, she went on, *I wish Fazire was here to see me married. I wish Tash could have a wish from Fazire and her child too and on and on, forever. That's what I wish for myself, for my daughter, for my line but mostly it's what I wish for my beloved Fazire.*

The door opened and Nate came out with the girl from the Registry Office.

They were, Lily was not surprised to see, smiling.

"There's been a cancellation," the girl announced.

There were cries of happiness and cheers of joy. Tash jumped up and ran across the room, throwing herself bodily at Nate who grinned without reservation at his daughter. He picked her up and swung her around as Tash laughed with sheer delight. Along with his unguarded grin, Nate's face was relieved and joyous.

That was when Lily knew she did the right thing.

However, she couldn't help but think it was wrong.

NATE AND LILY SAT IN front of the long, gleaming table.

Victor and Maxine sat at one end, the official witnesses to the marriage. They'd eventually sign the marriage certificate. The Registrar sat opposite Nate and Lily.

"Shall we get started?" the Registrar asked, smiling at the couple.

Lily nodded and turned her head to Nate. He was sitting beside her but seemed far away. As if he felt her thoughts, his hand came out and grabbed hold of hers in a strong, reassuring grip.

Lily bit back tears.

Fazire, can you see me? She silently asked no one.

There was no response.

I hope you can see me, see what you've done. She thought.

"Ladies and gentlemen, we are gathered here today—" the Registrar began.

That was when pandemonium struck.

The closed doors at the back of the room slammed open loudly, banging with force against the walls, and a man walked in.

Not just any man.

He was a man wearing a gold fez, gold earrings, gold armbands, a gold bolero vest, gold flowy pants and gold curly-toed shoes. He had black hair, a black, pointy goatee and what looked like black kohl around his eyes. He was walking on the ground but he looked disgusted at this act, as if his feet should be treading on clouds.

"Excuse me! We're in the middle of a ceremony," the Registrar was standing and Lily noted belatedly that Nate had let her hand go and was also standing.

Lily also noted, with some alarm, that Nate had a face that could only be described as *thunderous*.

"What on earth?" Lily heard Laura ask.

Behind the golden genie came more genies, one, two, three, a half a dozen, two dozen, four dozen, all in the same outlandish outfit but in different, vibrant, contrasting, *loud* colors.

They filed in, as the Registrar blustered, "Excuse me! What is the meaning of this?"

More genies came through until they filled the room, sitting in the open chairs, squeezing around the sides, down the aisle, along the back of the room and all of them craning their necks to see, staring unashamedly at Lily, Nate and even Tash.

Lily slowly stood, watching the Spectacle of Genies along with everyone else.

"This is absurd. Who are you people? You must leave. I'm marrying this couple," the Registrar announced.

"You!" the Golden Genie, who had plonked himself down right next to Tash in the front row, spoke pompously to the Registrar, "Can *wait* a moment."

"I will *not* wait," the Registrar told him.

"You will," the Golden Genie commanded.

"I will *not*," the Registrar returned.

The Golden Genie ignored her and his dark eyes fell on Lily.

"You are Lily Jacobs," he declared.

Nate had moved to her side, his arm slid around her protectively and he glared at the Golden Genie.

"What's going on?" Nate demanded to know.

"And *you* are Nathaniel McAllister," the Golden Genie proclaimed.

"Yes, I am. Now what in bloody hell is going on?" Nate snapped.

"I am the Great Grand Genie Number One," the Golden Genie stated pretentiously.

Lily gasped, Maxine gasped and Tash clapped happily, staring up at the genie beside her in awe. The Golden Genie spared Tash a glance and, Lily could almost *swear*, he winked at her daughter.

"I don't care who you are. You're interrupting our—" Nate started then stopped, his eyes scanning the room, jumping from genie to genie.

Lily felt his body grow tense beside her, his fingers digging into her waist. Then his head jerked to Lily and his brows drew together.

"Where's Fazire?" he asked.

Lily opened her mouth to speak but she didn't need to. Nate's face moved from alarmed inquiry to understanding. Slowly he closed his eyes and turned her into his strong body. He dropped his forehead to hers and opened his eyes.

"Lily," he murmured, staring straight into her eyes, "you didn't."

She nodded and she felt the tears again coming. How one person could cry so much in one single day was beyond Lily but she was proof it could happen.

"I knew you wanted it," Lily whispered, "and Tash would have been devastated."

"We could have waited," Nate said, ignoring the genie army. Ignoring the fact that he'd driven like a maniac (well, not *exactly* like a maniac but close to it) to get them to the Registry Office. Ignoring the fact that he'd given in to Lily's dare at the entrance and told her about her lovely, unbelievable, amazing surprise honeymoon. She would never have not actually gone into the office until he'd told her about their honeymoon, she was kidding, but he was that impatient.

He didn't want to wait, she knew he didn't. For goodness sakes, eight years ago he got her pregnant to bind her to him. Lily of all people knew that Nate would stop at nothing to get what he wanted. Visions of him forcing the Registrar to marry them at gunpoint were dancing in her head (*that*, she admitted, was a *wee* bit dramatic, but she certainly didn't want him to blow his stack in front of Natasha).

As for Tash, even to think her father couldn't move mountains was something Lily, if she could help it, simply would not tolerate.

Nate pulled Lily deeper into his arms, cutting off her thoughts.

"Will someone tell me what's happening here?" the Registrar demanded.

Nate and Lily ignored her.

"He told me to," Lily said. "I didn't want Tash . . . we've waited so long . . . I knew you wanted . . ." She stopped and then went on, "He *told* me to," she repeated, her voice finally breaking and she shoved her face in his chest.

"Darling," Nate whispered against the top of her head.

"What's happening here?" the Registrar shouted. "Who are these bizarre people?"

"They're genies," Natasha chimed in, her voice angry. "And they're *not* bizarre."

"They are *not* genies," the Registrar retorted.

"They are," Tash shot back.

"They are *not*. There's no such thing as a genie," the Registrar returned smartly, staring at Tash like Nate and Lily should get a handle on her.

"There *is* such a thing as a genie. You're looking at, like, a *bazillion* of them!" Tash, finally losing patience, yelled.

Lily took her face from Nate's chest and looked at her daughter.

"Tash, don't yell," she remonstrated quietly.

"Mummy, that lady's crazy. How can she say there are no—?"

"Tash." Nate's voice was firm and Tash's mouth snapped shut, her arms crossed on her chest and her face settled into an obedient yet rebellious pout.

Tash didn't only get her quirky smile from Lily. She also got a bit of a rebellious streak.

Nate's eyes moved to The Great Grand Genie Number One.

"Why are you here?" Nate asked.

"To judge the Wish of the Century Award, of course. This," the Great Grand Genie Number One gestured about him, "is the council, plus, er . . . a few other genies who just wanted to see you get married." He finished slightly less grandly but still in pronouncement mode.

"Fine," Nate clipped. "Would you mind then if we actually *got* married?" he asked wryly.

The Great Grand Genie Number One inclined his head regally.

"A thousand expressions of gratitude," Nate muttered with dry humor and Lily felt a hysterical bubble of laughter rising in her chest.

Nate threw her a look that said he was again *not* amused and the giggle escaped. Lily clapped her hands over her mouth to stifle it.

"Lily," Nate said warningly.

Lily took her hands away. "I can't help it. Oh, Nate!" She put her hands on his shoulders and went up on tiptoe to look him eye to eye as best she could. "I *so* wish Fazire was here to see this. He'd laugh and laugh and—"

"Your wish!" the Great Grand Genie Number One announced in a booming voice, a voice that made Lily jump and Nate scowl, and both Nate and Lily's eyes swung to him, "Lily Jacobs, granddaughter of the Great Sarah Jacobs, is *my* command!"

Then he lifted his hand and snapped his fingers and in a dramatic poof of swirling grape smoke, Fazire appeared not two feet away.

"Fazire!" Lily shouted, pulling from Nate's arms and throwing herself into Fazire's.

She vaguely heard astonished murmurs as her body hit Fazire's for she had no idea that genies rarely, very, *very* rarely touched humans and humans *never* touched genies.

"Lily-child!" Fazire exclaimed. "What, where—?"

Fazire was looking around him then he stilled and stared at the Golden Genie.

"Great Grand Genie Number One!" he cried, disengaging from Lily and dropping in a deep, low bow before his master.

"Fazire," the Great Grand Genie Number One stared down his nose at the bowing Fazire, "arise."

Fazire straightened and Lily took his hand. The Golden Genie's eyes dropped to their clenched hands and he closed them in obvious despair and shook his head.

"Great Grand Genie?" Fazire called, clearly confused at the turn of events.

The Golden Genie's eyes opened.

"My friend," he said softly but his voice still carried, "you have served this family well. The only genie who ever served *three* generations of humans. And you have performed the two best wishes in genie history, the creation of this girl and binding her to this man who needed her."

Fazire nodded, still confused but trying to pretend he wasn't. Lily clenched his hand tighter and her genie returned the gesture.

"Therefore, I think, Great Fazire," the Golden Genie declared, "if it is *your* wish, you will serve them through eternity."

Gasps were heard all around but Lily barely registered it, her own and Fazire's were so loud.

"Truly?" Fazire asked, his face wreathed in hope.

"Do you wish it, Fazire?" the Golden Genie demanded.

Fazire looked to Lily then to Tash then to the Great Grand Genie. Without another moment of hesitation, he nodded.

"So it will be," the Golden Genie decreed. "Your wish, Great Fazire, is my command!"

And, just like that he lifted his fingers and he snapped.

And it was done.

Lily threw her arms straight up in the air and shouted with joy.

"Yipeeeeeeeee!" Tash cried, rushing forward and jumping up and down, her arms around her mother and Fazire.

Lily hugged Fazire. She hugged Tash. She hugged Maxine who'd come around the table. She hugged Victor then she hugged Laura. Finally, she turned and threw herself bodily at Nate who lifted her off her feet in an automatic half whirl as he took her weight.

Nate set her down and looked at her, shaking his head and touching her cheek as he absorbed the pure, unadulterated delight emanating from her gaze.

His gaze moved to Fazire.

"Do you mind if we get married now?" he asked with sham courtesy but his lips were twitching.

Fazire's eyes narrowed. "Don't let *me* stand in your way. It was only *me* who brought you together in the first place," Fazire grumbled. "We shouldn't let *my* little wish have any time in your busy human lives. Not that it's unprecedented for a *genie* to get a *wish*. Not that we shouldn't revel in the fact that this has *never* happened *before* all through *eternity*. Not that we should glory for a moment in *my* joy and everlasting gratitude to the Great Grand Genie Number—"

"Fazire," Nate cut him off.

"What?" Fazire snapped curtly.

Nate put a hand on Fazire's shoulder. Fazire looked at the hand then looked at Nate.

"Tash," Nate said quietly and Lily's heart melted.

She never expected she could love Nate more, not in a million years, but at that moment she did.

Fazire's face softened. Then he hid it and rolled his eyes.

"Fine. I'll sit down," Fazire said with feigned harassment and his eyes cut to Lily. "Lily-child, get married for goodness sake. I'm hungry."

Again Lily giggled but this time she could hear Nate join her with soft laughter.

Fazire took Tash's hand and walked her back to the seats.

Everyone sat except some of the genies who floated.

Nate took Lily's hand. When he did, Lily squeezed his.

Then Lily looked deeply into Nate's beautiful, dark, beloved eyes.

Ten minutes later, they were married.

EPILOGUE

Nate

*Eight years later, Nate is forty-four, Lily is thirty-eight,
Tash is fifteen, Jon is seventeen, Fazire is too old to count . . . again,
it's early in the month of May . . .*

THE ROLLS-ROYCE GLIDED TO a halt outside the massive bookstore
on Oxford Street in London.

Nate noticed the line out the door and around the corner.

He turned to the young man at his side.

"Looks like we're going to be here awhile, Jon," Nate told his son.

The young man shrugged his shoulders and looked at his father then
he rolled his eyes.

Nate smiled.

They'd been in this situation before. Lily's books were very popular
and she gave a great deal of time to her readers.

Seven years earlier, Lily published a novel about a war widow, her
fatherless daughter, the intense but loving man she married, the daughter
that came from a genie's wish and *that* daughter's romance with an impossibly handsome but hard, cold, forbidding man whose heart she had
to mend. A romance filled with trials and tribulations.

It became a bestseller and Lily, often with Nate, Tash and their newly adopted, ten-year-old son Jon in tow, traveled the world signing books and speaking to rooms filled with her fans.

The first bestseller was almost always the fan's favorite, however, they usually had Lily's series, which consisted of book after book of romantic lovers and their perils, each filled with humor, touched with sadness and always, there was a genie.

Nate and Jon moved through the crowd to the table where Lily sat behind a stack of books and smiled her quirky, effective smile at the next person in line.

Even after eight years of seeing it every day, Nate's body (and heart) still reacted to that smile.

"Dad!" Tash called and ran forward from her place beside Fazire who was standing behind and to the right of Lily, shadowed, hidden but always at his Lily's side.

Tash threw herself at Nate, her tall, lean body rocking him back on his heels.

She'd never changed her habit of shouting his name and hurling herself in his arms every time she saw him.

Late at night, some years before, lying in his arms in the dark, Lily shared with some sadness that she thought Tash secretly feared every time Nate left her presence that he'd never come back.

Nate had long since worried the same thing.

He leaned back from his daughter, tucked a heavy curtain of her black hair behind her ear and smiled down into her eyes, *his* eyes, and she smiled back. He read the relief in them, as he often did since the very first days he came into her life before she quickly hid it.

"Jeez, Tash. Knock him off his feet, why don't you," Jon muttered from beside Nate.

Tash pulled out of Nate's arms and shoved her brother's shoulder. "Shut up, Jon."

"*Grow* up, Tash," Jon shot back.

"*You* grow up," Tash returned.

Jon turned beleaguered brown eyes to his father.

"Stop," Nate said quietly but firmly and both of his children, as they had for years when their father spoke in that tone, immediately obeyed.

Though, it must be said, Tash did it with obvious reluctance and Jon did it with extreme arrogance, an arrogance Lily maintained he got from Nate, pontificating, sometimes at great length, of the prevalence of nurture over nature.

Nate had been wary of adopting a child older than Tash, a street-tough kid just like him.

Lily had insisted. So had Laura. Maxine had demanded (dramatically). Victor had, surprisingly, sided with Lily, Laura and Maxine. Fazire had, surprisingly, sided with Nate.

Not surprisingly, Lily had convinced Nate as well as Fazire.

It hadn't been easy going.

Jon was a good-looking boy, tall, lean, strong, with dark-brown hair and eyes. He was smart, not as smart as Tash but he was street smart, sharp as a tack and a quick learner.

Jon was also rough, foul-mouthed, ill-mannered and had a deprived life that equaled and even surpassed Nate's.

Tash, with her open heart, had taken to him immediately. She loved having a brother and it was Tash's months of unrelenting exuberance that broke him down. That and, of course, Lily's unwavering but not overbearing love, just like Laura had shown to Nate, and Nate's firm guidance and innate understanding. Not to mention Fazire's outlandish but caring regard, Maxine's dramatics and definitely overbearing love, Laura's gentle affection and Victor's gruff kindness.

It took a year but Jon settled in then he accepted them and finally his status of "adopted" melted away and he allowed himself to become one of the family.

The only one who knew his full story was Tash. Or Jon thought Tash was the only one who knew. Fazire had overheard them and he'd called down Lily who'd waved at a passing Nate and they'd all listened in until Nate, realizing what they were eavesdropping on, had forcefully pushed both his wife and her genie down the hall as they silently struggled but eventually relented.

Jon had bared everything to his new sister.

And Tash had kept his secrets and they were close, truly close, as siblings should be.

Even though, to Nate's gentle annoyance, they fought constantly.

They stood, the three of them, and watched Lily sign her books.

"I wish these crowds would go away, I'm hungry," Tash mumbled impatiently.

"Careful with your wishes, little sister." Jon threw his arm casually around Tash's shoulders and she leaned into her brother, "Fazire's watching."

Fazire, Nate noted, wasn't watching, he was scowling. Then again, Fazire always scowled.

Jon knew about Fazire. Jon had even been granted his own wish though he, as with Tash, had yet to use it. This wish had been granted two years ago, after a visit from the Great Grand Genie Number One. For some reason, these visits came regularly, usually when Lily baked Nate a cake, something she did each week of their first months as husband and wife (as promised) then each month after his first-ever birthday party, then yearly without fail on his birthday—and other times besides.

The rules of Fazire's magical attendance on their family had been made at their wedding reception. Each direct descendent of Nate and Lily's line had one wish, if Fazire wished to bestow it, and Fazire would live with the first-born girl unless he had another favorite, that was entirely up to Fazire.

Fazire and Jon had a relationship that rivaled even the one the genie had with Tash. Then again, Fazire loved anyone that Lily loved. Even, Nate realized some time ago, Nate himself.

Fazire stomped up to Nate and his children but, as ever, he directed his glare at Nate.

"Do *something*. I need a coffee. I need cake. I will *die* if I do not have cake this *instant*," he demanded of Nate.

"You won't *die* Fazire. You *can't* die," Tash pointed out, wrinkling her nose at her genie.

"Well, I'll experience a fate worse than death," Fazire shot back.

"What's that?" Jon asked, grinning as he always did at Fazire's eccentric behavior.

"*Extreme hunger* and *lack of cake*," Fazire answered and his gaze swung to Nate. "Nathaniel, do something."

Nate looked at his watch. Lily had stayed forty-five minutes past the time she was supposed to stop.

He turned his head and looked at his wife.

Every day, she got more beautiful. So much so he wondered vaguely if he'd been bewitched.

He didn't ask, mainly because he didn't care.

"Lily," he called, his deep voice carrying across the expanse that separated them.

Lily's head shot up from signing a book and she smiled at her husband.

Nate's gut twisted but it wasn't at all unpleasant. In fact it was *intensely* pleasant and anyway, Nate was not only used to it, he liked it.

"Yes?" she called back.

"Fazire wants cake," Nate told her.

"I do not *want* cake," Fazire announced loudly and all eyes that had not turned to Nate (and stared, he was used to the women who stood in Lily's book signing line staring at him, then again, he was long since used to most women staring at him), turned at Fazire's announcement and the genie finished, "I *need* cake."

"We'll shut down the line," an employee offered to a groaning audience.

"Ten more," Lily put in then turned her smile at the line and explained, "I have to see to my family."

More heads turning, more stares at Nate, the incredibly handsome Jon, the extraordinarily beautiful Tash and the bizarre Fazire. Then heads swung back to Lily.

Most of the line disbursed good-naturedly and with thoughts that the strange man looked *exactly* like a genie, and also, of course, that Lily McAllister's husband was *impossibly* handsome.

Lily finished her ten books, shook hands with the bookstore manager, spoke briefly with employees then moved with her usual unaffected grace toward her family.

Upon arrival, she kissed Tash's forehead, Jon's cheek and, up on tiptoe, eyes warm on his, she brushed her lips against her husband's cheek.

"Sorry, sorry," she mumbled, finding Nate's hand. "Now, cake."

"*Finally*," Fazire grumbled as if he'd been waiting millennia rather than forty-five minutes.

They moved to the door, Nate engaging his phone and calling their driver. His hand left Lily's but only so his arm could slide along her shoulders, pulling her to his side as they walked. This he did a great deal and Lily's step fell in practiced tandem with Nate's.

While speaking to their driver, Nate watched as Tash shoved Jon then Jon wrapped his arm around Tash's neck and pulled her against him much as Lily was against Nate with obvious differences, mainly Tash exclaiming loudly, "Let go!" even though she clearly didn't want him to.

"Children! You're *making* a *scene*," Fazire declared even more loudly, making his own scene.

Nate flipped his phone closed after he'd told the driver they were ready for him and Lily's arm wrapped around his waist.

She tilted her head to look up at him. "Are we spending the weekend at the penthouse or going back to Clevedon?"

"London," Nate stated.

Lily nodded and looked to the ground.

"Lily?" Nate called.

She tilted her head back to him and her lips tipped up at the ends in a ghost of her quirky grin. "Yes?"

"I love you."

He didn't say it often. He preferred to show it, though Lily did both and often.

Therefore, when he did say it, she reacted, extraordinarily so, gratifyingly so. Her eyes lit then warmed before they softened and filled with wonder and awe, though the last bit was normally how she looked at Nate . . .

Still.

"I love you too," she whispered.

Abruptly Nate stopped and so did Lily.

And he thanked time for his children were old enough that they no longer needed to be shielded from Nate's intense affection for his wife.

He turned Lily in his arms and he gave her a kiss, a real kiss, a kiss that made her breath catch (Nate, with satisfaction, not only heard it, he felt it) and his heart beat powerfully in his chest.

He had no idea that people were staring at the beautiful, loving, happy couple and a few took pictures.

And he couldn't have cared less.

The End

Connect with
KRISTEN Online :

Official Website: *www.kristeashley.net*

Kristen's Facebook Page: *www.facebook.com/kristenashleybooks*

Follow Kristen on Twitter: @KristenAshley68

Discover Kristen's Pins on Pinterest: *www.pinterest.com/kashley0155*

Follow Kristen on Instagram: KristenAshleyBooks

Need support for your Kit Crack Addiction?

Join the *Kristen Ashley Addict's Support Group on Goodreads*

Made in the USA
Middletown, DE
13 January 2024

47792870R00255